CW01021263

FOR THE LOVE OF VIETNAM

To Jim
With love
from Rang Keanleyeide.

For the Love of Vietnam

Huong Keenleyside

JANUS PUBLISHING COMPANY
London, England

First published in Great Britain 2007
by Janus Publishing Company Ltd,
105-107 Gloucester Place,
London W1U 6BY

www.januspublishing.co.uk

Copyright © Huong Keenleyside 2007

British Library Cataloguing-in-Publication Data
A catalogue record for this book is available from the British Library

ISBN 978-1-85756-603-1

All rights reserved. No part of this publication may be reproduced,
stored in a retrieval system or transmitted in any form or by any
means, electric, mechanical, photocopying, recording or otherwise,
without the prior permission of the publisher.

The right of Huong Keenleyside to be identified as the author
of this work has been asserted by him in accordance with the
Copyright, Designs and Patents Act 1988.

Cover Design: David Vallance

Printed and bound in Great Britain

Foreword

Storytelling has always been a big part of my and my siblings' childhood. We would be told of heroic stories of the Vietnam War at bedtime, but no other story has captured our hearts more than the story of my uncle, Ngoc Lan and his life as a spy, otherwise known as Agent 022. My sister Lan-Anh, was the one who originally gave me the idea to write about our uncle, as she has always said, 'Our uncle's story is very beautiful.'

Although our uncle's story is one without a happy ending, I wanted to write and tell the world about him and his dangerous life as Agent 022. Rich in Vietnamese culture, this book is dedicated to the Vietnamese people who lived under the carpet-bombing, and those who travelled along the Ho Chi Minh Trail. Many war documents are still kept in Vietnam and they amount to many tons of information. After four years of collecting information and accounts from thousands of Vietnamese people, this book is from the soul and is indeed a very true story.

When the book was first published in Vietnam, it had an overwhelming response, so much so that the police had visited one of the newspaper's headquarters to try and prevent them from writing and reviewing the book. The journalist merely asked them to read the book. And they did. In response, the Vietnamese Army ordered thousands of copies to be placed into their officer colleges.

After reading the book, Thomas Keenleyside was astounded by the courage of the Vietnamese people and their love for their country, as he and other Westerners only knew about the Vietnam War from America's point of view.

My uncle is still alive today and in his heart, he is still searching for his second wife – the French lady who never came back – and does not know whether she is even still alive. Does anyone know anything about her?

I hope he finds her and I know one day he will, either on earth or otherwise.

Huong Keenleyside

In 1968, Vietnam was divided into two countries, but had three governments: North Vietnam, South Vietnam and Free Vietnam. The North received support from the communist countries of the Soviet Union, China and Cuba; the South had support from America and Australia. The 'Free Vietnam', otherwise known as 'Vietcong' by the Americans, had support from both the North and the South. The Vietcong often bought weapons and food from the Southern troops, which were all made in America.

Prologue

Can Tho City, South Vietnam, 20 August 1969

Fifteenth Avenue was the most beautiful street in Can Tho City. In the distance, villas loomed behind centuries-old Bang Lang trees. Villa No. 25 was modelled on French architechure and was surrounded by a large private garden. It was once the home of the former chief of the Can Tho Province, Mr Nguyen Van Bay. He, his wife and daughter had died in a car accident and the former chief's only son, Police Lieutenant Nguyen Van Tu, now lived alone in the huge villa. Tu worked in the police special branch office and the South Vietnamese used to refer to them as 'white uniform', because they wore white jackets as opposed to those worn by criminal or traffic police officers. As a member of the special police, he was responsible for investigating the Vietcong and other agents of the North.

It was ten months ago since his family had died under suspicious circumstances, and during that time, Tu had spent most of his time searching for clues. He did find a witness, who told him that the lorry which had hit his family car had been seen parked in the area a few days beforehand, and when the driver had driven off, it had crashed into his father's car. Tu, despite the witness's evidence, could not come to terms with the death of his family and he believed that the Vietcong had murdered his family. Tu loathed the Vietcong and only needed a slight indication of a person being a sympathiser of the Vietcong in order to arrest them and fabricate evidence against them. Many of those suspects did not survive imprisonment.

Police Lieutenant Nguyen Van Tu had just started in his new job and was busy packing for his impending move to the capital of Southern Vietnam, Saigon. Commander General II Corp Nguyen Huu Co, who later became Minister of Defence, had heard good reports about Tu and thought that Tu would be better placed in the Special Department of the Military Intelligence Service at the police headquarters. Although Tu had not recovered from the shock of losing his family, he believed that moving to Saigon would probably be good for him.

Fifteenth Avenue was deserted and the air was heavy and close. The shadows cast by the Bang Lang trees seemed to brood ominously under the dimly lit streetlights, and a feeling of tension pervaded amongst the people living in the area because of the recent spate of deaths.

By seven o'clock that evening, everything had been packed and Tu finally relaxed and enjoyed a cup of tea whilst waiting for the removal company's van to collect all the boxes, so they could leave Can Tho early the next morning. Tu had been waiting for a small van to arrive but instead, a lorry pulled up and stopped in front of the villa. The lorry driver, who wore black trousers and a hooded jumper pulled over his head, got out and knocked at the front door.

Tu answered the door and when he saw the lorry, he asked, "What is this? I only asked for a small van. Why have you brought such a big lorry?"

"I'm very sorry, brother," replied the driver, "the small van is not available today and this is all we have left. It's not a problem, is it? Anyway, brother, you may be thankful for the extra space by the time we've finished loading all of your things."

"I suppose so," said Tu, who still seemed a little put out. "You'd better come in."

The driver followed Tu into the spacious hall with stained-glass windows, but no sooner had they reached the stairs than a cord was tightened around Tu's neck. As Tu struggled for his life, he used both hands in an attempt to loosen the cord, but it was futile. He may have been a man of strength, but the driver was bigger and stronger than he was. It was an uneven contest and Tu was soon dead. He never even had the chance to realise that two other men had entered the villa – one of them closely resembling him in appearance. Inside the villa, the man who looked like Lieutenant Tu opened the wardrobe, took out a police uniform and put it on. Then he opened another wardrobe containing a huge selection of ties and belts, plus two pistols.

"You've got such a lot of clothes. Just how many ties do you need?" enquired the driver, earnestly.

"May as well pack them all," said Ngoc Lan, "I've heard the apartments for single men at the police headquarters' command in Saigon city aren't exactly small." Then the fake Lieutenant turned to the driver, "Do we not look like two peas in a pod?"

The driver glanced at the body on the floor. "Indeed, you do! Well, Ngoc Lan … I would never have believed it! Plan Z18 has gone much more smoothly than we expected, in spite of the vehicle mix up."

The other man turned to Ngoc Lan.

"This is only the start, and we should not allow ourselves to become complacent."

Ngoc Lan glanced at the stranger's body and his light-hearted emotions vanished as he asked himself why this stranger had to die. Ngoc Lan had only been informed of his mission the night before, when he'd finished a course of training under the Cu Chi Tunnel, and he would now live his life as this stranger. Up until now he had had his own life, which included his family and his new wife; however, his family had to be left behind in North Vietnam when he took on a new identity. There was only one way that he would get to go home now and that was for the war to end, but as to when that would happen was anyone's guess … Ngoc Lan had no idea how he would be able to cope with the new situation in which he now found himself. He knew very little about this police officer's life, apart from the fact that he was single and had no family. During the past four months, Ngoc Lan had been training with special programmes; he'd learnt how execute a "perfect murder" and also how to survive ... Now, it was all becoming clear that he was to become a spy, who was to live the life of another person under an assumed identity. Ngoc Lan's boss told him that he needn't worry, because everything was under control and the Bietdong was already preparing the way for his new life. Distracted from his thoughts, Ngoc Lan looked towards the driver.

"I will have to go and say goodbye to my neighbours, so that I can memorise their faces."

"You haven't got any neighbours!" replied the driver.

"Didn't most of them die recently? These are times of war, Ngoc Lan," said the second man, with a shrug and a knowing look. "Anyway, from now on, you are Lieutenant Tu." Then he jokingly added, " … or Agent 022."

"Yes, sir! Police Lieutenant Tu; Agent 022," the two men barked, simultaneously, bursting into roars of laughter as they did so.

"We have to deal with your body. How about I hide your corpse under the blossom tree in the back garden?" the driver asked.

"While we are dealing with this body, Ngoc Lan, you'd better take a good look at your house. It would be a tragedy if you were to get caught out one day because you did not know where your bedroom was," said the second man, in a low voice.

Ngoc Lan walked around the huge house, which had four reception rooms and five bedrooms upstairs. There was a cup of tea still steaming on the side in the kitchen and next to that was a piece of rice cake, which, strangely enough, was one of Ngoc Lan's favourite foods. Outside in the garden was an empty cottage and a greenhouse and, as Ngoc Lan took time to reflect, he could not believe all that was unfolding around him in this ... his new home, in his new hometown, assuming a new identity. It was only a few months ago that he'd just got married and here he was now now joining the army and the Ho chi Minh Trail to the South. He had been forced to say goodbye to everyone in his family, promising them that he would return home safe and well. That was one late afternoon ...

Chapter One

Two years earlier, Ha Bac – North Vietnam

It was late afternoon and the corn leaves, which were ripening in the field along the edge of the village of Phu Xuyen, were rustling in the light breeze. The sky was a deep blue and the birds were flying back to their nests for the night. A narrow, grassy path ran in a zigzag pattern to a mulberry field at the edge of the forest, where two men were going for a walk. One was Ngoc Van, a building contractor, in a trendy white suit, white shirt and a felt hat, and the other, Ngoc Lan, who was just twenty-five, was wearing a soldier's uniform; his helmet bore the insignia of an artillery warrant officer. Ngoc Lan had invited his brother, Ngoc Van, to talk privately for the last time before joining the army's fight in the South.

"I will be going to South Vietnam the day after tomorrow," Ngoc Lan informed his brother.

"How do you know? That should have been kept secret; if our army knows where they are going, the Americans are sure to bomb them. How do you feel about being sent to the battlefield?"

"You don't think that I'd come here to say my goodbyes to everybody only to desert from the army, do you?" said Ngoc Lan, raising his eyebrows at Ngoc Van. "Anyway, I'll be back in three years."

Surprised, Ngoc Van asked, "What makes you think it will be three years?"

"Sometimes, secrets take on a funny nature. The day after tomorrow we will gather in Thanh Hoa and from there, we will speed-march to Saigon to fight, conquer and return! We will be back by the end of 1969, or at worst by the beginning of 1970."

1

The Northern people shared the very same hope as that of President Ho Chi Minh and General Commander Vo Nguyen Giap ... that the war would end as soon as possible. In 1954, General Giap had beaten the French in the Dien Bien Phu Campaign in just 56 days, but this time, the Americans were a lot stronger than the French, and their army was better trained and equipped.

"I disagree. Do you know how dreadful the battlefield is? I think it is too early for you to be so optimistic. According to Uncle Ho's (the popular name for Ho Chi Minh, the natural leader of the North; even today he is both revered and cherished in a way that Stalin never was) prediction, it will be at least 1976, or even 1979, before we can reunify the country. However, as the American people are also against this war, they may withdraw their troops at any given time, and then your prediction would come true. Anyway, it may take you three years before you can even enter Saigon, because the Ho Chi Minh Trail is the most dangerous road in the world."

Ngoc Lan dwelt on these thoughts without pleasure. He had been so excited about the journey to join in the fight and hopefully bring peace back to the nation, that he hadn't even considered the latter prospect. The Americans had recently gone all out and seemed determined to win; they were bombing everywhere in the North. There was nothing left; no factories and no electricity. Even the fields had been damaged by bombs and the economy was in a terrible situation. Like everyone in the North of Vietnam, Ngoc Lan just wanted the war to be over as soon as possible.

"If that is so, then it may take longer to reach Saigon than initially planned, which would mean that it would be even longer before I could return home. I already miss our family ... I will miss this cornfield at sunset and the old tiled roofs, and all the times you and I have wandered through this field."

"The only person you will miss will be your new wife, Nhat."

"Yes, I will miss her the most," admitted Ngoc Lan. "I have been in love with her ever since I was fifteen years old. We only got married last month and now I am to leave her side for a life in the army; how can I not miss her? She is really weak and frail, Ngoc Van. If you have time, I would be grateful if you would call at our house and help her occasionally while I am away. My parents are old and my younger brother Mai is still living and studying in Germany ... "

"Don't worry," interrupted Ngoc Van. "Go to the battlefield and to the danger of the bombs and the shells. The people that remain behind will look after and support each other. After all, there are enough of us."

"I know, but ..."

"No buts. Have you finished saying your goodbyes to everyone?"

"Almost everyone."

Ngoc Van interrupted: "I don't think I told you, Nga, my wife, wants to settle near her family home."

Ngoc Lan pretended to be horrified. "Don't you mind living next to your wife's family? I don't mind joining the army, but living near my mother-in-law – never!"

"Peace will soon be here. I have plans to expand our village into a town, or even a new city. The village roads will become busy trading streets. The countryside would be a good place for city people to come to relax and buy agricultural produce and locally made goods," Ngoc Van thought, aloud.

"You have modern ideas. Your thoughts are creative. Nevertheless, each country has its own customs and traditions. It will take time and patience to introduce new developments. You see, our people just don't have sufficient experience to prepare them for such radical reforms. They're still not convinced of the benefits of joining cooperatives, much less ..." Ngoc Lan wondered.

"You are still quite young," said Ngoc Van, "and because of that, you are afraid of change and progress. When peace arrives, come back and see how well our homeland has blossomed under socialism. You must remember to write letters home. Make a success of your career. In our clan, we still don't have a hero, but we also don't have a deserter, either."

"I am proud of that," said Ngoc Lan, removing some letters from his bag. "It will be difficult for us to post letters on the march, so I have already written some letters for my wife. Please take them and send one to her once a month. I have pencilled the dates on the back of the envelopes."

Ngoc Van groaned inwardly; he knew that he would have to travel to make sure that the postmarks would show different provinces and this would prove both time-consuming and expensive.

"Are they full of compassion and love like a novel? Are they so full of tears that you can wring water out of the pages?" he teased.

"No, they're not," snorted Ngoc Lan, "They're encouraging her to get along with the other women in the cooperative. They tell her not to be worried about me, and that I love her. Come on, we've only been married just three weeks; no more, no less. What more do you need to know?"

"Enough, and remember, take care of yourself. I know you are as nimble as a squirrel and as strong as a tiger, but the important thing is your sixth sense which will help you to survive more than anything else, so try to develop that."

"I will try," answered Ngoc Lan.

"And I have bad news. Mui, our cousin, has died on the way home in the Quang Tri Province. The council have decided not to tell Uncle Tap until after the New Year."

"I don't know how his father will cope with this news; our family has lost too many people already this year."

"Every family in our province has lost somebody," Ngoc Van corrected.

"The war must end. I will do whatever I can to make it so."

Ngoc Van told Ngoc Lan all this bad news, because this was a time when everyone must look forward in order to decide what was good for Vietnam. Ngoc Lan must know that he was fighting for his family and his country. Wherever he may be, he must remember where he came from and that his family would be waiting for his return.

The two cousins walked along the countryside lane in silence. From the west, the perfect, round moon, signifying the fourteenth day of the month, emerged through thin grey clouds. Moonlight filled the fields with a silver glow.

There are so many beautiful things in my country that are worth fighting for, thought Ngoc Lan, on their return to Ngoc Van's house.

Everybody in Nguyen Ngoc's family had gathered at Ngoc Van's house for a farewell feast; to say goodbye to yet another member of the clan who was going to fight in the South. Most of the people left behind in the village were old, because the young were either in the army or had been sent to work on the Ho Chi Minh Trail. In the middle of the main hall was the family altar, where incense was burning and in front of the altar was a beautifully carved ebony bed. Some of the older men were sipping tea and discussing current affairs and some of the older women were sitting outside chewing betel nut. Flower rush mats had been laid on the ground and women were cooking in the kitchen, their faces red from the heat of the fires. Mrs Loc checked her brown *Ao Dai* and flannel waistband holding her silver betel mortar to ensure that she was tidy. She then walked formally towards the front of ancestral altar, hoping and praying that the ancestors would protect Ngoc Lan now that he was in the army and help suppress the American rebellion. She hoped that the ancestors would deflect arrows and bullets from striking Ngoc Lan, and that he would return safe and sound.

The village of Phu Xuyen looked peaceful and evocative in the light of the waxing moon. People were sitting sipping their drinks and dinner was just about ready. The old women enjoyed their gossiping and, while they would never admit to it, the old men enjoyed a good chinwag as well.

"Our villages are running out of men! We are afraid that there will be no one left to bring in the harvest this year."

Mrs Loc was quite scathing when she spoke.

"There is nothing to worry about. It only needs three responsible women to plough and harrow. We may even do better than the young men, who are not even capable of catching a chicken."

The old Mrs Nguyet slowly picked up a spittoon and, in a womanly, genteel way, disposed of her chewed betel nut. When she had finished, she placed the spittoon by the wall and said:

"So many cows, oxen and buffalo are being killed or wounded by the bombs. Farming will be difficult this year. The land is hard to work by hand, so rice will not grow very well. Moreover, this year we are asked to give more rice, vegetables and meat for the cause of the army."

"I've been watching the full moon. I am afraid that there will be a drought," continued the old man, Mr Tuan, taking up where Mrs Nguyet had left off.

"There will be no drought! I think it's more likely that there will be flooding. If that happens, then we'll have nothing to eat and we will go hungry. Drought does not hold out the same fears for me. Does anybody agree with me?" asked the old man, Mr Luong.

"That is the reason why people in Ha Bac are in a hurry to carry out maintenance work on the irrigation ditches and drainage canals. They have not been done for several years. A shortage of people meant that there was nobody left to scoop the water into the fields. It's as simple as that. When I was younger, I had to bail water until my arms felt as if they were breaking," remarked the old lady, Mrs Thuy.

"Bailing water is such hard work," Mrs Nguyet agreed. "My arms ached after twenty minutes but I still had to do it, hour after hour. You can get used to carrying loads that are too heavy, you can get used to bending over and planting rice, but you never get used to bailing water. In fact, no one can!"

"The country will soon be unified," said Mrs Loc, when she had finished the ceremony of giving food to their ancestors. She was escorted to a rush mat and sat down. "Once the fighting is over, our young men will come back and they will help us to rebuild all that we have lost. In the meantime, we'll just have to manage as best as we can. Our men are sacrificing so much at the front that we have to do all that we can to support them. It isn't easy," Mrs Loc continued. "The American bombing has played havoc with our villages, hospitals, factories and schools. There is nothing left for us. Everything we have is given to the men on the front line. I am afraid that when our children return, there will be nothing left for them but ashes. We ought to be ashamed of ourselves."

"Why are the Americans so angry? Terrorists have used many pounds of explosives in their country and yet they have no qualms about dropping hundreds of thousands of tons of bombs on us," Mrs Nguyet asked.

No one could answer. At last, Mrs Nguyet decided that it was men's territory that they were venturing into. The party around them warmed up as the stories became noisier and more interesting. Mr Tap happily told everyone that his son, the young soldier Mui, would return to celebrate the Vietnamese New Year. He often sent letters home and many people were in awe of the things he wrote in his letters to his father. He even told of some infantry battalions full of students from Hanoi; many of whom had never even fired a gun before.

Ngoc Van glanced at Ngoc Lan. He had said nothing to Uncle Tap about the terrible news of his son, but inside he felt like crying. Ngoc Lan wanted to go to the South right now, to fight with the South Government and the Americans and to ask how they could commit such atrocities.

Earlier that year, Ho Chi Minh had said he was willing to lose ten men for every American soldier in order to bring peace to his country. So every young man in North Vietnam had been recruited to the army, bringing the numbers up to 3 million. There would be serious fighting ahead.

At last, Ngoc Lan entered the magic road – the Ho Chi Minh Trail. It was not as Ngoc Lan had imagined. No books or reports had mentioned that the Ho Chi Minh Trail had no clean water or how primitive the conditions were, so Ngoc Lan kept diaries and eventually he became used to jungle life. Ngoc Lan knew that the Ho Chi Minh Trail had been under attack from American bombs but what he didn't know was that there had been bombing every day. Rather than go straight to Saigon, they decided to take detours of many hundreds of kilometres to avoid the carpet-bombing. Sometimes, there was no food, so the soldiers had to eat jungle leaves and bamboo shoots. Ngoc Lan lost weight. Life on the Ho Chi Minh Trail was much more difficult compared to the training they had received in the North. Ngoc Lan was forever hungry and longed to know when he would be able to eat enough food again. If Ngoc Lan wanted to have a shower, he needed to wake up at 4.00 a.m. only to have to stand under a tree and then shake it for the water to fall on him. As the Americans were unable to use aerial photoreconnaissance to look for troop movements because of the jungle cover, they used different kinds of detection devices. The most common were microphones. Another was a machine which could detect human urine. Like all of his colleagues, when Ngoc Lan urinated, he retained the urine, so that a soldier would be able to remove it far from Ho Chi Minh Trail as a decoy, in the hope that the Americans would detect the urine and bomb that area instead. Sometimes, Ngoc Lan's unit would have support from an elephant team, and they were used to carry the equipment and supplies. Once, when especially hungry, Ngoc Lan stole the elephant's sugar (used as a reward), so the next day, the elephants refused to move until they received their sweet drink. Ngoc Lan recalled feeling rather embarrassed at the time.

On Ho Chi Minh Trail, it was not easy for the mail to get through to the troops. However, Ngoc Lan was one of the lucky ones, as not only did he receive a letter from his family, but also one from Nhat. Ngoc Lan read Nhat's over and over again, until the paper finally disintegrated and he could no longer read the words.

Ngoc Lan witnessed thousands of soldiers and officers working under the bombs every day. Sometimes, the American army used as many as 700 planes to bomb the trail in a week. Thousands of tons of bombs were dropped, killing many of the young soldiers. Despite the death of so many, no one was intimidated by the Americans. Some soldiers referred to the Americans as 'monsters', and they wanted to force them out of Vietnam. Sometimes, after a long day's trek, everyone was able to relax beside the river. After a simple meal with jungle vegetables, Ngoc Lan sang his favourite song for his colleagues, *Love song*, which was written by Hoang Viet, who went along the Ho Chi Minh Trail singing his song for the soldiers:

When I sing my love song,
To send back to my girlfriend at home.
My strong voice could drown out the sound of the bombing.
My strong voice drowns out the sound of the storm.
Darling, do you know that my song is from my heart.
I hope my song could stop the war ...

Chapter Two

Saigon 1968, Tet Offensive

By January 1968, and after several months on the Ho Chi Minh Trail to the South, Ngoc Lan's unit was finally closing in on the southern capital of Saigon. The unit stopped in the jungle, just 60 kilometres from the centre on the northern side.

Ngoc Lan heard that his unit was to be part of one of the four main axes of the attack to open the way to Saigon. That day, everyone, including Ngoc Lan, knew they were about to enter into a very important fight. By the twentieth, the day that marked the start of the Tet Offensive, Ngoc Lan's unit was located at Dong Du. For the first time, the North attempted a full-scale set-piece battle against the South, rather than the guerrilla warfare that they had been carrying out so far. It was hoped that the sight of a major victory against the South would trigger a general popular uprising amongst the people. If these people could be persuaded to take up arms in support of the Northern forces, the war would be almost over. Open-style fighting was something the Americans had been wanting for many years. They would then be able to introduce the superior firepower of the B-52s, helicopters, warships, tanks and modern weapons.

For the Vietnamese, Tet is the Lunar New Year and is as important as Christmas, Easter and all other holidays rolled into one. In previous years, there had been both official and unofficial ceasefires. It was also hoped that the South would be caught off-guard by a major offensive at such an important time (as with the Yom Kippur War in Israel) and that the holiday traffic from people travelling to see family would disguise the movement of their troops. However, Colonel Nguyen Ngoc Loan reported that the number of young people entering Saigon for Tet holiday were far more than usual. Agreeing with him, General W. Westmoreland ordered more troops from outside Saigon to return to the area as soon as possible. No one on the northern side knew what was waiting for them in Saigon; Ngoc Lan had even thought about the impending victory ... when he could go home to reunite with his new wife and of the time when, hopefully, no more bombs would fall from above on to his hometown.

When the attack came, the war entered one of its fiercest periods. Many people died and a lot more were dying from the injuries sustained from the bombing and artillery attacks. In the first week, the fighting seemed to be turning to the North's advantage.

Ngoc Lan's team celebrated New Year earlier than usual, before marching rapidly from the jungle areas to the suburbs of Saigon. The fighting was fierce and bloody. Initially taken by surprise, the Americans recovered swiftly and they began to inflict huge casualties. The fighting was not just in Saigon but Nha Trang and Cam Ranh, along with thirty-seven other cities and bases. Rumour had it that the fighting was fierce everywhere, especially around Hue, Da Nang and Saigon, and the northern armies suffered huge losses. Ngoc Lan's unit suffered huge losses too, and bodies of the North Vietnamese soldiers lay everywhere. However, there was no time and nowhere to bury them, so the corpses were simply thrown into the river, and, on occasion, rivers were dammed with bodies and streams ran deep red with blood. Otherwise, if there was a body nearby, it was simply left for the rats and crows.

Rather than retreat after the huge losses, Ngoc Lan's new team (reduced from three units to one through heavy losses), along with all the other surviving units targeted against Saigon, continued with their mission on the orders of General Giap. Ngoc Lan knew that it was a suicide mission and doomed to failure, but it was too late to turn back. The Tet Offensive attack would have to be a total surprise if they were to win, enabling the North to take over South Vietnam, in the near future.

Initially, things went well for the Northern side; some teams even reached the television station and started to transmit a recording of Ho Chi Minh, calling for a general uprising of the population of Saigon. Unfortunately, they were unable to broadcast the whole transcript because power was soon cut by the Southern forces.

Other units managed to scale the wall of the American Embassy. A short round of fire took place, resulting in the deaths of the Southern army guards. The Northern army units used RPG anti-tank rockets to blow up the main doors to the embassy, but they held firm. By this time, US Marine troops were firing from within the embassy at the Northern troops, who had no cover and were eventually forced to retreat.

Meanwhile, South Vietnam and the Americans had moved huge numbers of troops close to the areas of the expected fighting from the Cambodian and Laos borders, especially in the areas around Saigon. By the time the Vietcong and NVA troops entered Saigon, they found themselves surrounded by American troops. They attacked with great force and it was now the turn of the Northern troops to be taken by surprise. Early that morning, Ngoc Lan and his colleagues were woken to the sound of a massive attack. There was heavy gunfire everywhere and the battlefield was thick with smoke. Ngoc Lan's colleagues were dropping like flies.

After days in Saigon under the rain of gunfire, Ngoc Lan knew that the North had no chance of winning the battle. The South Vietnamese army, with excellent help from American troops, were fighting back. After two days of fighting, bad news was received on the Northern side; the first being that there were no more bullets and the second being that there was no food. Everyone, including Ngoc Lan, knew that if the North continued to fight they would suffer huge casualties.

Everybody on the Northern side could see that the Southern Vietnamese were not rising up and supporting the North in they way that had been hoped. The Vietcong and Bietdong (Southern people against the Americans; Bietdong meaning special) were in trouble, because both had also lost huge numbers. All the Northern armies were dropped into action with very few supplies of food, water and medical help from the local population.

Ngoc Lan's unit was down from hundreds of men to only eighteen, due to the Dong Du battle; he knew that his side was in a dire situation. Even though they were so low in numbers and had to leave all their shells and artillery behind, they were ordered to reform and prevent other units from retreating from the battlefield.

Armed only with AK47 assault rifles and RPG grenade launchers, Ngoc Lan's unit held out for a few more hours. Ngoc Lan and his colleagues saw the Southern army and the American troops with many different types of modern weapons. Many of those killing machines were shooting out bullets as though it were piecemeal and the Northern Vietnamese soldiers fell heavily under fire.

"Run," Ngoc Lan's friend Tuan told him, "just run," he said, having just been shot.

Being the last surviving man from his unit, Ngoc Lan ran. Suddenly, he felt something smash into his left ribs. Then he felt the pain; the pain of a thousand knives cutting into his muscles and his breath was knocked out of him. In his semi-consciousness he wondered when the pain would diminish. Why would anyone want to invent weapons that hurt humans like this? Damn all of them to hell, he thought. He looked around and felt desolate, alone in the middle of a battlefield surrounded by bodies. Nobody was alive; there was nothing apart from his companions' corpses strewn across the ground at the back of Tan Son Nhat Airport. Darkness swept before him as he was overcome by nausea and smoke. Ngoc Lan could feel the lukewarm blood oozing from between his ribs. He began to shiver from shock and became dizzy from the loss of blood. He managed to pull off his coat before he became too weak to tend to his bullet wounds.

If I am still alive at sunset it might be possible to escape, he thought to himself. He only needed to crawl about eight hundred metres further towards the hangar, and then he would be able to disappear into the wild, grassy field to safety. He was desperate not to fall into enemy hands.

Never before had Ngoc Lan waited so eagerly for sunset. The minutes felt like days. He was in terrible pain and was suffering from hunger and thirst. His lips were parched and his teeth were numb. There were provisions around him, but he dared not move for fear of being caught. He had a throbbing headache which he willed to disappear and was also conscious of a wound to his jaw. He felt sure that he was going to die and prayed to God for a miracle, even though he knew that God could not change the length of the day. His awareness of God's presence and protection from the shadow of death was what would get him through …

At last sunset came, heralding a ceasefire. For the first time since the battle had started, there was silence – an eerie silence – and he shivered from fear. He could hear the distant noise of a plane's engines and lorries as the Americans tried to regroup and regain communications and control. Ngoc Lan knew he needed to get away now if he wanted to survive. In pain, he crawled slowly towards the hangar. To this day he never understood how he managed to crawl his way through the layers of barbed wire, and how so many Americans, perched high in the defence watchtowers, never saw him. At times, he was so exhausted that he simply had to rest, whether it was lying at the foot of the sandbag walls or just outside the enemy's defence works. On the other side of the field lay the city.

Ngoc Lan had never been to Saigon before, but he was confident of finding help there. He crawled to the edge of a stream and, unable to stand his thirst any more, he bent his head to the water and drank as much as he could. He then hid himself in the middle of some wild bushes and passed out.

Ngoc Lan awoke to a burning sensation from his wounds as they were cleansed with alcohol. A beautiful young girl was looking at him with large worried eyes and next to her stood an older Vietnamese woman wearing a pale yellow silk dress. He could tell by the way she was dressed that she was cultured and she went on to address him in a friendly manner. As he tried to sit up, he wondered where he was and who they were.

"Lie down, son," said the older woman, "we're on your side and we are trying to help. You are in the hands of Saigon Special Troops."

Ngoc Lan felt relieved. These people were highly trained, carried out dangerous tasks and had been fighting for many years against South Vietnam and the Americans. If the Americans infiltrated the Saigon Special Troops army, it would have been disastrous. However, for Ngoc Lan, it was good news, because they were all in the same boat. Ngoc Lan felt at ease, because the Americans and the Southern armies would never be able to find him here.

Ngoc Lan looked around and realised for the first time that he was in a cellar. The young girl introduced herself as Little Lien and the other woman was Mrs Tam; Little Lien referred to Mrs Tam as "Mum", which meant that Little Lien was not Mrs Tam's daughter.

The young girl sounded concerned as she washed Ngoc Lan's wound.

"His wound seems to be getting better; it's certainly better than it was yesterday, but I am still concerned that it might take up to a fortnight to completely heal."

"I have other things on my mind. I am worried because the Americans are out in force looking for Northern Vietnamese citizens and those helping them. I don't want you to get caught. You must remember to be on your guard, Little Lien," replied Mrs Tam.

"Yes, I will," replied the girl. "Perhaps, we ought to ask Doctor Tan to do a few stitches so the wounds can heal quicker. We need some more painkillers ... Oh dear," she said as she pulled back the sheet and uncovered more cuts on his body.

"He must have crawled through layers of barbed wire. Look at his white skin. He must come from the North. So many of our soldiers have died. It was only this afternoon that I passed the American Embassy, and saw all the dead bodies of special troops that had still not been disposed of. It was heartbreaking."

"Mum," said Little Lien, "we are all suffering. I, too, have lost six of my friends. Do you know how I felt when I saw Vietnamese bodies littered across the city? I felt sick."

"It was May 1963 when the Americans supported General Duong Van Minh in order to kill President Diem and that was when I lost my husband and my sons ..."

"This offensive has seen the worst fighting of the war so far. This morning it was announced on the radio that up to five thousand of our soldiers have already been killed and the police have arrested hundreds of suspects during the last few days."

After Ngoc Lan's treatment, Little Lien opened the bamboo box to remove a cake, a banana and a canteen full of hot chicken soup; the smell was delicious.

Ngoc Lan was still on his guard and was unsure as to how much he could trust them, so he pretended to sleep as he listened carefully to their conversations. He glanced up at the ladies looking after him, wanting to say something or to thank them, but he was unable to move his lips, as he was suffering from exhaustion and pain. He was still feverish and he subsided into sleep once the stinging from the alcohol on his wounds had eased off.

Over the next few days, Ngoc Lan's health improved. He had many conversations with Little Lien and she told him more about Mrs Tam, the amazing woman who was fighting for her country; she, too, had lost her family in the war.

Through Little Lien, Ngoc Lan learnt that Mrs Tam's house was a revolutionary base as well as an important contact point between Saigon Special Troops (Bietdong) and the guerrilla bases in the North. In 1965, while both sides were engaging in the fighting, many innocent people had died in the crossfire, including Little Lien's family. Little Lien had left her family home to come and live with Mrs Tam, who had also suffered the same loss. These two victims of war found that they both had a common cause to fight for; both were in the same situation. Ngoc Lan had the same feelings; he, too, was alone and far away from his hometown and family. But here were two women who yesterday had been strangers and yet now he felt so close to them. In these two women he found his temporary family, and he felt like he was at home again. Mrs Tam was just like his mother, and he started to call her just that. Little Lien, whose mission was to work as a street barber for the American troops at Tan Son Nhat Airport, had found Ngoc Lan whilst patrolling the airport area.

Little Lien had burnt all Ngoc Lan's belongings, including his only photo of his wife. Initially he had been upset, but she explained that it was for his own safety; the photo of Nhat with her Northern dress could put him and everyone else in danger if it was found in his possession. Ngoc Lan knew Little Lien was right, but nothing could quell the upset that he felt now because the only photo of his wife had gone.

Little Lien brought him newspapers every morning to bring him up to date on the progress of the Tet Offensive. There was news of defeats everywhere. Ngoc Lan had thought that the attack on Saigon was the only operation, but he was shocked to discover that over sixty other operations had taken place. The fighting in and around Hue had been especially fierce. There, the old imperial city had become a killing field. He was equally horrified to learn of the scale of losses on the Northern side. Ngoc Lan agreed with Little Lien that this would be the last time that the North would carry out an operation on this scale. General Giap had to return to the guerrilla style of fighting that had been so successful in the past if he were to succeed. The Saigon newspaper reported that General Giap knew that the Offensive had lost the element of surprise, but he had still gone ahead with the attack and many thousands of people had died as a result. It proved to be a very expensive lesson.

One morning, Ngoc Lan looked at himself in the mirror and asked Little Lien if she could help him to cut his hair.

"I can't," she answered. "But I can shave your head."

"She has never cut anybody's hair before, dear," Mrs Tam told him, bringing a smile to Ngoc Lan's face.

"It's not funny," Little Lien said crossly.

Ngoc Lan did not laugh, of course; how could he. He admired Little Lien too much for all she had done to save his life, so he decided to let his hair grow instead.

Sometimes, Ngoc Lan would talk to Little Lien about the North. He told her that life in the North was always busy. The youths were fervent and conscientious, and the young women volunteered to become labourers or "assault youths". It was their job to carry ammunition boxes or repair bombed and mined out roads; jobs which were normally done by the soldiers. All of the volunteers were very brave and the women who remained on the home front were as heroic as the soldiers were.

The day would start early in the morning, with the Northern people exercising together. The clang of the gong at the cooperative barnyard would mark the start of the working day, when everybody went to his or her allotted tasks. All the fields and barns, along with the animals such as oxen, cows and bulls, were common property. People worked together and divided the profit between themselves. Everything was shared according to need. Although she had not been to the North, Little Lien still wanted to live amongst a community like that; it must be interesting, she thought. But it was the wounded and war-disabled soldiers that she and Mrs Tam hid and fed that made her feel cherished and valued. She was working towards reunification and this was far more important to her than her own desires. She wished that one day the people in the South would have a normal life under the communist party and Uncle Ho. Uncle Ho – these two words were so sacred to her. Ngoc Lan loved Little Lien's innocence and warmth. At the age of nineteen she was still inexperienced, but he admired her idealism. She wanted Vietnam to be at peace and to know justice, and was prepared to take tremendous risks to help the wounded soldiers from the North, who were paving the way for Vietnam's future. Her own mother and father had fought and died as she was now fighting; as did all of Mrs Tam's own children. She knew that if she was caught and shot there would be many other youngsters ready to take over where she had left off, and to help fulfil her dreams. She genuinely believed that the South would eventually be free.

Little Lien told Ngoc Lan that her views were simple. She did not fight for her family for the simple reason that there were no living relatives left on her side of the family. She did not fight for her children, because she was not yet married and because it was too far into her future. She fought and would sacrifice everything for what she believed in, for justice. Her beliefs gave her strength, courage and patience. She was no different to all the other young people who loved their country, and Ngoc Lan respected her beliefs.

Ngoc Lan thought back to the frenzy of the Tet holiday, just as if it had happened yesterday. His companions who had fought with him had all died and he vowed that he would never forget how courageously they had stood their ground and their bravery which helped protect him as he escaped to safety.

One night, Little Lien told Ngoc Lan that he would have a surprise visitor; the visitor being the Minister of Defence of South Vietnam. Ngoc Lan was worried that Mrs Tam was going to turn him over to the police for a reward, but was relieved to discover that Little Lien was just teasing him.

It was another week before Ngoc Lan recovered his strength enough to walk again. Doctor Tan was surprised at how quickly Ngoc Lan had recovered and put it down to the several months of walking along the Ho Chi Minh Trail that had kept him fit and strong. Leaning on Little Lien's shoulder for support, he climbed the stairs to the living room. The room was large and the walls were covered with wood panelling. Towards the back of the room was a large sofa, which was covered in rich, burgundy velvet. The floor was laid with shiny white tiles with intricate patterns, like a roman mosaic, and there were pictures with beautiful landscapes hung on the wall. Ngoc Lan recognised the names of the famous artists and knew that a couple of them must be at least eighty years old. Looking through the door to the dining room, he could see a long, dark table with six chairs down each side, each embedded with mother-of-pearl motifs. At the end of the dining room were some french windows that opened out on to the long garden where all different kinds of fruit trees were growing. It was such a relief to be able to see the sky after a week of being cooped up in the cellar. Ngoc Lan now realised why the house was so safe; the Southern police would not even begin to suspect that such a rich family as Mrs Tam's would assist the Vietcong or the Northern army.

The said visitor arrived later that morning, and this was the first time that Ngoc Lan had met his boss, who agreed to keep him in Saigon. As a soldier, Ngoc Lan was used to obeying the orders of a superior immediately and without question. Ngoc Lan's boss ordered him to stay inside Saigon for the new mission, where he would be closely involved with the Bietdong. The Bietdong in Saigon had a network of many small groups; they attacked the Americans from inside Saigon and were used to working undercover. They were also well connected with the Vietcong, who were fighting against the Americans. The Vietcong and Bietdong already had very good intelligence as they had many spies, but placing an agent with this amount of access to top secret information was priceless. Ngoc Lan's mission would mean he would have access to vast amounts of important information, which could be used in the fight for reunification and would be worth ten of their normal spies. Little Lien explained that the reason why the Bietdong's boss wanted him was because he looked the image of someone else, and she asked how he felt about becoming a member of the Bietdong.

"I am surprised, but I'd love to work with the Bietdong of Saigon."

"You'll have lots of fun working for them, I'm sure."

"I have no idea how I will be able to cope. Surely they must know I have no experience or knowledge about anything like that," he added, with a note of worry in his voice.

Little Lien dropped her head down, trying to hide her smile.

"You'll need to learn quickly then."

Ngoc Lan told Little Lien that he would do his best, because the only way he could go back home was if the war was over and Vietnam was unified. However, Ngoc Lan had had no time to be homesick. So many things had happened in the past few months and with his new mission having been revealed to him, he had to give it his full concentration. Ngoc Lan began his new mission immediately after his boss had left, when Little Lien gave him a long list of things to learn; he found everything new and exciting.

In preparation for his mission, his first lesson was to learn how to behave as a Saigon citizen. For a month, Ngoc Lan learned to act and speak like one of them and to eat spicy food, which Ngoc Lan hated the most. The second lesson he had to learn was to act as a very modest upper-class Southern Vietnamese citizen, who loved the Americans and their style, and approved of their actions in Vietnam. He also had to pretend to people that he hated the North and the communists, which was proving to be very difficult, as Ngoc Lan had been brought up to be very proud of his Vietnamese culture and traditions, and his love for the North – his home country – was not easily allayed. The third lesson was easier, which was to learn to make women fall in love with him, and Ngoc Lan enjoyed "practising" with Little Lien. The fourth lesson was learning to use a gun. He had to be equally good and fast with both hands. Each day, after dark, Ngoc Lan would go out, while Little Lien stayed at home with Mrs Tam, as he was being taught how to drive a car by Doctor Tan.

One month later, Ngoc Lan was sent by another boss to a training school, in Cu Chi for further instruction. Ngoc Lan never met him before, but was able to contact him via a secret letter box. Their first meeting took place in the middle of a field, after a Vietcong supporter had gone with him from Mrs Tam's house. From there, Ngoc Lan was told to close his eyes by yet another man. Ngoc Lan was then escorted beneath the earth to an underground city.

Ngoc Lan was astounded by what he saw in the tunnels. There was a carefully hidden trap-door leading into a dark, cramped tunnel, barely three feet high and two feet wide. As he followed his guide, he would occasionally warn Ngoc Lan not to step on a certain place, otherwise his foot would fall through into a booby trap of some kind. One of the favourite methods used was that of wooden spikes, which had been smeared with human excrement. These were used to injure any American troops that were brave enough to try to follow them. The spikes alone would be enough to put an unlucky person stepping on to them in hospital for a while. The Vietcong people told Ngoc Lan that the sight of the infection caused by the human excrement would shake the morale of other troops tasked with the job of clearing the tunnels.

The tunnels constantly changed direction and level, as did the type of booby trap. They also seemed endless, and Ngoc Lan eventually learned that they formed a round circuit of 185 kilometres. Every so often they opened out into rooms, where troops and their families slept. Other rooms formed operation-planning areas, schools or hospitals. The kitchens had special chimneys that carefully dispersed the smoke and smells of cooking. Everybody living underground had to wash with western-style soap, so that the tracker dogs used by the Americans would be confused and unable to distinguish from the smells of their handlers and the tunnel inhabitants. Ngoc Lan was proud to learn that 5,000 men, women and children, including himself, were resuming a normal life in the tunnels.

Parts of the tunnels were located under the airport and, occasionally, at night, the Vietcong would raise their guns above ground and shoot towards a perimeter sentry box. Southern troops would be led to believe that they were under attack and return fire. It would result in a fire fight, with Southern forces shooting at each other. The Vietcong would be long gone by the time discipline was restored, and not before there were many Southern casualties.

Ngoc Lan was filled with encouragement, for the undertaking of such a huge construction job could not have been done without the support of the local Vietnamese. In the three months of living in the Cu Chi Tunnels, Ngoc Lan learned to speak as a Southern Vietnamese person and he learned to become a Southern Vietnamese police officer. In the following months, Ngoc Lan worked hard, as there was much to learn. Sometimes, Ngoc Lan felt so tired what with sixteen hours of learning each day for his exams that he lost a stone in weight, but people said he looked a lot better for it. Ngoc Lan learned to become a charming, smart young gentleman, and he learned to become an intelligent, hard-working, skilful police officer. Ngoc Lan could never imagine how he could learn about all the court procedures, which would normally take five years to complete at university. However, the training gave him confidence and he eagerly anticipated the start of his mission, even though he still did not know exactly what he would be doing or who he would be. Life in the tunnels and all the training was so interesting that Ngoc Lan didn't have time to miss his family and his only love, Nhat.

When the training was complete, Ngoc Lan was set straight to work. He and his team went to Can Tho and, after the murder of the policeman

Chapter Two

Nguyen Van Tu, it now became clear that he would take on that man's identity. Ngoc Lan never forgot the night of the murder, and that night heralded the start of Ngoc Lan's new life.

Chapter Three

After the Tet Offensive had been set up and the arrests that followed, the number of profiles in the secret documents of Vietcong room increased dramatically. The increase in numbers was mainly due to the Vietnamese people who had helped the Northern armies or were simply against the Americans. A record number of extra staff had either been recruited or transferred. Lieutenant Tu was one such officer who had been transferred, moving from Can Tho to the Communist Public Record Office (PRO). Lieutenant Tu was Ngoc Lan's mission, and he would assume his identity. Tu's CV was perfect and in a short time it was to open up even more opportunities. Ngoc Lan's boss hoped that Agent 022 would be able to integrate quickly and win over his colleagues' hearts and respect. The Bietdong team had great expectation for Ngoc Lan, along with everyone else who was involved, including Little Lien, who was looking forward to his first day at work. Everything was running so smoothly for the false Lieutenant Tu that he began to feel more confident with the impending operation. Perhaps everything had been arranged too perfectly. The Intelligence Agency had prepared everything with consideration and wisdom. The move from the Cu Chi tunnel to the beautiful apartment in the upper-class area of Saigon was a huge jump for Ngoc Lan, and he quickly became accustomed to nice food, the comfy bed, the air conditioning and the hot water for a shower. However, the first day at work did not go as they had hoped, as "Police Lieutenant Tu" had overslept.

"Sorry I am late."

That was the first thing that Agent 022 said to his colleagues. The previous night he had tried to think about what he would say the next day, something like "How do you do," "Nice to meet you", and "my name is ...", but this was not to be.

"You are ...?" his boss, a fat man called Major Vuong Duong Vinh in a white uniform, asked, as everyone looked at Ngoc Lan expectantly, waiting to see what the outcome would be.

Ngoc Lan hesitated and tried to remember his name.

"My name is ..." Ngoc Lan paused, then continued, "is Nguyen Van Tu. I have been transferred from Can Tho and these are my orders."

"Welcome to the secret documents department of the Vietcong office," Vinh said warmly.

Later that day, Vinh took Tu on a tour around the office, and introduced him to everybody. Tu was introduced to Lieutenant Mai, Lieutenant Rang and Lieutenant An. It also gave him a chance to look around his new office, which was medium sized with American office equipment; Tu even had a new desk and leather chair. Vinh also took the opportunity to point out some of the more important rules and customs such as the safe.

"This safe," Vinh indicated, "is where we keep all the secret documents about the Vietcong and details of all the people we believe to be working for North Vietnam within our country. We must never remove any documents from this room or take them home."

Tu could not believe his eyes. He was so close to the entire secret documents held on the Vietcong, Bietdong and the Northern people that he wished he had a lighter to burn it all. However, he simply said, "I'm going to love my job," which made his new colleagues laugh.

Tu's first week went well and he felt as though he was living a Hollywood film. It had only been a week since Ngoc Lan had been taken out of the Cu Chi tunnels, when he had been blindfolded, and loaded on to the back of a lorry with two other men with whom he had been training. And he was now playing the role of a Southern Vietnam policeman. It all seemed like a dream, because it had all gone so fast.

For the first month, Tu spent all his free time exploring Saigon. Coming from a farming village with no electricity, the bright lights of Saigon were a major culture shock. The shops were open all night; the bars and the cinemas were all new to him. Everybody whizzed by on motorcycles or in American cars. In his village in the North, there had been no secrets and everybody had to behave themselves. Saigon was different to the North, and Tu tried to get his bearings. He had lived for the past few months in the cellars of Mrs Tam's house, and he had seen very little when he was learning to drive with Doctor Tan. Tu was now rather excited about the prospect of discovering Saigon in his own way. Here, it meant nothing if Tu wanted to go into a bar, get drunk and pay for the company of a girl for the night. The lack of rules here compared to the strictness of the village was like a flash of realisation for Tu. The amount of money he had to spend compared to the bartering economy of the North was a further revelation for him.

The capital of South Vietnam looked more like an American city. Many of the streets had American names, and everything came from America: clothes, food and household furniture. There was even an advert for an American film with Bob Hope, and Marilyn Monroe's picture posted to the walls all over the city. There were American soldiers, officers and their families everywhere. Tu knew that America was pouring more troops into Vietnam than ever before – five hundred thousand. However, he was still surprised to see Saigon with so many American people and he enjoyed watching the Americans in Saigon's streets – something he had never seen before. The dress sense of Saigon's citizens was equally as smart as that of the Americans. Everything was new to Tu and it seemed as if he was in a different world. However, the situation unfolding in front of Tu's eyes worried him. The North was strong and they used hand-held weapons and had huge numbers of troops, but here, in the South, he could see far more modern weapons, including tanks, lorries, planes and armoured personnel carriers, all of which were manufactured in America.

The picture that Saigon presented to Tu of city life was vast, and he could see a huge difference between the rich and poor with nothing in between. Saigon District I was for the rich, with smart-looking villas, hotels or offices. However, not far from Saigon's District I were poor people who lived in poorer areas. Their houses were made from bamboo trees and there was no clean water. During the summer months, children and elderly people were used to living in the streets.

Tu's mission didn't involve too much work. New cases arrived in the office every day, and he would report it in such a way that it was less hazardous for the Vietcong. To cast off any suspicion, he would tell his colleagues that they must be careful, because if the case was wrong, then the Vietcong and the North could use it against the country. On occasion,

Tu would come across important documents giving detailed information about certain suspects and he would try to send messages warning them, so they could hide or move on before the police came to arrest them.

Tu lived comfortably on the salary of a lieutenant and experienced the freedom of the South. He had the use of a chauffeur-driven car well as his own private car, which he enjoyed driving. However, Tu had many questions that needed answering about the South. He had always been taught that non-communists were bad, but the evidence that he had seen and the freedom that the people had been given was so very different to what he had been led to believe by the Northern government. As to whether one should follow the communism or non-communism path was something for the government and the leaders to decide. They were the only ones who had the authority to make decisions. For the moment, Tu was happy and enjoyed his salary and his new car.

With his new-found freedom, Tu was able to travel everywhere, say hello to anyone and, on occasion would stop at a Vietnamese tea shop to treat himself to a tiny a cup of green tea. The tea shops in the North, and South have similarities. Both would be small, either set on the street or pavement. Sometimes, if it rained, the tea shop owner would protect their stalls and customers by throwing a large sheet of clear plastic over the stall.

One day, Tu met Little Lien at Ben Thanh Market. She scolded him and told him that he should be more careful, because spying was not a game. Once again, Tu disagreed with her, so he jumped into his car and sped away, leaving a worried Little Lien behind. Tu certainly enjoyed driving fast and wondered why women, like Little Lien, liked to complain and to stop men from having fun.

Tu had lived in Saigon for a while before he had been sent to Cu Chi, so it very much felt as if he was returning to his hometown. He felt a strong bond between himself and Saigon. Everyone said hello to him and sometimes he bumped into people and they would introduce themselves, simply because they were relatives of his colleagues. Despite the war, the people in Saigon were very friendly and Tu was proud to work and fight for them.

Tu was single, of course, and because he was from Can Tho, he had been given a one-bed apartment at the police headquarters. Being single, like Tu, Rang had the room next door. He led a typical bachelor's lifestyle, often playing practical jokes, and he had many girlfriends; but he was an angry man, devoid of any human kindness. Maybe it was because of his job. When he first applied to be a special police officer, he had been turned down. Rang assumed that this was because he came from a poor family, so he hated all his white-collared colleagues, who had all come from rich VIP families. However, Rang was a Christian and when he found out that Tu was a Christian, too, he immediately formed a friendship with him. Sometimes, on a Sunday morning, Rang would drive Tu to the church in his jeep. One day, after church, Tu met a beautiful young girl and Rang told Tu all about her. It turned out that Vinh had once been infatuated with her and he also discovered that she was the daughter of Charles and Ann Philippe, the owners of a rubber plantation in Dau Tieng and a shipping company. The Philippe family were very influential. Many of their close friends were VIPs in the government, and Ann Philippe was the ex-lover of the president and was still very friendly with him.

Rang then added, "We all fancy Nicole, I'm afraid."

"I don't, I'm afraid," Tu replied.

He thought of Nhat, his much-loved wife in the North, and he missed her a lot. The last letter he had received from her was when he had been on the Ho Chi Minh Trail. When the American bombing campaign of the Trail had ceased, there would remain the danger of unexploded bombs. It was crucial to clear the road and the driver would often ask all his passengers to climb out and unload any cargo. He would then drive close to the bomb or, if needed, over it, to make it explode. If he was very lucky, he would be flung clear, with only minor scratches and bruises. If he was lucky, he would be killed outright; and at worst, he would be a mangled wreck, far from any medical care. The mangled lorry would be pushed clear of the road and the traffic would flow south again. After the bombing raid, Ngoc Lan's team had needed to move on, so after a difficult day, he had opened Nhat's letter and read it aloud to everyone. His wife had given birth to a baby boy, which meant that the North could potentially have another soldier; this concept was amazing and he felt so proud.

Nhat had not received any news from him since the Tet Offensive, so he knew that she would be worried, but she would know that he was still alive because she would not have received an official notification of his death. All he had been through over the past few months was something he hadn't yet come to terms with.

"Anyway, you don't stand a chance," Rang finished, interrupting Tu's thoughts as he entered the church hall for a cup of tea. That month, the church had two young girls helping in the kitchen, so Rang used to stay for a cup of tea after the service.

One afternoon it poured down quite unexpectedly, so everybody in the street ran for cover to avoid getting wet. Tu put his hand out of the window to let the rain collect in his hand. Rang delighted at seeing people's clothes getting wet and joked about how silly the white-coated police officers were about not wanting to get their uniforms wet. It was only that week Rang had received a letter from his mother who was a farmer. She had written saying that they were in desperate need of rain, as the rice crop was parched. Phan Thiet, his hometown, was in an area renowned for its hot and dry weather, and it was therefore difficult to grow rice there.

"Farmers have been waiting for this rain for a long time," Rang explained.

Tu agreed, "It hasn't rained for two months. Most of the rice is parched and dying. Perhaps this rain can save the harvest."

Rang looked at Tu with astonishment; he had always thought that the policemen in the general office came from rich families, rather than from farming stock. He had never come across anybody who had the faintest idea about farming, which made Rang view Tu in a different light. He started to warm to Tu and two weeks later, he asked Tu to join him for a drink after work. For Rang, going to the bars meant going with call girls. However, for Tu, who came from an area that had no bars, it meant an evening of expensive drinks, which were ten times more expensive than they would be if they stayed at home.

They entered a quiet bar in Le Thanh Ton Street; sentimental music could be heard in the background and there were quite a lot of young women lounging around in revealing clothes. Two young women sat together at the lieutenants' table, wearing red skirts and nothing more apart from red bras to match their skirts. The dancing girls on the stage were replaced by a naked floor show, something Tu had never seen before. A waiter brought a bottle of whisky and four glasses with soda and ice to the table. Tu gave the waiter a tip and asked him for a receipt.

Pouring the whisky, Tu said, with an air of annoyance, "Rang and the rest of you may think that I am mad, but this type of music isn't my scene. Music is a very important part of our country's culture, and is indispensable in our spiritual life. Through music, this country's civilisation can be shown in different lights. How would the world see our country's customs, traditions and civilisation in this modern, hippy, sentimental trash?"

"Teenagers love it … so do I," chipped in Rang.

"I don't," Tu said, but remembered back to when he was young, when he liked, noisy music, too.

"I think Brother Tu is right," said Rang. "Bottoms up!" Tu finished his drink in one gulp. "I've found my new best friend," Rang said, as he poured himself another glass of whisky.

Tu said nothing. He was finding it so easy to become friends with this police officer that he felt he could make one hundred new friends every evening. He smiled at the thought although it appeared that he was smiling at one of the girls.

"Why are you laughing at me?" one of them asked Tu.

"Am I?" Tu asked.

"Of course he is not," Rang answered for him. "He fancies you; would you like to go out with us tonight?"

"Maybe," the girl answered. "Where are we going?"

"The police headquarters," Tu replied.

"No thank you," said the girls, and immediately left the table.

Rang looked at Tu with astonishment, wondering at Tu's stupidity. It wasn't just Rang who thought this; everyone at the office thought this of Tu. Even General Co and Loan; but they were fond of Tu, because he was dependable and reliable, and they knew that if they were in need of something, they could depend on Tu first and foremost.

Chapter Four

After several months of lying low and trying to integrate, Tu became more confident and active in his role. He now felt able to visit Mrs Tam at any time of day or night. Tu confided in Mrs Tam that he was concerned that one day someone who knew the real Tu might suddenly realise that he was an impostor.

"Tu's family are all dead and almost all of his close friends are dead, too. Don't forget, you could always be suffering from poor memory and I'm quite sure you could bluff your way out. I honestly don't think you have anything to worry about, dear."

Mrs Tam also told Tu that it could be long a time before he would be able to return to the North and therefore Tu should consider starting a new life for himself in Saigon. He was single, an eligible bachelor and he needed to marry into the right social circle, in order to be able to eliminate any suspicions. Tu could not believe what he had just heard; he couldn't marry again – he was already a married man.

"I know it's not easy," Mrs Tam continued, "but it will help you adjust to your new life. I want no more than for you to be safe and well, Tu. We will try to find you a rich girl, very rich, so if you wanted to you could live a life of luxury, which will perhaps help you to forget all about Tu's old friends. You once told me about Nicole. What do you think of her?"

"I don't know," Tu answered. He recalled that terrible party where everyone had looked down on him.

"Do you like her?" Mrs Tam asked again.

"Of course he likes her," Little Lien answered for him.

Mrs Tam and Little Lien helped Tu as much as they could, which made Tu feel as though he was working with them as a team, rather than strangers giving orders. His boss was very powerful and if Tu needed anything, a

Mercedes or money to act the part of the son of a rich family, for example, his boss could immediately despatch it to him via the secret letter box. Knowing the power behind him, Tu became increasingly confident in the operation. After a long day at work as a police lieutenant, Tu used to visit Mrs Tam and Little Lien instead of going to the pub with Rang.

One particular summer's night, Little Lien had made some spring rolls and she served their dinner on the floor, rather than at the dining table, because she knew that Tu liked to retain the traditional ways of Vietnam. A large mat of cane strips was rolled out on floor with a large rotating wooden platter in the centre; Little Lien tried to do everything with the correct etiquette especially for him. Once the dishes of food had been placed on the platter, everybody sat on the mat with their bowls and chopsticks. There were Vietnamese spring rolls, fresh fish cooked with chilli and pineapple, and pork cooked with onion, garlic and spring onions, all of which smelt delicious. The last thing Little Lien did was to place a mixture of chopped chilli and fish sauce on a couple of tiny saucer-shaped dishes.

After dinner, Tu helped her with the washing-up.

"What are you thinking about?" Little Lien asked, after Tu had dropped some china onto the floor.

"I am thinking about my next marriage," said Tu, as he swept up the broken pieces.

"You should be happy," she joked, laughingly.

"Are you joking?"

"No, I'm not," Little Lien said, thinking what fun it could be to tease Tu. This would be something about which she could joke for many months to come.

A short while later she voiced her concerns with Mrs Tam.

"Mum, tell Brother Tu to get married and be done with it," suggested Little Lien, in her typically cheeky tone.

"Well," answered Mrs Tam, seriously, "Tu's future wife must have rather special qualities if she is to help him, Little Lien. And Tu must be attractive enough for the girl with whom we want him to fall in love."

"Then he will become snobby and forget us," Little Lien said, sulkily.

"I doubt that. But certainly I'm attractive and handsome; I can make any girl fancy me if I need to," said Tu.

However, it was this, more than anything else, that made him realise how much control he had lost over his own life. But if his bosses were to tell him to act the part of president or disappear, then he would be forced to obey orders, no matter what the personal cost.

"Don't you like that idea?" Little Lien asked Tu, as she continued to quiz him; she knew that Tu needed to marry a girl from a known anti-communist family, or at least a family with one or more young men in the army. A family that helped with the war effort would also be an advantage.

Little Lien cherished Tu. Ever since the day that Ngoc Lan had become Agent 022, even if it was a big mistake, he had duly acted the part of Lieutenant Tu. He did everything with such professionalism, as if he had been doing it all his life, that Little Lien could not help but admire his courage. He demonstrated a true actor's ability and she idolised him. She would never have admitted it, but there was a possibility, a suppressed daydream, that maybe one day he could be something more to her, but for now, brotherly love was enough. However, such bittersweet moments passed quickly, to be replaced by a sacred friendship, which can only exist between fellow comrades-in-arms.

"What do you think of my getting married for a second time?" Tu asked Little Lien, as everyone sat down for coffee.

Little Lien smiled happily.

"You are lucky; as far as I know you will be marrying another, and then another!"

"I'd rather kill myself."

Little Lien felt sorry for Tu, so she stopped teasing him. "You are only doing it for the cause. It doesn't actually mean anything, but I never understood why our boss ever included you in this important mission."

"Do you think I am stupid?"

"Well, I never thought you were intelligent, Brother Tu. Being in love or marrying another beautiful girl isn't exactly hard work, is it? I thought most men would be pleased to take on another wife. Just look at you. Stop acting as though you are any different to any other man in this world ..."

At first, Tu thought Little Lien was a little over the top, but when he thought about what she had said, he calmed down somewhat. Little Lien was young, and young people were always happy; they saw the world in a different light. Their knowledge of life might not be from experience, but they were intelligent, and Tu loved to work with them. Take Little Lien, for example, she made life a lot easier for Tu, and sometimes, when Tu was stressed, he would talk with her, for without knowing, she would alleviate his stress.

"I don't know," Tu pondered. He was a pawn on a chess board, and was unable to see the humour in Little Lien's joke. "I am a communist party member ..."

He stopped himself in his tracks immediately and looked at Little Lien and Mrs Tam. He had just made a major slip of the tongue and, being an intelligence officer operating inside enemy territory, he could not afford to make such mistakes.

"Whoops," he said sheepishly.

"Don't worry. I'm sure that this will be the last time you will make that mistake," Mrs Tam reassured him.

Tu looked at Little Lien, who was amused by the slip of his tongue.

Then Mrs Tam turned to Little Lien, "What did you do to him, I asked you to help him, didn't I?"

"I am helping him, Mum. It is very simple for a girl to fall in love with Brother Tu, if he just follows my advice. He needs to wear smart clothes and bring flowers every time he visits. Women love to hear how much they are loved, so just say you love her ten times a day; that is all."

"Ok, ok," said Tu. Then he turned to Mrs Tam: "I have been invited to the Philippe's for dinner next week," he said, changing the subject.

"You should go," Mrs Tam answered with a smile.

"I have to go. I am expected to be General Co's guest."

"I know," Mrs Tam said, but Tu did not understand her until he discovered the real story ten years later.

Mrs Tam, realising she had said something she shouldn't have, became flustered.

"I mean, I know General Co as everyone does in Saigon."

Then Mrs Tam proceeded to tell Tu more about General Co. He was one of thirteen generals who had helped Prime Minister Nguyen Cao Ky gain power in 1963, when Ngo Dinh Diem had been killed by General Minh's bodyguard, which is why he was popular in Thieu-Ky's government.

Tu was very worried, and he wondered whether General Co knew the real Tu. If so, his head might not stay on his neck. However, Tu said nothing, because he knew that Little Lien would think he was scared. Instead, he kept looking at himself in the mirror to check if his eyes, nose, and even his hair, really looked the image of the real Tu.

Chapter Five

President Nguyen Van Thieu stood rather impatiently with his chin jutting out as his servant made final adjustments to the collar of his tunic. The servant sighed inwardly, hoping the president would choose this one. He had tried on five suits so far and this, the worst one, had caused peals of stifled laughter when the servant had told the wardrobe mistress of his latest choice. Thieu was restless, because he was awaiting the arrival of someone special. In order to be alone, he had sent his wife Thu Thuy, to attend a meeting with the mayor of Saigon concerning a so-called "Women's Liberation Association".

The expected car, a white Rolls-Royce, pulled into the drive of the Presidential Palace and came to a halt outside the main entrance. The chauffeur, dressed in a smart uniform, hurried to open the door. A woman in her mid-forties stepped gracefully out of the car. She was elegantly dressed and whilst not beautiful, she had an aristocratic allure. She had a tall and slender figure and she wore a perfectly tailored white dress. The dress came to just below her knees and had a wide, plunging V-neckline, displaying a pearl necklace, along with a pearl hairpin clasped to her neatly tied-up hair. Her red lips gleamed under the bright sun. She was Mrs Ann Philippe, the wife of a Frenchman who lived just a short distance from the palace. For a long time now, some of the police officers from the Intelligence Department, which was responsible for security, had wondered why the French family were able to live so close to the secret emergency tunnel from the palace. Very few people knew that Ann had been a girlfriend of Thieu when they were teenagers.

Thieu was at the door to welcome her in person.

"Hello, younger sister Ann," he said seductively.

"Good morning, Brother Six," replied the woman, referring to him by his common nickname.

"Good morning, Ann, you are looking lovely," he proffered.

"And you look decidedly nervous!" said Ann.

"I am ok, thank you; I thought you might walk here." Thieu said with a smile. "Come in," he added, as he made way for her to enter. Ann seemed to be familiar with the palace as she crossed the big hall and made her way towards the main living room. From there, he guided her into a private room, which was only used for his closest friends and family. Ann seated herself on an ivory chair upholstered with silk. Thieu, with his ever-ready smile, sat opposite her and was eager to talk to her, even though they had last met only two weeks beforehand.

"How are you, Ann? How is everyone, and how about your daughter Nicole? The one I like to call Thu Cuc."

"She's fine; she loves her Vietnamese name, Thu Cuc. Sometimes even I have to make a concerted effort to call her Nicole."

"I'm not surprised. When I was eighteen, I, too, liked American names ..." He paused briefly, then continued, "And it was at that age that we first met," the President volunteered, with a forced smile.

Ann laughed sweetly: "Brother Six, that is an old story; anyway, General Co told me that he knew someone at police headquarters who would be a perfect match for Nicole. Apparently, the man comes from an upper-class family in Can Tho. I believe his name is Nguyen Van Tu; son of Sir Nguyen Van Bay."

"Promise me you will not follow the old Vietnamese custom of choosing a husband for Nicole. You should let her decide for herself. I don't think General Co has any idea about Nicole's boyfriend. However, I do know that Mr Nguyen Van Bay was a hero of our country; I would love to meet his son."

"That's why I like Lieutenant Tu, darling."

Thieu said nothing; he had heard only too clearly what Ann was trying to say. He remained quiet for a while, then changed the subject. "Anyway, how is Charles?"

"My husband is fine, but he is concerned as to why you keep changing generals," said Ann, whose eyes now matched her worried tone. "You're changing so many things in such a short space of time, brother."

"Things could be worse," replied the President gravely. "It is a complicated story, because it involves Mr Khiem and Mr Diem, as well as the Vietnamese ambassadors in Washington. For the past few years we have sent them hundreds of millions of dollars, and yet their bank account is empty. The embassy can't explain where the money has gone. We believe that they have used many millions of dollars, which were supposed to be gifts to the Kennedy family and some VIPs in the White House. It also includes a suitcase with one million dollars in cash, addressed to the Vice President of America, which was sent as part of a 'diplomatic package', which is why there is no documentation. They were lying and this scandal has been linked to some of the people in my government. Darling Ann, if someone does not agree with my policies and those of the White House, then they will have to leave."

"I do worry when you let the White House step their feet into your government," Ann said.

"I don't believe our country is strong enough to defeat North Vietnam; yet some people like what the Americans are doing, and others do not; I can't do anything about that. However, we are lucky to get excellent support from America and America is our ally; let's hope things will go well."

Ann gave him a nice smile: "You are very clever; I am proud of you."

Ann stayed for lunch with Thieu and when she was about to leave, he asked her when he could see her again. For Thieu, seeing Ann was the highlight of his private life and for Ann, Thieu would always have a special place in her heart. She felt sorry for the situation he was in and she wanted to help him, so she decided she would remain in Saigon to be there for him.

"Do I need to make an appointment to see you?" Thieu asked jokingly, as Ann was about to leave.

"Yes, you do," Ann replied, with a smile.

"Darling …" Thieu said, a little awkwardly, "I love you."

Ann remained silent. Thieu had been waiting for many years just to hear Ann say that she loved him one more time.

Over the years, Thieu had developed a cold and brutal personality. This was probably due to his thirst for power which had consumed him over the years. Thieu had changed so much from when he had been a soldier to where he was now. Ann had always been enchanted by his charm and seductive voice, and this was still the case. Their story went back a long way. Ever since Thieu had been very young, his one wish had been to become President. No one but Ann had taken him seriously. Twenty-four years ago, Ann's father had ordered, as a condition of Thieu marrying his daughter, that Thieu should give up his post in the army. Ann's father did not want his only daughter to become a young widow. He had been forced to choose between his love of Ann and his job in the army – he chose his job – which Thieu saw as a stepping stone to power. So their relationship was over. However, those people who were close to Thieu knew that he had always loved her. The newspapers, however, always gave the impression that Thieu and his wife were the perfect family.

Thieu stood outside the palace and waved goodbye to Ann, standing there until her car had disappeared from sight.

"Mr President," his bodyguard's voice cut through his reverie. "You have someone waiting on the phone, Brigadier General Cao Van Vien, I believe, sir."

"Tell him I will call him back later," he replied, with a tone of exasperation as his private secretary approached.

"Sir, your letter for President Nixon is ready."

"Bring it to my office."

"Sir, we have had news …"

"What news?"

"I am very sorry, sir; our campaign in Quang Tri was …" He paused as he tried to think of the least shocking words "… heavily defeated."

"Damn!" Thieu shouted, before turning back towards the palace.

Chapter Six

Ann and Charles Phlippe who owned Rose Villa in Mac Dinh Chi were hosting an important dinner for Prime Minister Quat. The villa was brightly lit and the servants were bustling around in preparation until six o'clock when the servants retired to their quarters. Ann had prepared green Thai mango to be served with vintage whisky.

It wasn't long before Ann heard the noise of the heavy iron gate opening, heralding her guest's imminent arrival.

"Good evening, my dear friend," said Ann, as Prime Minister Quat arrived.

"Good evening! How are you?" The prime minister's tone was friendly.

"We are all fine, thank you," said Ann. "Come in, Brother Quat."

"I hear you've had a meeting with the President Thieu?"

"I had hoped to be able to glean some information, but things didn't work out the way I'd hoped. I am sorry, Brother Quat," Ann replied.

"Then it is with regret that I must inform you that I am left with no other option than to hand in my official resignation tomorrow," he announced sadly.

"Oh, my dear friend, I am very sorry to hear that."

"Nguyen Cao Ky is going to take over my position," said Quat bitterly.

"I know," said Ann softly. "Have you got any plans? Have you thought about living in France?"

"Possibly," answered Quat hesitantly.

Quat told Ann there was a good likelihood that Ky would order his forces to assassinate him. He wondered whether their previous relationship would bear any weight on how he was viewed now. It was not likely though as recent history has shown that Vietnamese ex-prime ministers fared very badly. It was unrealistic to expect special treatment from him, especially being aware of the fact that the CIA and the Vietnamese Secret Agencies would be following his every move.

"If the situation becomes any more complicated," said Ann, "I will be forced to sell up and move back to France with my husband and daughter."

"Perhaps that would be the right thing to do," replied Quat. "I always held onto the fact that peace would reign, but I no longer have the courage of my convictions. The government has been rendered powerless, and the more the Americans give, the more they feel within their rights to manipulate the situation to their advantage." Quat poured himself another whisky. The surplus money that the Americans had sent over for the cause, had been viewed by Quat as being available funds for the taking.

Ann looked around warily. The prime minister's guards were standing watch, guns at the ready. Rose Villa was safe, but you never knew if someone was watching.

Ann pointed to the Tien Phong newspaper on the edge of the table and said, "There's an article in the paper that says that all the army campaigns and operational plans seem to be known by the North even before our own officers hear of them. It also suggests that there are North Vietnamese spies in our government, and in the Ministry of Defence, as well as in police headquarters!"

"I have nothing more to say on the matter!" replied Quat. "I have sent my resignation mainly because I have issued a list of five generals who I suspect of being communist, which is why they have forced me to step down. You mustn't believe what the media are saying about me! In my opinion, the Americans seem to be on quite good terms with South Vietnam, but they have been mislead since they have followed Minh's way."

"They have reason to, and everybody knows why that is."

"Do you think Thieu welcoming Minh back it is a good idea? I've heard a rumour going around, saying that Minh is selling American weapons to the Vietcong. Now that I have retired, if Vietcong take over the country then it isn't my concern any more … Anyway, where is Charles?"

"He went out to meet Thieu. They have some business or other to attend to."

As it happened, Quat had been so ineffectual that his resignation the next day didn't in fact cause much of a stir. During his time as prime minister, the country had been anything but safe. The Americans always had the final say in the country's affairs. The Vietong and Bietdong (special South Vietnamese partisans fighting against the Americans) had carried out constant guerrilla warfare and the North Vietnamese army continued to harass the northern borders, leaving behind scores of dead soldiers. As leader, he should have let his people's interests govern his actions, but, unfortunately, he had not. He was not the first leader who had unwisely led his people to war. Everything he had done had been driven by his insatiable greed for power. He commented that sometimes he felt that he was just a figurehead and it was others who did all the real work. Nevertheless, as long as he was able to satisfy his own vanity, he was content. For these reasons, handing in his resignation was a good move on his part. However, letting Ky take over as prime minister was like setting the fox to look after the hens.

Later that night, Ann was waiting for her husband in the bedroom and when he finally arrived, she put down the book she was reading: "I have been so worried about you. I don't know what I would do if anything happened to you. You must phone and let me know next time you are going to be late. There's gunfire everywhere."

"There were armed police patrols along Hong Thap Tu. Apparently, they believe that they've discovered the hideout of some fifty or so Vietcong."

"How was your meeting?"

"The president has forced me into a dilemma."

Ann looked at Charles anxious to know more, but there was nothing she could do except wait until he was ready to tell her.

"He said he wanted me to bring him a shipment of weapons instead of clothes, household goods and other such materials. I declined his request ..."

"Unfortunately, I have no influence over Thieu. He is now too powerful and you will not be able to refuse him," Ann replied.

"I know. I am also concerned of our situation here. You know my views on the war," Charles looked pensive. "These are dangerous times and I fear for our safety. I am aware of your reluctance to leave Vietnam, but we should seriously think about returning to France."

"We are spending millions on our companies, but I can't think of anyone who would want to buy them, especially while the market is so unstable." Ann explained. "Besides, my mother is still here. She is ninety years old and I couldn't bear to leave her here on her own."

Charles sighed, "Ann, I won't speak of it anymore, until you are ready to consider."

"Thank you, darling. Oh, and another thing …" Ann hesitated.

"What is it?"

"Mr Lam the butler has brought his family here. I have already arranged two rooms for them next to the garage. I told them that I had to ask for your permission though. Are you happy to let them stay with us for the time being?"

"It is up to you," Charles said, as he started to get undressed for bed.

"That will mean that Mr Nam will have to move into your smoking room, won't he?" Ann passed her husband a dressing gown as she spoke

"Oh!" Charles finally began to understand what she was asking.

"Anyway, darling, it is actually better for you to smoke outside, isn't it?"

"You are right." Charles had no other option than to agree with his wife. "But what about my pipe collection? Where have you put them?"

"Mrs Nguyet, the housemaid, has already put it in your drawer in the library."

"Anything else you might like to tell me while you're at it?"

"That's all," Ann replied, with a mischievous smile.

"Shall I turn off the lights?"

Charles did not often talk about the weapons business with his wife. What he did know was that he did not have any alternative but to agree to work for the president. Thieu was capable of killing anyone, who would not comply with his demands. All his generals, except Minh, were expendable, and a foreigner like Charles was no exception. Suddenly, he remembered something, and turned to his wife:

"By the way, General Thi has invited us both to lunch next week. He told me he hadn't seen you for a while."

Chapter Seven

Mrs Tam said she would find a girl for Tu, but Tu resolved to find his second wife by himself as he arrived at Rose Villa with General Co. There were so many beautiful girls at the party. The life of a spy was fun and gave one the opportunity to meet lots of interesting people and beautiful girls, Tu thought. He certainly saw a lot of Southern generals, VIPs and the former Prime minister, Quat. General Ngo Van Phu, commander of the Cam Ranh Tactical Area – an extremely important area – was present and he was somebody that Tu desperately wanted to meet.

Everyone at the party appeared to be happy and relaxed, until an ear-splitting siren unexpectedly sounded outside. Two jeep loads of police officers in white uniforms stopped in front of the villa. Soldiers, who were bodyguards to the generals, quickly formed a guard of honour. General Cao Van Vien had arrived and was attended by a large number of followers. Among them were leaders from police headquarters, including the notorious thug, Loan. Tu greeted the Colonel with some trepidation.

"Good day," Quat responded to Loan and Tu moved closer in order to hear what they had to say. He understood from the conversation that Loan would be responsible for monitoring Quat's every move instigated by Vien's orders.

"We are terribly sorry that you have retired, and I am sure that you will soon settle down in America," Vien said to Quat.

"Well, I think it is time for younger people to take over power. I am too old to carry on. However, I will remain living here in Saigon."

It was obvious that the smile on Quat's face was false.

Vien was also a political operator. He went around greeting the guests as if it was his own party. He said a few words in Quat's direction to show his sympathy for his situation, then he lingered a little longer with Colonel Binh, head of the Khanh Hoa Police Department, and they briefly exchanged stories that had recently appeared in the local newspapers. They spoke of Mr Richard Nixon, congratulating the surviving soldiers who had been at Chu Lai, and the number of ice-cream factories for the American troops in South Vietnam, which should make a Guinness World Record this year. It was all propaganda for all the Southern Vietnamese children who wanted to join the American Army. However, Westmoreland had still complained about how difficult it was for his troops to get used to the heat in Vietnam.

Over the previous few years, under Westmoreland's new search-and-destroy policy, the American Army and Vietnamese Republican Army (ARVN) (the army of Southern Vietnam) had fought battles and killed without hesitation. Many villages and communities were destroyed and the young and old alike were slaughtered. The population at large had become discontent, resulting in disorder and disagreement amongst the leaders in administrative sections of the Vietnamese Republic. Quat's aunt had accosted him whenever newspaper articles appeared about children being killed. However, the former prime minister had ignored all these grievances. Three hundred thousand people had lost their lives during the last three years. Therefore, he could not expect his rank to protect him, and the possibility that Thieu had been trying to eliminate all the supporters of Ngo Dinh Diem was a great cause for concern.

Westmoreland was an extremely arrogant man. He would never accept that the American forces were going to lose the war against North Vietnam. Thieu had just signed a proclamation of martial law which surprised no one, given that the Vietcong and North Vietnamese armies had joined forces and were pushing towards Khe Sanh, Bien Hoa, U Minh Forest and the Saigon suburbs. The Southern forces had already lost five thousand soldiers, and the American forces had lost three thousand, one hundred and fifteen soldiers. The whole of Saigon was in a state of nervousness. Defence works, sandbag walls and barbed wire fences appeared all over the city, turning it into a fortress.

Before the party, Thieu had held meetings with some of the higher-ranking generals, including police General Co from police headquarters.

Thieu had insisted on maximum security, with checks on all identification, regardless of rank. He suspected that there were at least three, possibly as many as ten, agents within the system. The agents may have been money-grabbing politicians working in the government system, and they might even have been Vietnamese Nationalists, who believed that the North offered the best opportunities for a unified country.

"We should never ignore General Vo Nguyen Giap," stressed Thieu. "He won the Dien Bien Phu Campaign spectacularly. He has earned tremendous respect as commander of the North Vietnamese army. All documents, as well as profiles that I have read about him in France, show that he is a real leader of men – a professor of human nature. We must not underestimate him. According to our spies' reports, the total muster of the Northern Vietnamese army is only five hundred thousand. In addition, there is only one way to get to the South, and the road is narrow at Cam Ranh.

"If we bomb the Ho Chi Minh Trail intensively and continue fighting there to cut the Trail, then General Giap will not able to reach and capture Saigon."

"Mr President, in your opinion, General Giap is talented, but I don't agree," said General Le. "Look at the way he handled the Ho Chi Minh Trail. His methods are quite transparent. There is just one main road with no alternative routes. See how he sacrifices the lives of his soldiers so easily. These mistakes show how 'talented' he is, Mr President."

"General Le, I understand your reasonings," said General Co, "but I say that we should take more care for our troops' sake. Our agents may be wrong, and the number of North Vietnamese troops may be more like a million. That doesn't include the few hundred thousand soldiers of the NLF (National Front for the Liberation of South Vietnam), guerrillas, self defence, and other groups who are against us."

"Actually, the strengthening of our intelligence service is the thing I want to mention today," said Thieu. "You know the saying: 'Know yourself and know your enemy; you will come out victorious in a hundred battles'. Let me have reports on the weapons that the Soviet, China and other socialist allies are giving the North Vietnamese on my table, as soon as possible!"

"Yes, Mr President," the two generals replied in unison.

"According to a trustworthy source of information," said Thieu, "there is a North Vietnamese agent in the police headquarters. General Co, how do you explain this to me?"

"At the moment, I can't, but obviously the information handled by the department searching for suspected communists is of the highest sensitivity. I am most concerned at this time, Mr President, about that area. Not least, because it is the area where an agent could do us the most harm," replied General Co. "And that is why I have planted espionage agents in police headquarters by means of a circuitous manner. The new agents will all be from the provinces. They have been well trained, so that they can be infiltrated into the departments that we suspect the most. At the moment, I am currently looking for an agent I can trust; I already have some policemen from Can Tho."

Thieu nodded in agreement. "I am going to Honolulu next month," he added, "and I am looking forward to hearing good news from you both when I get back."

Their meeting was at an end.

Thieu phoned through for Vien:

"Hello, Brother Vien. How are things?"

"Hello, Mr President, everything is ok so far as I am concerned," said Vien, sounding unhappy. "I would like to raise something with you. It's about former Prime Minister Quat's close friend, Charles Philippe, the head of rubber plantations in Dau Tieng and owner of the MSP Shipping Company."

"I am certain," said Thieu, "that the relationship between Mr Quat and Mr Philippe is perfectly innocent. The French no longer have any influence here; they are no longer important to us, I would like to tell you to ask Nguyen Ngoc Loan, your filthy agent, to leave the party at Rose Villa immediately."

"Of course, sir," Vien replied.

His tone was respectful, but he could not help but wonder whether there was no limit to the lengths that the President would go in order to protect his lover, Ann Philippe.

"Right, remember, Charles is not to … err … disappear. Ever," Thieu continued.

"Of course, and I have had no reason to think otherwise, Mr President. However, it's the plan to bomb the Ho Chi Minh Trail that really concerns me."

"Put into operation the plans that we made some time ago."

"I still think we should bomb North Vietnam first."

"That is a good idea," said Thieu. "I will talk it over with the American President. I agree with General Westmoreland about the cutting-off of the Ho Chi Minh Trail through Laos."

"How about the fact that the North Vietnamese don't consider that our soldiers are prisoners of war? And bear in mind that this includes the downed American aircrew," Vien queried.

"The American Ministry of Defense has this matter in hand. As I understand it, Senator Robert Kennedy has already sent a letter to the United Nations requesting them to intervene. We just have to be patient for now, until the end of the war, at which point we will negotiate the return of our prisoners of war."

"I understand," answered Vien.

At least, he understood that Thieu had little concern for the lives of the American troops.

Thieu bid farewell to Vien and then hung up. General Thi's fate had been decided, but the Philippe family was top of the secret list ...

Since Thieu had come to power, he, along with Thiem and Ky, had formed a triumvirate of dictators sharing all the key government posts. As with all men who hunger after power, a triumvirate was never likely to satisfy Thieu, or either of the other two for that matter. The North Vietnamese wanted to know what was going on in Thieu's government and how Minh was ... This time, General Commander Thi was not in agreement with Thieu about the battle of Khe Sanh and using South Vietnamese soldiers in place of American soldiers. Both Thi and Hue were in Da Nang, but nobody could believe that Thieu or Vien could murder him, as they never did anything right.

In fact, the American Senate refused the request for more aid and troops in the minutes before Thieu left Vietnam for talks with the American President.

Thieu received another phone call from Ky. He advised Thieu to ask for aid and weapons only. His reason was that Westmoreland's policy was not getting anywhere, so no matter how many American troops were provided, the American army would still be ineffective. Thieu knew that if he asked the Americans for money for weapons, he would be able to use part of that money legitimately and filter the rest into his private accounts in Switzerland. He needed to talk to Charles Philippe in order to decide on the best and most secure means of laundering the money.

Back at the party, Tu was not as happy as he had been earlier on. Everyone was too busy to notice a poor, young police officer. Almost all of the girls were enjoying chatting with an American officer, who was tall with blond hair and blue eyes. They wore smart suits as opposed to their small Vietnamese counterparts, who looked hard and unfriendly in their white police uniforms. At that point, Tu felt he should be free to leave. All he wanted was to return home to his wife and family. He thought about the Ho Chi Minh Trail, the one-way road to the South. He knew that he would be shot as a deserter if he was seen going North along that road. He couldn't just scarper like a rat. He had to stay; it was the only sure way of returning home safely. He was here for the duration, until peace came.

Chapter Eight

Tu entered Rose Villa as General Co's guest, only this time he wore an evening suit instead of a uniform.

Rose Villa looked beautiful. The big front doors had been opened invitingly to welcome the guests as they arrived. The three main reception rooms on the ground floor of Rose Villa had been combined into a single large room for the party and a large vase had been placed in the middle of the living area. Flowers decorated the villa and were placed in the windows, on the tables and even up the stairs. Tu was relieved that he had not brought more flowers for Nicole. In the dining area, servants moved quietly around, offering guests champagne. Charles was the perfect host and was constantly moving amongst his guests, welcoming them as he went. He always had a special word to say to each one. However, he was concerned because his much-loved daughter still hadn't arrived home. Eventually, Ann told their chauffeur Mr Nam, to go and collect Nicole from university. When at last the green Cadillac arrived at the villa, and Nicole climbed out, she was wearing a long, ivory, silk dress with glass beads and sparkly gold thread sewn across the bodice. She was exceedingly pretty with her light brown hair covering her forehead; her beauty outshone all those around her.

"Father," Nicole called, in the sweetest voice she could muster.

"I was so worried," said Charles, as he gave his daughter a kiss. "Come here, love. I will introduce you to everyone, darling."

They first walked towards General Co and Tu:

"I would like to introduce you to my daughter Nicole. This is Lieutenant Tu; one of General Co's aides."

"Good evening, Uncle Co," Nicole said, as she greeted the General, before turning and saying to Tu "Good evening, sir."

Tu shook hands with Charles and greeted Nicole in the traditional manner. He was more comfortable this time, because Charles was a lot friendlier towards him than before.

General Co greeted Nicole as if she was still a sweet little girl; he also told Nicole all about Tu, whom he hoped would follow in his footsteps one day. Then the general left to speak with Ann. Nicole looked at Tu and wondered whether he really was general material.

"I'm sure that I've seen you at church, but I never realised that you worked for the police until now."

"I have just been transferred from Can Tho. Please excuse me," Tu said, as he moved away to greet another guest.

Nicole was annoyed by Tu's rudeness. Yes, he was certainly handsome, but there was no need to behave like that towards her. She had never had a boy treat her so rudely before, never! Who does he think he is? Damn him to hell! Nicole thought.

While he was talking with the other guests, Tu glanced in Nicole's direction. She admittedly had all the special qualities of a Eurasian girl – the beauty of a secluded princess. If Tu had not known that her father was French, then he could have mistaken her for Spanish or Italian. She was tall and slim and her waist was tiny, which was highlighted exquisitely in an *Ao Dai*, the Vietnamese traditional costume. Even her fingers were tiny. Surely, those fingers have never done anything more energetic than holding a pen, he thought to himself. She had high cheekbones and a long neck, which she clearly inherited from her mother. Her nose had a high bridge and she had her father's big, deep-blue eyes.

General Co was standing next to the old sideboard and was telling Ann about Tu. He believed him to be a hardworking officer, who had the potential to climb the ranks and to become a general. Ann was quite enthusiastic about Tu and had designs on pairing Nicole and Tu together as husband and wife.

It was customary in Vietnamese culture that the bride always went to live with her husband's family. Ever since Ann's elder daughter had left home, she had been dreading the thought of losing Nicole and was unsure how she would cope in the big, empty house. Charles also knew that he would feel Nicole's absence. Ann would still have her friends and connections, but Charles felt that he would be losing his last connection with France. But Tu had no family, so if Nicole married him, he could move in with them. Eventually, there would be children to fill the house with happy voices. Suddenly, the future looked bright and happy, rather than the bleak emptiness of a house without family. Tu came from a high-ranking family, but they were all deceased and he was now living in Saigon as a mere lieutenant police officer. Ann was sure that he would quickly climb up the ladder. The bribery rate for each official rank was high. However, she knew that Charles would disagree. He believed that women thought that money could buy everything, but in the military, things were very different. Nevertheless, Ann refused to believe this and still wanted Tu to marry Nicole.

Ann found General Co and Tu were mingling in the living room, and Ann observed Tu carefully, like a lion about to pounce on its prey. She was very impressed by the modest manner of the young Tu and thought that with such a good-looking man, he must inevitably attract many young girls. She wandered over to her husband and whispered in his ear, "We are holding a party next Saturday. Remember to invite that police lieutenant for me, dear!" she said, pointing her finger towards Tu.

"What? Since when were we having a party next week? Today's party has still not begun."

Ann signalled to her husband to quieten him.

"Shhh."

Of course, Charles obeyed his wife's order at once. In this world, there are only a few men who are not afraid of their wives; unfortunately, Charles was not one of those lucky few.

Chapter Nine

At nine o'clock in the morning, Tu walked into his office to check some of the "Suspect Vietcong" files, when there was uproar as all ten of his fellow workers simultaneously congratulated him vociferously:

"You must take us out for a drink to celebrate your marriage to Nicole."

"Tu, how did you meet her? Tell us what she's like."

"What's going on?" Tu asked, surprised.

Vinh brandished a letter with the prominent dark green seal of Rose Villa.

"Miss Nicole's butler came to the office early this morning and left a letter for you. This office has become popular since you were posted here, Tu."

"I haven't got a clue what you are talking about," said Tu, somewhat confused. "I don't even know who Nicole is."

"She is Mr and Mrs Philippe's daughter," said Rang.

"Oh! Now I understand. I met her once at her home. I said hello and went on my way. That was all. That's no secret."

"Open the envelope!" everyone urged.

Tu opened the envelope made from silk paper; not just any old envelope, but something special as one would expected from Rose Villa. Inside was a letter which Tu duly opened:

"It's from Mr and Mrs Philippe," he announced, at which everyone laughed, as they went back to their work.

That morning, when General Co came to visit the office, he asked after Tu and teased everyone that Tu might become the Philippe's son in-law. Like everyone in this office, Vinh could see that General Co also was fond of Tu. Everyone in the office liked Tu; he was an amiable man and he was the only person who could get away with commenting on Vinh's weight. Vinh guessed that Tu came from a family that shielded him from normal life, which was why he was so stupid and naive at times. His naivety made Vinh want to take him under his wing, which led them to become close friends.

Tu reflected on General Co; he had been so kind to him, and he wondered what would happen if General Co discovered the real truth. However, if Tu married Nicole, then it would eliminate any suspicions about him and he would, therefore, be able to do more work for the Vietcong. She would be able to give him access to important connections, which could potentially lead to important information that he could pass on to his bosses. He would, however, need to be careful, as the prospect of being discovered did not bear thinking about. He knew that marrying Nicole was the next step forward, so he remarked to Vinh one day how fond he was of Nicole.

"Tu, when you get married, let me be your best man. I will bring you lots of luck, if I am your best man."

"Enough," Tu embraced Vinh.

However, that was enough to make Vinh continue teasing him.

"General Co told me that her family likes you. It's remarkable that her family chose you," laughed Vinh. "She is well known for her snootiness. If she surrenders to an idiot like yourself, then it serves her right!" Vinh paused for a moment, because he was laughing so much that he couldn't breathe. Then he continued, "General Co told us to be careful around her and not to come on too strongly. However, I am happy for you, honestly!"

"Let's talk about something else," said Tu, wanting to change the subject. "It is about suspect F15. I want to question the prisoner directly."

"Good idea," replied Vinh. "I am writing a note to Chi-Hoa Prison this afternoon, so I will arrange it for you at the same time."

Tu had been informed by his contact that Prisoner F15 was from his own group of Bietdong and he was to do what he could to help him.

At the prison, Tu felt rather nervous while he waited for the prison officers to escort prisoner F15 to him. After a few minutes, he heard a noise of someone or something being dragged along a concrete floor. Eventually, a man appeared in front of Tu. He was black and blue and covered in blood. His clothes were rags, and he looked so hungry that he could almost have been a ghost. Tu wasted no time in commencing the interrogation.

"Name?"

"Nguyen Van Thoi."

"Age?"

"Twenty-five."

"Wife's name?"

"Le Thi Mai."

"Home address?"

"Lane 15/6 ... District 3."

"Job?"

"Driver."

"Committed to the Vietcong?"

"No, I am not!"

"You are a traitor!"

The prisoner did not respond.

"Lieutenant, he is a very stubborn man. It would be quicker to use electricity to encourage him to talk ..." said one of the prison officers.

"No!" replied Tu sharply.

He then turned back to the prisoner and, in an unexpectedly soft voice, asked, "Mr Thoi. Why do you make your life so difficult? You've recently got married, have you not? Also, your mother is ill. She needs somebody to look after her. If she were to see you now, she would die of shame. Why don't you admit that you are Vietcong? We all make mistakes. If you confess that you have fallen for their propaganda and tell us all you know, then I'll have you released as soon as possible. Think about it."

Tu, then turned to the two prison officers, and said, "Why are you just standing there? Bring Mr Thoi a cup of tea, and bring him some fresh clothes. I will also need some paper and a pen so that Mr Thoi can write down everything he knows."

The two prison officers were impressed by the way in which Tu carried out the questioning and left. Taking advantage of their absence, Tu continued to question the prisoner, "What else would you like? What about some Bau Da whisky?"

On hearing this, the prisoner's eyes opened wide with delight. Bau Da was a secret password for the Northern forces. He felt relieved to have allies here in this very prison and relaxed a little. It had been the first time he was able to let his guard down since the day he had been arrested. They had been torturing him continuously every day over the past week.

The prisoner gave the second part of the code by saying, "I do not drink. However, if you have lemonade and a pep pill, I would like to have 'two' glasses."

"Two" was the correct answer. Tu responded quickly and in a very low voice, so low that the prisoner had to lip-read.

"Do you know prisoners 133 and 1365, from your cell? Both have been turned and are now working for the South. For your safety, you will feign ignorance and say you know nothing; absolutely nothing."

Tu finished and broke into a cold sweat. He didn't want to think of the consequences if prisoner Nguyen Van Thoi had also been turned; what would he do? If he had been turned, then Tu would be tortured and interrogated. For a brief moment, he realised how hard his task was going to be. He quickly pulled himself together and realised that in a prolonged war, it made no difference as to what form death would take. He was a soldier and continuing the fight – whether it was out in the jungle with guns or seeking out information in the city – death could come either way. At the end of the day, death is death, Tu told himself, in an attempt to allay his fears.

He sat up straight and smiled. Thoi felt as though he had been released momentarily. Prisoners 133 and 1365 had been under suspicion for a long time, and senior leaders of Saigon's Bietdong had stopped exchanging information with them. Sitting in front of him was a lieutenant in military uniform with a military insignia, and he turned out to be his ally. His information had to be correct.

The two prison officers returned with milk and clean clothes, and Tu ordered the prisoner to be moved into the prison clinic.

"You are so kind, Lieutenant Tu," one of the prison officers said.

A short while later, Tu left the interrogation room. He knew that he would have to be on his guard at all times. It was like walking along a tightrope. Any one of the prisoners could betray him, and if they did, it would be Tu himself being tortured that night. The weight of his responsibilities and the stress of never-ending danger bore down heavily on him, but the feeling disappeared just as quickly as it had arrived.

Chapter Ten

Ann had heard many more good things about Tu, which made her believe that she had found a suitable match for Nicole. She even started to tell people how much she wanted Tu to become her son-in-law, and that she wanted to give him the opportunity to have a loving family again. Tu now started to spend most of his free time with Ann and her family. He would give Ann a lift to wherever she wanted to go in his new Mercedes, so that Ann would arrive in appropriate style. Ann took Tu to almost all of her important meetings and she introduced him to her powerful friends. And it was because of this, that Tu became acquainted with most of the generals and leaders of the South, which was something he would not have been able to do as a mere police lieutenant.

Ann even took him with her and Charles to Thi's private home for lunch. Thi was the one of the four highest-ranking officers in the Southern army, and Tu was delighted to be given the opportunity to meet him.

Thi's villa was located near the Ministry of Industry and was one of eleven villas belonging to Thi's family. The guests were Charles and his wife Ann, and General Ngo Van Phu, who had flown from Cam Ranh to Saigon. Phu was a compulsive man and Saigon army officials admired him, because he was a talented leader and because of his immense knowledge of military defence strategy.

Cam Ranh housed a very important port which was considered to be one of the best in the world, because it had a vast, long lake which opened out on to the sea. An immense bank of white sands, hundreds of metres wide, sheltered shipping on the lake from the roughest of seas. The surrounding terrain was mountainous and the road from north to south passed very close to this vital military base. During his four years in charge of the army fort in Cam Ranh, Phu had established a defence line there. McNamara, as well as Nixon and Westmoreland, all thought that Cam Ranh was the best barrier in the South, and valued the strength and importance of this defence line.

The military airport was to be enlarged and the sea port had become increasingly crowded; all of this served to make Cam Ranh a wealthy town. The town was bustling with all of the usual camp followers catering for the needs of the soldiers, sailors and pilots, for both the Americans and South Vietnamese.

Around the big dining table, Tu was pretending that he was shy by concentrating on the delicious food that was placed in front of him. He never expressed an opinion, but he made sure that he was listening and made a point to remember everything that was said. Even something that appeared to be unimportant could be of vital importance to another agent reporting to headquarters.

Ann complimented Phu, "You have made Cam Ranh such an important base, which is now almost impregnable."

"I didn't do a thing. Some hundred thousand soldiers under my command have done little more than clear the grass and cut down Trung Ca and banana trees."

"Are there many banana trees in Cam Ranh?" asked Ann, in surprise.

"Countless! This type of tree thrives in stony, sandy land and grows amazingly quickly," answered Phu.

"Did you say that the communist forces are unable to pass through the Cam Ranh defence line?" asked Thi.

"I have never said that!" replied Phu. "We have already learnt from our costly mistakes. The communists have attacked the Cam Ranh defence line many times, so now we now have placed yet more landmines and electronic fences along the shore. The American navy has an aircraft carrier on constant patrol. However, I didn't agree entirely with the President's ideas when he made a tour of inspection in Cam Ranh last week."

"In my opinion, President Thieu and General Minh are leading our country into a blind alley," Thi stated tentatively.

"I agree," said Phu thoughtfully. "President Thieu is intelligent and talented. However, his lack of experience is an increasing problem.

Leading a country at war with very limited experience is not a good idea. I definitely think," continued Phu, "that North Vietnam is stronger than we first thought. We are sure to lose if we don't have the people's support; it is hard to tell the genuine from the false."

"I have always supported you," said Ann, without thinking.

"Ann," replied Phu, "I have always been aware of your support, and today is the first time I have actually had a chance to meet you. I must say, your reputation and your support have preceded you."

"That's so sweet of you. Although, I couldn't have done any of those things without the help of my husband," she replied.

"On behalf of our military friends, I thank you both," continued Thi. "We should have all women generals, because they would make up their minds faster than men. Am I right?"

"You mean, my wife could be a general?" Charles asked. "We will almost certainly have to be careful if we make women generals," he added.

Everybody, with the exception of Ann, who was irritated by her husband's comments, burst out into laughter.

"I am only a housewife. I do not dare to talk about military affairs."

"You are the only one worth listening to at this table," said Phu, as he tried to appease her.

"If only I had the flexibility of thinking like a woman. I would win every battle," Thi added, with candid honesty.

At this point, the atmosphere became relaxed and happy again.

Suddenly, noises were heard from outside the front gate. Phu seemed indifferent, as if it was nothing. Only Thi appeared to be worried. The captain in charge of the security guards entered.

"What's going on out there?" Thi asked.

The captain of security answered, "Sir, there was a minor misunderstanding between the security guards and some white-uniformed police from headquarters."

Phu realised for the first time that Thi was in political chaos and believed that he was on the way out, because, normally, the police did not dare to interfere with the military, especially with the special security guards of high-ranking generals. Without further ado, Thi asked everybody to relax and enjoy their drinks.

Phu turned to Charles and said, "I would like to invite you and your family to join us for a holiday in Cam Ranh and Nha Trang. You would be most welcome there."

"Thank you; we would be delighted. You can't beat the sea views in Nha Trang," Charles replied.

"We'd be able to enjoy walking on the beach in the late afternoons and at nightfall we could go sea fishing for some squid. Have you ever done these things?" the general asked.

"That would be great!" said Charles with enthusiasm.

A Servant knocked at the door to confirm whether the diners were ready for the main course. The butler checked the food and the presentation of the dishes before handing them to the servants to serve to the guests.

"General Thi has such an excellent cook," enthused Phu, as he tried the spicy beef. "I have ten soldiers in the cook house at my quarters and yet still I have to be satisfied with boiled noodles!"

He turned to Ann and enquired: "I hear that your butler, Mr Lam is wonderful at his job and his speciality is baking the fish dishes of Ca Nuong Trui. Is that true?"

"Yes, it is true," Ann replied. "Mr Lam can also make many other dishes. I hope he doesn't ever leave us to become an engineer again."

"I know how faithful he is to you. If you wanted him to jump into the fire, he would. So he would never leave you," said Thi.

Thi knew all about Mr Lam's history, but he knew he would never be able to divulge any of this to Ann. For when the general, then a junior officer, had been on patrol, a Vietcong soldier had appeared, aiming a gun at his head. The soldier then lowered the gun and disappeared into the jungle as quickly and as silently as he had appeared. Many years later, Thi recognised Mr Lam as the Vietcong soldier who had spared his life. Out of gratitude, Thi kept silent about the incident. However, since Mr Lam had come to work for the Philippe family, he had given up his Vietcong work, because all he wanted for his family was to be safe and well fed.

"In my opinion," Thi announced, "in both the Presidential Palace and the White House, people have been totally blinded to the truth surrounding this war. Just look at the way they control it. Did you know that Nixon has declared that he would be interested in going into Cambodia? The fact is that the number of soldiers in Cambodia that he refers to is only a figment of his imagination. I suspect that only a number of soldiers know the unexaggerated truth. What about the news of 'continuous victories' from Khe Sanh, Phu Loc and Buon Ma Thuot, that were all a figment of the imagination? By the time the press have exaggerated their version of the facts and the editors have 'corrected' them, the story that appears in the paper bears little resemblance to the facts. For instance, the number of food stores that they supposedly took from the Vietcong was simply farcical."

"Oh!" exclaimed Charles, as he began to understand how straight-talking Thi was and why the Americans and South Vietnamese authorities wanted rid of him.

Phu added, "I am really worried. Last week, I had a conversation with Mr Hai from the Information Research Department. If such a talented man like Prime Minister Ky is taking over as vice president, then the situation for the research department is becoming untenable, for they are compelled to provide reports which brief the situation as those in power want them to be described, rather than how the situation really is."

There was a distinct irony in his voice as he described Ky as talented.

"I don't hate the Americans," Ann maintained, raising her voice, "but I'm not sure how they are helping things and why they are still here.

They all burst out laughing, as everyone at the party knew that Ann was only sympathetic towards France. She would have been quite content for France to have ruled Vietnam; if her husband was an American, then she would have been in favour of their current involvement. Ann didn't like being laughed at and was annoyed.

"Is there anything funny about what I just said? I'm afraid that I don't get the joke."

"I'm not laughing at what you said," replied Thi, "I am laughing because I myself have often wondered why the Americans are still here. They have helped us enough already, and that's why the armed forces of South Vietnam alone are strong enough to smash North Vietnam's military. Their initial thoughts about this war have started to go amiss," Thi paused to drink.

"From a Frenchman's point of view, and I'm sorry to say this, but the Americans will be the next to face defeat here," said Charles.

Phu looked him. "We love to hear about Americans doing things wrong; come on, tell us more."

"Oh, Brother Thi knows better than my husband," Ann smiled.

Thi continued, "It is ok when the country is on an even keel. However, whenever North Vietnam attacks us, our President seems to be at a loss. I cannot understand why our government has not found someone else to replace him. When our country is finally at peace, we will need leaders who are good at economics, healthcare and education, because this is what our country needs. And when the country is at war, we need an experienced general in charge and many other talented generals to support the President in order to save the country. President Thieu does not trust his generals. He is afraid that they may become too strong and then overthrow him."

"I see what you mean. It's quite logical," concurred Ann. "I think that anyone who takes over from President Diem would always be worried that someone else would want to take control."

"I agree, Ann," said Phu. "Within the military hierarchy, many disagree with the strategies carried out by President Thieu and General Westmoreland."

"As far as I am concerned, dear Brother Phu, I have always given my support to you, Brother Thi and General Minh," said Ann, who was happy to support anyone who was prepared to help her sustain her lavish lifestyle.

After the servant brought in a large dish of fruits and some cakes for dessert, Tu left the table to join the other generals in the smoking room. He was a non-smoker, but he needed to know what Thi and Phu were talking about concerning the plan of the attack on the Ho Chi Minh Trail.

When Ann left the party, she felt compelled to share her views with her husband:

"General Thi will soon be nothing. He will retire and move to America," she announced, "so then we will support General Minh. My dear, I love getting involved with the army. I have no desire to meet General Thi again, and I think I should make an appointment to see General Minh next week."

"As a businessman, I think you are right," agreed Charles.

Tu was pleased with himself, because he had more information to pass on to his boss and he now felt less guilty about his impending marriage to Nicole.

Chapter Eleven

In the early stages of his mission, Tu needed to learn how to initiate contact via the secret letter boxes, which was difficult because they never stayed in one place. It always amazed Tu how the Vietcong's infrastructure worked.

One day, Tu needed to pass on some information that he had copied from the office together with some documents he had obtained from Ann's friends. He tied these up in a sweet paper and placed them into his top shirt pocket, ready for the exchange.

He met Little Lien at Lon Market, who was shopping on behalf of Mrs Tam. She was wearing a T-shirt with the logo 'VB the Best'. The locals knew that the 'VB' meant 'Vietcong and 'Bietdong, but the Americans were told that it meant 'Vietnam-Britain'. The T-shirt business was booming.

The state of Lon Market was heartbreaking. Everywhere looked neglected and the roads were nothing more than ruts, holes and bumps. Houses and shops were deserted; only in the area near the market could he find even the slightest sign of life – some skinny wild dogs roaming on the streets. There were disabled people begging for money, which made the place seem even more desperate and in the middle of ruined apartment blocks, wild grass grew amongst the litter and loose bricks. The street was blocked at both ends of the street by watchtowers manned by soldiers, who looked menacingly at people who passed by.

Tu had been informed through his secret letter box that he had to find the "tenth" mushroom stall, where somebody would take the documents from him. The stalls that sold mushrooms were at the end of the market; however, when Tu counted, there were only "nine" stalls. At length, he found the right stall and bought some dried mushrooms for Mrs Tam. Having given the correct signal, he stood looking around for a few minutes. The information he was sending to the North was very important. The Americans and their puppets had been informed about a crack commando unit and were actively searching the north of Saigon. They knew that they were an extremely effective force, and didn't rule out the possibility of North Vietnam using this unit to mount an operation against Saigon, as they had done during the Tet Offensive.

Tu thought that if the commander-in-chief, Nguyen Van Trung, knew of the enemies plans, they would be able to divide the army and disperse the groups along the eastern provinces and take them by surprise, but that was for the people in headquarters to decide and to give the appropriate orders. All that was expected of Tu was to collect as much information as possible and to confirm its authenticity.

At the side of the market there was a group of travellers who were putting on a circus show with kung fu, magic and acrobatics. They were all smartly dressed and greatly skilled. The man with the top hat removed his hat and showed the audience that it was empty. He put it on the table and then took out ten white doves in quick succession. He then asked if anybody could lend him a dollar note, which he proceeded to carefully fold and unfold; it had turned into $10. The next performer approached Tu and from his top pocket and trouser pocket he took out many scarves all tied to each other. Everyone gasped and cheered after he had finished. When Tu was about to leave the market, he realised that his secret documents had gone. The street performer must have taken them. It was easy to see why the Americans constantly complained that they never knew where and how the Vietcong worked.

Tu now had no choice but to spend time accompanying Little Lien shopping, but he hated it. He could never understand why the need for only a few groceries involved her calling at all of the forty stalls. There were also more stops at various other stalls to decide on the right hair clips, ribbons and clothing. In comparison, when working, Mrs Tam was very decisive and authoritative, but when she was shopping for clothes, she could dither for hours. He could never figure out Mrs Tam's likes or dislikes. The row of stalls selling flowers next to the market was full of roses that day and Tu bought a big bunch of them as a present for Little Lien.

"This is for you!" said Tu, as he gave the bouquet to Little Lien.

Little Lien took the bouquet and gave him a radiant smile as she smelt the flowers.

"They smell lovely!" she declared.

"What kind of flower do you like best?"

"Roses, gladioli, violets and carnations," answered Little Lien. "I usually buy carnations and violets because they last longer. As for roses, I like them very much, but I rarely buy them. Oh, let me help with these bags."

"OK," replied Tu.

A couple passed by, hand in hand. The man was an American and the woman was Vietnamese. She turned back to look at Tu.

"Perhaps she's admiring your good looks," whispered Little Lien.

"It's because I'm carrying so many bags," he answered.

Little Lien ran her hand slowly through the petals and asked him, "Girls like flowers, but what about men? If you were given a present by someone, what would you like?"

"Aftershave, maybe," answered Tu casually and suddenly remembering that he hadn't shaved that morning. His thick sideburns got on his nerves and it took him ten minutes to shave each morning. But it was the thickness of his beard that was so like the original Tu's that allowed him to take his place.

"Really?"

"Are you buying something for your boyfriend?" Tu asked.

"No, I haven't got one and that's not because I am ugly," she shouted, indignantly. "All the men in Saigon have joined the army and I don't think I want to date a teenager."

"You know," said Tu, "you are just the kind of woman that men are looking for."

Little Lien wasn't happy when she heard these words. She knew Tu was only joking and trying to cheer her up – but he was failing miserably.

"Why are you suddenly so quiet?" Tu asked.

"Because my morning has gone, and I still can't find the last thing that I need."

"What about me? I was planning to wash my car. And here you are making me visit every single stall!"

"Why do you men love to complain so?" Little Lien asked with surprise.

Chapter Twelve

It was Nicole's birthday and the party that was organised on her behalf was to be held on the following Saturday, at the Philippe's rubber plantation in Dau Tieng, about 15 miles from the centre of Saigon. That day, Tu went to buy a big bunch of Da Lat yellow roses and a beautiful gold necklace.

"Oh, wow! They look gorgeous!" said his chauffeur, when he saw the gifts.

Tu suddenly felt terribly guilty, because he had never been able to afford flowers for Nhat, let alone a gold necklace. There were many occasions when his heart almost broke when he thought about how much she cared about him.

"Do you remember the American who worked with you this morning?" the chauffeur asked.

"Yes, I do."

"He is CIA."

"We are letting the CIA control us too much. They are everywhere," Tu said, to cover his initial shock. He had not thought of John as being CIA before and that worried him. He had to be more careful, as any similar slip-ups in the future could result in his torture and certain death.

"The CIA has asked us to summon experts to discuss and analyse the irrigation situation of rice production; anything to avoid telling the truth. Although I am only a driver, I get to hear everything. Anybody who sits in this car, no matter what their rank or position, seem to tell me their secrets and conversations. The latest is that John the CIA man is going to move into the general office."

"I like John," Tu said. "He said that lots of his colleagues have fallen in love with Vietnamese girls, and I believe him. Just look at how many American soldiers have family in Saigon."

"We Vietnamese are a lovely race. Anyway, where are we going, Lieutenant Tu?" the chauffeur asked.

"Take me to the office. You can have the evening off and I will go to the party on my motorbike."

"Thank you very much, sir," said the chauffeur gratefully, as he headed in the direction of the police headquarters.

The small drive from the highway to Charles and Ann's rubber plantation was festooned with flowers and flags. Even the rubber trees along the path leading to the house were covered with balloons and ribbons. Plants were arranged exquisitely and red carpet was laid out on the steps. Hanging on the front of the house were the flags of the Republic of South Vietnam, France and the United States of America.

The French-style living room looked magnificent and extravagant what with all the decorations. Crystal lights shone on rows of tables covered with spotless white cloths and yellow silk bows adorned every corner. In one corner, there was a table covered in a sumptuous purple silk cloth with bottles of champagne and a three-tiered birthday cake. Waiters dressed in suits and waitresses wearing pink *Ao Dais*, glided through the crowds, welcoming the guests with smiles.

In the morning, and under close supervision of Mr Mac Colin, all of the house servants had been busy with preparations for Nicole's birthday party. They had collected groceries and drinks from Saigon and the caterers had brought in local specialities, such as chicken, duck, fruit and vegetables. Everything was ready for the big celebration.

The day before, to express their gratitude for their mistress, who had looked after the workers on their plantation, the servants had brought presents to their adored mistress's daughter. Some of their families had worked as labourers on the plantation for generations, and many clearly remembered the old days, when Charles was an arrogant playboy. He had lived in Paris when he was a child and, after he had graduated from Paris University, Charles came to the plantation on holiday.

Workers at that time had lived together in low, damp huts in the middle of a rubber forest. After eight hours of work, they had gathered to gamble and drink. Many lost their whole month's salary by the end of the first week, so they started to steal the latex on the plantation. It reached such epidemic proportions that Mr Philippe Senior had to employ supervisors to restore order.

Charles was a cold man with little understanding, and he looked down on the workers, until he met Ann, the daughter of a great, rich landowner, Nam Vang. After their marriage, Ann worked hard to change the structure of the plantation, including that of the workers and their living arrangements. She encouraged the workers to get married and helped them to build small houses, instead of gathering round to gamble and drink alcohol each evening; the workers now spent time with their families. Ann didn't only teach Charles how to care for his workers; he learnt many things from her. In return, Ann and Charles were rewarded by increased loyalty and performance from their workers. As years went by, Mr and Mrs Philippe Senior eventually passed away, and the dealings of the plantation had naturally passed on to Ann.

As a young girl, Nicole had always played with the children from the workers' families. She had brown hair, a pale complexion and wore clean pink dresses. She was always the focus of the workers' children's attention, who had never had seen a foreign child before. Nicole had grown up in the lap of luxury, but she had also inherited her mother's kind nature. She respected those less fortunate around her. As a result, the plantation workers thought of Ann and her daughter with great affection and respect, and their villa in the rubber plantation never needed to be locked at night.

On her daughter's birthday, Ann ordered that each worker's family was to be rewarded with a bonus of an extra third of a month's salary. Many workers' wives volunteered to work in Ann's kitchen that evening to show their appreciation.

A VIP from the Presidential Place had accepted an invitation to Nicole's birthday party, so, at eight o'clock that morning, the local police commander had sent a group of police to check security at the rubber plantation's villa. The first group of guests were Nicole's friends, including Josephine her best friend, who had grown up with Nicole and who lived in the farmhouse next to their plantation. Like the Philippes, the French couple had spent most of their lives in Vietnam and spoke fluent Vietnamese. Next to arrive was Tu and shortly after, members of Ann's family drew up in two shiny black cars. The Karenna family from the neighbouring plantation drew up immediately after in a horse and carriage kissing everybody in the orthodox French style.

After Charles and Ann had warmly welcomed everyone, the guests were invited to look round the gardens, or, if they preferred, to relax in the guest rooms. The gardens of the rubber plantation were large and beautiful, with a path paved with stones, and the bushes and plants were pristine.

As the sun rose higher, the humid atmosphere made the guests feel uncomfortable. The mosquitoes came out in abundance, causing the gentlemen to retire to the living room to enjoy champagne and cigars, and the women to retire to the small guest room to talk over the latest fashion and the many items they had brought for Nicole's birthday.

Suddenly, there was huge commotion outside. A car with darkened windows pulled up outside the villa, followed by several other cars. When the cars came to a halt, policemen jumped out and surrounded the building. Everyone guessed that it was the President, so they all hurried out of the villa to form two lines of welcome for him.

A policeman dressed in a white suit, kepi hat and yellow crossed epaulettes, together with three other policemen, walked towards the President's car. Thieu had brought a present for Nicole's birthday in person.

That was the first time Tu had seen Thieu in the flesh. Instinctively, he moved his hand to his pistol. He already knew that the President was very young but he had not expected him to look as young as he actually did. Although he was over forty, he had the face of a man much younger. Even the Republic of Vietnam didn't have leaders who looked so youthful. Tu observed him carefully. He had a smiling face with a welcoming expression, and he had an aura of power around him. He shook everybody's hand, regardless of status. To show interest in the other person's life, he even added a friendly comment to each. Tu wondered how a President who killed so many people could have such normal face. His hand then moved to the stock of his pistol and gripped it tightly. General Co had seen Tu's reaction and immediately approached him to warn him not touch his gun, because if Thieu's bodyguard saw him, he would be shot dead without a second thought. Tu was sweating and he realised just how stupid he had been. Killing Thieu would not have achieved anything, because the

Vietnamese people only wanted the war to end and the Americans to leave their country. Tu was at this party to win Nicole's heart, not to fight.

Nicole formally greeted Thieu by crossing her arms and politely stood back. However, General Co, eager to greet his friend, pushed Nicole to one side.

"Brother Tu, have you ever met President Thieu?" asked Nicole softly.

"I have never had that privilege, miss."

"Please, do not call me miss," said Nicole. "You should call me Nicole, if that is ok?"

"It would be my pleasure, miss," replied Tu, deliberately trying to provoke her.

Thieu handed Nicole's birthday present to her, smiling while the cameras flashed continuously all around him.

"My dear girl, you have grown up so much! I still remember the time when you were very little. You came with your mother to visit me in hospital. You gave me a very beautiful bunch of flowers!" he said.

"Really?" Nicole asked shyly.

"Then, you asked me to give them back, so you could take them home." Everybody burst out laughing.

"You are twenty-one today, dear. Happy Birthday."

"Thank you, Uncle Thieu," replied Nicole.

Ann then politely asked the other guests to find a comfortable place in another part of the house, so that Thieu could relax in peace.

When they were in the drawing room, she asked Thieu whether he would like to stay for lunch.

"Of course, I'd love to," answered Thieu. "I am always busy but I miss you so much and lunchtime spent peacefully with you will do me good."

"I miss you, too, my old friend. How is Lady Thuy?" Ann asked; she never forgot to ask about Thieu's wife.

"She is fine," Thieu answered, and then he continued, "she has always respected you. A little while ago, she found a photo of you. She asked me to hang it in my private room or in my office in the palace. Do you remember the photo we had taken on the day of my graduation?"

"I do remember, and I remember how much we loved each other." Ann said, quietly. They both stared at each other in silence. Finally, she said, "You are looking tired."

"That's because, I am," answered Thieu.

"Can you reduce some of your workload? You have black rings under your eyes," Ann observed.

"I'll try," replied Thieu, seriously.

His heart was overflowing with love; a feeling that he only ever had when he was with Ann. There had been nobody else in his life that had compared to her. However, he had to hide that love and the pain he would have to carry with him forever.

"I heard on the news about the disagreement between the American President and yourself."

"Nixon doesn't think the Ho Chi Minh Trail through Laos is going to be a danger for the South."

"Wrong," Ann said, "that means the Trail will never be cut."

"I know," Thieu said, "and now is just the right time. It will be too late if he and General Abrams leave it until next year."

The servant brought in a tray and Ann noticed that Tu was stood just outside the door, so she called to him to join them.

Chapter Thirteen

That summer, the Philippe family stayed at the plantation. Even though the security there was not very good, their friends still visited them. Nicole invited some of her classmates from university to stay for a week, but when they had gone, she started to yearn for the hustle and bustle of Saigon once again.

Nicole was on the verge of returning to Saigon, when Tu came to visit her. He arrived unannounced, but his timing was perfect, for he came at a time when she was alone and looking for companionship. To begin with, Nicole was still cold towards Tu. However, Tu was so nice that Nicole was starting to enjoy his company and she even invited him to stay for lunch.

Ann scolded Tu for not giving enough notice, as they would have prepared something special for their guest if they had known. As it was, he had to join them for a simple lunch. However, for Tu, this was no ordinary lunch. The dining table was laid beautifully; the servants brought out the china, silver chopsticks and knives and forks only used for special occasions. The chef served hot soup from a 24-carat gold bowl and the delicious chicken was especially imported from America.

During lunch, Tu recalled his days on the Ho Chi Minh Trail. He remembered wishing he could have a hot meal with just enough salt. The rations, which used to be sent along the Ho Chi Minh Trail sometimes, were often destroyed by the bombing raids and the army lived on leaves for months at a time. Sometimes, Tu's team would burn grass and eat the ashes for the salt they contained. Tu missed his intake of salt so much that he sometimes even dreamed of having plenty of salt with a hard-boiled egg.

After lunch, Nicole invited Tu to have to look around the Philippe's rubber plantation. This gave him the opportunity to spend some time alone with her, and he had always wanted to see the rubber plantation. It was a beautiful sunny afternoon with the bluest of skies. The road among the rubber trees was dry and was perfect for a long walk. Kim, the house servant, gave Nicole a Chinese white umbrella to protect her from the sun and readied herself to go with her, but Nicole instructed her to stay at home, so she could walk with Tu alone. Tu felt awkward and was unsure as to how to start a conversation with Nicole. The words "I love you" did not come easily to Tu, although he knew he must tell Nicole how he felt as soon as possible. Nicole was talking about the war and about how many people had died, so now was not the right moment to repeat the romantic words he had learnt from Little Lien. Nicole told Tu all about her family's history, the farm and the rubber plantation all of which had been purchased by her grandparents, and how they now employ hundreds of workers, and how Mr Mac had been the acting manager for her family for thirty years now.

They were almost a mile from home, when a forest guard passed by. They stopped to exchange greetings and Nicole enquired after his family. He told them in a low voice that his wife had not been in good health, because she was ill with tuberculosis. As for his daughter, she had grown up and was about as tall as Nicole's shoulder. She had still kept all the toys that Nicole had given her when she was a little girl.

Nicole smiled and said, "She is such a sweet girl. I would like to see her sometime."

"You are so kind to us, miss. I will ask my daughter to call on you soon."

The forest guard finished talking with Nicole and went back to work. Listening to Nicole and the rubber worker talking, Tu found Nicole to be kind and thoughtful, a quality that he liked.

Nicole turned to Tu. "When I was a little girl, I used to use latex to catch red dragonflies and butterflies. It's fun when you are young and living amongst the rubber trees, because there are so many of them."

"As for me, I like to play in the fields. I prefer cicadas to butterflies."

"I have never seen a cicada," observed Nicole.

"Your parents love you so much that they try to protect you. You do not get out into the countryside much, do you?"

"I usually live in Saigon," answered Nicole, "but I used to live here when I was little. As you can see, there is only rubber here. Not much else to see or do."

"Maybe, when you have time, we could venture into to the western forest area to discover more. Would you like that?"

"Maybe," said Nicole, as she turned to Tu. "It's getting late, I think we'd better go back home."

Nicole tripped and, looking down at her shoes, she said, "These are the worst shoes imaginable for walking on the bumpy plantation roads."

She was wearing shoes with five-centimetre-high heels at the time.

"Are you ok?" Tu asked, as he helped her to remove her shoes and check her feet.

"You may have sprained your ankle, but I don't think it is anything serious. Give me your hand and I will support you. Will you be able to make it back home?"

"Yes, I will be fine. It was only a scratch," answered Nicole.

Nicole's hand was warm and soft in his strong hands. It was the very first time that Nicole had let a man hold her hand before.

"I wish I could hold your hand forever," Tu blurted out. Nicole said nothing.

"Nicole, look at me," Tu asked.

"I am looking at you!"

"I love you," Tu said, thinking about his mission.

"That's just because my leg hurts."

Tu burst into laughter and let go of her hand. She tottered backwards and fell on to the ground, spraining her other ankle.

Nicole went pale from the pain, but she couldn't help but laugh. The forest guards who had been following immediately appeared on the scene to help the young mistress. Tu had been on the verge of kissing Nicole, but now, much to his annoyance, he had to restrain himself.

Charles and Ann were waiting for their daughter and her young guest on the top of the steps to the house.

"Father!" shouted Nicole.

"What's wrong with you, my dear?" Charles asked his daughter.

Nicole turned to Tu and looked meaningfully at him.

"Father, Mother! We have a personal matter to talk to you about."

Nicole was so happy that she did not have time to think before she spoke; it was love at first sight!

Tu looked at Nicole with his eyes wide open. Things were happening so quickly, he had simply said he loved her, and now she was telling her family that they were to be married. Tu could never understand what went on in a girl's head.

Chapter Fourteen

Mrs Tam was sitting on an old, hand-carved chair. She used a handkerchief to dry her eyes, which were red with tears. She had done nothing but cry since she had heard the news of Tu's engagement.

"Mum, I am only getting married. Why are you crying?"

"I am crying because I am so happy, you daft thing. Next year, I might even become a grandmother."

"Hmm!" Tu answered.

"I have to say that I'm slightly worried though; we are not of the same social standing as Mr and Mrs Philippe; they are so wealthy and respected in Saigon. I fear that I will have to do up our house in order to welcome my future daughter-in-law."

"Mum, Nicole is very modest and kind, even though she is French."

"But you have only known Nicole for a short space of time. How can you be sure what she is really like? You should bear in mind that she has a French father, which will mean that she is always polite. She might be using it to hide her true nature and have her own secrets. Remember that you are also hiding a lot from her."

"Mum, you are so hard to please; you are just like a real mother-in-law!" said Tu, half-jokingly and half-serious. "I think the French people are nice; they are charming, intelligent, they dress smartly and their cooking is delicious."

"You do love her, don't you?" Mrs Tam asked, with smile.

Tu avoided the question by changing the subject. "You don't need to decorate the house just because I am getting married; the cost would be prohibitive. Anyway, the money is needed for the war."

"Don't worry about that," said Mrs Tam. "The senior leaders are just pleased that you are going to be a part of Nicole's family. It is the ideal opportunity to gather information. You will learn so much more than where you are now."

"I will try my best," said Tu.

"You should try to love Nicole. The poor girl; I feel awful that we are using her like this."

"I don't know what else to do!" He was torn between the loyalty for his wife back in North Vietnam and his loyalty for his country.

Little Lien gave him a mean stare, "I beg your pardon? I really don't think you feel that sorry for the woman for one minute. "

Mrs Tam raised her voice, interrupting Tu's train of thought.

"Will you two stop fighting; you are distracting my wedding plans. So, Tu, back to the issue of decorating the house. If I don't, it will look drab and I would be too embarrassed to entertain here."

"No, Mum. She is a good person and she will accept you for who you are. I would like to have a traditional Vietnamese wedding, not a French one."

"I agree. I will talk to Mrs Philippe about the planning. I have already had a brief discussion about it and she said she would like the wedding to take place at the Rex Hotel."

"Really? Will Little Lien help us?"

"No, she will very busy next month. She is helping the smaller traders in Rex Market, Tan Binh Market and the SKL Clothes Market to spread the freedom party's ideals. Like me, she will do whatever she can for the sake of the Revolution. In the end, my dear, it's the party with the most people on their side that will be victorious. We need to win the support of the people, because we could never beat the South and the Americans by fighting alone, darling."

"You're right ..." said Tu. "By the way, I should mention that our secret password is no longer safe, especially when I am in the office, because it is likely to be exposed. The CIA have been keeping a close eye on my files and examining different profiles. They are looking at various Saigon and Nam Vang drug dealers, concentrating on those who have American or CIA connections. They are also looking for profiles which have been 'lost' and which I haven't been able to account for. I am afraid they will discover the changes that I am making to these files and I will be found out."

"Don't worry," smiled Mrs Tam. "It's unusual for them to do anything about false information, because officials concoct hundreds of fake agent profiles every year in order to claim money and they then share it amongst themselves."

"Mum, you're great!" exclaimed Tu with relief.

"One more thing," continued Mrs Tam, "next week, don't go into any bars or places that Americans usually frequent. Do you understand?"

"Yes."

"What about plan MB20?"

Tu explained that he had just received instructions via his secret letter box and that the final details were being kept secret.

Mrs Tam informed Tu of what she knew of the plan. "Someone is to deliver a bouquet of flowers that you are supposed to have sent to Mrs Philippe. When you speak to him, he will say 'Flowers from Captain Tu to Mrs Philippe; I am sorry that I am late'. You will then have to respond: 'I am not Captain Tu, yet', at which point the man will give you final instructions. Alright?"

"Yes. I will try my best."

"Are you sure?"

"Sure."

"It is not a small job, so, in order to complete the plan, you will need 500 kilos of explosives. I still remember the time when you blew up our own tunnel rather than the South Vietnamese army office, so I have no idea why your boss wants you to do this. You will have to make sure that you succeed this time."

"Don't worry; in two weeks time, you will see the reports in the newspapers."

"Mum will pray for you."

"Thank you. Have you decided on a day for my engagement yet?"

"Little Lien is consulting a fortune-teller as we speak."

"This is not a real wedding, so why is she doing that? And I have not heard anything about Doctor Tan; do you think he will be able to come to my wedding?"

"The moment you said he was a suspect, our senior leaders asked him to move to our outside base."

"Is there anything I can do for him?"

"You are already doing enough, dear. We need to keep you as safe as possible. And I am not happy that our bosses are using us as terrorists;

where are we going to find hundreds of kilos of explosives? It is a dangerous task and you are at risk of exposing yourself. You are too important to risk on such a hare-brained scheme."

"I know, Mum, but we must carry out our orders. We have no choice," said Tu.

He knew his boss was clever and would have thought through the plans first before making any hasty decisions.

Chapter Fifteen

Everything went according to plan. The contact that brought the flowers to Rose Villa also brought more details about Mission MB20. The operation was to take place two weeks before the wedding.

Following General Co's suggestion, Vinh tried to help Tu with his preparations to marry Nicole, but Tu had a mission to fulfil and Vinh would have prevented him from doing his duty. Eventually, Tu informed Vinh that on Saturday he would be going out with his friends, and, therefore, would not be able to see him until the following Monday.

That Saturday afternoon, a car carrying two men picked Tu up at the police headquarters. They were heading towards the Mekong Delta. It was a long and horrible journey along the bumpy, bomb-cratered road. After four hours, the car dropped him in the darkness next to the Mekong River. From there, he travelled for another couple of hours by boat to the organised meeting point, where he met a group of people holding on to bamboo floats in the river. There were five fishing boats around the floats, which were there to protect the rafts.

Two of the men explained how to fuse the bomb that was attached underneath the bamboo floats and when they had finished, they left Tu alone to do his duty. He knew that he had to be organised and do everything in the correct order, otherwise he would not survive. Looking death in the face, he suddenly realised why his boss wanted him to take part in this mission. If he died, it would come to light that a spy had infiltrated the South Vietnam police, which would be a huge embarrassment to the Southern government. He was a pawn in a game of chess, but he knew that he would do anything for his country, and do it well. If he survived, then he could return home to see Nhat and meet his son for the first time. It would certainly make an interesting story, that is if he ever got the chance to tell Nhat, and their friends and family.

Tu swam for a kilometre towards the bridge. Once there, he attached the explosives to the base of the bridge and set the timer. He jumped back into the river and swam as quickly as possible away from the bridge, until he came to the next meeting point, where he was pulled from the river by a group of strong men. A huge explosion was then heard. Tu had just blown up the Saigon Bridge. Someone gave him dry clothes and put him in the back of the car to take him back home. The air was warm inside the car, which made him feel tired, and within minutes he was fast asleep.

Tu woke near the Cambodian border; however, in order to cross the border, they had to wait until nightfall and wade through a rice field, because nobody had a passport. Tu was unsure whether the bridge he had blown up was in Vietnam or in Cambodia; so he would have to wait until he could read about it in all of the newspapers. At that present time, all he knew was how exhausted he was, but he was pleased, because he had accomplished his mission perfectly. Once over the border, Tu asked whether they could stop at a restaurant for dinner and grab a bottle of whisky. There was another car waiting for him, which was full of shopping bags.

"It's your shopping for your wedding," the driver told Tu, "including a new suit for the groom. We've only just got back from our shopping spree in Le Thanh Tong."

"Yes, we have. It was nice shopping there," Tu answered, going along with the subterfuge

The driver drove the car back to Saigon and stopped outside Tu's office. Rang came to greet him and gave Tu a hand to unpack his shopping. "Wow, you've done a lot of shopping today. Just look at all this; how did you manage to buy all this stuff in such a short space of time? You should help me to do my shopping, Tu. And look at this … that suit would look better on me than you."

"Get away, that's my wedding suit!" said Tu, taking the suit inside.

It was Vinh's birthday and everbody at work was getting together to go out for dinner. However, Tu remembered the warning from Mrs Tam about not going to any bars, especially where Americans drank, but refusing to go to Vinh's birthday party, even with a valid excuse, would draw unwanted attention towards himself. Terrorism was not a good thing, because, even if one American died, hundreds of people would be arrested, tortured or even killed. However, without bombing, how could the peace message be relayed? The Americans did not want to see a united Vietnam and did not respond to letters such as "Dear Sir, please withdraw your troops from my country", Tu thought.

The Caravel Hotel was busier than usual. Men gathered around the bar to smoke and drink, and at the corner of the bar was a group of Westerners wearing black suits and black ties. It looked as though they had been to someone's funeral. The bar attendants were busy, so Tu had to wait a while to be served. He chose a long table that was large enough to seat all of his colleagues, at the same time thinking that if the Vietcong wanted to plant a bomb, this would be an ideal target.

"What would you like to drink, sir?" asked the waiter.

Tu looked at the waiter. He noticed that a few of the buttons on his shirt were of a different size; not something to be expected in a five-star hotel.

"A glass of whisky, and, if possible, I'd like a slice of lemon and some salt."

"Excuse me, sir, we have yellow and green lemons, which would you prefer?"

Tu answered, but from the way he spoke, Tu thought the waiter might be Vietcong trying to tell him something. He needed the toilet and made a mental note to chat to him when came back out. He made his way down a long corridor to the restroom, when suddenly there was a massive explosion, followed by screaming. Tu immediately understood what had happened. The hotel had been bombed! Tu instinctively laid down on the floor and a door fell top of him, hitting him hard on the head. The lights flickered on and off and outside the building, the sirens of the emergency services could be heard in the distance.

When Vinh arrived, he saw six of his colleagues lying dead amongst the tables and chairs. The rescue forces promptly arrived at the scene, and gave emergency aid to the American soldiers first. Two American experts that had been Vinh's guests had been killed outright. Their broken bodies lay on the floor and their injuries were so severe that Vinh was unable to identify them, even though they were lying on their backs. Some of Tu's colleagues were also dead; they had been so kind to Tu and one of them was looking forward to the birth of his first baby next month. Tu felt lucky to be alive and prayed to God to ask him to put an end to the fighting.

Vinh approached Tu, who was sitting on the ground in the corridor.

"Are you ok?" Vinh asked.

"A door fell on top of me. It saved my life. I'm glad you missed all this."

"Thank goodness, indeed," he answered.

"I think the Vietcong were aiming at the Americans, don't you?" Tu asked.

"Yes, and perhaps they were planning to kill our boss, who is difficult to please …"

"Is Colonel Loan really that difficult to please?"

"Very. You're from Can Tho, so you do not know him like we do."

"I have an awful headache," said Tu, groaning.

He decided against wishing Vinh a happy birthday.

"You should go to hospital and get checked out."

"I will," said Tu, as he stood up. "Vinh?"

"Yes?"

"I was wondering whether you would like to be my best man," Tu asked.

"Of course I will; I am flattered."

"Vinh, be careful while you are here," said Tu, pausing to hear his boss's reply.

"I will. We will search for clues in Thi Nghe tomorrow, in Gate 13, District 1; and then there's always the Lao Dong village next to Saigon River. We have received information that groups of Vietcong and Bietdong have been seen in Lao Dong village."

Tu was pleased to hear what Vinh had said and he knew what he had to do next, and he needed to do it alone. Tu had to pass the information he had just heard to Mrs Tam and Little Lien as a matter of urgency. But that would mean that Little Lien would probably have to go and meet her contact in Lao Dong village, which would put her in great danger. He had never contacted the Vietcong directly before, but he hoped they would recognise his secret password.

It was half an hour before the curfew started and Saigon was already deserted. Tu, who was looking for his contact, walked on a track alongside the Saigon River. The river was dirty and there were many half-Vietnamese and half-American children, who had been discarded by their families, asleep on the banks. It was a heartbreaking sight. These children, through no fault of their own, were despised and were left to fend for themselves. In order to remove the children from the streets, the government periodically gathered up the children and put them into orphanages. However, the orphanages were heartless places; for there was neither love nor care for the children. The children often escaped and returned to the streets, preferring life on the streets to the cold and uncaring orphanages.

The moonlight lit up the Saigon River and the on the other bank, people could be seen queuing for the last ferry. It reminded Tu of home. Home. Tu suddenly missed his home and he wondered how the harvest was progressing, because there had been more typhoons reported than usual, whether or not his family had enough food to last until the next season, and whether or not everything had been destroyed by the American bombs. He also wondered how his family and friends were, and whether or not they had missed him as much as he missed them. Being an agent, he could never be sure about his fate, and it was like having a knife held to either side of your throat. If the South discovered that he was spy, it would take a miracle to save him and they only happened in fairy tales. Tu's fate was in the hands of others and it taught Tu to not trust anybody and suspect everyone, which was a tiring business. The rewards for denouncing a spy were great, and any of his friends may even have been tempted to betray him had they been in urgent need of money.

That morning, Tu had heard more news about a forthcoming attack at Vietcong Zone 9 (Tactic III), which would happen in approximately two weeks' time. The Americans and Southern government were outraged, because the Vietcong, with support from the Northern army, had declared a new Southern government (Chinh Phu Lam Thoi), which was fully against America. All they knew was that the chairwoman was called Nguyen Thi Dinh and Thieu's government had put a price on her head of 50,000 US dollars.

It was now the eleventh day of the carpet-bombing and the Americans had dropped 100,000 tons of bombs in the North to date. The electricity plants, petrol dumps and weapons factories alike had all been bombed, and the Americans were unconcerned that hospitals, schools and residential areas had also been wiped out in the process. Vietnam's people lived in constant danger and Tu realised how lucky he was to still be alive.

Tu sat on a stone bench and requested a bowl of Bun Bo from one of the street vendors. The street vendor's helper, a young boy, was watching Tu with curiosity, and wondered what this smartly dressed stranger was doing in this poor area. The boy brought him a bowl of hot noodles and put him to the test with the Vietcong's secret password.

"My Mom said if you would like some fish eggs, she will bring them to you. Oh, no," the little boy corrected himself, "... a chicken egg."

"I do not eat chicken eggs, fish eggs only," Tu answered, realising that fish eggs were something that would never be sold in this restaurant.

The little boy turned out to be one of the contacts, and so he gave him two coded messages, which contained addresses that were going to be searched by the police in the morning. It came as a surprise to see a small boy rather than an adult. The combined forces of the Vietcong and Bietdong certainly worked well together. Tu paid the bill and told the boy to keep the change.

When Tu arrived back at his apartment, he felt miserable and sad. At this rate, the war could last forever which meant even more time away from home. Tu often thought about running away from his mission to return home, but he knew he would be shot dead on the way to the North by either side if he did so. The Ho Chi Minh Trail was for men on their way to fight, not for the man who simply wanted to go home because he was homesick. Tu went to the kitchen to look for some beer or whisky, but he was fresh out, so he went to Rang's room instead.

Rang opened the door wearing just his shorts; behind Rang, on the sofa, were two girls with even less clothing on.

"Come in, Tu," Rang said. "Meet my darling Lin, she needs you."

Rang winked, then pulled Tu down on to the sofa next to one of the girls.

The girl called Lin came up to Tu and allowed her shirt to fall from her body. She stood in front of him with her large breasts positioned next to Tu's face, and whispered, "You are looking tired. Let me massage you."

Rang let the other girl sit in his lap as he spoke to Lin; "Brother Tu is still a virgin, so you will have to teach him, sweetie."

"Please excuse me," Tu said, as he moved to leave the room.

"Sorry, Tu, it was only a joke," Rang shouted, as Tu closed the door behind him.

The following week, Tu was planning to take some time off work, but he was unable to do so, because of a Vietcong member that had been arrested the previous night. He looked at the profile of this latest member, but it rang alarm bells. The profile in itself was suspicious. It looked brand new, as if it had just been written, and all the papers had been written up with the same coloured ink. He suspected that this man might be an impostor of the Vietcong. If so, why was he involved, or were the police just testing him? Why had Vinh given this case to him and not Rang? Tu knew he had to tread very carefully.

The prison officers brought in the prisoner. There was an air of defiance about the prisoner, but he looked clean and well and Tu was pleased that he had not been beaten.

"Name?" Tu began.

"Le Van Mien," answered the prisoner, irritated by the question.

"Age?"

"Thirty … erm … twenty-eight."

"Job?"

"Car and motorbike mechanic."

"Hometown?"

"Saigon."

"When did you join the Vietcong? It is better for you that you confess to everything. If you do tell me everything, I will help you. I repeat! If you work with us, you will find us to be generous. Our government has a policy of welcoming back with open arms those who have seen the errors of their ways, so tell me about the Vietcong, where are they?" The prisoner did not answer. "It will not help your case if you are stubborn."

Tu turned to the prison officers from the torture room and nodded his head as a signal. They immediately dragged the prisoner out. Tu heard sounds of water being flushed away and groans of pain. The prisoner was unaware of the secret sign he used to identify fellow revolutionaries, but it did not mean that he was not working for the North. There were many groups of people working for the North. The prisoner could easily have been part of the Special Forces, South Liberation Front or a Commando Secret Reconnaissance Agent, so Tu needed to establish which side he was working for. Maybe he had just joined the Vietcong, or if he was a fake prisoner, he might have been placed amongst war prisoners to gather information. Alternatively, maybe he was there to investigate Tu.

When the prisoner was dragged back into the interrogation room, Tu could tell that the prisoner had not suffered too much at their hands. Perhaps the police already knew who Tu was; sweat poured down his back. He could feel the dampness of his shirt against his skin. He hoped that nobody had seen his reaction and to distract them, he finally ordered to the prisoner to be taken back to his cell. On leaving the interrogation room, Tu felt relieved. It was only when he was inside enemy territory, that he became aware of the expensive price of freedom. His feeling of loneliness, homesickness and a combination of confusion and worry, brought him close to tears. I will go and see Mum and Little Lien, he thought, as he tried to shake off the feeling of uncertainty.

Chapter Sixteen

It was seven o'clock in the evening when Tu arrived at Mrs Tam's house. He felt comforted to see the light through the window, because it felt as though he was back at his own mother's house. Through the window, he could see Mrs Tam had a visitor and Little Lien was dashing around inside the kitchen. The visitor was a girl, but Tu couldn't see who it was. The girl was slim and graceful, and she was wearing a blue *Ao Dai*. It was Nicole, his fiancée. His heart skipped a beat and his love for her was overwhelming. As he walked into Mrs Tam's house, he beamed at Nicole and forgot to greet Mrs Tam and Little Lien in his haste to see her.

"Darling," whispered Tu.

He was so happy to see her. She was to become his family and at that present time, he needed security of his loved ones.

Nicole turned round. Her wavy hair was twisted high into a bun and she looked more beautiful than ever.

"I came to see Mum Tam," said Nicole gently.

Tu walked towards Nicole, held her and kissed her on the forehead.

Mrs Tam and Little Lien were quite surprised and felt a little awkward at this display of affection. It was they who had encouraged his love for Nicole and, yet it turned out that Tu was even more romantic than any of the actors in the movies. Little Lien had never seen this side of Tu before and walked away into another room.

"Who brought you here?" asked Tu, because he hadn't seen Nicole's car outside.

"Mr Nam, I asked him to wait for me outside on the road while I walked the rest of the way here. I didn't want him to park the car in the lane, because I was afraid that the car would be in the way. My mother said she has something to tell you, but you have not visited us for a while."

"I'm sorry. I have been very busy with work," Tu explained. He was thirsty so he shouted into the kitchen. "Mum, where do you keep the water?"

Mrs Tam entered the living room, smiling, "Tu, surely you haven't forgotten the fridge that you put it in the dining room."

Tu took out a bottle of water and then went to the kitchen to make a fresh orange for Nicole. He greeted Little Lien cheerfully, but she didn't answer.

"What's wrong with you?" asked Tu. "Yesterday I went to Ben Thanh Market hoping to see you at the shop."

"Really?" Little Lien replied rudely.

"Yes, I did."

"Anyway, how's work going?"

"Everything is fine, except that I'm not getting on with Rang."

"Why? Tell me; I might be able to help you."

"No, you can't." Tu answered. He was reluctant to tell Little Lien the real reason why he wasn't getting on with his colleagues.

They were interrupted by Mrs Tam, who came into the kitchen and quietly informed Tu that there was a policeman from headquarters outside to collect him. Tu looked out of the window so he could see who it was.

"It's my chauffeur," he told Mrs Tam. "For him to come here, it must mean there's some sort of problem, Mum. If anything happens, will you tell my family that I love them."

He then walked into the living room with a tray of drinks. Behind him, Mrs Tam was ready and Little Lien checked that her gun was securely in place under her T-shirt. She knew that if they had been found out, she would fight her way out and take Mrs Tam and Nicole with her.

"What's the matter?" Tu asked his chauffeur.

"I have news that affects you," said the chauffeur. "The new Vietcong prisoner has been beaten to death by the other prisoners, so you have been ordered to come back for the autopsy."

"I have to go," said Tu. He turned to Nicole: "I will visit you next week." Then he added, quietly, "I miss you."

On his way back to the office, his thoughts returned to Nicole once more. She had looked so beautiful when he had seen her at Mrs Tam's. He needed her at that moment. No, he was desperate for her, but she should not be with him. He was a spy. It wasn't fair to her and she should be discouraged from loving him. That would be in her best interests.

Tu felt uneasy at the sight of the corpse, but the killing of the prisoner actually solved a problem for him and he wished that most of his problems could be as straightforward. But it still left open the question of who actually killed the prisoner. Was it the work of a criminal? A prisoner of war? Or possibly an agent planted by his enemies? Either way, it didn't matter; he was in the clear. He felt sorry for the man. He had heard that he had had a good strength of character and was an ordinary civilian, who, like everybody else, had been caught up in the war.

A few days after the incident, Tu found himself in the interrogation room again when the prison officers brought him two further prisoners. He immediately recognised one of the men as being from the Cu Chi Tunnels.

"Welcome to the special Vietcong examination room," Tu began.

"But, sir, I am a criminal prisoner, not a political one," corrected one of the prisoners.

"So why you are here and what did you do? Tell me."

"Dear sir. I lost my job six months ago. I sold all my belongings to buy food, because I have my parents, wife and three children to support. I went to the Work and Pensions Centre, but all the staff were too busy doing their make-up or chatting on the telephone to be bothered to help me. I couldn't wait for any longer, sir. Two weeks ago, I saw a big woman with a bag full of food, so I stole it, and that is all. In my opinion, all the people who work for the W and P should be arrested."

"Stop," Tu said. Then, turning to the other man he said, "What can I do for you?"

The prisoner answered immediately, "I want to go home and I want to know if my family are ok. I committed a crime, but my family know nothing and I am not with the Vietcong."

"So why are you here?"

"I am just a bank robber," he said, "and didn't even do that right. I did nothing, but because I had my son's toy gun in my pocket, the banker called the police."

Tu read the case. When this man was arrested at the bank, he had had a letter in his pocket, which the police thought might be a password used by the Vietcong.

"So you are the bank robber?"

"Yes, sir."

"And you are the thief?"

"Yes, sir."

"If you were freed, what would you do?"

"Rob banks and steal, sir," they answered, in chorus.

"Not Vietcong?"

"No, sir."

Tu signed the agreement to let them go.

That afternoon, Vinh came to meet Tu as he was concerned about Tu's decision.

"You have gone too far this time. You know that I am your friend, but I must tell our boss."

However, many things happened in the following weeks and the department became extremely busy. Outside the police headquarters, the Americans, the North, the South, the Vietcong and the Bietdong were at combat with each other. Everybody in the office was working so hard and was so tired that Tu's case was forgotten. But even so, Tu could not make up his mind whether or not his boss was just being kind to him. Maybe it was the protection he was gaining by marrying into the Philippe family that was making everything go so smoothly for him. Either way, he took advantage of that help and allowed many Vietcong people out of prison.

Tu was following Little Lien's advice on how to court Nicole to the letter. Every Saturday, Tu bought flowers for her and if he was busy or on duty, he sent his chauffeur to take her shopping, or simply to deliver his love letters to her. Nicole had no idea her love letters were actually written by Little Lien with Tu's signature on them. She retained all of his love letters in a beautiful box, which she placed on the top of her dressing table, so it would be the first thing she saw in he morning. The love letters were filled with sweet nothings, such as "I love you so much and want to do everything for you and 'You are always in my dreams and I love you forever and a day'".

Sometimes Tu was embarrassed by the things Little Lien wrote in her love letters, but she just frowned. "I know what a girl wants from her boyfriend, trust me."

"But I don't want to lie to her."

"You're lying to her already. You're not able to live a proper life under the circumstances; besides we have no choice in the matter."

"I know we have no choice, but I still feel bad about the lies and deceit."

"Brother Tu, everyone in Vietnam, we all want life to be perfect, but we are at war. Sometimes we must sacrifice what we want out of life. I wanted to go to university, I wanted to have a boyfriend, I wanted to have lovely family, but I can't."

"I am sorry," Tu said.

He knew Little Lien was desperate for a boyfriend who was a Vietcong supporter, but they had to remain hidden, which made it impossible for Little Lien to meet anyone.

To make Little Lien happy, Tu used most of his free time to take Nicole to the cinema or shopping, and in the evening, he would escort Nicole to an elegant restaurant for dinner. Tu also sent Charles boxes of cigars and Ann fresh food, which he said he had bought in her hometown, but God knows where Little Lien had really bought it.

One night, at Mrs Tam's house, Tu said to Little Lien, "Now Nicole is so in love with me, are you happy?"

"That is your happiness, not mine," Little Lien snapped back.

"She rings me every day and my colleagues just laugh at me. She cries even if I just look at another girl in a short skirt. Every day she asks me if I love her! You are so clever, so skilful in love."

"And do you kiss her every night?"

"Of course."

"Did you know your expenses for courting Nicole are the dearest item on our bill?"

Tu was unaware of how dear it was to court Nicole and the Bietdong team never complained about the money side of things. They bought expensive cars and furniture for Tu's house, or gave money to dine, sparing no expense on a forty-year old bottle of champagne, which Tu ordered by accident; the most expensive restaurants never displayed the prices. Tu also used up all his salary during his courtship of Nicole and thought better of telling Little Lien. He resolved to marry her soon, before she made him bankrupt.

But the truth of the matter was that Tu enjoyed Nicole's company. She was so kind and beautiful that he found it hard not to spoil her.

Chapter Seventeen

Mrs Tam arranged the traditional *An Hoi* engagement ceremony for Nicole and Tu. The previous day, Mrs Tam and her sisters had prepared five offerings, which were placed into five red lacquered boxes trimmed with gold and covered with red crepe, to give to Nicole's family as a mark of respect.

At eight o'clock in the morning on the day of the engagement, Mrs Tam's sisters met at Mrs Tam's house and the entire groom's family set off to the bride's house in order to wish the bride and groom a long and happy life together. They all wore red *Ao Dais*, embroidered in gold with the Chinese character for "happy". Two boys, wearing traditional Vietnamese clothing complete with pleated turbans, walked in front of them and held firecrackers in their hands. A roasted pig, dyed red, was placed on a copper food tray to be carried by Tu's friend, directly behind them. When they reached the bride's house at the arranged time, Mrs Tam and her sisters, who represented Tu's family who had all died, gave the five gifts along with Tu's gift of 24-carat gold jewellery, which he had spent all day trying to find something that Nicole would approve of, to the bride's family.

Tu welcomed Mrs Tam and whispered, "Where is Little Lien, Mum?"

Mrs Tam continued to smile and answered quietly, "It seems that Little Lien is under suspicion."

"Why?"

"She has been foolish. She and some student friends at Thu Duc University attended a meeting, which was protesting against America in Saigon. Unfortunately, they were seen, so today, she is staying by the radio to ensure everything is alright. She may stop by later."

"I heard about that meeting ... Why did you let her get involved with something like that? Is there anything I can do for her?"

"You're already doing enough," said Mrs Tam. "And you know what young people are like; they just do things without thinking of the consequences of their actions. Becoming the son-in-law of Mr and Mrs Philippe will enable you to help the country more ..." Mrs Tam paused, and then she continued, "... and Little Lien."

Tu remained silent.

The sun was shining as guests arrived for the engagement ceremony. It was already very hot and Vinh opened an umbrella to protect the roasted pig from the hot sun. Rose Villa's gate was beautifully decorated with colourful flowers and there were two huge strings of firecrackers; one hung from each side of the gate. Mr Lam, set them off to mark the arrival of the groom's party.

Once Charles and Ann had welcomed their guests, everyone sat in the living room waiting for the ceremony to begin. Mrs Tam spoke first to Charles to explain that Tu had come to ask for his permission to marry his daughter. Then Tu made a formal request to him for his daughter's hand in marriage. Once that was given, Tu opened the box containing the ring, and he turned to Nicole to propose to her,

Everybody stood up cheering and Ann promptly burst into tears as she stood up to accept Tu's gifts. The five red boxes were opened by two people from each family both at the same time. The gifts included a hundred couple-cakes; special cakes used for an engagement day. Ann took out just a few small items in order to follow with old Vietnamese custom as a mark of acceptance. She closed all the boxes containing the gifts and gave them to Mrs Tam to take home.

"Thank you, Mr and Mrs Philippe," Mrs Tam said. "I would be delighted to accept these gifts for our relatives and to announce their engagement. Such wonderful news should be shared."

Charles stood up and approached Tu, the smile on his face vanishing. "May I offer you my congratulations ... "

Ann had been delighted to learn of her daughter's love for Tu. However, her husband was uncomfortable with the whole situation. He was losing his most prized possession; his daughter. When Tu had asked Charles for his daughter's hand in marriage, he had felt jealous of this young Vietnamese man who had won his daughter's heart. When he had first met him, he found Tu to be cold and reserved, and it had never even crossed his mind that his daughter would choose a police officer as her husband.

He had lived in this colonial outpost for twenty-five years, solely for his wife and daughters, and now that Nicole was leaving him, he felt lonely. Nicole had French blood in her; her hair was French, her nose was French and her accent was French. Nicole made him feel less homesick. When she was in his company he did not miss his grandmother and mother's vast vineyards in Bordeaux, where, during the wine harvest, he had sampled his first glass of wine made from the finest of grapes.

Fate led him to this far-flung colonial country with only a container of miscellaneous items from his family home. All those things had been put to one side, because Ann had had the house decorated in the American style and now they seemed out of place. As for Nicole, this girl was his only connection between Vietnam and his home country. Charles missed France more than ever. In France, he could live the life of a French gentleman. In Paris, he would frequent bistros and restaurants and he could mix with people who had similar tastes and attitudes, where tables were laden with beautiful-tasting wines and sweet-smelling food. He missed the weekends at the chateaux, the hunting, the fishing, the balls and the festivals.

He now had the extra worry of his daughter marrying a boyfriend she had barely even known for a month. The upset of Nicole getting married to a strange man started to make his hair turn grey and he began to drink more.

Nicole knew her father did not agree with her choice of husband, but he never showed his dislike of Tu. Nicole taught Tu how to win Charles' respect and Tu followed her advice very carefully, from insignificant points of etiquette at the table, to French grammar and the way to speak, in order to please her father. Tu knew his father-in-law would be a difficult man to satisfy and although Tu had made every effort to be agreeable with him, Charles still seemed to be unhappy.

Charles found it hard to believe that his lovely daughter Nicole could be happy with a second-rate policeman. One day, when they were in the office with Mr Lam, Charles consulted his wife.

"What is your opinion of Lieutenant Tu's proposal of marriage to Nicole?"

"In times of war, we are lucky that she has not fallen in love with a soldier. Tu works right here in the city. At least he is safe and can spend more time with Nicole. What else are you worried about?"

"I'm afraid he is having difficulty getting accustomed to our family."

"Do you mean he is of a different class, or that you don't like his attitude?"

"It's not just that, I also have the feeling that our daughter is in some kind of danger. Everything seems to be so rushed. Do you not think? And I wonder why General Co is so kind to Tu – a mere, lowly police lieutenant. I hope he is not trying to spy on us."

"No, dear, I think he loves our daughter and he knows that Tu is a good man; that is all. However, I think the sooner they get married the better. Anyway, when our daughter and Tu are together, it is clear how much they have become attached to each other. Our daughter is not only attractive, but she is also intelligent and gentle. I have also taught her how to run a household effectively and she will know how to get the best out of life. Don't worry about her too much, dear. Anyway, we will still be here to help her. I have also organised somebody to investigate our son-in-law's adoptive mother. Mrs Tam has a great reputation in business and I have met her, and I believe that our son-in-law's mother is a good woman. Oh I forgot to tell you, General Minh has already promised to source the food, which has been imported from France, for the army via our company and ships."

Charles interrupted his wife, "I do not like him at all, so this is the last time we will do business with the army. I wonder when your good friend, General Minh, or General Thi will become president."

"Why is that so important?"

"Because it is – it is desperately important," snapped Charles.

Then he stormed from the villa to drive somewhere … anywhere … just to calm down. Charles had supported Minh because he hated Thieu; the ex-boyfriend of his wife. If Minh became president, Thieu would probably disappear …

Nicole rushed into the office and bumped straight into Mr Lam, who was polishing the bookcase.

"Why did my father leave home so early? Is he angry?"

"No," Mr Lam answered, "everything is just fine."

"Is Tu coming over today?" Ann asked.

"Yes, he is. He is coming to take me to church. Mother, you do like him, don't you?"

"How much do you love him?" asked Ann.

"Mother?"

"Tell me. Do you really love him, or is it just his handsome face?"

"Both. Whilst we are on the subject, why do you love Father? Tell me about your love …"

"It is because your father has a nose bigger than most and a stylish manner that I wanted to win his heart; I have always admired the French," said Ann, and smiled at her daughter.

For Ann, her daughter's wedding day was to be one of the greatest days of her life. Everybody in the villa had been preparing every single day for two whole months. After the wedding, Tu would move into Rose Villa, so Nicole's room would need to be redecorated and the old things would have to be removed and placed into storage within the grounds. Bricklayers, carpenters and decorators had been working hard for a month to complete a huge modern room for the new couple. The curtains and drapes were ordered from France, the ivory wooden bed with yellow and silver edging matched the dressing table, and the two little heart-shaped tables, which were placed at both ends of the bed, were all designed by Nicole. On the top of the table was a clock, a framed photograph and a lamp.

Ann loved redecorating her daughter's room. She enjoyed moving things around and deciding whether pink or peach walls would suit the ivory bed better. As it happened, the decorator eventually painted the room in the two different colours.

As a present for his daughter and son-in-law, Charles bought them a new car. Tu managed get a promotion before the wedding and had planned to wear his police uniform with the new rank insignia on the day instead of his suit.

Just beforehand, Tu took Nicole and Ann on holiday to see his house in Can Tho. They both loved the villa and had a relaxing time, sunbathing in the afternoon and discussing the preparations for the wedding. It was clear that Tu and Nicole were in love and Ann was very pleased that Tu loved her daughter as much she did.

The holiday in Can Tho went well and time flew quickly. By the time they returned to Saigon fully refreshed, the wedding day was just two weeks away.

These two weeks were heaven for Nicole. She spent most of the time kissing her husband-to-be and hugging him, and she couldn't bear to be apart from him, even for a short while.

Ann was so happy about the marriage of her daughter, that nothing would upset her. If the dinner was not ready on time or her wardrobe in the bedroom was untidy, Ann would just gently remind the servants and laugh, rather than shout at them like she usually did.

The reception was to be held at the Rex Hotel in Nguyen Hue Street and Ann organised for the hotel chef to visit her house to discuss the menu. So at nine o'clock in the following morning, the maid knocked on the lounge door and informed Ann that Mr Bon the chef had arrived and was waiting for her in the drawing room.

Ann wore a traditional black velvet *Ao Dai* with the back embroidered with a peacock's feather and was accompanied by Charles to welcome their guest. She also wore a three-tiered pearl necklace and her hair was twisted high in a bun, which was decorated with a gold hair comb.

Bon stood up and greeted the Charles and Ann politely as they entered.

"Thank you for sparing the time to come here, Mr Bon," said Ann.

"Dear Brother Charles and Sister Ann," said Bon, as he opened his case, "these are the proposed menus. You have a choice of three, and I have been fortunate enough to find some more unusual and special ingredients."

Ann glanced at the menus, and was pleased to see the dishes that she had requested included swallow's nest soup, abalone, forest chicken, deer's nerve and shark's fin soup.

"Ann, you will be pleased to know that I have also managed to obtain bear's meat for you."

Charles spoke in French to his wife. "I don't think we should have that particular dish. I am totally against the killing of bears for food."

Ann translated in Vietnamese, "My husband said that the dish would be an excellent choice. We will certainly order that."

Bon understood French, but he did not wish to get involved in an argument. It was obvious that Ann would have the final say. Charles seemed displeased, but he made no further comment.

"I will briefly explain the order in which the dishes will be served," Mr Bon volunteered.

"Please do," replied Ann.

"We will commence with champagne; all the special foods will be served as canapés before the main supper. Chicken salad and swallow's nest soup will be for the Vietnamese guests and your American guests will have smoked salmon with a cheese sauce. The main courses will include steamed chicken, Chinese roasted ducks, fillet of beef and shark's fin soup. The desserts will include cream cakes, cheese and biscuits, and grapes. The reception room for the president and the VIPs has already been booked and we have been advised by their private offices as to which dishes will be required. Would you be able to tell me how many American guests you will be inviting? And whether they will require separate dishes for the main course?"

Ann turned to her husband, "Darling, tell me how many guests will be having European dishes."

"Ten guests from France, ten others from Dau Tieng, some Americans, although I believe they have been to Vietnam before and will therefore be quite happy with Vietnamese dishes."

"Darling, I want our guests to be happy."

"In that case, I will leave it to you," said Charles.

"We have invited twenty American guests ... we have many friends and I could invite some more ..."

"It's up to you," said Charles, making his excuses to Bon before leaving the room.

While his wife, daughter and servants were busy preparing for the wedding, Charles went out to have a drink. He was no use to his family at present. He was not trusted to organise anything for the party, the decoration of the house, or the choosing of the dress; the only thing that he was allowed to become involved with was the security of the villa on the day of the wedding. Ann was in charge of everything else. Even the invitations of the guests from his family's side were arranged by her. It was best, therefore, for him to go elsewhere and stay out of the way.

Two days before the wedding, Rose Villa had already been fully decorated and the rose bushes in the garden which were brought from Da Lat were starting to flower. Hundreds of lights were switched on day and night to ensure that all the rose buds would bloom and emit a powerful scent on the big day.

Tu loved Nicole, but was racked with guilt that she loved him so much. He went to work as usual and even stayed in the office after work to give Vinh a hand.

Before becoming manager of the Communist Suspect Record Office, Vinh had been in charge of cases connected to civil law, and it was because of his experience in examining different profiles and files that he was promoted.

"Why did you move to this office?" asked Tu, when he had read the documents of a new case from Buon Ma Thuot.

"Surely you must realise that nobody comes here with bribes."

Vinh was a good man who detested corruption. So it was with this in mind that Tu understood why Vinh had been moved from the civil law office, where a corrupt official could make a lot of money, to the Communist Suspect Record Office, where there was no chance of corruption as the Vietcong supporters were generally very poor, and had no spare money for bribes.

In the case of Buon Ma Thot, someone had brought an action against the government, because his son was not able to do simple addition and subtraction, due to the incompetence of his son's teacher. Vinh felt that teachers were not qualified enough outside of the city.

The Americans brought many new jobs into the country and people's lives had become far easier as their income had increased. However, most of the money went towards the war, which meant that education was last in line for receiving funds. The skills of the well educated were needed for the rebuilding of the country which meant that people like teachers had not had the chance to finish their education and in some instances not even high school. They taught in old fashioned ways and the students didn't understand their lessons. This led to situations where, after one or two years of going to school, pupils barely knew the alphabet and, if they were absent from school for even a short time, they forgot what little they had learnt and became illiterate again.

"I prefer a government that takes care of people's lives to one only making war," Vinh said.

He was skilful in dealing with civil law and when the office had a difficult case, they could pass it over to Vinh. However, Vinh was not good at dealing with Vietcong cases, for this was Tu's area of expertise, and he always seemed too lazy to follow the cases through.

"General Minh wants friendship between North Vietnam and the South government, and I support him. The Vietnamese people are of the same descent," continued Vinh. "By the way, I had a suit made for your wedding, and I am sure that I will be the most handsome man present!"

Tu laughed, "I know Nicole's bridesmaid and she is very pretty, perhaps she will marry you."

"Yes, I know," Vinh sighed, "but it is difficult being a major in the police force; I am always a target and the Vietcong have me as a marked man. It is too dangerous for a girl to love a guy like me."

"We cannot afford to make mistakes," said Tu, meaningfully.

Chapter Eighteen

When the wedding day finally dawned, the weather was perfect. Dawn broke to reveal a cloudless sky and there was a fresh feel to the air. It was neither too hot, nor too humid, and the weather forecast had reported that it wouldn't rain.

Following the Vietnamese tradition, the guests from the bride's family were to wait at Rose Villa for Nicole to get ready, so they could follow her to the church.

The reception room at the Rex Hotel was fully decorated with white flowers and white ribbons. Sixty tables had been carefully laid out and they had golden roses in the middle. Mrs Tam, Little Lien and Vinh arrived early to ensure that everything was in order. Rang, who Tu had come to hate, looked overdressed in a navy suit with a pink scarf and sunglasses.

Tu and Vinh wore black suits and striped ties. The flower on Tu's lapel was the only feature that differentiated them. Friends from work wore their white police uniforms as they waited outside the hotel smoking.

"You are looking very smart," Tu complimented Vinh.

"Of course, what would you expect?" answered Vinh, with mock pride.

At Rose Villa, everyone was happy and looking forward to seeing the bride in her new gown. Charles wore a pinstriped navy suit, with a white shirt and a black bow tie. He looked so proud whilst waiting to take his favourite daughter to the church.

A gasp went out as the door to Nicole's bedroom opened to reveal her in all of her glory. Nicole looked as beautiful as a princess in her spotless white dress. It had been made in Paris and had been sent to Saigon from Charles' aunt. Nicole wore the necklace which Tu had given her on their engagement day and she looked perfect. Charles had to fight back the tears as she walked down the staircase. It only seemed like yesterday that

Nicole had been his little baby girl and today, she was a grown woman. Charles was so proud of his youngest daughter and he couldn't help but tell his guests how beautiful she was.

As the mother of the bride, Ann also looked incredibly beautiful. She wore a long black *Ao Dai*, embroidered with two splendid yellow dragons. Around her neck, she wore a pearl necklace with a matching bracelet on her wrist. Her black hair was twisted high in a tight bun and was fixed with a diamond-encrusted gold pin. Her high cheekbones had been accentuated with dark rouge, and she wore a light pink lipstick. Even her eyebrows had been carefully plucked and pencilled in brown. The famous artist Lee Ha, had done her make up in person.

Earlier that morning, Thieu had phoned Ann, informing her that he would be coming to the wedding in person, but for his own safety, she could not tell her husband or her daughter that he would be there.

Charles and Ann's eldest daughter Hue, a millionaire, had arrived in style not long beforehand. She and her husband Chau Chinch were the new owners of the largest transport company in Saigon, and she was the most overdressed person at the wedding. She wore the traditional dress with a long green velvet top, and white trousers. A gold bracelet encrusted with huge diamonds reflected in the sunshine and the handles of her handbag were made of solid gold. Her high-heeled shoes were also speckled with diamonds and two guards accompanied her wherever she went.

Guests of the family arrived early and gathered in the front hall of the villa, where they had a light breakfast before leaving for the church. Most of the guests from Ann's family were pleased to know that both Ann and Tu's family had organised a traditional Vietnamese wedding. Hue's wedding had been a French occasion which had upset most of the elderly relatives in Ann's family.

The newlyweds' bedroom at Rose Villa had already been prepared, but the bride and groom's families had also booked the honeymoon suite at the Rex Hotel, in case the couple got drunk and wanted to stay. Everything was ready, except for Tu, who was looking miserable.

Vinh handed the white wedding bouquet to Tu, who took it gently, but with mixed feelings. Tu felt like a traitor to his wife in the North, and he also felt sorry for Nicole. He loved her, but it could never be a true marriage, and he was now going to stand in front of God to accept another woman as his wife. He was going to betray everything he believed in because of his mission. He was deceiving them all. The only way he could justify it was to keep telling himself he was doing it for his country.

Absent-mindedly, he withdrew a flower from the bouquet and placed it on the table. Little did he know that Rang was watching his every move with curiosity. He was in deep reflection of his past life and was startled when Rang's voice called out from behind him.

"Look! Lieutenant Tu is daydreaming. Are you thinking about what you will be doing later on tonight? If you are too drunk for the task, why not allow me to help?"

Everyone burst into laughter.

Tu pretended to laugh along with them, then, readjusting his clothes, he entered the reception room.

"Is everything ok?" he asked Vinh.

"Yes, everything is fine," Vinh said proudly.

He had certainly done an excellent job.

"My treasure, how handsome you look!" Mrs Tam told Tu, with a huge smile.

Little Lien wore a traditional pink *Ao Dai*. She stood next to Mrs Tam, smiling gently.

"Congratulations, Brother Tu!"

"Are you joking?" Tu replied.

"No, I am not! Why would you think that I am?"

"I'm sorry," replied Tu, grinning.

Vinh approached the groom. "Everything is ready. The guest list has already been given to the guards at the entrance. The president will be coming as well, so the palace will send a security team to check this room again. We have a private living room for him and there will also be some CIA and French dignitaries, who are guests of your future mother-in-law. The car has been decorated and is ready to leave for the church in three minutes."

Vinh stopped in his tracks and his eyes were drawn to the loud speakers. He couldn't remember whether he had checked them, so he walked across the stage towards the microphone.

"Switch that amplifier off," he ordered the guards.

The guards jumped up and obeyed. The buzz from the amplifier ceased, but something was wrong. There was a faint ticking!

"A bomb!" shouted Tu and Vinh in unison

Tu, forgetting who he was, quickly opened the fascia of one of the speakers. Little Lien was worried, because Tu hadn't worked with explosives for a few months, so she quickly walked up to Tu. "Do you know how to deal with it?" she asked, noticing that the bomb was hand-made and could therefore be easily defused.

"Why must you always think that I am stupid?"

"Get out!" Vinh shouted to them.

At that moment, Rang knew for sure that Little Lien was Vietcong. It was only minutes before that she had been flirting with him. There was no other explanation as to how she could turn into such a serious character when she came face to face with the bomb. Rang wondered how well Tu knew Little Lien and whether he was aware of the truth about her. He also remembered Thieu's warning to police headquarters about spies within the organisation, and he also had his own reservations about Tu and his marriage to Thieu's lover's daughter. Rang struggled with his thoughts; he needed to talk to his boss later.

"She's ok," Tu said to Vinh after he commented about Little Lien's involvement. "She didn't realise that I knew what I was doing. But she is right; we shouldn't be scared of the terrorists. We were lucky that we found it in time," he finished.

The bomb was set to go off in two hours time, which would have coincided with the guests' arrival. As the most senior officer present, Vinh ordered the bomb squad to remove the bomb and search the room once again; even the thousands of roses used to decorate the room were rechecked.

In the meantime, Tu went to talk to Mrs Tam and Little Lien. Mrs Tam was standing outside looking worried. Vinh came out to tell them it was all just a mistake. The blood drained from Mrs Tam's face; she now knew the truth, that both Little Lien and Tu were both fully conversant with bomb disposal techniques. But thank God it had been found early enough. As Little Lien helped her to climb into the car to go to the church, she wondered who had ordered the bombs to be placed there. She wondered whether it had been placed by somebody working in the hotel, who wanted to murder all the American guests.

Thieu's bodyguard informed people that they would not be allowed to bring weapons into the wedding venue, so another room was used to store all the guests' weapons.

"I think that we should keep this incident secret," suggested Tu.

"I agree," replied Vinh.

Vinh then picked up a betel nut to chew. As he spat it out, he wondered why on earth the Vietnamese still adhered to such an awful tradition, even though the country was now ruled by America.

"We'd better go," Tu told everyone.

"Come on, every groom needs to be late," Rang joked, as everyone jumped into their cars to drive to the church.

The church had been beautifully decorated with roses. The left-hand side of the church was full to capacity with Nicole's family and friends, while the right was almost empty with the exception of Tu's colleagues, Mrs Tam and Little Lien. Tu found the service boring and was eager for it to finish. Finally, the priest invited Tu to kiss his bride. Tu was an emotional turmoil because he knew in his conscience that the wedding was a farce. Tu kissed the bride and forced a smile as he took Nicole's hand and walked back down the aisle to the cheers of all their guests.

Outside the church, two lines of police in white coats waited with swords raised to form an arch. The newly wedded couple emerged through the arch to the grins of the police guard of honour, even though they were under strict instruction to remain impassive. They climbed into the bridal car to go back to the Rex Hotel for the reception with family and friends following. Thieu was in one of the three black cars at the end of the line.

At the party, Tu welcomed Thieu warmly. However, he really wanted to do otherwise because Thieu's government had been bombing the Hanoi Capital and the Habac Province, and Tu had no way of knowing whether his family was alive, dead, wounded or homeless.

Nicole stood next to her new husband to welcome the guests and invited them to come in and help themselves to a drink. There were seating plans up on the wall and people naturally talked about who was sitting where and why. There were also people who were upset as to why they were not seated at a higher table, but the presence of the president meant they could not complain too vociferously. The hotel waiters wore black suits as they walked around with trays of champagne. Betel nut was also on offer and there were spittoons strategically placed throughout the welcoming room for the guests' use. After half an hour or so, the mâitre d' announced that the meal was ready to be served and people started to move through to the dining room. People sat down at their allotted places, where many dishes of delicious food were on offer. As in any Chinese-style meal, they would help themselves to the dishes they most preferred. Whilst there were places set at the top table for Nicole and Tu, they had other duties to attend to and together, they went round the tables welcoming their guests and Tu offered the men the choice of a cigar or a cigarette. Every table offered Tu a glass of whisky, which he had to down in one. The American and the French guests were sat on the right-hand side of the room; on the left, were the Vietnamese guests, most of whom were VIPs, generals and ministers. Tu could not believe his eyes and he almost felt sorry that the bomb had been removed.

The reception was a great success and many guests, including Tu, were drunk. Guests from both sides of the family enjoyed talking, eating, drinking and congratulating the newly-weds. Charles and Ann both looked serenely happy. Little Lien was sitting quietly at the end of the table talking to General Co. They looked comfortable together and Tu felt a twinge of jealousy. It was eleven o'clock at night before Tu left the Rex to take his new wife home and because of the bombs earlier that morning, he was anxious for his new wife to be safe.

Back at the villa, the wedding bedroom looked charmingly romantic and dreamlike. Mrs Lam had already lit the candles and lamps with scented oils and the bed was awash with white rose petals. A flawless white rose lay in the middle of a champagne tray, which was a little present from Mr Lam. Under the pillows were some Champak flowers that had been placed there for their pleasant perfume. There was a heart-shaped table next to the bed, on top of which were little white boxes tied up with white ribbons, which were a gift from Ann.

Tu felt a lot better after a shower and when he emerged from the bathroom, he saw that Nicole was still standing by the dressing table. She was still in her wedding dress, except for the flowers and scarf.

"Are you tired, darling?" Tu asked.

"Just a little," she replied, "the hair slides are agony."

"Let me give you a hand," Tu said, as he helped her with them.

He was feeling a lot better than he had been at the party. He watched his new wife in the mirror and wondered if it was all just a dream.

"You are so beautiful," whispered Tu. "I still cannot believe that the most attractive woman in the world is mine."

Nicole turned round and faced her new husband.

"I have present for you," she said, displaying the tattoo on her shoulder inscribed "I love you Tu".

Tu felt a wave of guilt wash over him as what he saw was not that of his real name; it was the special policeman that Nicole loved.

"That must hurt, please don't do that again. You do look even more beautiful with your tattoo though," he admonished.

"That was my best friend's idea, when I went shopping for your present."

"You are so beautiful, both inside and out," Tu said gently, as he recovered her slides and placed them on the dressing table, where he noticed a large envelope.

Nicole smiled at him, "I've just opened the letter. It is from Father. He has bought two tickets to Paris. It is his surprise wedding present for us both. We are going to spend two months in France."

"Really?"

Tu thought that it would be impossible to remain away from Saigon for a whole two months at the moment, because he was needed by the North. He hesitated, and then said:

"I was planning on taking you to Da Lat. It was to be a surprise. I had no idea that your father was thinking of giving us a holiday in Paris, darling."

"Of course, I would much rather to go to Da Lat. I have been to France with Mother and Father many times, so I would prefer you to take me where you feel fit, darling. After all, I am your wife now."

The words "your wife" made Tu feel feel that everything was real, and he forgot about his mission for the time being. He suddenly felt a certain warmth inside his heart.

"I love you," he said.

"I love you, too," Nicole said, watching her new husband remove his white shirt. This was a special moment and she felt very privileged; this was the first time that she had seen her man without any clothes on.

Tu helped his wife to undress, her shoulders were beautiful and her skin was ivory ... However, unlike Nicole, Tu wasn't the slightest bit nervous ... Nicole's young, virgin body was quite exquisite; her breasts were pure perfection. She came to him and he extinguished the light, so that his new bride would not see the tears in his eyes, which twinkled in the candlelight, down Agent 022's handsome face.

Chapter Nineteen

The next morning everybody at Rose Villa crept around on tiptoes so as not to wake the newly-weds. Eventually, the couple descended the stairs, hand in hand, and entered the dining room. Ann Philippe followed along with eight servants, a guard, Mr Nam and Mr Lam. Ann formally introduced the new member of the Philippe family to the servants as Lieutenant Nguyen Van Tu from the police headquarters. They congratulated the new couple respectfully and then went about their daily tasks.

The big table at the corner of the dining room was laden with wedding presents, wrapped either in pink or red paper and tied with ribbons. Tu was not really interested in them, as he only had eyes for Nicole, who looked radiant beside him. She opened every single one, shrieking with delight each time. She had so much and yet she was still excited when she came upon a small plastic car – a present sent from her aunt in France.

"I have arranged for your things to be packed," said Ann to her son-in-law, as they both sat by the table watching Nicole open the presents.

"I don't understand," Tu said, somewhat surprised.

"Father has paid for us to honeymoon in Paris," Nicole reminded him.

"Mother, I haven't asked my superiors for extra time off work. I struggled to get a few days for the honeymoon. I honestly doubt that they would agree to a couple of months; after all, we are at war," answered Tu, as he looked at his wife, his expression pleading for some support.

"Mother," said Nicole "let's postpone our honeymoon in Paris. Tu and I would like to go to Da Lat. Oh, and we can call at my grandparents. Father's family will want to see us, and so will your family, Mother! We will go around and visit your relatives first. And Tu needs to improve his French before he goes to Paris."

"Good idea," said Ann, "but your father ..."

"Mother," said Nicole, "since when has Father ever been the decision maker around here?"

"You are right!" agreed Ann. "Of course my family cannot wait to meet my new son-in-law. But my sister-in-law will just have to wait."

Then she turned to Mr Lam: "Mr Lam, please go upstairs to ask Charles to come down and have a cup of tea with us. Tell him that his golden daughter is waiting for him."

"Yes, of course, madam," said Mr Lam, with a smile.

Tu understood that Ann was the undisputed boss of Rose Villa. Breakfast was served as soon as Charles and Ann had sat down. Tu was amazed, for it was the first time he had seen four servants serving only four people. There were also five or six others busying themselves outside making sure that newly-wed couple had everything they could possibly need for their honeymoon.

For Nicole, her honeymoon was like being in a fairy tale. Her husband was handsome and she well aware that he was besotted with her. He took great care of her and Nicole was so proud of him. He was the object of desire of all the women whenever they went out for a walk. Even on a visit to the rubber plantation, Tu demonstrated his sweet nature and kind-heartedness in his dealings with the plantation workers. He seemed to disparage money and property. For him, it clearly wasn't the done thing for just one family to own so many hectares of land. She, on the other hand, did not agree with his egalitarianism. He called it justice and she thought it foolish, for it would make the people lazy. Of course, their disagreement would not spoil their honeymoon. They would wake before the sun rose and after having breakfast, they would go for a walk. In the evenings, they would sit at the poolside admiring the sunset beside the tables laden with fruit.

One morning, as they sat in the hotel dining room, Nicole said: "I wish your parents were still alive. I would be a good daughter-in-law." Tu had some mango to keep his mouth busy, so Nicole continued, "How would you feel if we were to spend a week of our honeymoon at your villa in Can Tho? I love your bedroom there, darling Tu."

Tu pretended not to hear and hoped that Nicole would stop talking about the house in Can Tho, because for Tu it was not his house. He hated that house; however, Nicole was insistent on making his house more welcoming. Tu wondered why women always talked too much once they were married.

For Tu, the honeymoon was an opportunity to relax after several months of being a spy. In this city, he could do anything without worrying whether it might turn out to be a mistake, and he enjoyed having time to himself. Tu felt in tune with nature and Da Lat's fascinating views. A day in the highlands began with the birds singing from the top branches of the apple trees; a breeze delivered an all-pervading sweet-smelling perfume, invisible and suspended in the air, of roses, orchids and apple blossom. Far away, in the east, the sun appeared to be planted in layers of silken clouds, some a hazy red, some pink, and others a light yellow. The early morning rays of sunlight illuminated the land with a fresh, soft golden light. Dawn in Da Lat brought peace ... perfect peace. Water murmured in small channels far away and the horses trotted along the streets, carrying tourists up mountain roads in open-topped carriages. It was calm without the sound of gunfire, which they had become accustomed to hearing in the city. Without the thunder of marching soldiers, without the nerve-grating screech of battle tank tracks on the move, and without the screams of people having been injured in bombing raids, or cries of orphaned children. Suddenly, in the midst of a war, Agent 022 enjoyed a little peace.

In Da Lat, the children wore beautiful and colourful clothing, and played in the playground. The high-street shops were all open, and people in the market talked about the cost of living becoming cheaper, and easier. In the hotel where Nicole and Tu were staying, the waiter would bring them cocktails and would stop to chat to Tu about horse racing. Tu had to rub his eyes to make sure that he wasn't dreaming. He wondered if he was in heaven ... but no, it was Da Lat, a highland city, and he was lucky enough to be able to leave the war behind him, even if it was for only a few short days.

Tu turned to look at his wife and as she woke up, she saw him looking at her and she smiled instantly; not just with her mouth, but with her eyes, too. He so wished that he could freeze that moment forever. He could not believe how fortunate he was. His bride was so beautiful; and she looked so sexy in her white silk kimono. He was unable to hold himself back, so he kissed her passionately. He slowly removed her kimono to reveal her smooth shoulders and her perfect, sensuous body. Nicole responded readily, returning his kiss slowly and tenderly.

Chapter Twenty

Nicole could never understand why Tu was in such a hurry to return home. Over the last few days of their honeymoon, his mind had been preoccupied by work, which upset Nicole. Leaving Da Lat, would mean that she would have to get up at five o'clock in the morning to begin their journey home.

Nicole was still sleepy when Tu finally managed to rouse her from her slumber, but when Tu gave her a big hug, her frustration soon passed.

On their return, Charles greeted them both with a smile, "My darling Nicole and my dear Tu, welcome home,"

"Hello, Father," Tu replied, shaking his hand as Nicole gave her father a hug.

The servants unloaded the car and took the luggage upstairs. The table was laid for a late breakfast, because Ann had wanted to wait for her daughter's return before eating.

"So, have you definitely decided to postpone your trip to Paris?" Charles asked in French, as he sat opposite Nicole and Tu.

Tu did not answer his father-in-law; he had too many things to do and he couldn't just up and leave and neglect his mission.

Nicole knew her husband was a shy man, and realised that his French may not be that good, so she answered for them. "Yes, Father, we unfortunately have; besides, Tu will need to improve his French before we go, Father."

Charles agreed, "You are right; perhaps we will all go together as soon as he is ready."

"Of course, Father; I have missed Paris."

Charles' face lit up when he heard his daughter say that.

Mr Lam brought in a tray of hot bread, butter and marmalade; they enjoyed the morning together with their new family member. Everyone at

Rose Villa was pleased to have Nicole and Tu back home. A few days later, Nicole was worried about Tu's manners around the house, as he never came to the dining room on time and he was always doing something at breakfast, lunch and dinner time. This annoyed her, because she so desperately wanted her father to approve of him and accept him. It was unfortunate timing, because Tu was usually locked in the bathroom secretly listening to Hanoi Radio.

Before Charles and Ann came down for dinner, the servants placed fresh flowers in every room at Rose Villa. Mr Lam informed the new servant that the pink napkins should only be used when Nicole's friends came for dinner.

"Brother Lam, shall we have dinner? I am hungry," she said to Mr Lam, as she sat down next to Charles.

"Of course, sister," Mr Lam answered, as he went to the kitchen to tell Mr Ba to get the food ready.

"How are you, Ann?" Charles asked his wife tenderly.

"I am fine!" answered Ann, impatiently. "I am afraid I have some bad news. Part of an urgent consignment from France didn't arrive on time, so I have had to give a ten per cent discount as compensation. In addition, the Dai Loi who promised to pay us the outstanding debt this month, phoned a few days ago to ask for a further extension to their credit. They said they were having problems with their bank in France and promised to pay next month."

Charles brushed the papers aside and consoled her, "Don't worry. I am going to the plantation next week and I will sort it all out then."

Mrs Lam brought in four small bowls of onion soup for their starter, but no one could start, because Tu was still locked in his bedroom. He was busy writing notes about all the information that he had collected from all the important people that had visited Rose Villa, including the president.

Looking at Nicole, who was somewhat embarrassed, Charles attempted to cheer her up. "When I was young, I was the just the same."

"You are still very young, darling," said Ann, gently.

"No, you are getting old, Father!" Nicole teased with a smile, winking at her mother.

Charles smiled and reached out for an ashtray. Mr Lam, ever attentive, went to the library to bring back a box of cigars.

"Thank you, Mr Lam, would you like one?" Charles offered his butler.
"No thank you, sir," Mr Lam replied, "They are too strong for me."
"You should give up smoking," muttered Ann.
"Mother!" complained Nicole. "You have been saying that for years. You know that Father has tried several times before, so whatever makes you think he could now?"

Ann did not reply, but cast her eyes down the corridor. She was becoming frustrated because there was still no movement to be heard. They were all hungry and still waiting for Tu to come down so they could start. Charles was starting to get annoyed; who did he think he was, keeping his father-in-law waiting. His new son-in-law had no manners. When at last Tu came down and found Ann and Nicole in the dining room, he was oblivious to the fact that Charles had already left the room in anger. Mr Lam nodded a knowing look in Ann's direction as he caught her gaze.

Mr Lam had been Ann's butler for seven years. Their paths had crossed one Sunday morning, when Ann had been on her way to church. She caught sight of a man lying beside the rear wall of the church and had been so overcome with sympathy, that she ordered the chauffeur Mr Nam to take the man back to the villa.
When the stranger had woken up, he had been surprised to find himself in a bed – one with a mattress covered in a spotless white drape. The wall in front of him had been painted light yellow and he had noticed a large picture, which he later discovered was a portrait of the owner's family. To his right had been a big window, with heavy yellow curtains, and some cake had been left out for him in a silver dish, with a glass of milk, on the white French table next to the bed. To his left was a small wardrobe, with a full set of men's clothing hung outside. The stranger had had no idea where he was, or how he had come to be there. Then he had heard a low, soft voice behind him: "Oh, you are awake! Drink your milk and then you can have a bath."
Glancing behind him slowly, he had noticed a small door at the back, leading to a room.
"May I ask where I am?" the strange man had enquired.
"This is your lucky day," said the man, "You must have been born under a lucky star! You were very fortunate that my lady came across you. You are

now currently residing in the villa of the Philippe family. Mr Philippe is the head of a rubber plantation. He is also the director of an African shipping and transport company."

"Really?"

"Yes, that is right. My lady saw you lying beside the church and brought you here. I'll never know how you didn't manage to get yourself arrested. What do you do? Where do you live?"

"If I told you, I doubt that you'd believe me. I am an engineer and a doctor by trade, but I am now out of work. It is very difficult for anyone to find decent jobs, unless you join the army, and companies and workshops are forever going bankrupt in this day and age."

"I agree. The economy is unstable and everyone is struggling to survive. It's terrible. By the way, my name is Sang, but people call me Nam," said Mr Nam sympathising with the stranger. "What is your name?"

"My name is Lam," the stranger answered.

Mr Lam told Mr Nam his life story. It had turned out that he had had seven children. The previous year he had lost his job, so he had been forced to pedal a rickshaw in order to earn a living to support his family. Two of his children had detonated a mine and lost both of their arms, and he had been left with no other option than to sell his house and rickshaw, to pay for medical care for his children. He had walked to Saigon to try to find work, but his money had run out and as a result his landlady had thrown him out onto the streets. The day he had been found, he'd had a high temperature and he had been more than appreciative to find such a kind lady in the middle of Saigon. Mr Lam, overcome with emotion, couldn't stop the tears from flowing down his cheeks.

At noon, the housemaid had brought Mr Lam some lunch. He had thanked her graciously and had assured her that he would leave the villa as soon as he had finished his meal, because he hadn't wanted to impose any further; although Ann had had other ideas.

"Mr Nam has already told me your story. You are welcome to stay here and work for me if you like, and once we get to know each other better, I will give some thought as to which job would suit you best. Do you know anything about rubber plantations?"

Thus, Mr Lam remained with the Philippes, looking after the business affairs of his greatly respected new sister. After their old butler had retired,

Mr Lam had taken his place. Mr Lam gave his all in serving Ann's family, and in return for his loyalty, Ann gave Mr Lam's family work. She offered Mr Lam's wife a job in the kitchen, as an assistant to the cook, and his sons were given jobs in the rubber plantation. There were times when Ann suspected that Mr Lam was Vietcong, but the feeling soon passed.

After a quiet dinner, Nicole discreetly asked Mr Lam if she could talk with him later, in private.

When they met in the garden, she spoke to the butler with frustration, "Please help me, Uncle Lam."

Mr Lam smiled. He knew that when Nicole called him "uncle" she wanted something.

"Dear Nicole, what is it? Is it serious?" asked Mr Lam, gently.

Nicole told him about her father's dislike of Tu and how different Tu's behaviour had been since they had come back from their honeymoon.

In Mr Lam's opinion, Nicole had married much too young and too quickly. He sighed, and realised that he would have to tread very carefully, because he certainly did not wish to offend Nicole.

"I don't know Tu very well, but he seems to be kind-hearted. We are servants, so we have to be on our best behaviour with him, miss."

"You know what my family are like; my parents are strict; manners and etiquette are important to them. For example, this morning, we had to wait for Tu to come down to breakfast, and last night, he ate a bowl of food on his knee in front of the TV, rather than sitting down at the dining room table with the rest of the family. My husband is living as though he is still single. I believe that because his family died, he has grown unaccustomed to normal family routine. What should we do Mr Lam? You are the only one who can help me. He listens to you. I have tried to talk to him, but he doesn't listen to me because I am only a woman."

Mr Lam tried to explain the situation to Nicole, "Well ... you are right, but I don't think Mr Tu's manners are that bad. Don't forget, you have grown up in a high-class French and Vietnamese family, and God bless you for thinking that every family is the same. But you must remember that he is working for the police and therefore he must know all the recent news. There have been many major events in the news recently; there has been continuous bombing of the North for the last eleven days. There are reports of chemical weapons being used and many American aircraft have been shot down, including B-52s. The negotiations for a ceasefire at the Paris Peace Conference are ongoing and the relationship between President Thieu and the CIA has been under scrutiny. People are angry because some of the American troops are playing games by reporting that they are under attack, when they are not. With all this going on, it's no wonder that he is glued to the TV."

"I am fed up with the war, when will there be peace, Mr Lam?"

Mr Lam said sadly, "I myself have wondered about that thousands of times. I'm afraid I don't have the answer."

"Last month, they bombed the Presidential Palace; this month, there have been many cases of people throwing grenades into American officers' quarters. For many nights now I have been unable to sleep; I find myself just staring at the ceiling feeling scared. I am afraid that one day they will bomb Rose Villa. What would happen then? I have had so many nightmares and I am so afraid that sometimes I can't sleep, Mr Lam."

"Nicole, Rose Villa is located in one of the safest parts of the city, we should be ok."

Nicole smiled pleasantly. "Our family were planning to go back to France, but I have persuaded them to stay here a little longer, for Tu's sake."

"Love changes everything, doesn't it?" smiled Mr Lam.

Looking towards the gate, Mr Lam noticed that a car was arriving. It was Mr Nam returning with the shopping Nicole had ordered earlier.

Nicole went back to the living room and saw that her husband was sitting in front of the TV waiting for the news. "I have something for you," Nicole said, pointing towards the main entrance.

Mr Lam was helping Mr Nam to bring in a brand new TV.

"I have instructed Mr Lam to carry it to the bedroom for you," said Nicole.

"It would be better if you had let me buy it!" snapped Tu, without looking at or even thanking Nicole.

Looking at her husband's long face, she burst out laughing. She was astonished at his rudeness.

"Why are you laughing?"

Nicole refrained from replying. Tu didn't ask her again; his eyes were still glued to the TV. The presenter with curly hair was speaking about the carpet-bombing on the Ho Chi Minh Trail. He added that this was a clever tactic on the government's part, because within a month, the 559 road would be cut off. In addition, provisions to supply to the National Liberation Front had been reduced from 9,000 tonnes a month to 900 tonnes a month, which was all due to the victories of the United States Army Intelligence Service, the South Vietnamese Army and the American Central Intelligence Agency. The commander-in-chief of the air force welcomed Westmoreland's visit to Saigon Airport, who then flew on to Cam Ranh, to inspect the work on the expansion to the airfield which would eventually become the biggest airfield in Central Vietnam. Many South Vietnamese troops, along with hundreds of American troops, had been waiting to greet him.

"Damn!" exclaimed Tu, as he switched off the TV.

Nicole looked at Tu, puzzled. She couldn't understand why he was so angry. It was good news for the South. He became aware of Nicole's surprise and realised his mistake, so he smiled and kissed her, and tried to distract her by asking if she remembered that he was taking her out to the cinema later on.

The next day, Ann was standing by the library window when she saw her daughter walking hand in hand with her husband around the garden. She was happy to see her daughter looking so pleased with life and it set her thinking about her own life. At the age of fifty, she had fulfilled most of her dreams and ambitions of her youth. She was comfortable and accepting of her fate. She had a sweet affection for Saigon, where her family, friends and relatives had been living for years. The only thing that gave her concern was that she made Charles unhappy by not agreeing to live in France. His love of Indochina wasn't as great as hers.

Earlier that morning, Charles had asked her to return with him to France; she had replied that she still didn't feel ready to leave Saigon. She wanted to remain to support her children, and she felt as though she still had more to do for her country. Minh wanted peace, but not at any price, which was why she supported him. She used her family's money to court supporters for Minh in parliament. She was grateful to Charles, as he had never said a word whenever the family safe had been emptied to support a political campaign for him. If Minh became president, Thieu would have to leave Vietnam and this made her feel guilty, because, by supporting Minh, she was betraying Thieu. She felt she needed to see him again to apologise and to reassure him that she still loved him.

Charles walked into the room. "What are you thinking?" he asked.

Ann looked at her husband. He was wearing a black suit and a felt hat, and he carried a case with him.

"You're looking smart," Ann said to her husband.

She was thinking about making a phone call to the palace, so she could talk with Thieu, and she hoped she could see him very soon; maybe they could even go somewhere together.

"I'm going out. Would you like to come with me?"

"Yes, I would," replied Ann, putting her head on his shoulder as she spoke to him in French.

"I think it's time for us to return to Paris."

"Are you sure, darling?" Charles sounded happy, eager and hopeful when he spoke.

"Maybe."

Charles fully understood Ann's discomfort and guilt about leaving Vietnam. They both loved each other with their hearts and souls, but the sacrifice that Charles had made in remaining in Saigon during war was because of his love for Ann. One does for the other; one lives for the other because of the bond of family ties. It was invisible but definite. He could feel the rapid approach of old age now that Nicole had grown into a woman. When the war ends and the plantation business is stable once again, he hoped that Tu would help her look after the family business, but for the time being, he could see that Tu was passionate about his job as a special police officer. Charles was starting to lose interest in the plantation, as his weapons business with the South Vietnam government was going so well.

Since Nicole had married, money did not seem to interest him any more. He wanted to relax. For him, relaxing meant going back to France, and he wanted to establish a permanent base there. The French people lived in stone houses and there were paved roads unmarked by war. He even missed the coldness of Paris in winter, and the busy atmosphere of the Christmas season. Papers in French were rare in Saigon, so he was forced to read papers in American English in order to follow events of the war. The Vietcong had recently become more active and both sides were involved in the fighting in order to seize land and people. North Vietnam suffered huge losses from mass bombing, while South Vietnam was under the rain of Agent Orange, and he could see that the Vietnamese people were destroying their own country.

That afternoon, Tu left the office early because Nicole had said that she was feeling unwell. When he got home, Ann welcomed her son-in-law home with a happy smile and spoke to him with reassuring words.

"It's nothing serious; your wife is in bed resting."

Tu noticed there was more food on the table than normal.

"Mother, are we having party?"

"Of course," Ann replied, with a knowing smile.

"Don't forget, next time you go to visit the president and General Minh I will give you a lift. It will look to the outside world as though we are a loving family, Mother."

"You are right; we'll do that, son."

Tu ran up the stairs two at a time to his bedroom, as he was eager to see his wife. She was still wearing the blue silk dress with a plunging neckline at the back, hemmed with lace and a little ribbon. She was lying on her front and looked tired.

Tu took his wife's hand and gently asked, "What's the matter with you, darling?"

"I'm fine," Nicole answered.

"You're looking tired. If you get up and get dressed you may start to feel better. Perhaps you would like me to go downstairs and get you something to eat. Would you like that?"

"Don't remind me of food. I feel sick enough as it is."

"Really? So what did the doctor say?"

"Can't you guess?"

"No, I can't."

"I … I'm pregnant," announced Nicole, in a joyful tone. She turned over and held him around his waist. "Maybe we will have a son, darling."

The word "son" made Tu forget who he was. That very morning, he had received bad news; the very first news in four years. His wife and son in the North had been hurt in a bombing raid. Both were out of danger, but, unfortunately, Tu took it out on Nicole and he became cold and remote.

"This is not a good time to talk about having a baby ..."

Nicole was not expecting that reaction. She felt overcome with emotion and suddenly, her surroundings darkened as she fainted.

Tu had been sitting beside Nicole's bed for hours. She lay motionless, in a state of shock. He reproached himself for his indifference. His wife's virginal love and her bitter disappointment had moved him deeply, reaching to the very depth of his soul. He craved for her forgiveness. He hadn't moved from her side and she was still feeling befuddled and desolate, because of her husband's crude and unexpected behaviour. His patient caring caused Charles' anger to ebb away. The servants went to their room without their dinner, for they were grieving for their mistress; everyone was worried, except Ann, for she thought that Nicole was exaggerating things a little.

Tu felt immense guilt. He had only married Nicole for his mission. In the beginning, Tu had liked the idea of having a family, of having dinner ready on the table, for when he came home from work every night, with everyone at Rose Villa waiting for him. It had made him feel very important. Now, he felt as though he had lost his freedom, especially with the baby on the way. He was in shock and yet nobody cared about his feelings; they all looked upon him as though he spelt nothing but trouble.

Nicole was much better by the following morning, but Tu was too late to make contact with the secret letter box, which meant that he would have to bring the documents and photos home from the office that night, so that he could meet up with Little Lien later.

After Tu had left for work, Ann came to speak to her daughter and Nicole told her mother what had happened.

Ann burst out laughing, "Was that all that made you so sad? Your husband had just got back home from work and was tired. I should really have warned you. You should always wait until men are relaxed before telling them something so important," she admonished.

"I only told him I was pregnant. That was all," Nicole replied in amazement.

"Having a baby is sacred and important. The fact is, men don't like shocks; they prefer to learn things gently as they can be bowled over by such unexpected news."

"Do you mean to tell me that men are stupid?"

"Men can be quite silly in the way they treat their wives and children, so you should take it easy on him for a little while. Poor Tu, he hasn't had anything to eat and drink since yesterday."

"Mother!"

"Yes?"

"You seem to love your son-in-law more than you do me," she said petulantly.

"I love you both equally, and I am convinced that a man like him would never betray his wife and children. If I hadn't been certain that he was good for you, I would never have agreed for him to marry you."

"Mother, I really miss him," said Nicole. "Can you get in touch with him to ask him to come back home?"

"I don't think Tu will return home early today, dear," Ann said sadly.

Chapter Twenty-One

That evening, Tu went to meet Little Lien in a pub called the Himalaya Bar at Central District 1, where the singer Thai Thanh sang every night. He took some important documents with him, which should never even have been removed from the safe. Tu wanted Little Lien to take them with her to the Vietcong.

Earlier that week, Mrs Tam noticed that someone who had been associated with the underworld was watching and following Little Lien, and for her own safety, ordered her to move out of Saigon and into the jungle. Little Lien assured Mrs Tam that she had not done anything wrong to upset the underworld of Saigon, and therefore she must have been mistaken. However, Little Lien agreed that maybe it was the best thing to do, but she did not want to leave Saigon without saying goodbye to Tu.

Tu sat alone at the end of the bar and had a drink. The bar was busy. The air was smoky and noisy, and there were many Vietnamese soldiers and American officers eating, drinking and talking about the news from the White House and from the Paris Peace Conference. Everyone in South Vietnam was talking about the war. However, Tu was trying to erase the word "war" from his head. He glanced around, looking for something to distract him. There were lots of girls dancing in very short skirts, so short that he wondered why they even bothered to wear one. His attention was caught by a rather attractive young girl with long flowing hair. She was chatting to some Americans and when she turned around to walk towards Tu, he realised that it was Little Lien.

"Little Lien!" Tu said, with shock and disapproval. "That outfit makes you look too sexy for your own good and I don't like it; and why were you talking to those Americans in the first place?"

"Stop acting like a big brother," Little Lien snapped, as she sat on the chair next to him. "I don't like your uniform, either."

"Ok, ok. How are you, anyway?" whispered Tu.

"F … fine," Little Lien answered, looking miserable.

"I am worried about you," he said, with a look of genuine concern.

Little Lien smiled, and then moved closer to him and whispered into his ear:

"I am ok; you're the one on the dangerous mission, not me. So you, too, may have to leave."

Little Lien said something that she shouldn't have, but she continue to tell Tu that she had overheard a story about the boss informing Mrs Tam that he might want to move Tu into the jungle, but, in the end, they had decided against it.

He wondered whether Little Lien knew a lot more than she was letting on.

"I thought that my position in the office was vital for us, so why does our boss want me to leave? Oh dear, I must have done something wrong."

Tu wanted to stay in South Vietnam more than ever. After all it was his duty and also, Nicole was expecting their first baby and he didn't want to just disappear leave her without saying anything.

"You're an important link, and if you got out now, we would never have another chance like this. Mum said she would do everything in her power to keep you safe, so that you could stay here. So please don't die!" she said.

"I will try not to."

"Our boss is worried about you."

"Who is he?" Tu asked.

"I have never met him," Little Lien answered truthfully.

Tu knew she was hiding something, but because it was part of the mission, Little Lien would only tell him on a need-to-know basis.

Tu sighed; the officials for the North wanted Agent 022 to remain safe, and would protect him at all costs. However, Tu knew that there were thousands of profiles of known suspects in the records office and many plans to kidnap and kill the leaders of the National Front for the liberation of South Vietnam.

Little Lien was eyeing up all the Americans troops in the bar, telling Tu how handsome she thought they were.

"Would you like something to drink?" Tu asked, in an attempt to divert her attention.

"I would love a glass of beer,"said Little Lien whilst still looking at the Americans.

"Beer is not good for you," Tu said sulkily.

"Ok, ok. Anyway, it's time I got on, I will have a drink with you next time," said Little Lien.

"Sister?"

"Yes?" asked Little Lien, her eyes revealing a deeper feeling that Tu could not understand.

"You take care," he said, as he held her small hand inside his.

He touched the fingers of the girl that he loved as his little sister gently. Her hands were cool to the touch and when he released her hands, she was clasping a tiny letter full of top-secret information.

"I will miss you," Little Lien said at last.

"I'll miss you, too, and I can't wait until I see you again."

"Peace will come soon, and then we will meet again, brother."

"Yes, sister."

Little Lien left the bar alone. Tu stood out of sight in the gloom of Vo Tanh Street, his eyes following Little Lien as she walked away. He could not help but worry about her. He shrugged his shoulders and told himself that he was being silly. The street looked quiet, so he turned around and was about to step back into the bar, when there was a loud bang. Tu instinctively knew that it was gunfire. He turned around praying that the shot was not for real.

He saw Little Lien lurch, as she turned to look back towards her last relative to whom she had just said goodbye. She slowly dropped to her knees and fell, face down. Tu understood her look of anguish and his heart ached. He would willingly have given twenty years of his own life not to have Little Lien shot. His first thought was to protect himself by hiding in the bar, but he knew that he would never forgive himself if he stayed there, so he turned back and rushed towards her, hoping somehow that he could save her life. He took the slip of paper from her hand, swallowed it and then tried to stem the flow of blood. Doors on both sides of the road opened, as people poked their heads out to see what had happened.

"We need an ambulance," said Tu, choking and hoarse.

Whilst some people went off in search of one, a crowd of hippy teenagers flooded out on to the streets, showing their anger and disgust openly.

Little Lien opened her eyes and looked at Tu. She instinctively knew it was him and that he would not desert her.

"Sister," Tu whispered.

Little Lien managed to give him a faint smile. Blood was flowing from her chest, covering his white police uniform.

"Come on, sister! Hold on. An ambulance is on its way," whispered Tu, as he quickly checked her pockets to remove her gun.

Instead of one gun, he found three; too many for such a small figure.

"I'm so cold," Little Lien uttered, barely able to move her lips.

"She's cold," Tu repeated, trying to hold back his tears.

One teenager took off his shirt to cover her in a futile attempt at keeping her warm. However, it was in vain; her body was now limp and without life.

"Sister!"

Tu called her name for the last time, glancing towards the sky above, hoping that God was looking down on them. Lovingly, he closed her eyes; eyes that had been radiant, full of hope and overflowing with belief. She was beautiful and, even in death, she looked like a holy angel.

Chapter Twenty-Two

Tu hated the meetings at the office. They had to attend somewhere between three and six meetings every week. This proved difficult for Tu, because he didn't have any previous knowledge about police work and had no idea what they were talking about half the time. In one of the meetings, Loan was angry and he shouted himself hoarse, which caused an unpleasant atmosphere.

"Yesterday, the Vietcong entered every representative deputy's house and attacked them. What did we do? We did nothing. Security in Saigon is our responsibility and yet they made us look like fools in the eyes of the people. They must have been watching the comings and goings from our office all the time to familiarise themselves with our faces. How many more of you will be killed? Many of our plans have been leaked to them and as a result, we never catch anyone in our raids. The luckiest we have been so far is to shoot an old cow!" No one in the room dared to laugh. "Why are our bombing raid plans being leaked?" Loan paused to sip his drink, and then continued, "Whenever we carry out our plans to raid a suspected Vietcong office, we suddenly find ourselves in the middle of newly laid minefield – laid out especially for our arrival. The big question here is whether or not we have a traitor in our midst! I want to know, and it is your duty to find the person who hides his face!"

"Look at this," Major Chin tried to calm his boss down. "District I has almost no problems. This shows that police there work effectively."

"In my opinion, we should send more forces to check out the suburbs of Saigon."

"I'd rather kill entire villages than let one Vietcong member survive!" Loan finished, with a roar.

All the officers started frantically shouting over each other, trying to blame each other and put their own views forward. Once order was restored, everybody worked together, reviewing the districts of the city one by one. They concluded that the districts of Thu Duc and Cu Chi were safe and were faithful to the government and the President. It was assumed it was impossible for Vietcong to gain support in Cu Chi!

At the end of the meeting, Loan approached Tu and asked after Tu's family and said that he hoped to visit them all soon. Then, without saying goodbye to anyone, Loan left the office. Loan was still very angry, because Tu was still alive after the plot to bomb his wedding had failed. The plan had been Loan and Vien's initiative and they had intended to kill everyone in the wedding party. Unfortunately, the bomb had been found and removed beforehand.

Loan was a man who hated the Vietcong and all the people who supported the North. If he suspected someone was Vietcong but was unable to prove it, his philosophy was better to be safe than sorry and he killed them regardless. He killed many suspects until a western photographer, Eddie Adams, had taken a photograph of Loan killing a suspect in the street without due legal process[1]. It had been published around the world and Loan had been forced to be more cautious and ever since then, he would use gangsters; including the gangster who was well known in Saigon as Fat Thanh and whose reputation preceded him. Thanh used to work alone and he would do anything if the price was right; he was a man totally without morals and for two years, Loan had used him to carry out a number of assassinations. Since Tu had been moved from the police branch of Can Tho to Saigon by Loan, Thanh had been watching him very closely. When Rang reported his suspicions about Little Lien, Loan had immediately wanted to kidnap and question her, to find out if Tu was Vietcong, but Thanh had shot her dead in error, because he had been drunk when Loan had called to give the order. Because of his incompetence, for killing Little Lien and for his failing to carry out his previous order by killing Tu at Rose Villa, Loan decided to visit Thanh with a few policemen in tow.

Thanh lived with his wife and his 8-year-old daughter in a newly built apartment block in District 5. When Loan arrived with his firing squad, he made them wait outside. Given all the mistakes, and the possibility that

Thanh may decide to talk to Western journalists, Loan decided that Fat Thanh's usefulness was over. He needed to be silenced forever.

Loan stepped into the sitting room and closed the door behind him. "Why?" he asked curtly.

Thanh had no idea what Loan was planning or talking about. He was confident that Loan and he were brothers in blood and that he therefore he had nothing to fear.

"Dear Brother Loan," Thanh said, still standing, while his boss dropped himself into a chair. "Rose Villa is so strictly guarded that I cannot penetrate it. If you wanted, I could kill Tu on his way to work. Besides, I don't believe for one moment that the Vietcong would ever use him. He is an idiot – a wimp – and the only thing going for him is that he is handsome!" he joked, trying to ease the tension.

Loan gave no reply. He had hated and suspected Tu for a long time, although he never had any proof. It was no use spending time and money keeping a close watch on every suspect, and it was unwise to kill Tu on his way into the office. His death would be undoubtedly be attributed to the Vietcong in that situation. His superiors would be angry that the Vietcong were able to attack one of their own, and because Loan was in charge of security within the capital, he would be the one to blame. Rose Villa was strictly protected by the most famous bodyguards equipped with the latest weapons. Charles Philippe imported many weapons and God only knew how many guns were within his villa. Furthermore, the CIA was keeping a close watch on the villa, because they suspected the Philippes as being French spies. It was therefore obvious that Thanh did not want to throw his life away on such a dangerous mission. What a coward, Loan thought.

"I have got a new, silent gun here for you. You may need a special one," Loan said, as he drew out a Browning.

"That's hardly the best!" Thanh blurted out, with disappointment.

"Is it not," Loan said as he shot directly at Thanh and his lifeless body fell to the floor.

His wife and daughter rushed out from the other room. As she tightly embraced her daughter, not daring to shout, she understood that Loan could kill her and her daughter without reason at any moment. The little girl stared at her father and tried to run to him, but her mother kept tight hold of her.

As Loan left the room, he indicated with his head that his job was done here.

Once outside, Loan said to the squad, "Thanh has gone; Chin, you stay here and do the necessary. The rest of you, follow me back to the general office."

Loan had no blood on his uniform and seemed quite in control; however, inside he was raging. Perhaps Tu had been born under a lucky star, because despite Loan's best attempts, Tu still remained alive; but he would never give up. He was sure that Tu was Vietcong or a spy. He just needed one piece of firm evidence. He knew that Tu was friends with Vinh and Rang, but he could not be sure that he could rely on them for support. Loan was aware that Tu had a two-week holiday planned in Cam Ranh next month, so Loan resolved to make maximum use of that time to gather evidence in his absence.

1. See www.digitaljournalist.org/issue0410/faas.html for the photograph

Chapter Twenty-Three

Nicole never got over her disappointment at Tu's reaction when she had told him of her pregnancy. She became introverted and cynical about life, and she would spend hours at a time sitting by the table, or by the window, wallowing in her own misery. She had convinced herself that her husband must have another woman.

Nicole became paranoid that Tu was cheating on her. At midday, if he did not come home, it was because he must be having lunch with some other lover. If he was late in the evening, she pictured him in bed with another woman. Slowly, the misery corroded her soul and she became bitter.

Sometimes, when they were in bed asleep, Tu would dream and call out a name of another woman. It hurt Nicole so much that she would hug her knees and rock gently. Occasionally, Tu would wake up and see her like this, but rather than comfort her, he would just heave a sigh and turn away. With all this evidence, what else was Nicole supposed to think? How could she believe that her husband really loved her when appeared so distant? Admittedly, nobody had ever seen Tu with another woman, but why then did he not behave as if he loved her? He had always acted with kindness and been a good son-in-law, but no matter how much Nicole tried to think of all his good points, she still did not believe that her husband genuinely loved her. To keep the atmosphere stable within the family, she had to play the role of a happily married woman. She never complained, cried or confided in anyone. She was sure that if she told her mother how unhappy she was with her husband, then her mother would immediately send for a psychiatrist. Nicole wondered if her unborn child would be a baby girl, so she would be able warn her about life's perils. Her baby would be the only person in the world who would understand her, who would love her with all her heart and soul.

She had heard somewhere that beautiful women would always have problems in love, so she wanted to be ugly, ugly enough to be able to trust the man who loved her. She felt sorry for those women who envied her and her position, her white complexion and her elegant lifestyle. All Nicole wanted was to be happy. Mr Lam was well aware of Nicole's unhappiness, but he didn't know how to help her. He felt that she needed to sort it out for herself, in her own way and in her own time.

One evening, Nicole waited for her husband to come home and, as usual, he was late.

"Are you still awake?" her husband asked gently, as he saw his wife sat on the chair next to the bed. It was one o'clock in the morning.

"I can't sleep. I was worried because you hadn't come home," answered Nicole.

"Darling, I had loads of work to do and, whilst I wanted to come home, these are times of war, which makes it impossible, however much I want to."

"Tu, don't lie to me. I'm not a baby. Nor am I so stupid as to not understand what is going on. Some nights, when you dream, you call some woman's name …" Nicole stopped in her tracks; her voice was full of bitterness. Then she continued, "I know you are cheating on me. Tell me, do you hate me that much? Why can't you say you love me any more?"

Tu said nothing. He was helpless, for he was unable to explain the true situation. It was better for Nicole to hate him than for him to reveal the whole truth. He knew that he had treated Nicole badly ever since the first time he had declared his love for her. Earlier that night, as Tu was travelling to his secret letter box to deliver a document, he had been shot at. Now, back home, he almost wished the bullet had hit him rather than face this argument with Nicole.

"Oh my God, punish me; but please, tell me how much she knows about me?" he prayed, silently.

Nicole saw her husband lower his head, which angered her:

"Why you don't answer me?"

"Darling," Tu spoke from his heart, "I am truly yours. I wish you wouldn't worry, in case it affects our baby. From the time I first fell in love with you and married you, have I ever been seen with another woman? I don't even smile at anyone else, and I certainly don't betray you, Nicole."

Then he came towards his wife and gently touched her back.

Half of the frustration in Nicole's soul ebbed away as she listened to him, but she still felt sad. Inside her soul, she felt her husband's love dying.

Tu held his wife tightly; his mind was full of disturbing thoughts. He sometimes felt like screaming at the sheer cruelty of life. Whatever he did seemed to hurt the ones he loved, but he could not tell anyone ... his duty was to keep his other life a secret.

"If you want, we could go over to the plantation this weekend. Maybe you should spend more time there. The fresh air would do you good."

"I've been listening to the radio and the news was awful, so I think we'd better stay here."

"Don't worry, darling. I will take care of you and our family; you will be fine with me."

Nicole felt better as she listened to Tu speaking in such terms. Maybe he did love her after all.

"Mother is worried. She wants to take Father back to Paris. The situation is so bad that Nixon is sending more American troops to Saigon."

"Do you like the way in which the Americans control our country?"

"I want a city without barbed-wire fences, tanks, guns, bullets, mines and bombs, so our baby can play outside. I want an end to the curfews; particularly in hot weather like this, and I want you to be able to take me out for a walk, so that we can breathe fresh air again!"

"What else do you want?"

"When the war ends, I want to live in a big house, with a big living room and a row of white pillars at the front."

Tu left his wife alone with her big spending ideas. He was different from her. Rich people needed symbols of their wealth. For Nicole, a living room with two sets of sofas was not enough, and if the library had space for five thousand books, it would not be large enough. Nicole had always had plenty of money. She thought nothing of spending more than most people would earn in a year on one item. Nicole had everything; indeed, more than she could ever need. He could see the injustice of it all. At Rose Villa, there were no less than ten wooden tables, all skilfully carved, scattered all around the house. His parents' house in the North had only one farmhouse table; a rough-hewn board balanced on top of bricks, and their table served many purposes. Tu had only one dream, and that was for the war to end so he could go home, work on the farm, grow crops, and keep some chickens, ducks and pigs. Tu would enjoy life without all the fighting; a free life, where he could do what he wanted and where he did not wake up in cold sweats from nightmares in which he had been arrested and tortured.

"When the war is over," Nicole continued, still thinking of the future, "we should return to France. I would like a large house in Paris. Mrs Tam has never been abroad, so we could take her with us. Do you think she would like that?"

"Of course she will. By the way, I'm going to see her tomorrow after work, in case you are wondering where I am."

"May I go with you?" Nicole asked.

"Better not; it would be much better if you stay at home, darling," answered Tu.

He had refused his Nicole's request because he had to make an exchange of documents. He had done valuable work in the past week and he had stayed late again that very evening because he had to finish copying all the documents in the safe. Vinh had left work early and trusted Tu to keep the key. Deep in thought about the huge amount of work he had copied for the Vietcong, he failed to notice that Nicole was upset.

Chapter Twenty-Four

"Darling Tu," Nicole said to her husband one morning, when they were in the back garden, "what name would you like to call our new baby?"

"If it is a boy, we should call him Trung; and the next baby should be called Hieu."

Nicole looked at him, somewhat confused. "Don't you want our baby to be named after you?"

"I am a man at war, and the names Trung and Hieu have a special meaning to me. I will give our babies those names, because they remind me of our wonderful country; a beautiful country with great people," Tu replied.

Of course, Nicole still did not know his real name, so how could he possibly name his son Tu? After all, Tu's body was under the tree by a house in Can Tho. He wondered whether he should tell Nicole the truth and when would be a good time to tell her, because as his wife, Nicole should be the first to know the true identity of her husband. But what would she think of him if she learnt the truth? Maybe his bosses were right, that he shouldn't tell anybody. Besides, it would jeopardise the mission.

"I didn't know you were that patriotic. Every time you talk with President Thieu you seem to disagree with the government's policies." Tu remained silent, a sure sign that he didn't want to talk about the subject any more, so she changed tack. "Do you miss Little Lien?"

Tu nodded in agreement.

"I miss her, too," said Nicole, "I'm not jealous, but I can see that you had a strong brotherly love for her."

"How well you know me," said Tu, smiling, remembering that all Little Lien had ever wanted for her country was peace.

Nicole was suffering from extreme tiredness and the hot weather did not help matters. Her bump was getting bigger by the day, and although Tu thought she looked radiant, Nicole would sometimes catch her husband looking thoughtful, and she knew that he was thinking of someone else. Nicole hoped that whoever it was had left this earth. Nicole made a huge effort to put all her jealous thoughts to the back of her mind. She was having a baby, and that was more important than jealousy. Romantic love, beautiful love, eternal love and faithful love, only ever happen in books and on the stage. In the real world, love didn't happen like that.

The following morning, Tu mentioned to Nicole that when the war had finished and peace finally reigned, he would like to live in the countryside. He had visions of living in a farmhouse, where he could grow vegetables and have chickens, so in the morning he could go with his son and collect the newly laid eggs. Nicole was confused and did not know where these ideas came from, because she certainly didn't share his views. Tu decided never to speak of such things to his wife again, because she could never understand about his desires or feelings, not knowing where he really came from, and nor could she understand the farmers' love of the land.

"We could do that at your house in Can Tho," Nicole told her husband in an attempt at to compromise.

Tu shook his head, and told her that he did not want to live in the city; the countryside was where he belonged.

"How do you know our baby will be a boy?"

Tu was thinking about his life in the North. Not hearing what Nicole said, he was not quick enough to answer her question.

"I think you should write your will," she said, finally.

Tu burst out laughing.

"Why are you laughing? Do you think that I'm mad?" asked Nicole.

"I wasn't laughing at you. I was laughing because with this stupid war, I could die at any time and I have nothing to leave you," laughed Tu.

"What do you mean?" said Nicole. "We have lots. Not only this building, but offices in the sea transportation company, the rubber plantation ... and shares in the Thanh Do estate company. Being son-in-law of the Philippes, you are worth a quarter of that fortune. I wrote my first will when I was eighteen; I inherited something from my grandfather in France and I had to rewrite my will right after our wedding."

"Ok, could you write the will for me? Then I will sign it," he agreed.

"Our family solicitor will help you. In the will, do you want to mention anyone apart from your immediate family?"

"I have no one else," Tu answered.

"Mrs Tam?" Nicole reminded him.

"Shall I leave her my uniform and weapon?"

"You are teasing me," Nicole laughed. "Apart from Mrs Tam, surely you would consider Vinh as a friend. A few hundred thousand piastres for him would not go amiss, for example."

Tu was unable to answer. Vinh was not in the same situation as he was. Eventually, when the country reunited, Vinh would become a prisoner.

"Let me think about it. I have a few months' salary still untouched in the closet. I would like to take Vinh out sometime to a bar, or a disco, or perhaps even a nightclub. Why wait until I die!" Tu joked.

"And what makes you think I'd let you go out every night?" she retorted.

"Then I promise I will place his name in my will," he finished.

"Is there anybody else?"

"You!" Tu lowered his voice. "I will leave you the sky."

Nicole felt sad, she didn't want the sky; she only craved his heart. But she knew she did not own his romantic, lively heart; she never had. Nicole was proud, and she would never beg for love, ever.

"If you write the will today, we should go and visit Mrs Tam at the weekend," said Nicole, changing the subject.

As Tu put on his shoes, he added, "I'll go to see the solicitor right now."

However, as he went to leave, he decided better of it; kicking off his shoes and pulling Nicole back down on to the bed beside him. The bed was far too inviting and Nicole looked ever so sexy in her maternity dress.

The solicitor Huynh Van Thanh was fifty years old and had been in the business for twenty-five years. He was one of the best known solicitors in Saigon and was well respected by his clients and peers. Charles and Ann were Mr Thanh's oldest and wealthiest clients. They were as loyal to him as he was to them, and he always gave a top class service in order to help them.

Tu appeared in his offices unannounced and Mr Thanh was notified at once. This was the second time he had ever met Tu – the first time had been at the wedding – and he came out to greet Tu in person.

"My young friend, come in," said Mr Thanh "How is your family?"

"My family and I are all fine. How are you, Uncle Thanh?" queried Tu.

"Am I old enough to be called an uncle?" Mr Thanh asked, after he had invited Tu make himself at home.

"You are my parents' friend, so I will call you uncle," Tu answered.

"Oh, it always pleases me when the younger generation keep up the old traditions and etiquette."

"Thank you."

"Have you ever worked on a rubber plantation?" Mr Thanh asked.

"No, I haven't, uncle."

"Your father-in-law told me that you have helped him a great deal. Now, for the will, I have a standard draft here, so I think we should look at it and discuss it first."

Mr Thanh then handed the papers to Tu.

Tu felt strange. Everything that was happening in front of his very eyes was a farce. He was fighting for the Democratic Republic of Vietnam. Under communist rule, everyone would be equal, and then his family would have a better life. The slave classes would be freed and the ruling class would disappear forever. For the present, he was in the ruling class with joint possession of hundreds of hectares of a good rubber plantation. Hundreds of miserable people worked hard by day and night, caring for the trees that produced the sap that other people just took for granted. He had once proposed an idea to reward workers and his wife's family had been polite, listened, agreed, and then made it clear that it would only work in the short term.

"Darling Tu," Nicole explained in a sweet voice, "this year's profits will need to be retained in the business. Next year, if the rubber is of inferior quality, or if there is a poor harvest, we will have to use this year's profits to pay their wages and repair their houses for them. If our people fight, gamble or are arrested by the police, we have to pay their fines to free them. We need to have plenty of money to look after our workers."

It made Tu laugh to think that the Philippes thought that they were taking care of their workers when really they were exploiting them. When the war ends, the rubber plantation will become a cooperative and the entire workforce will live and work together as a classless society – everybody would work hard for the common cause to make life better for all.

Tu was dreaming of the future and his principles could not be swayed by the prospect of a huge fortune. For Tu, the honour of becoming a soldier in the people's army of North Vietnam was sublime; nothing else mattered.

Tu promised Mr Thanh that he would look at the will and get back to him in due course.

"Yes, by all means. Take your time to look at it," said Mr Thanh, "then we can rewrite it in accordance with your requirements. I have already made some adjustments, which include fifteen per cent of your estate being left for your children, if, of course, you have any, and should you wish, you can alter this to a maximum of fifty per cent. Other than that, I can do anything else that you require."

Thank you," said Tu. He had a quick look at the will. Christ, he thought, how come this family was so rich? The Philippe's owned much more than he had ever realised.

That weekend, Mrs Tam warmly welcomed the couple, although it made Tu sad now that Little Lien was no longer around to talk to him and cheer him up. He felt very much alone now that Little Lien had gone, because it was she that had given him the strength and resolve to carry on.

Chapter Twenty-Five

During the summer months, before Nicole gave birth to their baby, Tu would take her to the seaside. Nicole loved Tu's villa in Can Tho and used it as a holiday home. If she had been allowed, she would have gone there every weekend. However, Tu was conscious of the fact that the real Tu's body was still under the garden, and wanted to avoid the place altogether, so he would always try to persuade Nicole to go to Vung Tau instead, because driving past the rice fields reminded him of home.

Tu looked at Nicole enjoying herself and wished that Nhat could see how beautiful the countryside could be. Nhat had always worked from early morning until dark; sometimes, she would even work under the carpet-bombing, so she had never had time to see the green fields and appreciate how beautiful they were before. He came to the conclusion that Nicole would never understand, unless she was made to plunge her hands into the mud and plant rice for ten hours a day, seven days a week, and in extreme temperatures. Farmers worked hard – unremittingly hard – throughout the seasons and in all kinds of weather. Nhat knew this all too well, but Nicole was from a completely different background. Nicole's indifference to the work, sweat and tears that were needed to make rice surprised Tu. He wanted to tell Nicole about Nhat, and about his real life in the North, and open her eyes to the world beyond Rose Villa, but it just wasn't safe to do so. The people in the North didn't eat the rice they collected; instead they saved the rice and everything they had to supply the troops fighting in the South. Assault youths take the rice with them from the North into Laos, then to Cambodia, and then on to South Vietnam. By that time, the rice would be stained with blood.

The Philippe family were fortunate enough to have their meals served in a cosy room, which was brightly lit under hundreds of crystal lights. On the dining table, there might be beef, duck, chicken, smoked fish and many vegetables all cooked in the French or Vietnamese way. Yet Tu could never allow himself enjoy such a meal at Rose Villa. To him, it was a sin. He felt that Nicole had everything; so much so, that he didn't feel as though she needed his love. Sometimes, he felt no guilt in deceiving the Phillippe family, because he believed that they could never understand the ways of the working class. However, although Tu and Nicole were from different backgrounds, Tu loved Nicole with all his heart and wished that he could have been her real husband. When the war was over, he would have to return to the North and to Nhat. The deception and the guilt, knowing that one day he would have to leave Nicole, consumed him.

As they travelled one day to their holiday home, Nicole asked Tu why he did not have any photos of Can Tho City, even though it was his hometown.

"I only like to look at pictures of you, darling," Tu answered.

"Thank you, but I'd like to take some photos of your home. But it first needs tidying up, darling," Nicole said, when they arrived at Tu's villa.

In the drawing room, next to the family portrait, was the photo of the real Tu on the wall staring down at him. Nicole preferred to have dinner with her husband in the back garden, but it made Tu feel very uncomfortable, knowing that the body of the real Tu was wrapped in a plastic bag beneath the soil there. Tu sometimes got the feeling that the ghost of the real Tu was standing right behind him whilst he ate his meal. Since the murder, the house had been empty and the only other visitor had been the gardener, who came to cut the grass and trim the trees in the spring. The gardener had also put in many new trees but the blossom tree, which marked the burial spot, had long since been removed.

One day, during one of their short breaks in Can Tho, Nicole met an old flame, Harry Jackson. He was in the American army and they had known each other since her student days, when she and some of her friends had been doing charity work for homeless children. Harry had also been a volunteer at the time.

150

Harry was handsome, friendly and very intelligent. He also had a good sense of humour and made Nicole laugh.

While Tu was busy meeting friends and colleagues, or visiting the tombs of his dead relatives, Harry would escort Nicole around Can Tho.

"Your husband is very popular here," Harry observed.

"He is, his old colleagues love to take him out for a drink," Nicole answered.

"Fancy having lunch in Saigon with me?" Harry asked.

"I'm afraid not, but you could always come back to my house; my father would be very pleased to play dominoes with you again."

Tu couldn't meet his friends as he had said he was going to, because most of them were real Tu's friends and others of them had been killed. There was always a chance of bumping into someone who knew the real Tu, and he could not afford to take that risk, so he had gone to a bar on his own, with the specific intention of getting very drunk, until he could no longer stand. In a drunken haze, he phoned to ask (or rather order) his wife and their driver to come and take him home. On the way home, Nicole asked after his friends, but Tu avoided the question by sleeping throughout the whole three-hour journey to Saigon.

On returning to Saigon, Harry occasionally called at Rose Villa. Everyone at Rose Villa liked Harry and he would play dominoes with Charles every Sunday, but it wasn't too long before the servants started to notice a relationship blossoming between Nicole and Harry. Tu was happy that Nicole had company – a good friend that could make her happy and keep her otherwise occupied while he was busy at work.

Chapter Twenty-Six

It was Sunday morning and Saigon was very busy and lively as usual. Many Vietnamese-American families and soldiers went out for breakfast, coffee and shopping. Saigon would be the perfect "Pearl of the Far East', had they not been in the middle of the war.

Nicole was standing next to the bedroom window looking out on to Mac Dinh Chi Street. A few Americans were taking their morning exercise and a little boy was walking along the street selling morning newspapers. Inside the iron gates of Rose Villa, Mr Lam was having a chat with the gardener and in front of the garage, Mr Nam, was cleaning the car. Nicole left the window to speak to Tu, who was still in the bathroom.

"Darling, shall we go somewhere today? Perhaps we could go to Can Tho," Nicole asked cheekily, knowing what the answer would be. She just wanted to see what his reaction would be.

"Well," Tu replied, as he left the bathroom, "I don't think that you should stray too far from the house in your condition. Anyway, could you kindly drop the subject of my house; you know I don't like going there."

"Oh, I'm sorry. I should have remembered," Nicole said, as she crossed the room to give her husband a big bear hug. "I will meet you downstairs for breakfast," she added, when she saw that Tu was nearly ready, and with that left the room.

Tu immediately tuned in to the North Vietnam radio to listen to the news while he was looking in his wardrobe to find something to wear.

Nicole loved shopping for her husband; the five-section wardrobe was full of shirts, ties and cuff links. At the bottom of the wardrobe was a box full of money – Tu's wages. Ann and Nicole loved to go shopping together, and they had plenty of money with which to do so; in fact, there was more than plenty. As a result, they had no interest in Tu's salary, or how he spent it. Nicole never rummaged around in her husband's wardrobe. Only the maid named Ms Thi, who did the washing and tidying up of their bedroom, knew of its existence.

Tu's eyes settled on the box. He hated to see that amount of money lying around. He remembered the day he had left for the Southern battlefield, when Nhat, his beloved wife, had put all their life's savings into his backpack. Times were bleak then. The money sitting at the back of the wardrobe would be very useful to Nhat, and he wished that he could send it to her. However, Mother Tam thought it too risky to send money back to the North, because she did not want anything traced back to Tu that may jeopardise his position. It was the cold and rainy season in the North, and Tu was naturally worried about Nhat and his son. Did they have enough warm clothes? Was Nhat eating enough? Did she have time to relax? Was she able to cope?

The news that was feeding through from Hanoi's radio was that the North was progressing rapidly to socialism, prosperity and happiness. There were always two versions of the war; in the North, the news from the radio said that the Northern people now had a better life since it had become communist and in the South, the Saigon newspapers printed reports of a Hanoi in ruins following American bombing. They gave only one-sided views such as killing hundreds of Vietcong, and parachuting into Khe Sanh and seizing control of the battlefield within a day. It was difficult to know what to believe. They reported that the Northern regular army was being weakened at an alarming rate and that the North was being bombed ever more fiercely, in order to force Hanoi to come to the three-sided negotiating table in Paris. The propaganda for the North was "All for the front line", and it made him wonder what remained for women and children in the North. When would their huge sacrifices be rewarded? The Northern women were sacrificing their lives in the name of peace, whilst in the South, women and children were victims of crazy and brutal raids. War ... Tu was unable to discuss his fears with anyone, or even express regret at the terrible loss of life. He had to remain silent and cold in the role he was playing. It was the inevitable price to pay in his mission as a double agent. Sometimes, Tu wondered to himself whether fighting for justice was such a great and glorious mission. Behind the glory, was the pain, the grief and the murders of all the innocent victims. He wondered if he would ever be able to find his own peace, even after the fighting had eventually ended.

Tu selected his Sunday best and went down to the dining room where he played a record. Nicole could not understand why her husband liked the army's songs. As he put on the record *Soldier's Love Letter*, the room was filled with evocative sounds:

> Since I gave up studying, I have put on the military uniform.
> Since I was away from home, I have had a thousand nights of melancholy in the open air.
> We have marched for thousands of nights and often rested in desolation.
> Sometimes we stopped for the night.
> Some are wishing, others dreaming, while I open and read your letters.
> I miss you … My post is by a river and we often bathe in the deep riverbed at dusk.
> My friends in my unit call me the dreamy soldier ...
> In the afternoon before yesterday, we stopped at a village and my squad had to stand guard by the road.
> There was a girl walking on the road; she was as beautiful as you are.
> I yearned to see your dress's blue colour on the evening road ..
> I ached for your lips.
> I want to jump in the Jeep to drive back home, so we could be together ...

Nicole listened carefully to each word of the song; but as to why it meant so much to her husband was simply beyond her comprehension. He had never been in the same situation as the hero of the song, so she was puzzled as to how he could identify with such homesickness ... Since they had been together, loved each other, he had never been far from her, not even for a day.

"Why are you smiling at me like that?" asked Tu.

"I smile because you seem to so completely understand a soldier's nostalgia for his lover!" she said lightly.

"Yes, I do understand. It means so much to me and that is why I like the song so much."

"Now I really am confused," Nicole muttered.

"How is our baby?" Tu asked, avoiding the subject.

"He is hiccupping," she answered, with huge smile.

She looked very beautiful when she smiled that way.

"Really? Let me feel."

Tu put his hand on Nicole's bump and he could actually see her skin move.

"I love to feel him move. It makes me feel so close to him."

"You wouldn't like it if he was inside you. It is very uncomfortable when he kicks me."

"I can't wait to see our baby," Tu said excitedly.

"Me, too!" replied Nicole, as she embraced her husband.

"I promise that I will be with you at the birth."

After breakfast, Tu drove to the plantation and Nicole waved goodbye to him before going back to bed. She felt so tired now that she was getting bigger.

That afternoon, Nicole started in labour. She stood next to the bed, sweating. The pain was unbearable and Mrs Lam and Ms Thi dashed around like headless chickens, not knowing what to do, while the men, including Mr Nam, went to the garage to play cards.

Nicole bit back the screams. She knew that this was only the start, and there would be much worse to come.

"Would you like a drink, love?" Mrs Lam asked, wanting to help.

"No," snapped Nicole, perhaps a little more fiercely than was necessary; but Mrs Lam understood.

"When will Tu and Mother come home?"

"Mr Nam will get them here as soon as possible," Mrs Lam replied, but the first car to arrive was that of the midwife.

Nicole was determined not to let the pain show; however, two hours later, she was screaming without giving a thought as to who might hear. Despite what Nicole might have thought, she did in fact have a relatively easy labour and after only a few hours, she delivered their baby.

"A boy!" the midwife cried joyfully.

The baby immediately opened his mouth wide to cry and everyone gawped at him. Two bloods flowed in his body – French and Vietnamese. He was a beautiful boy, and he had taken the best features of both his parents. Mrs Lam gently laid the baby in his cot after giving him his first bath.

In the nursery, was a huge pile of presents, along with a big box full of clothes and things for the new baby. The room was newly decorated and in the middle of the room was a hand-made wooden cot which was decorated with small teddy bears. In the kitchen, Mr Ba put all the everyday food in the fridge and went to the market to buy special foods for the new mother. He had been unprepared because he'd thought that Nicole still had another month before she gave birth, but he was determined to prepare delicious and healthy dishes for the young mother. There had not been a child in this house for twenty years now, and it was all very exciting. However, he wondered about the child's future in war-torn Vietnam. Being at war for so long, he wondered whether Vietnam would have anything to offer the child in the future? Mr Ba kept his thoughts to himself, because if the police heard his views, he would be sure to spend a night in cells.

The Americans said the war had already ended, but Mr Ba could not see any signs of peace yet. Several fire fights between the Vietcong and army units occurred daily. Every few days, the American troops and the South Vietnamese army would launch a raid. The noise was tremendous as the tanks and armoured vehicles set off with aerial cover from helicopters and jet bombers. On their return, the hospitals were flooded with ambulances, corpses and the wounded. The city was increasingly falling to pieces; the once busy vibrant market trading streets were now deserted. Many villages had also been burnt to the ground and in the forest, trees were left without leaves, due to the devastating impact of Agent Orange and napalm bombs.

Tu and Ann arrived later that evening and Ann immediately went to Nicole's side to help Mrs Lam and the midwife tidy up and make Nicole as comfortable as possible. Tu gently lifted the baby out of the cot and looked down on his sweet face. He carried the baby over to Nicole's bed. Nicole's face was red from exhaustion and her brown hair hung down over her forehead, which was bathed in sweat. Though very tired, she reached out her arms to receive the neat, spotless white bundle.

"I want to look after the baby myself, rather than hire a wet nurse," she announced, as she let the baby suckle.

"Our baby is so beautiful. Thank you, darling," Tu said kindly, with pride in his eyes.

"He is the image of you," she replied, as she softly lulled the baby.

When Nicole fell asleep, Tu sat beside the bed holding the baby, until Mrs Lam asked Tu to leave the bedroom so Nicole and the baby could sleep.

Nicole loved her baby so much that she paid less attention to her husband. Rose Villa was now in disarray. Even the mealtimes had to be changed – lunch was served too early and dinner was too late. Fried food, sweet vegetables and king prawns were served almost daily, because it was known to be good for nursing mothers. Little Trung slept during the daytime and cried all night and Tu had many sleepless nights, because Little Trung slept in their bedroom. He tried moving to the library to get some sleep, but it upset Nicole so much, that he reluctantly went back to their bedroom.

"We could leave Little Trung with the servants so we can have a break?" Tu offered his wife.

"No, I want us to look after him," answered Nicole.

"But I have to work ..."

Nicole stopped her husband in his tracks. "Darling, you could quit that job. You know Father wants you to become the managing director of our family's shipping company. Then you could work whenever you want."

Concerned that Nicole would push him even harder to quit his job as a police officer, Tu relented and said to her, "Nicole, I will help you to look after our baby if that is what you really want."

Thus, every night, as all the servants were sleeping, Tu and Nicole took it in turns to look after Little Trung. Although Tu was tired, he loved holding him and it made him think of his son in the North, whom he had yet to see. As he looked at his reflection in the mirror whilst holding a crying Little Trung, he wondered whether having a wife was such a good idea. He had the urge to sing a Northern lullaby to Little Trung which would have given him away. It was four years he had spent in Saigon now and he still hadn't had the opportunity to return to the North to visit his family or even received any information about them.

He had been given various nicknames "Super Hero", "The Stubborn", and "The Stone Man", amongst others. However, he was just a normal man, who sometimes simply wanted to cry because he was missing his hometown and felt lonely. Here, he had a family, but this family knew him as Tu, the police officer from Can Tho. Damn Tu to hell; he felt sorry for himself, because the fake Tu was already in hell.

As Nicole woke up, she glanced at them both.

"Is he asleep, darling?" asked Nicole.

"Our son is very handsome, isn't he?" he observed, passing the baby to his wife.

"I want another," said Nicole.

"What? What did you say?" Tu could not believe his ears!

"You heard me. I want another baby."

Chapter Twenty-Seven

Little Trung was ten months old when he first started to walk. He followed his grandmother from the sitting room to the dining room and then into the kitchen. He was adorable and his grandmother spoilt him rotten. He would even stain her long dress with chocolate, but she simply smiled and told the servants to clean up the mess with a napkin. Little Trung was very clever and, unsurprisingly, the first sentences he uttered were "I want toys.", "I want ice cream", "I want TV", or "I want my mummy."

His grandmother tried to teach him to say, "I am sorry" when he did something wrong, but he would always come back with "I want my mummy". When his father tried to teach him to say hello to adults before each meal, he simply said, "I want my mummy." When Little Trung was very naughty, his father would overlook it, but when his grandfather called him a naughty boy, he answered, "I want my mummy."

Nicole loved her son very much and so did Tu. After coming home from work, Tu would always play with him. Ann had fed him with French food since he was a baby, so he preferred it to Vietnamese. His favourite meal was pâté, chips and soup, so the cook had less and less work to do, because Ann usually prepared the French food herself. Little Trung made a huge difference to Rose Villa and everyone suddenly started coming home on time. However, Tu would often feel like an outsider, because there was such a strong French influence around his son. Nicole turned from being unhappy with her marriage into a very happy mother, and Tu turned from being a cold man, to a family man. Even Charles had become happier.

It was around this time that Charles proposed a possible move back to Paris. Tu was tired of the subject. Why did they try to propose something that they all knew would never happen? Ann was forever talking about the impending move, but everyone knew that she loved her lands, her villa, and her money in Saigon too much. Tu would never leave and he thought the family had too many businesses to oversee in Vietnam and keep them from returning to France.

When Charles was away, Ann waited for Tu to return one night to see what his thoughts on the matter were. However, on arrival, Tu seemed quite depressed, which was unusual.

"How was your work today?" she asked.

"There is trouble," Tu answered, while the servant brought him a glass of beer.

Ann drew his attention to the newspaper headline. "Have you read the news, the South have resumed the bombing of North Vietnam?"

"Yes, I have."

"I hoped they would settle for a peaceful solution. Now that they're bombing again, what was the point of negotiating?"

"I don't know; I really don't."

"Anyway, your wife is not very well."

"Oh dear, where is she?" Tu asked, turning to the door where Little Trung was toddling into the dining room. He had refused to go to bed and his grandmother had relented.

"Come here, son," Tu said, as he lifted him up.

He kissed the boy's chubby cheeks and curly brown hair. However, his mind was full of disturbing thoughts. America had started to bomb North Vietnam again: Hanoi, Hai Phong and Ha Bac. His house had a shelter, but his other son would still be in danger. He was unsure how the wooden shelter would cope with the bombardments of the B-52s. He just hoped and prayed that no bomb had hit it. He wondered why the American government was intent on slaughtering the North Vietnamese people.

Ann stretched out her arms to lift the boy. "Darling, come here, so that your father can get changed."

Tu gave his son to his mother-in-law and dragged himself upstairs.

The bedroom was shrouded in darkness, because all the curtains were drawn. Tu stood by the bed and gently took his wife's hand.

"Nicole, are you feeling ok?" he enquired.

"I am a little off colour, my love," she replied, wrapping her arms around his neck. "I feel tired because ..."

"... Because your son is so naughty?"

"Yes, how do you know?" Nicole said, trying to sound surprised.

"You have not told me what is really wrong with you."

"Are you ready?"

"I'm listening," Tu replied, with a smile on his face.

"I'm pregnant," Nicole smiled.

She had discovered that she was expecting another baby earlier that morning and she had desperately wanted to tell someone as soon as she found out. Her parents had been in the house at the time, but she had waited for Tu to come home so he could be the first to know.

The smile on Tu's lips faded. He quickly smiled again and embraced his wife tightly.

"Oh, Nicole, that is wonderful news, I am so happy, thank you."

"I will inform Mother. I can't believe that I am four months pregnant already," Nicole said. "I'm not sure if I am happy or not. Please excuse me if I say something out of turn."

"Darling …" Tu said again, as he tried to give her a big hug.

But Nicole spurned him and wandered downstairs to see her mother. Nicole excitedly told her the news while the servants prepared the dinner.

After dinner, Nicole spoke to Mrs Lam about Tu. She felt that there was a growing distance between them, including him keeping secrets from her, and the fact that she could never fully understand what was in his heart. Mrs Tam had been unable to shed any light on the matter and always proclaimed that Tu was the perfect gentleman. Her answers were always evasive, leading Nicole to believe there were secrets between them, resulting in her mistrust of Mrs Tam.

Mrs Lam spoke to Tu about her concerns and warned him against upsetting Nicole in her condition. Tu resolved to stay at home at the weekends whenever possible. He even had some days off to take his wife shopping for their new baby. Their second son, Little Hieu, was born on a cool summer's night and this time, Nicole let the servants care for the baby.

Chapter Twenty-Eight

To congratulate the new father, Tu's colleagues took him for a magnificent dinner at their favourite restaurant. They decided to go to Le Thuy Restaurant, as it was renowned for its American dishes rather than Vietnamese ones. Consequently, the majority of customers were Americans. They had a private room to themselves and, after ordering a drink, Mai, in his white police uniform, started to tell everyone an interesting story.

"One of my friends, who worked for a special military intelligence unit, told me something in the strictest confidence. Of course, he made me promise not to tell anybody, but this is too good not to share."

"Oh, get on with it!" Vinh said impatiently.

"The National Military Intelligence, the CIA and DIA have some special agents who are actually British SAS."

"The British, is that what you said?" Tu asked, with surprise.

"Do you know Great Britain?"

"I know it very well!"

"Really?"

"Of course, I have seen it on maps thousands of times. I know it very well. If I remember correctly, it is an island!"

"Apparently, these agents are very effective and ten of them have infiltrated the Ho Chi Minh Trail and the North."

"Really?" asked Rang, in disbelief.

"Why are the SAS active in Vietnam?"

"It's very simple, really; just like the Americans, Australians and New Zealanders, they think that the Vietnam War is something special," Mai continued. "They are strong, quick and resourceful. They are well trained and equipped with modern weapons. Unlike their American counterparts, they look quite normal; they're modest and straightforward – but not as wealthy as many other white people. Even in my wildest dreams I couldn't envisage my staff being so well trained."

"What is their main task?" asked Tu.

"They are skilled in the art of infiltration, to evaluate the strengths and weaknesses of the other side. For example, they discovered that, after the eighty-one day campaign in Quang Tri, while we were basking in victory, there were still Hanoi's troops and Vietcong troops in the local regiment, K18, sheltering right in middle of the old town. In addition, SAS agents were also dispatched to the North, under the cloak of charitable personnel and journalists."

"Amazing!" Vinh exclaimed.

"I would give my right arm to have such personnel," Tu said.

"We cannot have such an army now," said Ah. "I have some more news. General Co's wife has just had his eleventh baby."

"Eleven! That is enough to form a football team."

Vinh smiled, "I wonder how he can manage to have so many children. After all, he stays at the Ministry every night."

"His wife visits the casino every weekend," Rang said.

"We must follow his example in all fields, ha, ha, ha!" Mai exclaimed, and burst into laughter.

"I don't think you can compare anyone at work to our chief," Tu said. "But I'm sure I can follow his example of having many children."

Everyone, except Vinh, laughed. Vinh had never been in love, let alone thought about having eleven children! Rang looked at Vinh and read his thoughts as clearly as if he was reading a book. Rang thought Vinh flirted too much with women, so they only viewed him as someone to have fun with, rather than a reliable family man.

Tu's mind was elsewhere. The public had long since known that Loan, head of the police department, was fanatical in his persecution of the communists and their supporters. His viciousness overshadowed the actions of his superior, General Co. When the war is over, people would recognise that General Co was more lenient towards the communists. A CIA agent once joked that communists were appearing everywhere; they probably made up of half of this city's population. Tu wondered which side General Co really supported, the Nationalist Party or North Vietnam?

Tu was weighed down with his thoughts; was General Co on the same side as Tu? Tu had visited General's residence several times beforehand; usually for festivals or holidays. General Co had a decent, gentle and righteous wife and their children were obedient, polite and very well behaved. General Co was good father and a good father must be a good man, there was no doubt about that.

Mai asked Rang why he had refused a cup of tea while they were taking dessert. "Why have you stopped drinking tea?"

"I can give up many things," Rang replied. "For example, if given the choice of giving up tea or whisky, I would rather give up tea! I would choose the company of a young lady if I had to choose between her company and that of a man; I would always choose gambling in preference to a game of chess."

"Stop it," Vinh laughed. "Don't try to bluff us. We should not be joking at such a serious time; let me tell you a story that someone once told me. During a flight, a French passenger opened a bottle of wine, took a gulp and threw it into the rubbish bin. Uncomfortably, the Russian man in the next seat opened a bottle of vodka, took a swig and threw it into the bin. Irritated, the Swedish passenger lit a cigar and cast off the entire box. Angry with rage, the American passenger sitting in the next row stood up, grabbed a Vietnamese soldier and threw him out of the plane!"

"I understand," Mai said, "America has abandoned us."

Everyone went silent. The Americans were super friends of the South. If they left now, South Vietnam could fall at any second and that meant all the police officers here would become prisoners of war.

On the way home, Tu dropped in at a flower shop to buy flowers for Nicole. He asked the sales girl to direct him to a French baker. The girl gave him an address and Tu took out his pencil and wrote it down carefully. Unfortunately, the pencil broke and he threw it into the dustbin in front of the shop. It wasn't just any old pencil, it was Tu trying to get information to the Vietcong. The pencil had been hollowed out and inside was a thin piece of paper full of information about Campaign MT308, which he had found out from Vinh. The campaign was due to start at ten o'clock the next morning, and he hoped that his contact would be able to get the message to the correct people in time. There was no other way of getting in touch with his contact; he didn't have a telephone number and because of the curfew, it would not be easy to get to the forest. It left him with no option but to break regulations and deliver the message himself to the Vietcong area. Campaign MT308 could potentially wipe out the whole village.

Tu made a U-turn and parked his car near the general office. He strolled along the road, which was full of parked cars. The streets were completely deserted. He came to a jeep, which had a special licence plate that allowed the vehicle to go anywhere without being stopped. Tu took out a master key and opened the door. After a few minutes, he hot wired the jeep and drove home.

When Tu arrived home, Nicole was in the bedroom. She was wearing a silk kimono and ready for bed. Tu gave her a kiss and then he opened the wardrobe and took out the skirt that she had bought in Paris and urged his wife to put it on.

"Where are we going?" Nicole asked.

It had become such a regular occurrence that she neither expected nor received an answer. Quite often, Tu would take her out only to be driven round and about with no apparent direction or place in mind.

"I am taking you out for some fresh air," said Tu, putting on his police uniform.

"At midnight, that's amazing, darling."

"I need to do something and I want you to go with me, Nicole," he said.

He led her to the jeep outside the gate of Rose Villa and while Nicole tried to close the gate quietly behind them, Tu opened the door for her to climb in.

With Tu driving and Nicole in the passenger seat, the jeep left Saigon, passing through various police posts without difficulty. No guard dared to stop a car with American plates. They even stood to salute! Tu enjoyed such missions; it gave him a sense of importance and self-satisfaction. Gradually, he left the suburbs of Saigon and entered the countryside. Tomorrow, at 10 a.m., Campaign MT 308 would attack an abandoned base again, Tu thought joyfully, and giggled.

"What are you laughing at?" asked Nicole.

"I love you, darling," he said, blowing a kiss to her as he accelerated away. "Go to sleep. After this trip, I will be promoted. Would you like that?"

"Why do you men like to get stripes and promotions?" Nicole replied sleepily. "All policemen are the same to me."

The road became narrow and bumpy and it was dark, because there were no longer any street lights. Tu was worried, because even though he was in Vietcong territory, he knew that any patrol units would attack him with B40 machine guns, because they would believe them to be Americans. Tu's jeep was also reaching areas where bandits operated despite the traffic police patrols. Whilst overtaking a powerful car, he realised it was a car used by special agents. Tu suddenly felt nervous. He gently stepped on the gas and started to speed up, but the car behind matched his pace.

Starting to get worried, Tu suddenly turned sharply on to a road to his right; the squeal of the tyres and the jerky movement woke Nicole. The car behind not only followed Tu, but also moved closer. Nicole saw the glare of headlights and turned around to have a look.

"I think someone is following us," she said nervously.

Tu, still concentrating on the rough road and the car behind, replied slightly distractedly, "Don't worry, love. I have everything under control. I'll sort it out."

He knew that the jeep would never be able to outrun the police car, so he pulled over to the side. The powerful car pulled in behind and stopped with its bright headlights still on Tu's jeep. Tu got out very slowly and gently, making sure that the people behind could see his empty hands. The white of his uniform jacket shone clearly in the headlights of the car behind.

An officer got out and approached Tu; the driver stayed behind where he would be close to the radio and where he would quickly be able to respond if Tu made a dash for it.

"Tu, I'm scared! What's happening?" Nicole asked through the open window.

"Don't you worry. All you need to do is speak with an American accent," Tu said, in an attempt to calm his wife.

"But Tu, I can't speak American; you know the French don't speak that language."

"French sounds the same to me," Tu said.

Closing the door, he walked towards the policeman. Tu could see the uniformed jacket of the man he was approaching and relaxed slightly.

The officer saw Tu's white police uniform jacket and said the password for the evening in a friendly tone, "There is a lack."

"In the morning," Tu answered, giving the correct response.

Of course, he knew the correct passwords for whoever might have stopped him that night.

"Good evening, brother. Can I see your papers?" the stranger asked.

Tu very slowly and carefully reached into his breast pocket and took out his police ID.

The officer continued: "Why are you out during curfew?"

"Well," Tu pointed to Nicole, who was still sat inside the car, "my American boss loves excitement, so I am simply trying to please her."

"But why did you go out after the curfew and why the sudden burst of speed?"

"You know these crazy Americans; they like to live life dangerously," Tu joked.

The officer grinned whilst he was studying Tu's impressive credentials. He walked round the jeep and saw the American embassy flags for the first time. He had a careful look at Nicole through the window and as he returned to where Tu was standing, he winked at Tu and said that he should take extra care in meeting every need of his boss. Tu climbed back into his car and when the two officers drove away, he breathed a sigh of relief. Nicole asked what they had been joking about, because she had seen them laughing together.

"He was just saying that I should be more careful, that was all," Tu replied, as he started up the engine and continued on his journey. Nicole fell asleep and was oblivious to the fact that Tu had stopped and got out of the car for a few minutes.

On the way home, he was in a happy mood and was having fun driving at speed. Tomorrow, at ten o'clock in the morning, his boss Loan would look very stupid, Tu thought to himself merrily.

Later that night, the American advisor's jeep was returned to its original position.

Chapter Twenty-Nine

A week later, Vinh arrived at the general office following his holiday with a long face. Tu knew he had been on call during his holiday, so he felt silly asking him if he had enjoyed the break.

"Last week was bad here as well," Tu said, after he made a cup of tea for Vinh and himself.

"I know. I have been dealing with scandal. Can you believe, the Vietcong sent a note to the radio and it was read out on the news!" replied Vinh.

"Really?"

"The radio has been giving out false and malicious stories about the aid money for hurricane-stricken eastern provinces. They have been reporting that aid money has been taken by corrupt officials. The officials are angry, because they feel that they are doing their best under such difficult circumstances and our political bosses think that the stories have been spread by Vietcong sympathisers to lower morale. I was ordered to arrest everybody involved, but I have been trying to get a fair trial, so that nobody goes to prison for an unfair number of years. I hate the way the law simply dictates a specific sentence for a crime without taking the circumstances in to account."

"I agree. The judges should be more understanding. So what are we doing today?"

Vinh sighed, "Today, we have to clear up a mess."

"Why?"

"Don't forget, police headquarters is the general dumping ground. All the cases that are either too politically sensitive or unimportant end up on our desks. The target of this investigation is under the protection of a very important person. Make a mistake on this one and we will incur the wrath of his friend." Vinh stopped and changed the subject. "Have you read the latest scandal in today's newspapers?"

"No, what is it?"

"A boy suffering from cancer underwent an operation to remove a tumour. The biopsy was sent to the labs for investigation. Unfortunately, the lab staff lost the sample. The boy died the day before yesterday and his family have taken the case to court. The district police will assign it to the general office, because the boy was a relative of the First Lady," Vinh uttered. "I hear you have cleared a number of files."

"About twenty."

"Well done, Tu."

"Unfortunately, they were all cleared. They were all supporters of the South and I was unable to extract any Vietcong."

"Oh dear, I often wonder what's going on," Vinh said. "We are all Vietnamese together and yet we find it so difficult to understand them, and it's even more difficult to find them. Where do the Vietcong hide? We have only arrested a few of them, but I'm sure that there are thousands more."

"I never seem to catch any Vietcong, but I know they are out there. Do you remember that case when somebody threw a fragmentation grenade into the Z-Nightclub? It was an 8-year-old newspaper boy. He found the grenade by chance and threw it as a joke! Remember the murder of two GIs at the 'Lan' pub? That dancing-girl had found out that her lover was cheating on her and killed him in a fit of jealousy. She was also involved with the Commercial Attaché at the American Embassy. I had to arrest her. I had no choice."

"Do you think I am a good detective?" Vinh asked. "As far as I know, no member of my family is Vietcong. But how can I be sure? What about my friends? What about you, Tu? For all I know, you could be their top agent. They are everywhere, you see. They are everywhere, but whenever you try to catch hold of somebody they slip through your fingers. Why don't our superiors want to face facts?"

"That's their problem; it's easier to be blind than to accept something painful," Tu shrugged.

"Right!" Vinh shouted. Then he started to eat his sandwich while reading some of the records scattered on his desk. "Soon, there will be nowhere for the Vietcong to hide," Vinh muttered to himself: "Saigon is now a strong blockhouse!"

Saigon was indeed like a huge blockhouse; only it was a malformed one. Interwoven barbed wires, layer after layer, inside and outside. The American bases were defended with strict security precautions enforced by large numbers of troops. The capital city swarmed with puppet South Vietnamese soldiers, secret agents, police officers and American "experts". Despite all these protective measures, everyone was apprehensive and waiting for the next unforeseen danger. After the Tet Offensive, there were rumours of a second Tet, after which the Americans understood that it was not going to be easy to crush North Vietnam. Some were saying that it would be impossible and that the Americans should withdraw all of their troops. Hanoi had agreed to come to the negotiating table in Paris again and the atmosphere was becoming increasingly despondent with each passing day.

Vinh had stopped eating. "Sometimes I miss the old Saigon, Tu. It was very peaceful. We were upper secondary students and we used to gather together and sing under sponge-berry trees in the park late at night. There were no bombs and no fighting back then. I never thought I would be a special policeman hounding fellow Vietnamese people, who just happen to have different way of thinking to my superiors."

"I hope the war will end soon."

"Everyone hopes so, Tu."

Tu suddenly felt sad. When the country was reunited, he would write a letter to the government to tell them about people like Vinh, who devoted themselves to their work and the people's well-being. For them, it did not matter who they were working for; only that they were working for the common good. He felt sure that the government of the North would employ people like Vinh after the great victory.

That afternoon, Tu lingered in his office after working hours. He rummaged through Vinh's heap of records and pulled out a particular file. He put it in his briefcase and walked out. However, unbeknown to Tu, Rang had been watching everything through binoculars from an office across the hall.

Chapter Thirty

Nicole had changed; she was constantly depressed and it didn't help that Tu was working such long hours. Their family doctor prescribed sleeping tablets, but they were ineffective. The only thing that eased her mood was when Harry came to visit Rose Villa. The servants at Rose Villa watched Nicole and Harry with great interest and it moved to the next level when Charles and Ann stayed at the plantation and took the boys with them.

It was a Sunday evening when Harry called round with the intention of playing dominoes with Nicole and her parents, but Charles and Ann were not at home. However, Nicole was very happy to see him and welcomed him into the villa. After dinner, they sat around the coffee table and played chess, while Mrs Lam made herself busy tidying the room. She was reluctant to leave them alone in each other's company, because she wanted to know all the details between Nicole and Harry. Gossip about Nicole and the American soldier had been circulating around the villa for over a month now and the servants would talk about them in the kitchen, or outside in the garden, and even in the rubber plantation.

Nicole was struggling to win a game of chess with Harry. Even Mrs Lam tried to help her by suggesting appropriate moves, but she lost twice in a row. She was angry and wanted to cry in frustration, but tried to suppress it. Finally, it all became too much and she burst into tears.

"Oh! I'm sorry," Harry murmured, as he came to sit next to Nicole and held her hands. "Please don't cry." Then he pulled Nicole into his embrace and hugged her close.

On Harry's shoulder, Nicole smiled and stopped crying. Mrs Lam was aware that Nicole was falling in love with Harry and she ran to the kitchen to give everyone the latest update.

A few minutes later, Mr Lam knocked on the door. He brought in a tray of light drinks and French biscuits made by Ann for her daughter before she had left. He decided to look after the guest himself, knowing how much his wife loved to gossip.

Harry left quite late, which worried everyone at Rose Villa, because he could so easily be killed when wandering around Saigon at night. Harry seemed to be afraid of nothing, and he looked very happy. He was oblivious to the fact that everyone at Rose Villa was watching them and that they knew of his love for Nicole.

Concerned about the inevitable affair, Mr Lam warned Tu that he should spend more time with Nicole. However, Tu had too many things to do and he couldn't spare the time. Nicole was beautiful, she had many men who found her attractive, and now another admirer had joined the long list, so why should he be worried? Peace for Vietnam was what was important. Preventing Vietnamese from killing Vietnamese was more vital than his own life, he thought.

As predicted, Harry paid another visit to Rose Villa. They had just finished a delicious meal that had been prepared by Mr Lam and Ms Thi and were having coffee in the library. Nicole looked beautiful. She wore a white, open-collared gown and her brown hair was coiled up in a chignon. Harry wore blue jeans and a white shirt without a tie. He had recently had his hair cut short, which suited his face. They were having a lovely evening, until Nicole suddenly missed her sons. Her hidden thoughts boiled to the surface and tears rolled down her cheeks once more.

Harry approached her and held her shoulders as he tried to console her.

"I miss my boys," she sobbed, in English.

"Oh," replied Harry giving her a big hug.

Nicole leaned her head against Harry's shoulder and he gently kissed her hair and told her that he loved her.

"I love you, too!" Nicole replied unconsciously.

"I love you," Harry repeated. "I have loved you right from the very first time we met. I have often dreamed that I will have you one day, Nicole."

Nicole looked deep into his eyes and she knew that Harry truly loved her.

Chapter Thirty

The following days were heaven for the pair of lovers. It seemed that nothing could spoil the time they had together. On the few occasions that they noticed the world, everything appeared to be marvellous and there was even good news from the peace talks in Paris.

"After the armistice, I will take you to visit my parents in America," Harry said.

"I long for peace more than ever," Nicole replied. "I hope that peace will come soon; it would be nice if one morning I woke up and suddenly found that I was living a normal life; one where there was no fighting, no bombing, no shooting and no more worrying. When I last visited Paris, I was jealous, because the people could walk around freely and they had no need to worry as to whether somebody was going shoot at them or whether the building they were walking past was about to be bombed."

Every single day that the war continued it increased the risk of Harry being killed or injured in battle, or being posted elsewhere. They lived as though each day was their last. The American operations departed in romanticism and glory, and yet they returned in black body bags or on bloody stretchers, which terrified her. Nicole experienced sweet days of love with Harry and in return, he offered her passion, with the all the ardent enthusiasm of a young man in love.

Outside the window, Saigon was grey and gloomy. It had rained incessantly for a week now and the radio and television broadcasts repeatedly reported that the Northern operations had failed due to flooding and rains. The photos of the Ho Chi Minh Trail were ample proof of the terrible weather, and appeared in every newspaper in Saigon, along with news from the peace talks in Paris. However, Nicole and Harry didn't care about any of it; they were too absorbed in their own world.

After a long kiss, Harry said, "Tell me the meaning of your Vietnamese name."

"A sad flower," Nicole answered, "that blooms in the winter, but Saigon has no winter."

"Darling, I love you," Harry murmured, as he kissed her hand.

"I love ..." but she was interrupted by a long kiss.

After he had left, Nicole rang her friend Josephine to tell her about the love she held for Harry. She had been unsure of her feelings towards Harry up until now and she now knew that he was somebody special. It was all happening so quickly. She had been so in love with Tu and had felt guilty betraying him, but Tu had become cold and indifferent in recent months. Nicole never knew if she could trust his love and although she could not prove it, she suspected that Tu had another woman. She was aware that he had shown more warmth and kindness towards her recently, but, nevertheless, it was too late. Nicole knew without a doubt that Harry loved her, and she returned his love readily. Nicole was oblivious to the fact that Mrs Lam was listening to her call from the master bedroom.

One night, after Harry had left Rose Villa, Mr Lam reminded Nicole that her parents were returning home with the boys tomorrow. Nicole understood that when her parents returned, she would have to once again become a good daughter, a dutiful wife and a caring mother. Suddenly, she felt guilty about her behaviour, especially towards Tu. After several days of living in torment, upon her family's return, Nicole resolved to stop seeing Harry. Whenever Harry called, Mrs Lam was instructed to tell him that Nicole was busy or otherwise occupied.

Chapter Thirty-One

Tu, accompanied by Ann, made a visit to Cam Ranh. Nicole remained in Saigon with the children, because she said that she did not want to visit a dangerous area. Although Tu knew that it was because of Harry that she didn't want to go, he still wanted go to Cam Ranh. It was an ideal opportunity for him to spy on the gate of death, which had killed so many thousands of Northern soldiers.

Whilst travelling from Nha Trang Airport, Tu was overwhelmed by the sheer size of the powerful military base at Cam Ranh, which was one of the biggest in the world. He travelled along the single road from Highway 1 to Cam Ranh Island. The American troops called Cam Ranh "Little Hawaii City", because it was beautiful and unaffected by the war, with few armed officers from either side. He could see the picturesque landscape with his own eyes, and it was clear that a great investment had been made in this military base. It was obvious that no expense had been spared in making sure that all of the most recent innovations and technology had been incorporated; not only in terms of the design, but also in the equipping of what had become one huge killing machine. The Cam Ranh airfield was crowded by day and night. Hundreds of jet fighters of all kinds stood in close proximity to one another in steel hangars, with half-metre-thick walls built to withstand mortar shells. A great number of barracks had been built and the open-air oil pipelines ran from the fuel dumps to the airfield and the seaport. Across the only path to the Cam Ranh Peninsula, the American army set up four self-contained citadels to prevent an overland assault or infiltration.

Phu greeted Ann and Tu with the highest respect and because the soldiers and everyone in Cam Ranh was expecting a visit from the President of Vietnam, they thought that Ann, because of her presence, was the First Lady.

"My sister," Phu said courteously. "In this fierce and dangerous location, your presence is truly appreciated."

"Your words make me very happy, and I should have visited you sooner. Saigon papers make frequent reference to the forthcoming visit of General Abram at the moment."

Phu smiled. "He will come here together with our president. He's presently in Da Nang and, because he has confidence in Cam Ranh, he intends to send in more reinforcements, sister, which will involve even more work for me."

Ann made a gesture to show her disapproval of the president's actions. "Do you think such a withdrawal of troops from Da Nang to Cam Ranh can be justified? The dry and scorching weather in Da Nang has made it difficult for the Americans to advance."

"The climate of the Cam Ranh Peninsula does not suit the Americans, either, dear sister. At midday, the temperature can reach 40 degrees Celsius indoors with the sunlight reflected from the white sand. There isn't enough vegetation here to give any shade. However, the Americans have built an ice-cream factory here; perhaps you should try an ice cream, sister?" Phu joked, and then continued, "Tomorrow, I will take you on a visit to the logistics headquarters before going to Nha Trang. This afternoon, we shall tour around Cam Ranh."

"What about a trip to the beach? Maybe there will be something for us to see there. Or a boat trip, perhaps?"

"That's impossible, sister. Anyway, Cam Ranh and Nha Trang still have places where you could relax. The Americans and I are trying to save Saigon for you," Phu said, as he pointed towards the horizon out to sea, where there was a fleet of American Navy destroyers and frigates, to demonstrate as to why they couldn't visit the beaches.

Along the coastline of Cam Ranh Bay, the 13 kilometres of beautiful beach were deserted. Ann and Tu could see the anti-aircraft guns by the side of the beach and the view hardly made Tu feel that he was on holiday.

"Oh, I see," said Ann.

"I could take you two to the lake over there; there is such a beautiful view from there."

General Phu ordered his chauffeur to drive himself and his guests to the Cam Ranh Bridge. From the bridge, Tu saw an amazing view of Cam

Ranh Bay. There were mountains all around and the three big lakes connected to the sea; the white sands looked so picturesque in the open under the sunshine of summer.

The lake which Phu took them to was quite large, covering at least 150 acres, and opened out into Cam Ranh Bay. The water was quite shallow and was thriving with sea life and in the sunset, storks calmly hunted for fish. There were rows of aeroplanes on the airfield, loaded with bombs and rockets, beside the path separating the airfield from the lake. Everything was silent.

Guessing what Ann was thinking, Phu started to speak. "The landscape is so bleak, my sister; very different from the busy capital city, don't you think?"

Ann agreed, "Yes, it is deserted, indeed. The barrenness prevents me from relaxing and admiring the landscape."

"What a pity!" said Phu.

"But I do like the quietness here," Ann said, as everyone climbed out of the car and walked by the lakeside. "Saigon is so crowded and noisy by comparison. You are so kind to take the time to welcome us, I can see you are very busy, Brother Phu."

"Thank you, sister. By the way, I heard from President Thieu that you will be going to France this Christmas?" Phu asked.

"This year, Charles is going to Paris alone. I do hope both sides will agree on a ceasefire during Christmas, so that Saigon could enjoy the festivities. If you return to the capital this Christmas, please do come to see us. Your family will be most welcome at my house at any time," Ann said.

"Certainly, my sister," Phu replied.

Ann went quiet. For the past few years, she had been unable to take long vacations because of Tu's work, and it was very difficult for him to arrange the necessary leave. She wished he would find a much safer job, but, as a young man, it was unlikely that he would follow his mother-in-law's advice.

"My son-in-law didn't want to go to Paris for Christmas; I am not sure why."

"I'm sorry, sister, but I agree with him," Phu laughed, loudly. "If I had followed the advice given to me by my mother and mother-in-law when I was young, I would now be a non-commissioned officer."

"You mean we women are always acting against the best interests of men? We just don't want them to come to any harm, that's all."

The very next day, Thieu arrived at Cam Ranh in his private plane with his wife, who was wearing a pink *Ao Dai*. Following her husband down the aircraft steps, they were greeted by Abrams and Phu. Hundreds of American and South Vietnam troops were lined up on the tarmac to welcome President Thieu and the First Lady.

Phu held a special party for Thieu and Abrams and both Ann and Tu had been invited. Tu found Abrams to be kind and charming and he seemed to understand about the North and was aware of what was happening to the troops on the ground. Thieu congratulated Phu as the hero of the country, because with Tactic Cam Ranh, the North could never enter Saigon unless they wanted them to. There would never be a need for another Tet Offensive again, and Phu promised Thieu that he would secure Cam Ranh at all costs.

For Tu, the trip to Cam Ranh gave him an invaluable insight and access to data about the military situation of the enemy. He had even personally counted and memorised the types and numbers of planes and warships. A direct attack would be prohibitively expensive in terms of casualties with little chance of success. A report from Tu, together with many corroborating reports from other sources, would be sent to the Intelligence Department to be thoroughly analysed. Then, the High Command and the Party Central Committee could make proper decisions on the methods to liberate South Vietnam. Tu was all for the liberation of the South and the reunification of the country.

When he returned to Saigon, Tu sent a warning letter via his secret letter box to warn the Vietcong not to directly attack Cam Ranh; at least, not until there was further information that suggested a way into the base.

In those early autumn months, the staff at police headquarters were unable to rest. Student demonstrations were taking place everywhere and if their leader was arrested or killed, three others would appear and take his place. Everywhere, Vietcong, guerrillas, and even seasoned commandos of the National Liberation Front of South Vietnam, rose across the whole country. Thieu ordered that every officer working there needed to be checked, but they were so busy, they could not afford the time, no matter how important the order. The normal investigations and administrative work within the general office all took second place to the urgent demands of the general uprising.

At present, it was impossible to wipe out the visible Vietcong, let alone hunt out the hidden secret agents. According to reports allocated the highest possible secret rating, all estimates about the quantity and quality of North Vietnam regular army troops were completely misleading. Everybody strenuously blamed someone else for the woeful discrepancies, until the blame finally shifted to the doors of the White House and the CIA. North Vietnam had an army of 3 million men, while the Pentagon gave an estimate of only 590,000 troops; less than the number of American soldiers sent to Vietnam, which was an incredibly illogical figure. However, the Saigon regime had not recognised that. Minh, or Big Minh as he was otherwise known, was right when he objected to the statements made by the young and inexperienced Ky. However, Minh's voice was drowned out by the rumours that he was vying for power with Ky. But Minh always ended any comments he made by admitting that for somebody so young and inexperienced, Ky was not so bad. Tu paid special attention to the military predictions of this big and handsome general.

The following weekend, Minh was invited to visit Ann at the plantation. Tu was excited and throughout the week, he prepared questions to try and find out more information.

Minh was very tall for a Vietnamese man and had a big pair of thick glasses that tended to soften his penetrating glare. He was very popular with the army and despite his numerous plots to overthrow the government and Thieu, he managed to keep his head on his neck.

When Minh arrived by helicopter and Ann greeted him warmly, Tu was surprised at how open and friendly he was and by the fact that he had a good knowledge of the police system. He was also especially quick to show his genuine respect and admiration for the Northern general, Giap. After the death of President Minh, General Giap was the only worthy opponent. The Secret Service and the Intelligence Section of the North often leaked out information and it was rumoured that Minh was on good terms with some of the high-ranking officers of the Northern forces. But the information could not always be trusted, so unless it was given official credibility by the CIA, these rumours were dismissed as a deliberate attempt by the North to spread distrust in order to lower morale.

Whilst in the living room, Minh was complaining about the police. "In my opinion, the police have been so busy concentrating on spies, fifth columnists and guerrilla, that routine crime solving has suffered. Many notorious gangs of robbers are now free to operate on the streets of Saigon in broad daylight," Minh told Tu.

"I agree. The police force cannot cope physically with the workload. Our boss Tay seems to have only one priority and that is arresting and torturing Vietcong followers. Now that the students are demonstrating so violently, it makes it impossible to follow up on smaller crimes that are taking place in Saigon. We need more policemen, but it is difficult to recruit new officers. They are too frightened to be the targets of Vietcong supporters."

"Brother Minh," Ann interrupted, "do you think it will be possible to reunify the country and establish a bilateral government?"

"Yes, I believe it might very well be," Minh answered.

A servant brought in a silver tray of tea and, while Ann poured, Minh ordered his bodyguard to bring a large gift box into the room. Minh opened it and there, on the red velvet, was a gold-rimmed tiger fang and two jade necklaces.

"These are for you, Ann," said Minh. "Last week, on my trip to Pleiku, the Provincial Chief presented me with these. I have had them embellished at a goldsmiths."

Ann beamed, placing one of the necklaces around her slender neck.

"Brother Minh, you have a good memory to have remembered that I love traditional jewellery. Who on earth would be able to catch such a big tiger? What a fang!"

"The hunting of this tiger makes for a quite a sensational story," Minh explained. "And whilst tracking the beast, we discovered evidence of Northern troops around Pleiku."

Tu listened intently as he ate one of the cakes and looked out of the window at Minh's helicopter.

"The Northern regular army is not as small as predicted by the CIA. In my view, North Vietnam has an army of one million men. They are marching southwards along the routes known collectively as the Ho Chi

Minh Trail. They also take some roundabout routes through Laos, to transport weapons and provisions."

Tu knew the Trail very well. On the muddy trails along high mountains and through thick jungles, he and his companions had eagerly marched to the front. The Ho Chi Minh Trail was 1,100 kilometres long and was made up of a number of rough roads from North to South. Sometimes, they walked in single file, and other times, when they were available, they got lifts on Russian lorries camouflaged in green leaves, which were few and far between. Most of the soldiers travelled by foot, carrying around 60 pounds of food, medical equipment and weapons. It was worse in the rainy season, when the Trail became a quagmire and the humidity was unbearable. To keep up their spirits, they used to sing.

Thousands of young girls with bright smiles would volunteer themselves to keep the Trail open at all costs, by repairing roads damaged by floods and landslides, clearing broken-down lorries and bomb craters as they went. Their arms, pale due to malaria, would wave until the lorries disappeared towards the South. Among those faces, he still remembered two young girls in particular. They had immediately rushed out to fill in a crater that an American bomb had created, but no sooner had they touched it with their shovels, than the bomb exploded. Tu would never forget the smiles of those girls as they had died such a painful death. He wondered whether he would have enough time to smile before his own death. When the country was reunified and at peace, he wanted to drive along the Ho Chi Minh Trail. He would burn incense sticks at every milestone, to commemorate all the young people who volunteered. To him they were the heroes.

"What are you thinking, Tu?" Ann asked. "Come over here and have a drink with us, dear."

Tu turned back to Ann and Minh and said that he was impressed by his helicopter.

Ann and Minh burst out laughing. Minh asked Tu if he would like to go for a flight with him some time over the four Tactical Zones, and Tu was very pleased to accept. By the end of the visit, Minh was talking to Tu with great fondness and even referred to him as "son".

"Well, it's time for me to go; I hope I will see you again sometime, son." Then Minh turned to Ann. "Next time, if Charles is not busy, I shall invite him and your son-in-law to inspect Central Vietnam with me."

"My husband loves to fly everywhere. He has always wanted to purchase a plane, but I don't think he should, because I think that small planes are unsafe."

"How right you are; but it only applies to the civil planes. Military aircraft like the Phantom are extremely safe, but they are only designed for military activities," Minh answered honestly.

Ann and Tu escorted Minh to his helicopter and watched him take off.

"Mother, I've never known anyone who was so well connected as you. How do you manage to make friends with so many high-ranking officers?" Tu asked.

"It's very simple," Ann explained to Tu. "I once became friends with someone and he introduced me to others. We are upper class, so everyone wants to be our friends, dear!"

Chapter Thirty-Two

The two countries, North and South Vietnam, had agreed on a ceasefire during the New Year festivities and firecrackers echoed everywhere. Mr and Mrs Lam were given a few days off and they returned to their hometown to celebrate the New Year with their family.

Rose Villa was busy with their preparations. Ann made all the traditional dishes for New Year's Eve, including roasted pork, fermented meat, sticky rice cakes and spring rolls. Meanwhile Nicole busied herself preparing the New Year's gifts of red envelopes and filling them with new money. Her sons were "helping" in the way that small children help. Tu bought plenty of firecrackers and firewood, and Mr Ba spent four days shopping to make sure that he had enough food for the three-day celebrations.

The Presidential Palace sent Ann a big package of gifts that Mr Ba now carried into the kitchen. On the top was a branch of sponge berry. It reminded her of when she was nineteen all those years ago and of when Ann and Thieu used to stand beneath the sponge berry tree in his grandmother's garden in Ninh Thuan. Thieu used to climb up the tree and break off the flowers to give to her. Suddenly, she felt an overwhelming nostalgia for her old flame. Ann's husband would never accept presents from Thieu, but Charles had already left for the plantation and Tu was visiting the tombs of Ann and Mrs Tam's relatives, so would be none the wiser.

The cemetery where Little Lien's grave lay was massive. The South Vietnamese, no matter how poor, always spent huge amounts of money to ensure that the graves were big and ornate, as it showed just how much the deceased person was loved. Mrs Tam did not spend much money on her other children's graves, but Little Lien's grave was beautiful, because Tu wanted a special commemoration for her.

Tu paid only a small amount of attention to the graves of Ann's relatives and quickly moved on to the tomb of Little Lien, where she was resting beside Mother Tam's own children. Mother Tam had prepared all the necessary votive offerings of food and drink in advance. There was New Year's cake, coconut jelly and some French biscuits that Ann had baked in the early morning. Nicole sent white lilies for Little Lien and Tu brought some white roses with him.

Tu sat next to her grave and told Little Lien everything he had been doing over the last year. Mother Tam invited Little Lien's soul to come back home to celebrate New Year.

Whenever they visited Little Lien's grave, Mother Tam and Tu often stayed there for quite a long time. Little Lien's death had broken Tu's heart, and when the incense sticks died out and Mother Tam had packed up the votive offerings, Tu felt miserable. The bundle of white roses and lilies lay on the tomb, with the loose rose petals slightly dancing in the evening breeze. Mother Tam stayed near the tomb; she did not want to leave; this was Little Lien, her husband and her children's graves, all of which she treasured greatly.

Mrs Tam stood up, trembling. She had cried off and on throughout the day and the tears began to flow once again.

"Shall we go home?" Tu consoled Mrs Tam. "Peace will come soon, you know, of that I am sure."

"I am sure that you are right."

"The Paris Conference has reached many agreements in our favour."

It had turned dark in the graveyard, so Tu picked up a rose, brought it to his lips and placed it gently back on Little Lien's tomb.

"Mum and I must go now; I still feel great sorrow at your death, my sister. The tombstone also senses my pain, Little Lien," he murmured to the silent portrait of Little Lien, encased in glass on the tombstone. He stood up and helped Mother Tam to the car.

"After New Year's Eve, I am going to be the first person to step into your house and, after worshipping the ancestors, I will take you to have lunch with my parents-in-law."

"It's up to you," Mother Tam replied, hesitantly.

"Maybe you should retire next year, Mum," Tu suggested, as he saw Mrs Tam wince at the pain in her back.

"I still want to earn money to support our side. It is not yet time for me to retire; there is a still lot of work to be done. Our side is so poor in comparison, that we need to raise all the money we çan raise. I know you worry for me, but I also worry about you. Remember to take care of yourself, Tu."

"Yes, I've always been cautious."

"Don't take my advice for granted, my dear!"

"Mum, I have this pistol," Tu stretched an arm to grasp his gun. "If I am discovered, I will commit suicide."

Mother Tam's six children had devoted their lives to the Revolution, and she had witnessed the death of dozens of young people who called her "Mother". What Tu said was nothing new to her. However, she had no desire to witness the death of any more youths. Too many had already died. They had had so little time to enjoy a life and had not been able to live for themselves ...

"When the war ends, I will take you to visit the North," Tu continued.

"I long for that day, so I can visit Uncle Ho's mausoleum, and then I could visit your family," said Mrs Tam. Her eyes glittered with happiness.

"My family will be honoured to welcome you, Mum. They will want to thank you for giving me my life back again."

Tu became excited thinking about that day. He couldn't wait; life would be so much better if peace came to them.

Nicole took Little Trung for a stroll in the park. She wore a red beret and a red silk dress reaching down to her calves. Ceasefires were few and far between, so she did not want to waste the opportunity to take her son out. The weather was perfect for a day out. Nicole hoped that one day Tu would agree to travel to France with her, so he may experience the cold winters of Paris. Earlier that morning, Nicole had asked Tu to take her out, but he had been too busy. He was always busy with work. Nicole hoped that when they eventually moved to France, Tu would have more time for her and their sons.

Nicole held her son's hand tightly, and Little Trung carried a basket of apples and tropical fruits bought by his mother in his other hand.

"Mummy, the sales lady said I am a good boy," Little Trung said, in stilted Vietnamese. However, his mum still understood him.

"Yes, you are good, Little Trung," Nicole replied lovingly.

"I like to help you carry things," Little Trung said, as he bent down to pick a wild flower, which he then gave to his mother.

At home, when playing in the garden, Little Trung often gathered wild grasses to give to her. Nicole was delighted to receive these gifts from her son. She would arrange them in a bowl of fresh water, which she placed on the table in the drawing room. Little Trung knew that his mother loved all the presents that he gave her and all the servants understood that Nicole loved his flowers so very much, that they never dared to clear away the bowls of wild grass and left them for Nicole to dispose of.

"Mummy, I will always do as I am told," Little Trung continued.

"I know," Nicole agreed, "and Mummy is forever grateful, because God has given you to me. Mummy needs nothing more than you and your little brother," Nicole confessed to her son. The truth was, while she was unsure whether she believed that Tu loved her any more, she had no doubt that Little Trung really did.

"We'll take a short cut along the path to the car," Nicole said, as she led Little Trung along another track. "Would you like an ice cream before we go home?"

"Will the ice cream man call me a good boy?" asked Little Trung.

"He certainly will, if you're obedient," Nicole replied, smiling.

She looked around as she had the sudden feeling that someone was watching. Harry, in camouflage combat clothing, was standing by the path. Nicole was surprised, but very happy to see him. She quickly approached him, asking why he was there.

"Oh, I am just ambling along," Harry smiled, as he lifted Little Trung up. "Wow! Look how fast you're growing! You must be big enough to be able to help your mother now!" As he put Little Trung on the ground, Harry turned to Nicole. "So, how are you?" he asked.

"I'm fine, Harry," Nicole replied. "My son and I have just taken a ride on the Ferris wheel, but we're on our way home now."

"It's unbelievable that a whole month has gone by since we last met. Time flies so fast; anyway, how's your family?" Harry asked.

"Everyone is fine, thank you. I heard the news over and over this week; will you return to America?"

"I don't know. Over 100,000 American troops have gone home already. Unfortunately, I was not one of the lucky ones," he answered, sadly.

Mr Nam was waiting by the Rolls-Royce when they reached the main road. He opened the car door and stepped to one side for his young mistress. Nicole helped Little Trung to clamber in and she reluctantly said her goodbyes to Harry.

"Goodbye, Nicole," he said with a smile, "and a Happy New Year."

Nicole whispered back, "Happy New Year to you, too."

As they got in the car, Nicole started to weep, because she would much rather have stayed with Harry than have returned home. Mr Nam shook Harry's hand to say goodbye. Before turning the key in the ignition, he asked Nicole, for the last time, if she really wanted to go home.

"Brother Nam, please go," she answered, closing her eyes.

She wanted to retain that moment of love and compassion for a moment longer. She had decided to part and never to see Harry again ... she suddenly felt a deep feeling of grief. Returning to her family, husband and children might be out of habit and, perhaps she was even being defeated by the temptation of a peaceful life but she knew it was what she must do.

Mr Nam looked at Nicole through the mirror. She looked lost and her eyes were full of tears. However, Tu was waiting for his wife at home, and he knew deep down that she'd made the right decision.

Tu wanted to retain as many of the Vietnamese traditions as possible, and he knew that Nicole would not have been taught all of them. On the first day of the New Year, the parents would sit on chairs, while their children knelt to wish their parents good health and longevity. Then the parents would thank their children, or give them money as a New Year's gift. At Rose Villa, things were slightly different, because there were huge numbers of people working for the Philippes. Ann told Tu and Nicole that she would cook Vietnamese food on the last evening of the old year and the first day of the New Year. However, on the first evening of the New Year, it was imperative to prepare a French meal with seven courses: three appetisers, one main dish, two desserts and, finally, cheese served with grapes and biscuits, because Charles was expected to return and celebrate with them.

Every year, Charles and Ann would fly to France for Christmas and would return to Vietnam for the traditional New Year festivities; this year was the first time Charles went alone.

Nicole was not listening to what her husband was saying, because her mind was on Harry, wondering if he was enjoying the Vietnamese New Year.

"How are you, Nicole?" Tu asked his wife, as he noticed how unhappy she looked.

"I don't know," she answered. "I feel sad."

"Oh, I am sorry. Is there anything that I can do?"

Before leaving the room to go upstairs, Tu gave her a hug to comfort her. Tu simply believed she was sad because another year had gone by, and women didn't like to think that they were getting another year older.

Chapter Thirty-Three

When Vinh and Tu returned to the office after their holiday, they immediately noticed a change of atmosphere in the office. Everyone seemed much more relaxed, happy and there was a general feeling of mischief.

"Something must have happened," said Tu.

"Are you sure?" asked Rang, with a mocking voice.

Tu nodded.

"There is a flower pot!" Vinh cried out in astonishment.

"We have a new colleague," Rang revealed, with a smirk on his face. "Her name is Han, and she is beautiful."

"I've heard all about her, but I've not yet met her," Vinh told Tu. "I had to settle some affairs in the West last week and was told that our chief had recruited a real beauty. What a pleasant surprise!"

According to Rang, the newcomer was an acquaintance of Loan and came from Go Cong area where they were renowned for their good looks and were portrayed as the perfect woman.

"Are you sure she is beautiful?" Tu asked.

"Very!" answered Rang.

"She's late," Vinh commented, with disapproval in his voice.

"Typical woman," Rang replied.

"Can she organise files?"

"No," Rang replied.

"Can she answer the phones?"

"Uh-Uh."

"Can she type?"

"Nope!"

"Then why was she recruited?" asked Vinh. "I need a qualified employee."

"You need a qualified employee. Oh, dear boss, if you need a secretary, you have one now!" Rang burst out laughing. "She is a relative of our big chief. More importantly, she is beautiful. What further qualifications could you possibly want?"

"For me, beauty is enough. Oh, come on, Vinh, apparently she is a beauty," Tu grinned.

"What does she need to do that will require knowledge? Brother Tu can help her find files. I can type for her. We have a pretty woman in this office, that's all we need!" Mai said, smiling.

"Agreed!" shouted all the others in chorus, and they all burst out laughing.

"Who interviewed her?" Vinh asked.

"Why would she need to be interviewed?" Tu joked.

Vinh sat silently with a glum look on his face. The previous week, he had suggested to the new chief, Tay, that he needed to recruit a secretary for his section. Where on earth was the office heading if they were selecting employees like that, he wondered.

"Watch out! She's coming!" whispered Rang.

Vinh looked up as the door opened and there stood a stunning woman, with long, slender legs in very high heels, and a very short miniskirt. Her blouse was so low-cut that there was just a hint of pink peeping up over the top of her bra, suggesting that she should have bought a bigger cup. Tu agreed with Rang; she was incredibly beautiful. She had short, black hair, which was permed in the American style. She had big black eyes, with long eyelashes, and high cheekbones. Even her lips were luscious and inviting. Vinh was unsure whether she was just an acquaintance of the big boss, or his lover. Tu wondered if this secretary had been placed in the office to spy on the Archive Section. It was certainly plausible. He admired Loan's talents, even though this made him a very dangerous opponent. He was a general well versed in strategy, despite his hot temper, and it was not without reason he was called the "The Killer of Vietcong".

More than one hundred suspicious safe houses had been cleared as being nothing more than a bar, a hotel and coffee shop, and Loan had begun to suspect that the unusual lenience of the Archive Section was due to the presence of a spy. This was the reason behind Han.

Tu was now faced with the dilemma of all double agents?; the more successful he became, the more the evidence was accumulating against him. Whilst working at the section dealing with records of suspected Vietcong, he had already achieved tremendous results. Hundreds of suspects had already been cleared and were no longer under investigation. He knew that he was a link in the chain, engaging in an important and dangerous mission. The Intelligence Department deserved the most credit, but the many individual agents involved should not be ignored. He was now playing a small role in a drama with a carefully prepared script. In this play, he had to fulfil his performance without an understudy or stuntman. If he was merely good, then he would lose his life. He had to be perfect one hundred per cent of the time. Therefore, he had to be extra vigilant over this new, pretty employee, but he had to admit, she was beautiful. It had been a long time since he had met a woman as attractive as Nicole. However, Han had more of a sexual allure than Nicole's noble elegance.

"Why are you all looking at me?" the new secretary said, as she threw her half-smoked cigarette on the ground and rubbed it with her heel. "Get back to work, right now! All of you!"

Everyone looked, with their mouths wide open. Was she a secretary or the new boss? Tu wondered, and burst out laughing. Han turned back, throwing him a sharp glance. Rang whistled and Vinh handed her a couple of short letters to type up. Two hours later, she brought them back to Vinh. The words were misspelt and in the wrong order, with practically no punctuation. They were a mess. The Archive Section is not a typing class and a tortoise could type faster than she does, Vinh thought.

Vinh, however, was quite polite and openly flirted with her. However, after a week, everyone knew that it was Tu that Han had a crush on. Not wanting to hurt her feelings, he talked to her about things he thought women would be interested in, like hairstyles, brands of famous perfumes and children. Tu liked to talk about children. He was proud of his two beautiful sons and Han showed a special joy when hearing the stories about Little Trung and Little Hieu. They talked about how Han had once loved an American soldier called Johnny, and after serving in Vietnam, he had designs on getting a job as a newspaper photographer. He had taken every opportunity in Vietnam to build up a great portfolio of photos to show to potential employers. However, on patrol, he been concentrating on his shot and he didn't see the tripwire set by the Vietcong. His friends came to Han's house to break the news as gently as possible to her. Seven months later, she gave birth to a strapping boy and Han's family had disowned her when they had found out about the pregnancy. Having no means to provide for the baby, she had left him on the doorstep of an orphanage. Later, she had gone back to the orphanage to find that all the babies had been sent to America. She knew her son had been given a new name, so she had no means of tracing him.

"I miss my baby so very much," Han told Tu one day, in a voice choked with emotion.

"I understand, Han," Tu replied.

"How can you understand when you've never been far away from your children?"

"I read novels …" said Tu.

"Phew, that's just reading other people's stories! You have no idea, do you?" Han burst out laughing, "Many have said that it was my own fault for loving my country's enemy and I was unable to cope with their disgust and contempt when I gave birth to Johnny. If I had ignored them, I would never have lost my son. In the west of Vietnam, where I come from, people hated half-blood children, but in Saigon, women are proud to have an American partner."

"When did you give birth to your son?"

"When I was twenty."

"At that time, you were too young to go against the pressure of public opinion. You are still young, and I'm sure you will have a lovely family with beautiful children one day."

"I don't want to have any children now," explained Han. "Who can guarantee that my child will not be killed? I see so many children dying every day because of mistaken bombings or raids. Who benefits when those children are killed? Who arranges their killing? And yet nobody is blamed."

"Do you want something to drink?" Tu asked, bringing her a glass of water.

Their love of children made Tu comfortable enough to invite Han to have a meal at Rose Villa. The other diners included Thu Thuy (Thieu's wife), and Colonel Binh, a close subordinate of Vien. It was obvious that

Han was flirting with Binh during the meal and he seemed to be flattered by her attentions.

A month later, Han and Binh flew to Da Lat for a holiday. Tu could breathe a sigh of relief; she had obviously not been sent to the office with the sole intention of watching Tu. She couldn't have been an agent and Tu was growing fond of her himself.

"You should stay away from Colonel Binh," Tu told her, when she returned to the office.

"What do you mean?"

"You see, his influence is great. He has a loyal army; even President Thieu has to tread carefully around him. His minions are ready to wipe out anybody who threatens their boss's career."

"You don't need to look after me," Han said, sulkily.

"Look, you can have a good husband. The colonel is twenty years older than you." Han stared at Tu giving no reply. He continued. "I know his wife; she is notorious for her jealousy. Do you know any wives of generals and military officers? They are crack shots. I will share this with you, but please forgive me. If they kill their husband's lovers, the killing will be covered up. It's wartime. Thousands of people are killed daily. Only American corpses are important. Who will be bothered about an unidentified corpse?"

"Who do you think you are? Are you trying to preach to me?" Han said, becoming touchy.

Tu looked deep into her beautiful eyes. "I think of you only as a good friend."

Han refrained from answering. Her eyes glistened with emotion; she was touched by Tu's sentiments. Tu was a man of honour, and his wife was extremely lucky. Han saw his expertise in his work and his loyalty to the country. On the wall close to his desk, hung the portraits of the Head of State and the American President, Nixon. Han thought about her mission; she was not merely the secretary they had all come to know and love …

Two weeks later, Loan called Han to his office.

"Good afternoon, boss," she said in a jokey voice.

"Have you found out anything about Lieutenant Tu?" Loan asked, as soon as she entered.

"He is on our side," she answered.

"You're lying to me!" Loan shouted. "You're not falling in love with that idiot of a man are you?"

Han tried hard not to burst out laughing; everybody was scared of Loan except for her. Han's father was Loan's father's best friend, and it was Loan who had put her into the mission in the first place, so she pulled a long face and started to cry. "I will tell my Daddy. I just can't spy as you ask of me, Uncle Loan, but I did my best."

"Very well ... but in the next few weeks, I want you to tell me as much as you can about Tu, and remember, no family business at work, ok?"

Han went silent. They couldn't just arrest and imprison people who believed that the war and the Americans were wrong. She really had no idea which side Tu was on, but she did know that Tu was a good man, and she couldn't put him in prison, even though she knew Tu occasionally helped the Vietcong. She even told Tu that if he wanted to steal documents, she could lend him a helping hand. She was always taught to be good to the good people, and she knew that Tu tried to save people's lives, which was good in her books.

Chapter Thirty-Four

Minh had a stream of unwanted guests. The big news that became common knowledge was that Minh was to become president, which unsettled everyone, because they all suspected that he would throw out all the people working under Thieu. In the hope that the people currently under Thieu wouldn't lose their jobs under the new regime, Minh received constant visitors. No one knew he was considering having a small government consisting of up to six people. Today, he was expecting a visit from Ann, and she was bringing along her son-in-law Tu. Minh ordered a servant to change the flowers and prepare coffee for his guests, and reminded them that his guests used French coffee and not Vietnamese. It was a welcome change to have guests this week who were not merely looking to improve their employment prospects.

Tu thought that Minh might be tempted to hand over the South to the North completely if he was offered a position of power in the new administration. If that was the case, Tu would be able to return home sooner than expected because the war would soon be over.

"Hello, Brother Minh," said Ann, as she and Tu got out of the car.

"Hello, sister, I am pleased to see you; do come in," welcomed the General. "How are you, my son Tu?"

Tu could tell that Minh was genuinely pleased to see them. Ann entered the living room and Mrs Minh greeted her and Tu and then left the room. Ann was here on business and therefore Mrs Minh did not need to be present at the meeting.

"I was listening to the radio in my car. The air force has been given orders to drop napalm bombs along the Ho Chi Minh Trail again," Ann said.

"I hope the campaign will end soon," said Minh.

"I'm very worried," Ann continued.

"It's too late. The whole of Vietnam knows. What has happened cannot be concealed."

"Brother Thieu told me that the White House knows nothing about this."

"When did you meet Thieu, Ann?"

"Last Friday."

The previous Friday, Thieu had invited Ann to attend a reception in Henry Kissinger's honour. Thieu had been happy to see her and told her how stressful it was being in his position, and as president, he thought he had everything; and yet he now felt that he had nothing. Everything he had done since entering the Presidential Palace amounted to a big, fat zero. He had been in power for eight years and America was no longer listening to him. They had pushed him to sign the agreement in Paris, and then they had cut off any financial support. Henry Kissinger, on his diplomatic visit to Vietnam, returned to America unexpectedly after Thieu refused to co-operate with a bombing campaign of Cambodia. Kissinger was furious with his decision and left Vietnam immediately afterwards - not attending the party Thieu had organised for him. This month, Minh wanted him to agree to leave the areas of Danang, Hue and Nha Trang if the North Vietnamese entered South Vietnam, and Thieu could not understand why. Ann told Thieu that he should not worry, and that this was only a small storm in the political hurricane. Thieu looked totally helpless that day.

"Thieu was very worried," Ann said, "about the test spraying of toxic chemicals in Central Vietnam. He was surprised to hear that the White House only knew that the American army had tried to use Agent Orange in Vietnam through an article by the reporter John Pilger."

"Many things are kept secret about the activities of the Americans in Vietnam. I don't see anything strange. This was the decision of the American army and strictly supported by Thieu. Anyway, I don't believe that the White House knew nothing."

Ann smiled, "Brother Minh, why do you want Brother Thieu to agree to leave the areas of Danang, Hue and Nha Trang for the Vietcong? Our country has spent huge amounts of money over the years to keep the communists out of that very area."

"May I ask why that bothers you, my dear young sister?"

"It bothers me because I am afraid we will lose! Brother Minh, do you think letting our troops leave is good idea? It just looks as though you are inviting the North to come here."

"Ann, my little sister, you seem to be accusing me?" Minh asked.

"Brother Minh, don't misunderstand me. I just don't think that's good for our country."

"It is time for Thieu to retire; he did his best for our country and he is a good man," Minh gave a straight answer to Ann's question. "Thieu is not strong enough to rule the country anymore. If the Americans left and the whole world is against the war, then why do more troops need to die?"

Minh still remembered that there was a history between Ann and Thieu, so he did not want to tell her too much, even though he was asking for her financial support.

"Would you like a cup of tea?" Minh finally asked.

Ann opened her handbag to remove a big white parcel.

"This is a small present from me to support your future work. Next week, I will give more. The shipment of weapons has arrived and will be directly escorted by Charles."

Ann had to stop herself from asking Minh why all the containers of weapons were sent to the Minh forest in the Vietcong area, rather than to the Southern army. She knew this because the lorries had a special certificate from Minh, "Passed", and had not been stopped at any Southern army check point.

"Thank you, sister!" Minh said. "My family have prepared a simple meal for us in the garden and I would like it very much if you were to stay and have lunch with us. My family will also be very pleased to dine with you two," Minh told Ann, in very old, traditional Vietnamese.

Four weeks later, at the office, Han lingered at Tu's desk to talk with him.

"You're right, Brother Tu! I should not have fallen in love with a married man. I was seduced by his power," Han said to Tu, but her eyes kept looking at his table and came to rest on the document case, which Tu had just removed from the safe.

"Did he travel with you to Da Lat and Cam Ranh?" Tu asked.

Tu had seen that she had noticed what was on his desk and started to worry, because it was not his name on the case. It belonged to Vinh, and it should have been sent to the boss, who would decide whether to put twenty people in the prison or to just send them to Con Dao Islands, which would mean that they would never have the chance to return home again. The information that he was told through the secret letter box was that these twenty people were very important to the Vietcong, more so than the police thought or knew. He had to do something quite drastic.

Han threw her handbag on top of the documents and started to chatter away. "General Phu intends to convert Cam Ranh into a 'gate of death', which Vietcong cannot pass through. You know, Cam Ranh has a superb terrain as defence. It is so terribly hot there with impenetrable mountains, that even a rat could not hide, let alone the Northern Army."

"But Colonel Binh has no experience about the Strategic Zone II." Tu spoke in an ironic voice.

"Don't dismiss him! He and General Phu have agreed on many important plans. More runways, including diversionary ones, have been built."

"General Phu commands a few hundred mediocre troops. How can he set up so many strategies and plans?" Tu asked.

"You idiot! Seven thousand old troops and 15,000 new reinforcements ... Since McNamara's visit, Zone II has become the most important area of the strategy for our military defence, dear Brother Tu."

"Vice President Huong will pay a visit there next month; though I cannot see why. I cannot see the value of Cam Ranh," Tu said.

"Really? You know, maybe I'm wrong, but you always seem to have a bad opinion of the military generals."

Tu gave no reply. Han did not stand on the same side as him. Thieu and Huong were enemies and compared with generals of North Vietnam. Someday, the generals whom Han was admiring would become the prisoners of the victorious army – his comrades. Thus, as a matter of course, Tu paid no respect to them. However, if Han kept having intimate relationships with these officers, she may find out other military secrets and pass them on to him.

Finally, he uttered, "My wife is organising an early Christmas party. If you are not busy, you are more than welcome to join us."

"I would be honoured to be your guest," Han gratefully accepted the invitation.

Han brought presents to Rose Villa and she paid no attention to any of the military officers. Instead, she sat with Vinh during the feast and they were chatting to each other for quite a while.

The day after the party, Tu was suffering from a hangover and phoned the office to ask for the day off.

"Hi Han," Tu said. "Could you tell Vinh that I am ill and will not be coming in today, please."

"I will," Han replied.

"Don't tell the others. I don't want them to make a fuss. And would you mind bringing around the papers I was working on, I need to check something?"

"I will," Han promised.

Tu had no authorisation to take the documents he had requested home, but as Han was connected to Loan, he knew that she would be able to take them without being questioned.

In the afternoon, Han and Vinh visited Tu at home. They were in the sitting room when the servants brought tea, and an orange juice for Han. Nicole was tired, but she came to the sitting room to greet their guests. She was slightly jealous when she saw Tu's pretty colleague wearing a rather short miniskirt, but the jealously soon disappeared when Han and Vinh announced that they were getting married. Nicole and her husband warmly congratulated them. "You must come to ours for dinner, so we can cook you a congratulatory feast."

Nicole called Mr Lam to prepare some champagne.

"Congratulations, you are joining the society of fools!" Tu said, as he lowered his voice so that Nicole could not hear.

After the guests had gone, Tu urgently needed to exchange information. There were fifty families in Saigon who had been recently discovered as Vietcong and were in imminent danger. However, Tu couldn't understand why the documents were even sent to the department; luckily, Tu had intercepted it.

Chapter Thirty-Five

On Sunday morning, Tu and his wife were having breakfast in bed. Nicole was quite comfortable and was enjoying a hot cup of coffee in peace when her husband tried to give her an unwanted kiss.

"What is our plan for today?" Tu asked, as he put on a dressing gown realising that Nicole fancied a cup of coffee more than him.

"I don't know. We could go out, or I could do some shopping?"

Nicole stopped talking at the loud knock at door from Mr Lam, "Nicole, you have someone waiting on the phone for you."

"Who is it?" Tu asked.

"Mr Jackson," Mr Lam answered.

"Uncle Lam, I told you that I don't want to talk to him any more!" Nicole snapped, getting angry with him.

"I have already told him that," Mr Lam replied, "but he said it's very important. He said that he has been posted to Khe Sanh next week."

The name Khe Sanh made Nicole jump up. "Please tell Harry to wait," she told Mr Lam. "I will be with him in a moment."

Her mind was spinning; the area surrounding Khe Sanh had been on the news every day that week. The fighting was so fierce there that many thousands of Vietnamese and American troops were dying every week. The helicopters were said to be constantly ferrying American corpses from there day and night. Why did Harry have to go there of all places?

Nicole put on a robe and hurried downstairs. She picked up the receiver and Harry lowered his voice, "I want to meet you. Can you find it in your heart to meet me?"

"When are you going to Khe Sanh?" asked Nicole.

"Next Tuesday. I have no choice. I am a soldier, Nicole. But I would like to meet and say goodbye to you before I leave."

"Perhaps that might be a good idea after all, Harry," Nicole murmured.
"Shall I come to your house?"

"No, I will pick you up from your place at lunchtime."

Nicole ended the conversation by hanging up, not wanting to be overheard. After the conversation with Harry, Nicole ran to the garage and she ordered Mr Nam to get her Cadillac ready.

"I need the car in one hour," she said.

Nicole then went upstairs to get changed. Tu called to his wife from the bathroom, "I could take our sons to Mother Tam's alone if you like? You could have a day of rest today or go shopping?"

"Yes, that's a good idea," Nicole answered and as an afterthought, added, "I may be late back."

Stepping into the bathroom, she used a towel to wipe some shaving suds from her husband's face.

Nicole picked Harry up at the main entrance of Building 63. She gave up the driver's seat to Harry.

"I thought that I would never see you again," Harry said, whilst fastening his seatbelt.

"I don't want you go to Khe Sanh."

"I know," Harry replied.

"Shall we visit my mother's plantation?"

Harry turned the car towards the outskirts of Saigon and asked Nicole: "I've been told I must go because Lieutenant Colonel Collin of the 7th Fleet wants me to assist some of the best Vietnamese pilots in the world. They're testing a new rocket there."

"Do you mean that the American army wants to turn Vietnam into a testing ground for their new weapons?" Nicole asked.

"I'm sorry. I don't agree with it, but I'm left with no choice in the matter."

Harry turned on the indicators before turning on to the highway towards the plantation.

At nine o'clock that evening, Tu returned to Rose Villa. He questioned Mr Nam when he saw that his wife's car was not in the garage. Mr Nam, embarrassed, tried to protect his beloved mistress by lying to his master. He told Tu that she had to go to the plantation to discuss some important issues with Mr Mac, which angered Tu. He scolded Mr Nam for some time, because he had dared to let Nicole drive to the plantation alone. He told the servants to take his children to their rooms, and then he proceeded to phone the plantation.

Mr Mac answered the call in person.

"May I talk to my wife?" he asked, in French.

"Please wait one moment," Mr Mac said softly, placing the receiver on the table.

He went upstairs to Nicole's bedroom and through the half-closed door, he saw Nicole and Harry entwined in each other's arms fast asleep. Not wanting to disturb them, he told Tu that Nicole was asleep after her long journey.

"Ok, let her sleep," Tu said.

Then he requested him to tell his wife to stay there until Mr Nam came to collect her rather than drive home alone.

The news of Harry Jackson's death arrived at Rose Villa one rainy afternoon, one week after he had travelled to Khe Sanh. The weather matched the news; there was a typhoon with dark skies, strong winds and torrential rain.

When Tu came home from the general office, Nicole welcomed him with swollen eyes.

"I know," Tu said slowly. "Mr Nam rang me this afternoon."

"I want to hold a memorial service for him," Nicole sobbed violently.

The handkerchief in her hand was damp and Tu led Nicole into the sitting room. After helping her to sit down, he consoled her, "Darling ... women sometimes, in their moments of grief ... I mean, you're too emotional now ... I mean, you're upset. I'm very sorry; however, he's not part of our family," Tu bumbled on, not knowing that Harry was more than just his wife's best friend.

"His helicopter was shot down and there wasn't anything left of him to send back to America. He is supposed to be an MIA. Brother Tu, I want to do something for him ..."

"The army will take care of him," Tu snapped, finally losing his patience.

"No; Harry has a lot of friends in Saigon. So I want a memorial service where his friends can pay their last respects and perhaps I will even build him a small tomb."

Shocked by what he had just heard Nicole say, Tu responded, "If you really want to build his tomb, there are some places still available next to Little Lien. But he cannot meet Little Lien, because she is in heaven. If he did get to met Little Lien, he would understand that she didn't belong there and that he should not have come here."

"Harry knew that he should not be here, too!" Nicole shouted. "He wished that the entire United States of America had never intervened in Vietnam."

"I really don't think it would be right that you want to do anything for him! Do you realise what you've just said?"

"Are you jealous?"

Tu looked at his wife and he immediately stepped out of the room rather than get involved in an argument when she was in this mood.

Nicole picked up the diary; the only thing of Harry Jackson she had left. A friend of Harry's had brought it round to Nicole after his death, knowing how close they had been. Nicole was so tired and upset that she did not know what was right from wrong. She wandered into the library and placed the diary on the bookcase beside One Thousand and One Arabian Nights. She decided to consult Mr Lam about the funeral.

Harry's funeral was organised for 8 o'clock on a Tuesday morning at the cathedral. Charles and Ann wore black suits but Nicole wore a white skirt and white top, which was the traditional colour of mourning in Vietnam. Her hair was tightened with a white band which was skilfully tailored as a hair ribbon. Only she understood how much she was mourning for Harry, because in Vietnam, a couple could be considered as being husband and wife by just sleeping together, which was why she wore mourning clothes for him that day.

Tu got angry when they returned home from the ceremony. This was the first time Nicole had ever seen him angry.

"You bring shame on the nation!" he shouted.

"You mean I bring shame on you!" Nicole retorted, in a gentle but stubborn voice.

"Yes! He was our enemy!"

"Our enemy? Or only your enemy?" she responded petulantly.

Tu was silent. Finally, he looked up: "You're right. He was only my enemy."

"I'm sorry!" Nicole whispered, immediately regretting her outburst.

"It's not your fault. He is only my enemy and I now realise that you have never stood with me in all our years together. It is not my heart that you hold a candle for."

Nicole opened her eyes wide; she was shocked. Tu was actually jealous. Nicole's grief for Harry opened Tu's eyes. He thought carefully about all that had happened and he knew that he had no reason to be jealous, but he still stayed at his office for a week, until he finally relented and went back to Rose Villa one night, quite by accident, in a drunken stupor.

That night, he staggered home after drinking several spirits in the bar. He felt more than a little merry and the streets seemed to be dancing in front of him. Even the street lights were hazy and moving around him. He made a mental note to tell his police friends to punish them for standing in disarray. They even dared to bump into a police officer like him! Even though the street lights tried to block Tu, by constantly jumping in front of him, he eventually arrived at the heavy, iron gates of Rose Villa. He burst out laughing as he wondered why they needed such a big and heavy gate. Perhaps it was second only to the green-painted bullet-proof gate of the American Embassy. But the embassy had good reason to fear. Tu was afraid of nobody. The Americans and their puppets would be driven away. The communists and Vietcong were his comrades. They gave him such strength in his heart that he feared nothing! He wanted to open the gate wide to welcome his comrades' return. My God, please forgive me, he prayed, this is my prayer: I pray for the safety of my comrades and family in the American raids and bombings. I pray to be assigned with more tasks by my superiors. If the war can be stopped by prayer, I will pray until I die. But I do not believe in God; God must obviously have a sense of humour, and this war is no joke. Tu finished his prayer and then opened the small side gate to gain entry. Rose Villa was quiet. The windows of the sitting room, kitchen and first floor were still bright. In the garden, Nicole was sitting in the swing by the pebble-covered path in front of a row of black and silent trees. All lights were suddenly extinguished.

"Oh, not another blackout," Tu told himself, as he sobered up a little.

"Welcome home, Tu. These are times of war, that is why everything is so dark," Nicole quietly greeted Tu but inside she was raging.

"Can you see all the stars?" Tu asked, looking up at the sky. "Tonight, the sky is so black, without a single cloud, all the stars will shine brightly," Tu told his wife, and he then asked if she wanted to go inside.

"I think I might stay here for some fresh air," Nicole replied.

"When I was a child, I used to lie on the grassy banks in the rice fields, absorbing the fragrance of the countryside and admiring the wonder of the sky. I used to wonder where all the stars came from!"

Nicole remained silent. What he said about the sky being full of stars meant nothing compared to her grief. High up in the sky, she wondered which star belonged to her Harry.

Tu dragged himself into the dining room. He was so thirsty he opened the refrigerator and removed a bottle of water. He gulped down a bottle, but his thirst seemed relentless. Mrs Lam asked him if he wanted something to eat, but the word "eat" nauseated him and he bent down to be sick.

Ann stood in the dark library and watched Tu. Seeing him drunk, she left the library and went upstairs. She wanted to keep Charles in his room as his disappointment in Tu certainly didn't need exacerbating. She wanted to prevent him from seeing their problems as he already had enough worries on his mind.

Nicole sat motionless on the swing. She had known Harry's love for just a few months and she still could not get over the shock of his death. Everybody thought that she was a lucky girl. She had many things; more than the ordinary person could ever hope for. However, she had fallen in love with Harry and she would have traded everything, except her children, to be able to love Harry a little longer. She wanted him to be there with her, to dry her tears. She wanted to be loved for just one more day. She would tell him how much she loved him. She was ready to go to hell for him and didn't fear it any longer. She did not even fear hell. Heaven would be very boring without love. Why did she not recognise earlier that Harry had loved her all along? He always encouraged her to help the nuns, and to take care of the wounded people in the hospitals. Now, she felt silly, because she was afraid of blood, bandages and limbless bodies. When he read books for children at the orphanages, he used to ask her if she liked the stories. He encouraged her go to discotheques and she missed their chance encounter, in the park or at the shops … wherever she went. She missed his kisses and wondered why the Vietnamese people didn't kiss regularly. She couldn't understand why they viewed kissing as a strange habit for only alien creatures to indulge in. Harry loved her, he loved Saigon, he loved the Vietnamese culture, and he loved the word Vietnam. Why oh why did someone have to go and kill him?

"My Lady," Mr Nam's voice broke the silence.

Nicole wiped away her tears: "Yes, Mr Nam?"

"The fog is thick now. Please go in for some rest; otherwise you may catch a cold." He paused and in a low, kind voice, asked, "Do you miss Mr Jackson?"

"Yes, I do," Nicole burst out sobbing again.

"I miss him, too," Mr Nam said in an attempt to console her.

"I don't know what to do with myself, Mr Nam."

"You should take comfort in the fact that Mr Jackson loved you." Mr Nam said, "his soul will always be near you. So, don't be so sad, my dear Nicole."

"Mr Nam, please give me some advice," Nicole said, softly.

"My dear Nicole, we men want our women to stand firm and strong and weather the storms of life, so when men cannot be there to help, we know that they can survive."

"Harry came and took my heart away. And God is punishing me."

"Don't blame yourself, everything happens for a reason," Mr Nam consoled her. With that he left, just as silently as he had arrived.

Sitting alone, Nicole felt yet more self-pity. Nobody could relieve her sadness. Nobody understood her. Why did her love have to be so short-lived? She would have revealed to Harry all of her secrets had she known otherwise. She would have paid no attention to gossip. She would have felt no shame about their relationship. She would have held his hand and they would have taken strolls in the streets of Saigon. She would have talked freely with him at the hospitals. She would have kissed him in the street, or whenever he had wanted. She would not have avoided him … ever! Who is lucky in love? Maybe nobody. Everybody is short of love. Is her sorrow now that of her husband? She now hated Tu for the way he treated her. Why did he not love her? Why did he push her into such a situation? Exhausted and with swollen eyes, Nicole dragged herself inside.

Upstairs, Ann pulled the blinds to cover all the windows. High above, the sky was full of stars, but the sky of Nicole, her daughter, was full of sorrow.

"What's the matter with you?" Charles asked when he saw Ann standing by the window.

"I really don't know," Ann answered, "but I am worried."

"You always did like to worry," Charles commented.

"I sometimes think I've become overcautious in my old age," Ann said, sitting down in the chair covered with ivory silk, next to her husband. She looked around the room; the room she had seen a thousand times before. Charles' private room was the largest one in the villa. It was furnished with a soft sofa, a tea table and a small television set in the corner. His large bed was always covered with brocade of the same ivory colour as the lining of the curtains.

"I think you are right," said Charles. "We are getting older and slowing down. I'm considering selling the plantation, but I know I would feel guilty, if I did."

It was understandable that Charles was reluctant to sell. His grandfather had worked hard on it for thirty years, converting the wild lands full of snakes and mosquitoes into immense gardens of rubber trees. His parents had spent their whole life in this alien, hostile colony to continue that vision. His mother used to take him for a stroll along the paths covered with rotten leaves on humid and hot mornings. She sowed in her young child the seeds of love for soil and rubber trees.

"Darling, do you think the North will win?"

"I do, especially if President Thieu's government were no longer supported by the Americans. Where would they get the money to maintain such a huge army? And with them being so dependent on steel and petrol, it would be impossible to achieve."

Ann was silent.

Charles continued, "If possible, you should tell General Minh that he should not pursue the president's chair. However, it would be interesting to see the two of them manoeuvre for supremacy. The Americans want to exploit General Minh and his neutral viewpoint. But in my opinion, America and your generals are about to be defeated."

"Why are you dismissing my country so lightly?" Ann snapped, becoming touchy.

"I'm not, but President Thieu should understand his real strength more than anyone. The Paris talks are a blow to the South. If Mr Huong or General Minh take the presidency, then President Thieu will bear no blame for the pitiful collapse of his Republic, and even the use of destructive chemicals. It would be a good time for him to be absolved from his crimes."

"Are you sure that the Republic will be defeated?"

"The truth is sometimes terrifying to face; but face it we must, my darling."

Ann shook her head. "I'm so bored with war. Sometimes, I wish that the North will win to bring a swift end to the suffering."

Ann's last comment did not surprise Charles in the least, she was without doubt very intelligent, but it was difficult to predict what she would say or do next. Initially, during the war of independence against the French, she had wanted the French to win. Then she wanted the South and the Americans to win; now she had changed her mind yet again, and wanted the North to win.

"General Minh himself wanted to negotiate with North Vietnam to establish a coalition government. If that happened, our country would have all the advantages of socialism and capitalism. It is a very interesting concept, isn't it?"

"Sometimes, I don't understand you," said Charles.

"Without this civil war, the Americans would not have come here, and our daughter would not be consumed with grief," Ann said frankly.

"Our daughter will be fine. She's made of stern stuff and takes after you," Charles replied.

Chapter Thirty-Six

The last of the Americans had cut their losses and started to leave Saigon, which had been plagued with insecurities and uncertainty for some time now. Many families had sold their houses and shops to seek shelter in other countries. As a result, there were few foreigners in the city and very few American soldiers were seen in the streets. The only remaining Americans were the abandoned children of irresponsible American soldiers. The relatives of the victims, who had been killed by the American army, hated these children, because their fathers had been the killers who had slaughtered their people, burnt their houses and brutally tortured the living.

Charles wanted his family to leave Saigon as soon as possible. Everyone agreed, but Tu had been at work when the decision was made and it was uncertain as to whether he would go with them. The whole family gathered in the sitting room, waiting for Tu to arrive home.

"Good evening, Father, Mother," Tu said, when he finally arrived home. He then turned to his wife and with a happy voice said, "Look at me, Nicole," he said pointing to his lapels.

"You have been promoted to the rank of a Captain!" Nicole cheered.

Charles, however, did not smile.

"Congratulations, my son!" Ann said, as she hugged him.

"Thank you very much, Mother," said Tu, then turning to his wife, he asked, "Darling, how is Little Hieu today? Let me hold him for a little while."

"Tu?" Charles spoke in French, "Your mother and I need to discuss something important with you."

"What's that?" Tu replied, looking up.

He was busy playing with Hieu when Mr Lam entered to tell everyone that dinner was to be served.

When the whole family were gathered in the dining room, Mrs Lam brought in onion soup for the first course.

"Your father and I have put the plantation up for sale and the whole family will be returning to France," Ann said.

Tu looked up at his father-in-law, then to his wife.

Nicole asked, "Why are you so surprised? You've always told me that you wanted to go to France."

"It appears that the North will win, and I am concerned that day is not very far off, my son," Ann continued.

Ann was oblivious to the fact that Tu had been praying for that day for some time now. How meaningful that day of victory would be for him. He had been working through many dark years to do everything he could to bring about victory for the North. It would mean that he could return home to the North and to see his wife Nhat and the son he'd never met. He would never go to France, and was unsure how he could explain that to this family. He loved his two sons very much, and he loved Ann and everyone at the villa, too. Nicole gave herself to him whole-heartedly, and gave him all the love a man could want, but he knew that this could not continue forever. For now though, he still needed to continue with his charade.

"I will come with you to France. I'd like that very much," he lied.

Charles looked at Tu. "Everything is not as simple as that. There is a big possibility that we may lose it all; the villa, the money and the plantation. I am a good businessman, but I can't foresee the outcome of the war and there maybe nothing that I can do to save what we have here. We will probably lose everything, son."

Surprised to hear her husband talk with Tu so openly for the very first time, Ann said, "I don't think the South will lose so quickly. Hopefully, we will have enough time to sell everything and send the money back to France." Then she turned to Tu, "My dear Tu, what are your thoughts on the matter?"

"I agree that the situation here is very chaotic, but who would want to buy our houses and plantation now… and what about our employees; how would they live after we left? Even if the North wins, we are still Vietnamese! The North just wants the war to end and to reunify the country. I understand your concerns now that the Americans have left, but we have changed governments many times before. Mother, Father, you have spent your whole lives here, so you may find France as it used to be. I still believe things will be ok here."

Tu stopped in his tracks, suddenly wondering whether this small family would be ok after all. The Vietnamese nation is altruistic and compassionate, he thought. They just didn't want to live under foreign power without freedom. The Americans had already been defeated, so there was no longer any reason for Vietnam to be hostile towards them.

"Your father and I are old," Ann said. "It wouldn't matter if we were killed, but we are worried about you two and the children. You are a police officer, Tu. What will happen if you become a prisoner of war?" Ann's voice was choked with emotion.

Ann had stopped talking, because Mrs Lam had entered the dining room to clear the dining table and serve coffee. Tu made a decision to reveal his real position to his family and wife, but when he looked at them, he was unable to say anything. Why was it so difficult to tell them the truth?

"Tu, are you going to stay here?" Ann asked.

"Mother, let Nicole decide. I will live wherever she wants to live." answered Tu.

"Father, Mother nobody is sure about the situation," said Nicole. She understood that Tu wanted to stay, so she decided to stand by him. "The North and the South are equal in troop strength. In comparing weapons, South Vietnam has more advanced technology. The air force and the navy now rank first or second in the world. We have hundreds of warships and thousands of aircraft. There is no reason why my husband should become a deserter, just because the American army withdraws from Vietnam." After a short pause, Nicole continued, "We have shared our successes, and I think I should stand by my husband. Father, Mother, I will stay with Tu in Saigon. If my husband is captured and imprisoned, I will take care of him."

"My darling husband," Ann asked Charles, "you frequently read French newspapers. What is your opinion?"

"I think North Vietnam will win. I just hope that we have time to move back to France," Charles finished.

One day, Vinh, Rang, Mai and Tu were having a discussion about relationships at work and were wondering why Tu was so loyal to his wife.

"That's because," Tu explained, "since meeting Nicole and getting married, I have felt completely satisfied. My wife is my companion and so I don't feel the need to look for another woman."

"Do you think your love is perfect?" Rang asked. "Surely, you don't expect me to believe that you actually love your wife! Declare your lovers immediately!"

"Maybe I have been too modest with my praise," Tu said, referring to Nhat who was taking care of his old parents at the time. She worked hard from dawn to dusk in the field, because everyone had to do the work of three in order to support the cause. "I love my wife and I am so grateful to her that I could never thank her enough for all she has done."

"Grateful?" Rang ridiculed him.

"You will never understand," Tu answered.

"We're just joking. Actually, I did want to ask you something. When we have been out to search and arrest the Vietcong, you never take your gun. Why is that? It makes me wonder if you can actually use one."

"You, don't move!" Tu said, and he quickly took out his two guns and shot straight at the wall just over the top of Rang's head!

Everyone went quiet. Han was standing outside the door. She looked up the ceiling and said: "If you two want to kill each other, then go to the stadium. No one here has any free time to clean up your mess! Anyway, you are not a bad shot, Brother Tu."

"Not bad at all," Vinh said, and they all continued working and talking about the war as though nothing had happened. However, Rang was so angry; he wanted to shoot both Vinh and Tu dead on the spot. They were rich and thought that life was so cheap that they could joke about it.

Later, Tu apologised to Rang for making him look like an idiot in front of everyone in the office. Then, speaking to Vinh, he said, "I am worried that we are going to lose. I overheard somebody say that we would let the North rule our country rather than stand up and fight. If that happens, then we need to save people's lives; even the Vietcong prisoners."

"I agree," said Mai, who was also a spy for the North. "We have had two changes of government this year alone, so if our country is ruled by the North, then I believe that we will still be ok."

Everyone in the office was worrying about the same thing. A ceasefire had been put into effect and the Americans had lowered the flag from their embassy for the final time, to signify their withdrawal. From the Northern front, there was news of defeat after defeat. The North Vietnamese regular army was marching southwards and was being joined by ever more Vietcong supporters. The severe bombings had failed to break the campaign of the North, and the Trail looked busier than ever. Thieu went on the TV to announce his imminent resignation.

Everybody apart from Tu left early that day, so Tu used this time to read yet more documents. The most important documents Tu searched for contained information about South Vietnamese agents, who would continue to work under the Northern rule if the South fell. Tu discovered that all of these agents had been placed in jobs such as doctors, teachers and factory workers. The South was still fighting, but maybe it would be wiser for them to prepare for defeat. Tu would soon be able to see his dream: peace, reunification and his return home.

After work, Tu sent documents via his secret letter box. He sought information about his parents and family – detailed information or even just a photo of his wife. For more than eight years now, he had not seen Nhat and the realisation that he couldn't remember what she looked like disturbed him. In his mind, he could picture her as a 10-year-old girl running in the fields, but the vision of her face now was unclear. He only remembered that she had long hair. As to why he could remember her in childhood better than when she had become his wife, would remain a mystery. Anyway, the war was almost at an end now and he would soon be home, but it was too early to celebrate as, behind him, from the window of the apartment opposite, Rang was watching.

Rang put a call through to General Co. He told his superior in an excited voice all about the documents and evidence that he had collected over the past few months to prove that Tu was a spy.

"This is very serious," General Co said over the phone.

"It's unbelievable," said Rang. "He comes from a trusted and wealthy family and is the son-in-law of our president's old flame, so I thought it would be better to report this to you rather than my Chief, Tay."

General Co interrupted Rang's chattering. "This is an important issue, which cannot wait until tomorrow. Tonight, at 9 p.m., you will meet me at the New York Restaurant in Vo Tanh Road," he said, terminating the call.

Rang was nervous about his meeting with General Co and made a special effort to look smart and professional. He wore a black suit with a red tie and placed a red handkerchief in his top pocket. Deep down, he was hoping that this information would lead to a promotion. Eventually, too anxious to wait in his quiet, single apartment any longer, he drove to the house of the high-class call girl named My La, who he had known for the past two years. My La's apartment was located in quite a wealthy area; however, the inside of the apartment was in chaos. The apartment was littered with clothes, handbags, cosmetics and shoes. On the table, there were mouldy loaves of bread and the ashtrays were brimming. The table was so dirty that Rang dared not drop his keys on it. The bedroom appeared to be marginally cleaner and the bed was covered with a smooth sheet. However, the floor was a jumble, with clean and dirty clothing scattered everywhere. Suitcases, old footwear and the uniforms of American troops were strewn in utter confusion. The four walls were full of photos of Marilyn Monroe and on the bedside cabinet was the framed portrait of a chubby child.

"My, you are looking smart today. Are you going anywhere special?" My La asked when Rang entered her disorderly bedroom. She was lying naked on the bed and watching a pornographic film. She was about 20 years old, and had a Bridget Bardot hairstyle. When Rang gave no reply, she continued, "Well then, why did you put on a suit on such a hot night as this?"

"I have a meeting with my superior later. Everything seems to be going in my favour recently," answered Rang.

"You need only pay me 5,000 dong today," said My La.

"My God, that's one-sixth of my monthly salary!"

"You men must work hard to support your lovers, darling!" My La joked.

"Free love is sometimes too expensive!" he said, taking his wallet out of his pocket.

Rang gave My La the money, which she counted and placed in the bedside cabinet drawer before proceeding to strip Rang.

Seeing her throw his jacket on to her dirty clothes, Rang winced; "Oh, mind my suit!"

"Don't worry, sweetie, I will iron it again if you ask nicely," My La told him.

An hour later, Rang sat up after kissing My La's yellow-dyed, rumpled hair. My La turned over to lie on her stomach.

"Do you have any marijuana?" she asked.

Rather than answer, Rang slowly ran his finger up her spine.

"Your skin is so soft," he said.

Rang wanted to stay with her a little while longer, but time was running short, so he got up to get dressed. He hurriedly put on his suit and tie, but the red handkerchief had disappeared.

"Oh no, where is my red handkerchief?"

"You'll find it," My La answered.

Rummaging through the heap of dirty clothes on the floor, Rang still could not find it. It had to be somewhere. How strange! The handkerchief had disappeared all by itself.

"My darling, please get up and help me to find it!"

"Take my red knickers!" said My La, ever the tease. She was also lazy.

"This is no time to joke. I told you that I must meet my superior."

"Your superior will never recognise that they are really a pair of knickers. I have a question. Do men like to see female knickers or handkerchiefs?"

"Ok, I give in. Take them off and give them to me, now!"

"You could always help me, my darling," My La said, turning over and arching her back.

Rang pulled them down and pushed them into his pocket. My La, still playful, wiggled her body as suggestively as she could manage. Rang gave her a quick kiss on her nipple to save face, but even My La could see that his mind was elsewhere. He let himself out and hurried to the car. He had just enough time to drive to the restaurant.

After parking up near the restaurant, Rang switched off the engine, but, before he got out, a smartly clad young man put his head in through the window and said, in very friendly voice, "Hello, brother! Have you got a lighter?"

Without thinking or looking up, Rang was about to put his hand into his pocket when the young man pressed a pistol against his chest and pulled the trigger.

A hot feeling spread from Rang's chest through to his back. He had no time to realise what was happening. He wondered why he'd been shot. Only General Co knew he was coming here …

After the curfew, military police discovered Rang's car. The investigators were sent to the scene to search for clues, but the only thing they found was a pair of red knickers in the breast pocket.

The next morning, Vinh arrived at the general office with a worried expression on his face.

"Tu, please find the files from 160X to 190X for me."

"Why? Those files are Rang's responsibility."

"Exactly, and that is the problem. Rang was assassinated last night."

"My God! Are you joking?"

"I can't believe it, either. I don't know how to break it to his mother yet."

Tu opened the cabinet, drew out a file, and passed it to Vinh, who opened it. After inspecting it, he gave a long whistle, "It's true. The file has been doctored already."

Tu's heart sank and his palms started to sweat.

Vinh continued, "For a long time now, our boss has suspected that there was a traitor among us. Last night, Rang was killed and Loan phoned and ordered me to check the files that Rang dealt with. This is the evidence. Clearly, Rang has been passing information to the Vietcong. Heaven only knows how many documents he has sold to them. The call girl who was last seen with him was arrested earlier this morning. If you want to question her, I will give you a note giving you permission to do so."

Tu, now relaxing a little, said that he would question her immediately. Changing the subject, he said, "Yesterday, Han and my wife went shopping for the whole day. They certainly have lots of ideas on how to spend your money. Incidentally, your wife-to-be has saved you 300 US dollars, because she bought a new dress for half price."

Hearing about his Han made him happy and eased his tension.

"You know, my parents-in-law have been preparing a huge wedding ceremony; nearly one thousand guests have been invited."

"Good God!" Tu said, "I had better to be nice to my wife – I certainly wouldn't want to marry again!"

Before he went to question the call girl, Tu read her statement and burst out laughing. As he entered the interview room, Tu found her to be very sexy. She wore a black dress, which suited her complexion, and black high-heeled shoes. White sunglasses hid her tired eyes and on the armchair was a black leather raincoat.

"I believe that you were the last person to see Rang alive," Tu said, as he began the interview.

Chapter Thirty-Seven

Tu took three days off work to assist with Vinh and Han's marriage. He was tired with his duties as both a policeman and a spy, so having the few days off was a welcome break. The wedding was to take place in Han's village in the west of South Vietnam, so it would give him a chance to learn more about the country. It was to be a traditional Vietnamese wedding and no expense was spared. Han's father, Mr Tran Do, was an influential man, who possessed 20,000 acres of land and a beautiful house. The house was set in the middle of a field surrounded by a stone fence, with columns, pan-tiled roof and wide entrance doors. Tu discovered that Do was a close friend of Loan's father, and it confirmed his suspicions of how Han managed to get such an important job in police headquarters in the first place.

Do had two wives. Mrs Linh Do, his first wife, was beautiful, decent and courteous and Mrs Ngo Do, the second wife, was polite and subservient, with a clear view of class distinction. Linh showed a friendly and open attitude to all relatives of her husband's family and those of her own. However, she kept herself at a distance from her husband. She did not live with her husband, but with her father, Mr Van, who had even more land and was noted for living a life of luxury.

All the land owned by Do had been given as the marriage dowry from his first father-in-law Van, who, at the age of seventy, was still very healthy. He was especially fond of traditional singing and every week, he invited a dozen singers and musicians to sing throughout the night. They mainly sang songs full of pathos, about love tragedies and doomed love triangles. These performers had a great passion for music and could perform up to six hours at a time without a break. The old house was filled with singing and musical sounds that carried over the immense, deserted rice fields.

Han had lived with her mother, Linh, and her grandfather as a child and on special occasions or important events, Linh would come to visit her husband's house.

Linh's bedroom was kept exactly as it was the day she had left her husband to return to her father's house. That day, Van had ordered his butler and the servants to take his daughter back home in a very solemn procession that could only be held by a rich man such as himself.

For the first time in ten years, Linh entered her old bedroom again to prepare a dowry for her daughter, in traditional Vietnamese and Buddhist tradition. The bedroom would also be the new couple's room after their wedding ceremony. Some maids tried to advise Han against doing so, because of unlucky associations, but she was adamant that they brought her belongings there. Her father's love for her mother had never diminished. Her stepmother Ngo was not a happy woman. She had never been respected by the servants and Han pitied her; she was like a ghost in her own house. Her father had followed traditional customs and married her after they had slept together.

After tea, Tu was standing on the wooden decking in the garden when Han came to him: "Do you think I'm stupid?" Han asked Tu, while lighting a cigarette. Tu threw Han a puzzled look. "I have played the part of a whore because I wanted to challenge my father," Han continued, wanting Tu to know more about her past history. "In his opinion, what is old is good. All traditional rules, customs and practices are better than the more modern ones. I don't think he should have two wives. My mother suffered a great humiliation, especially at his second wedding, when my father took a younger and beautiful bride home to Kowtow in front of the ancestral altar. My mother embraced me and cried when the firecrackers had resounded at the gate. I didn't understand at the time; all I knew was that I was happy to be wearing a white dress and a garland like a princess. My mother understands his needs and she knows it is not her fault, but she is a lonely woman, who no longer loves my father although she is still married to him. In this country, no decent woman gets married more than once; even if her first husband dies. I hate the old customs. I have adopted the hippy style with enthusiasm because I feel this need to rebel. I have worn miniskirts, used cosmetics, styled my hair and smoked cigarettes to anger my father. For me, rebellion means freedom."

"I see that your father still loves your mother very much."

"Loves and fears," Han replied. "My father only loves her because he can't have her back. Even though my father is a ladies' man, he is now a very lonely man," Han continued. "All the female singers in the band that will sing at my wedding have fallen in love with him at sometime or other."

"He is very dynamic in his outlook," Tu commented.

"He is rich and generous and has granted the singing troupe several acres of land as a bonus."

"Wow!" Captain Tu exclaimed, raising his eyebrows.

"Knowing my step-mother's respect for property, my mother ordered my father to compensate her with a further acre of land."

"Really?" Tu asked

"My mother knows that my father is fond of traditional singing. Therefore, she has frequently invited some troupes to perform here. These troupes respect my mother and even if they were very busy or staying somewhere very far way, they always tried to accommodate her if my mother invited them."

"Why have they stopped so early today?" Tu asked, nodding his head towards the singer and performers who were packing up their instruments.

"My father is not well," Han said. "He is usually very healthy, but for the past few days he has felt tired."

"He has been organising a superb wedding ceremony for you! What would you expect?"

Ngo approached Tu and Han and in her softest voice, she said, "I have prepared some snacks for you, my darling. Vinh has gone out hunting with the local villagers in the rice field." And with that she left as quietly as she had arrived.

Han's eyes followed her as she left and then she continued, "I don't understand how my stepmother has been able to suffer the life she has been offered here for so many years."

"Because she was taught to follow the old customs," Tu answered. "A concubine is always at a disadvantage."

"Do you want to have two wives, just like my father?" Han asked, half-jokingly.

Tu refrained from answering her question and Han smiled, "You men are all the same, but I know Vinh. He only has eyes for me and I am the happiest girl in the world. Given everything I have done in the past, I cannot believe that I have found such a good man as Vinh, who loves me with all of his heart."

"You are a good person, Han. Nobody can go through life without making some mistakes. So we should always endeavour not to complicate matters by constantly harking back to something that is best long forgotten."

Han said nothing. She was feeling better after talking to Tu. She had seen Tu exchange secret documents several times, but she had chosen not to report him to their superiors. A good colleague should not denounce his or her friend's mistakes. Anyway, Tu was a close friend of Vinh, the man she loved so much.

Tu left the crowded and busy house to take a stroll in the field. It was nine o'clock in the evening and some of the farmers were still working. They were pouring rice into bags and carrying them to the warehouse in the middle of the field, which was situated on stilts to protect it from flooding. Tu wondered what Nhat would be doing now, and whether she was still busy cutting rice at night. Perhaps she was building a stack of straw, or feeding the buffalo. Women in the North worked so hard. The huge gap between the North and the South was very apparent.

That night, the sky was full of stars and Tu reverted back to when he was young and started counting the stars. When he was eighteen, he used to count stars and dreamed of the wonderful things he would do and see in his future life. Now that he was approaching forty, counting stars no longer filled him with dreams and hopes for the future. The dreams of youth had been replaced with the hard realities of life, and army boot camps rather than university studies. Sunday lunches became small portions of dry, cold rice. The comfortable mattress was replaced by a wet bog; the fluffy pillow with a hard tree root, and the silk sheet by your canvas poncho by the side of the Ho Chi Minh Trail. The lithe body of a footballer was replaced by a cadaver racked by malaria. The comfortable office job turned into the lonely vigil of the sniper waiting for the opportunity to kill a fellow Vietnamese citizen. The pleasure of weekend motorbike trips became thousand-mile forced marches. The journey to the South was full of hardships. There was no hot or fresh food, and no clean water; only muddy sewerage poisoned by Agent Orange. The pleasant evenings at home with friends were no more, and were replaced with night-guard duty, looking for a silent assassin. The soft affection of the family dog became the rats at night chewing on toes whilst one was sleeping. The pleasant chirping of cicadas was replaced by the whine of artillery shells. His youth had been stolen from him and battles in which all of his comrades had been killed brought about a harsh reality. Thinking of his comrades made him smile with pride. Those days were so vivid and glorious.

Tu was unable to sleep that night and when he did finally drift off for about an hour, he was woken up very early by Vinh.

"Wake up, my best man. My father-in-law will kill me if I arrive late to marry his daughter," Vinh said, as he removed their suits from the wardrobe.

On her wedding day, Han wore a red wedding dress and Vinh looked extremely happy next to his bride. In the main house, all the interior wooden partitions had been removed to form a spacious hall for the vast numbers of tables and chairs and in the courtyard, a big tent had been erected for yet more tables and chairs. Firecrackers were burnt whenever guests arrived and the music was loud as the bride and groom welcomed their guests with traditional wedding food, betel nut and Vietnamese tea. All the guests were exquisitely attired in their traditional costumes. The men were dressed in white suits or traditional long tunics and turbans, while the women looked splendid in their colourful *Ao Dai*s. The bridesmaids wore long red dresses and printed in gold ink was the Chinese character for "happiness". In contrast, there were some guests from Saigon who were dressed in rather more modern attire. The men had long hair, flared trousers and tailcoats, and the women were wearing miniskirts, low-collared delicate tops and curly hair following the American hippy-style of 1970.

Tu was able to find out more about Vinh's family. His father was a retired civil servant with the Ministry of Industry. His mother Mi was a junior secondary school teacher and although she had retired, she spent time helping her neighbours' children to study. They were kind-hearted and loved by everyone, and Vinh was just like them.

Vinh had to drink many glasses of wine, given to him by the guests, which was an old Vietnamese custom. He spent a long time visiting each table, so by the time he reached Tu's table, he was slightly the worse for wear.

In his drunken confusion, Vinh asked Tu "Is this my wedding day or yours, Tu?"

Tu, who was also extremely drunk, couldn't remember who was getting married either. "Neither of us. I don't know who the stupid man is."

Chapter Thirty-Eight

Han completely changed character after marrying Vinh. Her husband's good virtues had a big impact on her. She became elegant and never wore a miniskirt again. Loan had been on the verge of sacking her; however, now that Han had married his favourite officer, he was no longer in a position to do so.

Han fell pregnant one month after the marriage and both Han and Vinh were ecstatically happy. Vinh could not express how proud he was of his pretty wife. Tu remembered Vinh telling him once that intelligence was unimportant for women, because it did not require an IQ of 160 to become a perfect wife. Only a madman would want a wife who was more intelligent than himself.

With the assistance of her husband, Han's qualifications and experience considerably improved and she began to be praised more often. However, Han's expanding experience and knowledge worried Tu. He was conscious that the files he replaced had to be kept safe from her prying eyes. Fortunately for him, Han asked for early maternity leave and, after her departure, the Section of Secret Archives became disorderly again, owing to the fact that she phoned Vinh every day. Everybody, including Vinh, got tired of her prolonged calls, and Vinh's impatience increased in proportion with Han's calls.

"My goddess has changed," he winced. "She used to be sweet and gentle before we got married. Now, she is much too talkative! Tu, why have you not gone mad after so many years of marriage?" he cringed.

Tu smiled to himself. If Vinh ever found out that he already had two wives, he would die of shock.

Later that day, Tu went home and noticed Charles looking tired and thoughtful. Charles invited Tu into the library for a chat. He was beginning to show signs of age and his hair had turned white over the recent months. This was the first time he had shared his problems with Tu. His plantation was to be deserted currency had devalued to a dangerous level. All banks were blockaded, because the government was transferring foreign currencies and gold abroad. His money had become increasingly worthless, due to massive inflation and corrupt business partners taking advantage of the chaos.

Charles also admitted that he had lived here for nearly half a century, and that he had grown to love the country, the people and landscape of Saigon. There were many things he would miss if they left.

"We have lost everything. The North is on its way to Saigon. Many streets in Saigon are empty, because almost all the foreigners have left," he said.

"Father, you should go back to France, because … " Tu paused. He refrained from telling Charles that because he was French, he might not be safe if the North came to Saigon, and that he knew they were already on the way … "Father, don't worry," Tu consoled Charles, "one day, under the new government, I will rebuild and reclaim all that you have lost."

"I don't doubt that for one moment. Your Mother doesn't want to leave; she wants to remain here, to be with you all, and … her homeland."

"Father, Mother is Vietnamese; we don't need to worry too much about her. You must go to France first. If the situation gets worse, I will take Mother and Nicole to Paris at once."

"Will you?"

"I promise, trust me," Tu said, overcome with emotion.

"I trust you, Tu. I will leave next week, by boat, to get everything ready over there, for when you all arrive in Paris. Our new home will look just like Rose Villa. I will miss your mother and all of you. I hope I am doing the right thing," Charles added.

After a moment, he gave Tu his first ever hug, and then left the room.

Mr Mac was in the hall and he quietly followed his master. Tu worried about Mr Mac; a man with black skin could be easily mistaken by the Vietcong as an American and be killed. Tu was unsure as to how he could save him, though he would try to help him as best he could. Mr Mac was a good man, and a clever manager; more than that, he was a man with a kind heart. Both Charles and Ann and Mr Mac belonged to South

Vietnam; a country that would disappear from the world map soon, which meant they would face great danger.

On the day Charles left Rose Villa, there was much sadness as they said their farewells.

Insomnia plagued Tu and for some unknown reason, he kept thinking about his childhood. In those days, everyone except the elderly and the very young went to the front. The men joined the army, while the women joined the voluntary youth force. Out of school, Tu and his friends worked in the fields and during those fruitful years, potato and chilli were experimentally planted in Tan Yen. The fields of chilli grew in the sunlight and with one pull, you could obtain many potatoes from a plant. To this day Tu still remembered how delicious boiled new potatoes served with herbs and coriander was. At night, Tu did his homework while his grandmother read the prayer book and she would look up to the sky to see if the American war planes were coming, and if they were, they would take cover in the shelter

Tu had grown up with Nhat, during those wartime years. In his village, people used to pull up young rice sprouts or water their fields under the moonlit nights. For reasons unknown, farmers always performed those two jobs at night. Tu's family were farmers and they owned only a few infertile fields, so his wife in the North could do nothing except farm work.

In 1965, when he left to fight for his country, his hometown still had no electricity, putting them at a great disadvantage. However, since he had been living in Saigon, he had heard many good reports about North Vietnam. According to reports made by Hanoi Radio, everything had changed. If that was true, his family in the North would have a better life and he could worry less about them. His village might even have access to electricity, or a new hospital, or a new school, and then there would be more jobs for the young people. The farm may even have tractors, or an engine to reduce the manual work. His wife may have time to relax and not have to work hard any more. He certainly hoped so.

Tu woke up earlier than usual. It was Monday morning and the first and ground floors were quiet. Mrs Lam and Ms Thi were already in the kitchen. Mrs Lam was boiling water to make tea and coffee and Ms Thi was preparing instant noodle soup. In the oven, a batch of croissants were baking and turning golden brown, which was one of the Philippes' favourite breakfasts.

"Good morning! It's a lovely day, isn't it?" Mr Lam politely greeted him, whilst cleaning the cabinet and bookshelves. He only felt satisfied when everything was polished to a high gloss.

Tu looked at the view outside the window through the part-opened curtains and wondered why there were no police raids or gunfire. Last night was the first time he had relaxed enough to sleep.

Mr Lam, however, would never be able to relax in Saigon; the President had gone to Taiwan, so Vice President Huong was in power. Events were taking place so quickly that Mr Lam could not make sense of what was happening to his country. Rather than worry, he tried to lead a normal life. The government was unstable and had changed presidents twice in the past week. And Tu, his younger master, was feeling happy because Saigon was losing. He would sing all day when he was at home. God bless him, his voice was quite awful … Mr Philippe was already on the boat on his way to France, so no contact could be made with him, and Ann was very upset. Mr Lam understood what Ann was going through, but he did not know what to do to help her. Besides, it wasn't just Ann that was worried, it was everyone. In the past ten years, South Vietnam had changed government many times, and Vietnam had been at war for far too long. We'll just have to see what happens; everybody has to die one day, don't they, Mr Lam thought.

Tu went to the kitchen to make a cup of tea. He liked his tea strong and found it difficult to find good quality tea in South Vietnam. Tu made a glass of fresh orange juice and, taking some biscuits, he put everything on a tray to take to Nicole in the bedroom. The sun had risen and the early morning dew adorned the rose bushes and ornamental trees.

Seeing Tu, Mr Lam rushed out to help him carry the tray of food. "Please let me take the tray upstairs for you. You must ask me for help next time."

"Thanks, Uncle Lam, but I will take it in for Nicole this time," Tu answered.

After placing the glass of orange juice on the heart-shaped bedside table, Tu entered the bathroom and saw that Nicole had already hung his police uniform on a chair for him.

"I'm going to visit the Children's Hospital with some nuns this morning," Nicole announced through the open bathroom door. She sat leaning against a heap of pillows. "When you are working on the night shift, I miss the orange juice that you sometimes bring for me in the morning,"

Tu smiled at his wife, "Would you like to go somewhere for breakfast before I go to work, or would you prefer to have breakfast with the children at home?"

"I think I will have breakfast at home, so you will have to breakfast alone today, darling!" Then she continued, "Can you try to contact Father, please. Mother is worried, because we haven't heard anything from him."

"I'll try, but if the weather continues like it is, it may take Father more than six weeks to reach the seaport."

He kissed his wife goodbye and then went to the garage, climbed in his car and drove away. Sitting in his car to wait for the traffic lights to change, Tu started to worry for his father-in-law. The North used to refer to the 1700 kilometres of Vietnam's coastline as the "Ho Chi Minh Sea Trail", and if fighting ships ventured into the China Sea, and even into the international sea area, they would be sure to attack the South Vietnamese ships. Charles' ship had sailed under the American flag and occasionally alternating to the French flag, which could increase the risk of being attacked.

Listening to the car radio, Tu heard that the Northern armies were approaching Saigon and the government was talking about surrendering, so more lives would be spared. In order to get to the office a bit quicker, Tu switched on his police siren. As he entered his office, it was as he thought. Everyone in the office looked worried. Vinh informed Tu that most of them had quit their jobs to flee abroad. Surrounded by chaos, Tu asked Vinh if they could do something for all the war prisoners they held. Vinh agreed with Tu, so that day one hundred people in their custody were freed. Their bosses had ordered them to destroy all the documents for their own safety, in case the North came into Saigon, but Tu tried to save as many documents as he could, as they may well be needed in the future. At lunchtime, Ann phoned Tu and said that Phu was paying her a visit. She was worried that something awful was about to happen in South Vietnam.

Chapter Thirty-Nine

Phu arrived at Saigon by helicopter. When he reached Rose Villa, he looked tired and different to the last time Ann had seen him. Ann had made tea and prepared some French cakes, which she knew Phu liked. Twenty years ago, when Phu had been a mere captain in the French Paratroops Regiment 6 at the siege of Dien Bien Phu, he and the French soldiers used to have French cakes with nearly every meal. Ann had often made these cakes and sent them to Cam Ranh as a present. Out of respect and her feelings for him, Phu visited her today to inform her of his next move. He had just met Mr Smith in the American Embassy to ask permission for his eldest son to settle in America. Immediately after this visit, he would fly back to Cam Ranh and he would remain there to the very last. His view was that a defeated general should die on the battlefield.

Phu enthusiastically drank the tea and ate the cakes as a mark of respect and to conceal his fears from her. It would probably be the very last time Phu would see Ann and Saigon. At that very moment, a big battle was taking place and, within a week, both sides would lose many thousands of soldiers. Before leaving for Taiwan, Thieu had signed a secret agreement to order the Southern army not to keep the Da Nang province and Hue city if the North reached the Midlands.

"Has your husband gone to France?" he asked.

"He left for France last week," Ann answered, "and I have not heard anything from him."

"Why are you still here?" Phu questioned.

"Tu has to report into the office every day. He and my daughter have decided not to run. With you and many of our friends still here, how could I possibly leave?" she replied sadly.

"You should go to France, I mean immediately," Phu uttered in a sorrowful voice. "You could come back when things have settled, sister."

Phu tried to minimise the seriousness of the situation in order to comfort Ann. The last thing he wanted was to terrify her. No one knew better than he that the corrupt regime which he served in, was about to collapse. Everyone knew that Minh would overthrow Huong and takeover the presidency. Huong had already said that he would be happy to pass the presidency to Minh if Minh had ideas on how to save the country.

"Brother Thieu has already gone abroad, and I doubt very much that he will return."

"Has he?" asked Ann.

"The president and General Vien went to Cam Ranh to see me before they left. They stressed that the Strategic Zone II would be abandoned in case of an attack by the North. You should go to France at once; that's the only advice I can give you at this time. Unfortunately, Ann, I believe that defeat will happen soon, and I feel no shame in being defeated by General Giap. Even De Castries was knocked out by him; not forgetting President Thieu, General Minh, General Vien and myself! All the most talented French and American generals have been, or will be, defeated by General Giap, never mind by a paltry general such as myself!"

"How did you manage to reach Saigon in such difficult times?" Ann asked, trying desperately not to show her emotion.

"I came by helicopter and left it in the stadium."

Mr Lam brought in a glass of water for Ann and for the first time, he realised just how worried and scared Ann was. His growing concern caused him to ring Tu at work, as he was now the master of the house.

When Phu had left, Ann burst into tears and sobbed; she felt as though the sky was caving in. Why hadn't Thieu told her anything? Was he embarrassed? Or did he not know what was happening? For whatever reason, Thieu had forgotten her; the man she had known for 30 years. How could their love, of which she had always been proud, end like this? He went to Taiwan without telling anyone; he ran away just like a rat; he left his country, his hometown, his family, and now Ann. He only cared for himself. Ann's father always used to say that Thieu was a selfish man. Her father was right; older people have more experience of judging others.

After receiving the phone call from Mr Lam, Tu came home to find chaos at the villa and Ann looking distraught. He eventually restored calm and he gave Ann and Mr Lam a North Vietnamese flag and Uncle Ho's photo. If the North came to Saigon while Tu was at work, he knew that the flag and the photo would protect them.

"Where did you get these from?" Ann asked.

"These are from our Vietcong arrests. They have been held in storage in our offices, as well as many other items," Tu admitted truthfully.

It was the spring of 1975 and most of the people in Saigon either lived in great fear or great exhilaration. Those who felt happy tried to conceal it, for it still would have been dangerous to show such glee. Overall, Saigon felt like a time bomb about to explode. News of defeats were sent to the city from Pleiku, Buon Ma Thuot and Khe Sanh.

Mother Tam accumulated food, as she had done during the Tet Offensive. There were many revolutionaries that had managed to enter the city to prepare for the final advance on Saigon. The more advances the North made, the more the Southern army became nervous, and in most places, cities and towns were abandoned. The enemy was invincible, and what had started as an orderly retreat became a full-blown defeat. It was clear that the end of the war was near.

To welcome and in preparation for the victorious Northern army arriving in Saigon, Mrs Tam amongst others had been making North Vietnamese flags and sticky rice cakes that were favoured by the Northerners. It was also decided that the Vietcong and the Bietdong were to hold a great banquet and mix the traditional dishes of the North with those of the South. Mrs Tam was so happy that peace was finally approaching. Tears flowed down her cheeks, for the loved ones that she had lost and who would never get to see that glorious day.

Mrs Tam had not known Tu's first wife in the North, but she knew through Tu that Nhat was a heroine of the war. She loved both of Tu's wives and had no idea how Tu was going to deal with his family situation after the victory, especially as Tu still kept his mission secret from Nicole. Mrs Tam silently burnt some incense sticks on the altar as she prayed for the end of the war, for love and unity among the Vietnamese people, and national reunification. She even prayed to Buddha and gods to bless the country. When the war ended, and after all the bombs and weapons had been buried and armoured vehicles and tanks had been dismantled to produce agricultural machines, she made a decision to quit trading and take a trip to the North, to see her adopted children. After many years of protecting and feeding liberation troops, she had dozens of adopted children from the North. She had lost count of how many wounded soldiers she had taken care of.

Mrs Tam remembered taking care of a wounded commando named Hai. When she asked him why he had been injured, he answered, "Mum, those American soldiers were so young, like my younger brothers at home, that I could not kill them. As a result I became injured myself."

She understood his predicament and readily agreed with him. Actually, she hated nobody. The death of any man, Vietnamese or American, would hurt their mothers, wives and children so much and, of course, Mother Tam. One thing for certain was that they would all hurt so very much at the loss of their loved ones. She was certain that the more lives that were saved, the better it was. Mother Tam never repeated Hai's story to anyone because she did not want to see Hai punished for his "aiding and abetting the enemy". His superiors would certainly not agree with his motives, even though she herself fully understood them.

Like many people in Thieu's government, Ann was beside herself with worry. The South were about to lose and the Americans who had initially offered their support, had deserted South Vietnam. She stood to lose everything, and there was a strong possibility that she would have to go to prison because she was in the owning class. That class had been excluded since 1945 under the Minh government's orders. Having killed many thousands of rich people between 1945 and 1946, the government apologised and the killing ceased. The government still had no laws in place to protect these classes and the government would never be sympathetic towards the affluent.

Ann truly believed that Tu would try to help her, but she was not sure if the government was as benevolent as Tu had said they were. As Tu got involved with the preparations to welcome the army to Saigon, Ann and Nicole were both overcome with worry. He had never seen Ann behave like this before. It was out of character for her to leave the running of the plantation to Mr Mac and without checking on their shipping company. It was highly unusual.

Nicole saw even more strange and unusual behaviour by her husband. He still went to work early and came home late. But after his normal working hours, instead of going home, he stayed away from home for hours on end. On occasion, Nicole found strange pistols and machine guns in their cars. She couldn't understand why Tu kept so many guns. This question constantly haunted her and she told Mr Lam that she sometimes felt as though her husband had switched alliances and now supported the Vietcong. Mr Lam told her that Tu believed in the saying "What goes around comes around". He believed sympathy towards others would come back in the form of good fortune for their children. Mr Lam, however, had had his suspicions a long while ago that Tu had been helping the North, and warned him about Nicole's doubts and anxieties.

Thinking she would be able to help Tu, Ann organised one of her gatherings. Whilst chatting to one of Charles' acquaintances, she found out that he was the owner of a stock and gold trading agency in Hong Kong. His company bought 24-carat gold from Dubai and reprocessed it into 9-carat or 14-carat, which would be resold at the price of 18-carat gold in Saigon. With his 40 years' experience in the stock market, he had a good insight into the falling value of all the companies in South Vietnam; especially small-scale rubber enterprises. However, he felt that to sell holdings and accumulate money was the best solution, because currency was devaluing at such an alarming rate. He felt sorry for Ann. It was too late for her, for Ann's cash had already stagnated in the banks and in the open sea, and her cargo vessels had been sunk by mines.

Many banks temporarily put a stop on international transactions, and the banking system had been neutralised, which made it impossible withdraw any money. The South Vietnamese aeroplanes were transporting gold and other valuables out of Vietnam day and night. Although General Co assured her that if anything happened, he would assist Ann and her family to travel by helicopter to Thailand, Ann told Tu that she was considering moving to France, but Tu promised her that he would be able to take care of the family himself. In the evenings, to obtain some normality, the Philippes still gathered around the dining table for dinner. However, on the other side of the big gate of Rose Villa, Saigon was under a black cloud, because the crisis point was drawing ever nearer.

News of defeats from the Strategic Zone I reached Saigon, making everyone anxious, and the whole city became disorderly under the impending attack. It was later followed by yet another piece of shocking news. Hue and Da Nang, the cities in the Midlands, just 700 miles from Saigon, had been liberated! (Or occupied, according to which side a person was supporting.)

The government and the staff of South Vietnam were in complete chaos. While Thieu was in power he made many decisions, which made it easier for the North to enter Saigon, and Minh helped even more by ordering the withdrawal of the armies from the Tactic Zone II, known as the "Gate of Death". Without aid and support from the Pentagon, North Vietnam easily gained control.

Chapter Forty

Then one day something amazing happened. Suddenly, there was no bombing, no gunshots and no cries of pain or grief. There were no arrests and no more flares. Saigon was quite cool for the time of year and the Saigon River was tinged with green and full of boats laden with fruit and fish. There were even some larger ships anchored, motionless, outside the port. At five in the morning, the church bell resounded to signal early prayers. After the session, Tu took his children for a stroll along the Saigon River. Of course, the riverbanks were still areas of high security, because all the army's major camps were located there.

Little Trung and Little Hieu were very excited to be going out with their father. They were dressed smartly, with sailor-styled uniforms and berets. Tu held Little Hieu in one arm and led Little Trung with the other. Little Trung's small fingers were sticky from a sweet which had been given to him from a passer-by and Little Hieu was mesmerised by the ships and boats.

"Daddy, look at that big ship!"

"Very beautiful, son," his father agreed.

"Daddy, look at that bird; it looks like grandma's gun!" Little Trung said.

"Where is it?" asked Tu, as he glanced around, but all he could see were black barrels pointing at him.

Automatically, he picked up Little Trung and ran to the Americans' office nearby. From there Tu phoned the general office to ask Vinh to come and pick them up. Vinh dispatched police officers and a jeep to escort him home. Tu knew that he would not be able to be a normal person, even on Sunday, as long as he was a police officer. He hated it; he hated not being able to take his sons for an innocent walk. The barrels pointed at him surely belonged to the puppet secret agents. The war was nearly over, so why and who wanted to kill him? Or perhaps it was as Tu's boss believed, as in the old Chinese proverb, 'If no rabbits are left, the hunting dog is no longer needed.'

Nicole rushed downstairs when she saw the car pull into the drive and smiled with relief when she saw Tu. "I was so worried," she said embracing him.

"We just went for a walk. Don't worry, darling, we had a great time," Tu replied.

"Mummy!" Little Trung said, in an exited voice. "Somebody chased Daddy. Daddy had to carry me and run away, it was fun!" he said, exaggerating slightly.

"It was nothing; just a game of tag," Tu explained.

"Do you think women are that stupid? Do you think I believe any of your little stories?" Nicole smiled. "You should not take our children for a stroll during these times alone. You know the communists hate the rich. We could be killed at any moment! Anyway, Mr Nam or your work's driver both have plenty of time to play with them or take them somewhere."

"I just wanted to have some time with our children and to live a normal life."

"And be pursued by Vietcong? Darling, being a special policeman, you could be killed. You should take more care."

"I accept! I lose, and whilst we're on the subject you should know that the Vietcong are not as bad as you think, dear," said Tu. Then he turned to the maid Ms Thi, "Please can you take the children for a bath," he instructed.

Nicole waited until Ms Thi had left with the children, and then she continued their conversation. "Mother has gone to the plantation. If you could take two or three days off, then we could follow her."

"For the past few days, I have been very stressed, so perhaps it would be a good idea. It's a long time since we visited our plantation."

"Mother has been meeting with a lawyer. All the houses and plantation will be left to us. I can't think why Father thinks you are good at business and why he has started to trust you."

"All women think their husbands are useless. Are you one of those women?"

"I think you are very talented. But since the Tet Offensive, the city has become a heap of dirty ruins. Even the plantation has been abandoned. You won't be inheriting much now, I'm afraid."

"We will start again," said Tu, with a note of excitement in his voice, but he also felt hurt to hear about their financial predicament. He had wondered many times why the Americans initially came to Vietnam. Why did they burn and destroy everything only to put Vietnam into the Stone Age, rather than helping to build the country like a good, big brother to Vietnam, as the South Vietnamese people called them? Nobody wanted to help with the reconstruction, nobody wanted to do business, and all the short-sighted people have run to foreign countries.

Nicole interrupted her husband's. America will help us to rebuild the country after eradicating all the Vietcong."

"How innocent you are!" Tu said to Nicole. "The enemy has always wanted to kill us. They have never wanted us to recover and stand up!"

"You mean America is our enemy?"

"For me, speaking honestly, a good government is the best solution for Vietnam at this moment in order to end the civil war. War has made our country poor. Nobody likes war. Do you think it's good for Vietnamese to kill Vietnamese?"

"I am ignorant when it comes to politics, but I agree with you, it's very illogical for Vietnamese people to kill each other."

Nicole stopped chatting with her husband when Mr Lam stepped into the sitting room to tell them that dinner was ready.

"Mother is not at home today. Shall we ask Mr Lam and the others to join us for dinner?" Tu asked.

Nicole shook her head, "He has never had dinner with our family. Not because our parents are arrogant, it's just because he would feel uncomfortable. In his view, we must observe family traditions and rules; otherwise, other servants will also behave with familiarity. Then ..."

"What's the matter, my love?"

"I wish to take care of him when he gets old. But now, even I cannot ensure the safety of our own family, let alone Mr Lam."

"You mustn't be so worried," Tu said, as he held his wife's hand. "Believe me, I will take care of you and our family."

Nicole said nothing now but Tu could read what she was thinking. For many years the South's special police officers had been continually hunted by Vietcong. Every day, some police officer or other was executed by Vietcong for their crimes against the people and the country. Tu was a police officer who was working within the Section of Secret Archives, and they had arrested many Vietcong and put them in prison, so Tu could understand Nicole's worry as to why she didn't believe him when he said that their family would be safe.

"I will write a letter to the American President to tell him to stop the war…" Nicole said petulantly, her eyes glistening with tears.

Tu wandered over to give her a hug; he liked her innocence and wanted to protect her, but he knew it was time to make her understand, "He believes in the war, my darling. You should know that in America militarists are very powerful, and sometimes, the president listens to them rather than the people."

"I think the American president will support a peaceful solution above everything else."

"He could never do that."

"How do you know?" she asked.

"Many affairs are considered secret in Washington. But here, in Saigon, nothing is secret."

"Darling," Nicole tried to stop her husband, "let's not talk about it any more. We should have dinner now, so I'll bring the children down."

As Tu opened the blinds, he saw it was already dark and he could see the tanks and armoured vehicles running noisily back and forth along the streets. He sighed, he had lived in Saigon for nine years now and every day, he grew to love this city even more. The people in Saigon were sincere and friendly, and everyone was fighting for the same cause … peace. Saigon citizens had loved and protected him from both sides of the conflict, and Saigon had given him its best. In return, he wanted the best for post-war Saigon.

After dinner, Tu asked Ms Thi to put the children to bed.

"I want Mummy to read me a bedtime story. I like to hear about the rabbit and the tortoise running a race," said Little Trung.

"Not your Mummy, my Mum," Little Hieu sulked, because his parents were so preoccupied with their conversation, that they seemed to forget him sitting at the other end of the table. He had never wanted to share his Mum with his big brother.

"You are a young man now, darling! You can read by yourself. Let's try it for just one night, son," Tu said to Little Trung.

"I want my Mummy," Little Hieu answered in an obstinate manner.

That was the miracle of the boy. Whenever he asked, Nicole would always pick him up instantly and she would kiss him on his sweet-smelling cheeks.

"If you don't want to go to bed yet, you don't have to," she said to him.

She turned and headed for the library to choose a book to read for her son. There, in the bookcase, between the old classic books, next to Vincent Van Gogh and One Thousand and One Arabian Nights, was Harry's diary. She had read it many times before, so she took the diary out again and, just as every other time she had touched the book, her eyes filled with tears.

Tu followed his wife through to the library and saw Nicole with a book in her hand. Tu knew it was the diary, as he had come across it before and read it himself, but he said nothing. For many years after, Tu blamed himself for what had happened. He had not been fair to Nicole. Throughout the many years that he had played the part of Agent 022, he held only Nhat in his heart – the wife who was looking after his elderly parents – his real wife. For Tu, Nicole had every right to take a boyfriend. He hardly spent any time with her and most of the time during the past eight years he had lived solely for the mission. Any free time he did have was spent having a drink or a business dinner with colleagues. He even kept his own flat in the office so he didn't have to drive back to Rose Villa after a night out. Nicole must surely be upset with the way in which he treated her, and Tu was surprised that she did not have other boyfriends. She must have loved Harry so much. However, at least he managed to accomplish one good thing; he turned a blind eye to it and refuted the servants' suggestions that they were having an affair, by telling them how nice their relationship was, and that Harry was merely Nicole's best friend. Tu had felt jealous when he read the diary, but he understood how much love Harry had for Nicole. If wasn't for the fact that he had a family in the North, Tu knew that he would have been free to love her, and love her he would have done. Tu gazed at her as she removed the Van Gogh book from the shelf.

"I am looking for a book to read to Little Hieu ..."

"A book with Van Gogh's paintings? That's good idea, he could look at the pictures," Tu said, as he left the library.

Nicole's love for Tu had returned and that night, she decided to burn all her mementoes of Harry Jackson, so she sat down to read his diary for the last time:

"Date...

Here, there are no flowers, just white sand and blinding sunlight. I sit in the combat shelter looking out at the plateau where there are no people; just trees in the far distance that look like black dots between the sandbags. I wish that one of those suspicious black dots over there were you; you coming to visit me, not the Vietcong ...

The night sky is dark but full of stars. Now and then, a flare is released, tearing apart the black sky. Your face, when we met for the first time, becomes bright in my mind ..."

"Date ...

My dear Nicole, sometimes I ask myself why I must stay here; in an alien land with only coffee and banana trees. The immense plateau is completely deserted and any villages are so very far away. The people in the village are strangers to me. Sometimes, I think I will go mad when I continually ask myself why I am here. Eventually, I think of how I met and loved you, and that soothes my inner soul. I thank God for bringing you to me. I feel at peace because I know now and always that you love me. It must be very difficult for you to overcome the many challenges to love me, my darling ..."

"Date...

Today, my platoon met a young boy. He was thin and small. His face looked older than his age. He had no shirt, and it reminded me of when you were taking care of the orphans. I missed you. If you visited Khe Sanh, you would understand how poor the local children are. The local people are so poor that, in my view, it is a scene you cannot ever begin to even imagine. But the landscape is picturesque! When admiring the natural views in Khe Sanh, I dream that I am on a summer's vacation in a remote country, beside an empty beach. Darling Nicole, I am very sad, because that feeling passed so quickly and is now replaced by anxiety. The Vietcong must be somewhere nearby. The situation becomes so tense that I must think of you every second of every minute to balance out my nerves. I often imagine when I can sit next to you on the flight to America some day. My parents would welcome us at the airport. Their happiness will be doubled, because I have returned home with you.

"Date ...
Today, four helicopters transporting provisions to the battlefield were shot at. My helicopter escaped, luckily. I know that is because you are praying for me ..."

The tears in her eyes made the words written by Harry illegible, and she cried harder when she finally burned the diary with the candle on the table. She remembered how many times she had prayed and cried when Harry had been posted to Khe Sanh, but God hadn't listened to her prayers. At that moment, Nicole felt empty and wanted to die. Seeing the diary turning into ashes, Nicole tried hard not to drop to the floor on her knees.

Chapter Forty-One

It was the end of April 1975 and Saigon was yet again in chaos. Evacuees flowed into the city from all directions. Weapons and military vehicles lay abandoned in useless disorder on the streets. Long currents of evacuees jostled against each other looking anxious, and children were exhausted, thirsty and hungry. The road to Saigon Airport was particularly busy, with hundreds of people flocking with their luggage, bags and suitcases, big and small, containing all their worldly possessions as they tried to flee the country.

The Saigon harbour was crowded and lines of cold-faced soldiers equipped with modern weapons hardly tried to prevent the stream of people rushing to already jam-packed ships and boats. Hundreds of people clung on to the sides of these ships, and thousands were turned back because there was no more space. But the more fortunate rich and influential people used military aircraft or helicopters in which to escape.

Those whose relatives had joined the Southern army or worked for the government fled in fear of their lives, along with neutral people, because they were merely frightened of the unknown.

At Rose Villa, luggage was packed and the heavy wooden furniture was neatly piled up in a corner of the sitting room and covered in white sheets. The other servants had already left and Ms Thi wiped her tears as she bid farewell to her master and his family. She walked alone with just a small suitcase, a present from Tu and Nicole on her last birthday. The EMI radio was still switched on, so Nicole could hear the latest reports. Nicole was so frightened that she could not think or move. Her hands were shaking as she embraced Little Trung and Little Hieu. Ann now spent most of her time in her bedroom, and Nicole was unaware that her mother lived with a gun in her hand. April the twenty-seventh was a bad day for Ann. She had received terrible news from the plantation. Some looters had entered the main house and removed all the valuables and when they saw Mr Mac there, they had assumed him to be an American and had stabbed him to death. After all the recent bad news, Rose Villa was under the cloud of depression. Ann went downstairs into the big living room and she appeared to look her normal self. She opened a box and took out the Northern flag. It was the box Tu had given her some time ago, when he had explained that one never knew when it might prove useful and save her family. Ann was never under any doubt that Tu was a clever man …

Nicole was scared, as more devastating news arrived. Mr Lam's family had died on the boat during their escape. Tu was at the office and had not been allowed to return home since the Northern armies had entered Saigon. The phone lines had been cut and the last message he relayed to Nicole was that she should not worry for him, because he would be fine. Nicole held on to that last thought. If he was lucky, he might become a prisoner of war. The distance from Rose Villa to police headquarters was not far, but Nicole was too scared to leave the comparative safety of the villa and find Tu.

At noon on April the thirtieth, Minh read out the declaration of the unconditional surrender on the radio.

Outside Rose Villa, the streets had started to become boisterous as people began to join in the celebrations now that the war was finally over! Red flags with a yellow star overshadowed the sky. For the first time in a long time, the Southerners could sing loudly praising President Ho Chi Minh. The melodious and moving sounds of revolutionary songs resounded uninterrupted, as if Ho Chi Minh was a hero of that victorious day.

The formal Southern armies removed their uniforms, so that they would not be shot by the North. They walked past Rose Villa, which angered Nicole, because her husband had still not been able to return home.

That night, more bad news was received at Rose Villa; Phu had been arrested by the Northern army and had committed suicide whilst being detained.

Since there was no news from Tu since he had left for the office and the Northern forces had marched into Saigon, the family assumed the worst. When he did eventually arrive home, he was wearing the military uniform of the Vietnamese Revolutionary Armed Forces, which confused Nicole.

For years now he had been wearing the white Southern police uniform, and yet here he was now dressed in the enemy's olive uniform. It didn't make sense. Tu was happy, because he would no longer have the need to use the name of Tu and he could reclaim his identity. Unfortunately, everything had happened so fast that he had been unable to explain anything to Nicole and his family. Although Tu was ecstatic to see them, Nicole just stood there staring at him.

"My darlings!" he called cheerfully to his wife as soon as he saw them. He had forgotten who he had been during the past nine years, and mistakenly thought of his wife as being on his side, along with everyone else in Saigon. "We have won, we have won!"

"What are you talking about? We have lost."

Nicole stepped back cautiously. The children stopped playing and came to stand close to her. They could sense something was wrong and sought comfort from her. Nicole had been crying with worry for the past two days now because she had no idea if Tu was alive or dead. Now he was back home alive, and it made her so angry; he had not even thought to let her know that he was safe! Was it not important to him that she might have been worried sick?

"Go to your room, children, I have something important to talk to your father about," she coldly ordered Little Trung and Little Hieu.

"May I ask who you are?" she eventually asked, once the children had left the room.

"My darling ..." Tu suddenly felt guilty, ashamed and sad, because he had not told her his deepest secret before.

"My real name is Ngoc Lan."

Nicole stood still; she was looking at a stranger. Ngoc Lan regretted being too excited that the North had won, as his family had no idea about the truth behind the police officer Tu yet.

"Darling, I am sorry for not telling you before. I'm ... a ... a Northern Vietnamese soldier!"

His last words were uttered clearly and proudly.

"Am I still Captain Tu's wife?" Nicole could hardly believe what her husband was saying.

"Aren't you glad?" Ngoc Lan asked. He knew it was a silly question. "At least our family is now safe." Then he told her a little about himself.

"My comrades have taken over police headquarters and because they are in need of more police, I am now a police officer for the new government. Don't worry, my darling! We are safe; our family will be ok."

"Do you think it is safety that I want? It is too late; Mr Mac has already been killed, because his killers thought he was American," Nicole said, starting to cry.

She did not know how to react. Her husband was Vietcong and, for the past nine years, he had kept it a secret from her. This person in front of her was called Ngoc Lan, who had been born in the North, and he had only been living in Saigon a few months prior to meeting her. If he was truly a Vietcong soldier, then why he did not try to save his family first? Nicole had never understood the Vietcong then and she never would now, either.

Ngoc Lan tightly embraced his wife. "I'm sorry," he murmured. "I am so sorry. Where's Mother? Have all the servants left?"

"Uncle Lam is dead, Ms Thi and Linh decided to leave, Nguyet has hidden under the bed and Mother is upstairs."

Nicole burst into tears and this time, she was sobbing even louder. Ngoc Lan looked up and he noticed his mother-in-law standing on the staircase with a gun in her hand.

"Welcome home, Tu," she said, turning to her daughter. "Nicole, your husband is not stupid; he did everything he could to try and save us, and we should be grateful for what he has done. Whoever he is, it makes no difference," she finished, putting the gun on the table.

Ngoc Lan wanted to thank his mother-in-law, but was speechless. Instead, he went over to give his wife a hug and Nicole brightened a little, thankful that her husband was still alive. The last few days had been hell for her, so she proceeded to tell her husband all the terrible news.

"Mr Lam is dead. He tried to escape with his family. His nephew is a helicopter pilot and he was flying to an American ship at sea. The helicopter was too overloaded and it plummeted into the sea. You must have seen the pictures in the papers!"

"I am so sorry, and there are no newspapers, Nicole. I am truly sorry; I should have been here at home with you."

"Ngoc Lan?" she attempted to say his name.

"Yes?"

"Can I call you Tu?"

Chapter Forty-One

"You love that name, don't you?"

Nicole remained silent. After a while, she added, "How about the general office?"

Ngoc Lan sounded unhappy when he spoke next, "I shouldn't tell you about that."

"Do you not think that I can hear and see everything that is going on with my own eyes? This war has deprived me of half of my relatives in one day. What can be worse?"

"In any war, there must be losers ..."

"Do you think I don't know that?"

"I could not believe my eyes when I saw the thousands of special police officers that came to give their name and hand in their weapon. I worked there for years and still don't know how many people worked for the CIA and us. Everyone has been arrested, or will be arrested, for re-education. Vinh included."

"I was fond of him." Nicole was already starting to talk of him in the past tense.

"Vinh saved my life many times. Vinh's friendship provided good cover for me. You, Vinh, Mum Tam, Father, Mother, all of you have ensured my safety," Ngoc Lan said. "It broke my heart when I saw Vinh being arrested and knowing that I could not help him. He was a good man, and I felt helpless."

That night, Nicole went to bed without dinner. She went to the children's room to sleep. Ngoc Lan felt less happy than he had been throughout the previous two days. He hoped Nicole would feel better and that time would heal the rift between them.

By August 1975, things had changed dramatically. Nicole had even started to do the housework herself, as she no longer had servants. Ann had donated her cars to the new government, and the rubber plantation and the big farmhouse, including all the properties which had been rented by the workers, had gone to the new council. From being ladies of the house, they had stepped into a strange life. Even the lives of Little Trung and Little Hieu changed now that there were no servants and as there were no boarding schools open, they were sent to a nursery. Ngoc Lan felt sad as he watched his sons go to school without a servant for the first time; they looked so small and vulnerable.

Although the fighting and bombing stopped, Vietnam faced other problems. There was a shortage of money, and because there was no longer any aid from America, food and inflation had risen four hundred per cent, which made it impossible to buy food and goods. Life in general had changed dramatically for the people of the South. All the formal Southern officers, and people connected with the South government and the Americans, were sent to prisons in the North, to live and learn about communism, and there wasn't a single person that could say life in the prisons was good. Families of those people had no jobs, and if they did have a job, it would have been taken away and given to the people who had come from the North. This, of course, led to the people's dissatisfaction and the situation remained quite tense as social order and security had not yet been stabilised.

A number of Saigon people were dissidents. They would chant the slogan: "Do and enjoy life together, everybody as equals, no more different classes". Nicole was not blind; she could see many opportunists looking out for themselves. For some people, it was said that being poor was a nice way to live, as they were able to enter Saigon and take over the expensive houses which belonged to the old government and the rich, who had fled overseas when Saigon fell. For other people, the poor people from the South still lived on the streets and the distribution regime turned honest people into thieves. For Nicole, however, she felt as though she and her family had lost all their freedom. Police officers could enter her house at any time and for no apparent reason. Occasionally, people from the plantation would visit her, and the police, as well as neighbours, would come to the house and demand the reason for their visit and ask whether they were from the losing side visiting relatives in the South. People looked at Nicole just as if she was the reason why they were so hungry. Nicole wanted to leave her beloved Vietnam and she wondered how many other Saigon people had the same idea.

During that time, Ngoc Lan did nothing to help Nicole, as he was busy at work all day, helping many other people. After the war, there were so many things that the police needed to sort out that Ngoc Lan simply forgot about his family. To Nicole, he was not Tu; he was Ngoc Lan, and therefore a stranger in her eyes. Nicole tried to be strong for Ann and her children, and she even still smiled every night when Ngoc

Lan came home, which made him come to the conclusion that his family were happy and content.

"Darling, I agree with you that the new government must deal with many issues," Ngoc Lan explained. "And, the government will, of course, gradually stabilise life, develop the economy and ensure social order and security. But the important thing is that there is no longer an invader in our country. Independence, freedom, national unity, great support from the progressive people in the world and the honourable sacrifice of the whole nation will be decisive factors. Firm foundations, as well as strategic motive, will force the people to build a rich and powerful Vietnam in years to come. We must believe in the future. None other than us can do that, because we are the real masters of this country."

"When will you take me to the North to visit my family-in-law?" Nicole asked suddenly.

Ngoc Lan panicked, he could not take Nicole to the North yet. His first wife was still waiting for him to come home, and his parents and siblings were also longing for him. It had been nearly ten years since he had last seen them. When the Provisional Committee came into operation, he would then ask for leave. Before he was demobilised, he had fulfilled his last duty in the role of the new General Director of the Phong Phu Textile Factory (Xi-co-vi-na Corporation). During his work at police headquarters, he had gathered important information about ringleaders, secret spies and reactionary organisations that were planted in the textile corporation and the surrounding residential quarters. All in all, some two hundred people had been arrested. His superiors suggested that he serve in the armed forces on a permanent basis. However, he refused; his parents were nearly eighty years old and his wife Nhat must have received the letter he had recently sent her and would be waiting for the day when he would return.

"When we will go, darling?" she asked again. Ignoring her husband's silence, Nicole continued, "I know your salary is not enough to buy tickets for me and our children. All banks are blockaded, but I have managed to keep some money aside, so we could take our children to visit your parents as well. Your mother and father must be very proud of their two grandchildren." Ngoc Lan gave no reply. "You are not looking very happy?" Nicole smiled. "What presents will we buy for my parents-in-law, my love."

"I think they have everything except Saigon-style cakes," said Ngoc Lan at last.

Under the knowledge of all he had heard via the Hanoi Radio throughout the past ten years, Ngoc Lan believed that after years of socialist construction, the North must surely be very rich by now.

"I would like to buy some presents for my parents-in-law," Nicole persisted, with a smile.

"Darling, don't buy anything! We can buy anything we want in the North when we get there. I only hope that the South will be made just as rich by the communist government," Ngoc Lan added.

Chapter Forty-Two

Once the police department went into normal operation, Captain Ngoc Lan arranged his trip to the North. He did not know what was waiting for him, so he was both extremely excited, but also very nervous. He had fulfilled his duties and the life of Agent 022 had ended. He was finally going home, and that was all he could think about.

Ngoc Lan had a good train journey. The train was full of troops on leave and each and every one of them looked happy. They each carried dolls, Japanese potteries, sweets and cakes as small gifts for those back home; all the things that citizens of the South had, but knew would come as a surprise to their relatives in the North.

People shared food and fruit with each other on the journey, and they exchanged stories now that the war had ended. Most of them couldn't wait to see the land of North for the first time in several years! Ngoc Lan wanted to be left by himself, away from prying eyes, so he crossed to the door to see the view outside. The landscapes out of the window were so picturesque; completely different to the Ho Chi Minh Trail. The blue sea stretched out to the far horizon, and thick forests full of mystery shrouded their path. From time to time, the train had to stop at various stations in the cities on the way North, and Ngoc Lan's eye was drawn to the many shops selling local goods. At the end of the three days, the train finally arrived at Hanoi Station; Ngoc Lan immediately started to see the horrible effects of war. The houses were in ruins, there were very few shops open and those that were only had the basics: salt, oil and needles. Even these were rationed by vouchers, which had to be handed in when making a purchase. The people of Hanoi only felt relief in the knowledge that there would be no more bombing. The death and destruction was over. The 60kilometre road from Hanoi to Tan Yen was deserted, and most of the villages had also been burnt and destroyed. Thatched houses were mere shells, with their roofs entirely burnt out by the incendiaries dropped by waves of B-52s and the roads were full of potholes. Buffalo boys looking after the cows in the fields nearby were thin and covered with sores caused by a lack of vitamins. Ngoc Lan was devastated to see that the North was nothing like the Utopia he had imagined when he listened to the radio of Hanoi.

Ngoc Lan felt his initial joy ebbing away and turning to sadness. For the first time, he started to miss Nicole and the children, and felt extremely guilty that he was coming home to his first wife Nhat.

Nicole had said nothing when he had bid farewell to her and their children, before taking the train to the North. Oh, why hadn't she just said something? The image of her motionless face haunted him. After nine years of living with her, he now realised how much he loved her. Whilst he loved his parents and siblings, he had been able to live far from them for more than nine years. He also loved his first wife and the son whom he had yet to meet. Finally, he recognised that perhaps one day he would look back and think that these last nine years were, in fact, the best years of his life. He'd had the love of a special woman and the trusting adoration of two children. In those years, he had lived with the dream of liberating the country. In those years, he had lived in the love of the Southerners. In those years, he had learnt so many things ... Why did Nicole say nothing? Why did she not shout and moan, so he could hate her just a little? She was perfect; she knew how to break a man's heart. Well, not really ... he was the one who had broken her heart. He had done it first when he had been so cold towards her when she had first told him that she was pregnant. And he had broken it a second time when he had told her that she could not go to the North to visit his family with him. Was it possible to shift the blame of all he had done to her on to duty ... could he delude himself? Was it easier to live without looking at the truth?

Ngoc Lan was relieved when at last the train pulled into Bac Giang Station and he was able to leave those uncomfortable thoughts behind for the time being. The first view of his hometown hit Ngoc Lan hard, as the fields and his village had been destroyed by American bombs. There was nothing left ... nothing! The fields were pitted with bomb craters, and grass was growing in place of rice. The village had gone and people were now living in straw houses, instead of the old wooden houses he had left behind. Gone were the famous hundreds-of-years-old Vietnamese traditional houses that Ngoc Lan and Ngoc Van had always taken their guests to for food and entertainment. These had been made from beautifully carved teak or cedars – the colour of the wood darkened with age. The designs of the houses had been treasured by all the people in the village, as they symbolised the long cultural traditions of Vietnam. All these had been destroyed by the incendiaries dropped by the B-52s. The road to his house was unpaved. He passed only a few people on the way; they all looked thin and wore tattered clothes. There were no cars or motorbikes. The only transport that they had access to were second-hand bicycles. There were no shops or markets by the side of the road as there had been ten years ago; everything he saw broke Ngoc Lan's heart.

It was starting to get dark and in the distance, Ngoc Lan could see his house. He was nearly home. The light in the window of his house marked his destination and another bright dot, as small as a firefly, came from the oil lamp in the neighbouring house. He stood there taking in the scene, savouring the excitement, the fears, and the joy of being home.

Ngoc Lan opened the gate and proceeded to wander down the passage towards the kitchen. There was no barking of dogs to give his presence away; only vague clucks from the chickens in the back. As he stood watching, he could see a woman in a brown shirt cooking rice by the straw stove. The flames danced and above the fireplace were large patches of black soot. A black cooker and a terracotta pot were boiling to one side. Nothing had changed in that kitchen for ten years; except maybe the woman in the kitchen ...

"Nhat? Is that really you?" Ngoc Lan asked, unable to fully believe that he was finally so close to his wife.

Nhat turned around, her face full of shock and disbelief. "Is that really you, Ngoc Lan?" Nhat rubbed her eyes as if in a dream.

"Yes, it is me."

These were the only words he could manage, as his throat was choked up with emotion. Nhat looked at him for a second and then she called for her parents-in-law; she wanted to tell them that Ngoc Lan had finally come back after all this time. For ten years now, she had lived with them and seen them pray for his safe return. Ngoc Lan was happy that his parents were still alive. He saw his death certificate hung on the wall along with the certificate that read: "The country will always remember Soldier Nguyen Ngoc Lan."

Ngoc Lan suddenly realised that his family had thought him dead for many years. And that the many letters he had sent to his family since April saying that he would be back had never arrived. Everybody was so happy that Ngoc Lan was home. Nhat sat on the floor and said nothing; she was in shock, and could not believe her husband was still alive. Ngoc Lan could not understand why his boss had sent a death certificate to his family. Nhat and his parents had been in mourning ever since.

"Come here, darling," Ngoc Lan said to Nhat.

All four of them hugged each other in turn, screaming, laughing and crying in the joy of their reunion.

Nhat wandered back into the kitchen to boil a pot of water to make tea for everybody, and started to prepare a welcoming feast. The rice and potato dish was replaced with a pot of white rice, and then she went next door to ask them if they could borrow some eggs. The entire family ate their meal together under the moon. His son Khai was excited with his gifts and equally excited about the prospect of having a decent meal.

The air was hot and humid, with no electric fans to provide relief from the heat. There were swarms of mosquitoes, but they only bit Ngoc Lan. He was disappointed to find that there was still no electricity in his village. However, it was an evening to remember with familiar food, family and catching up on all the local gossip.

After the dinner, Nhat smoked the house to drive the mosquitoes away. There were no cushions or mosquito nets, and her bed was covered with an old-fashioned, torn mat.

"Why are you crying?" Nhat asked her husband in the darkness.

"I'm relieved to be at home at last," Ngoc Lan said.

He refrained from telling his wife that he was actually crying in shock at discovering how poor his family was after the war. The family home had been destroyed and he was saddened that his family were now living in a building made of straw and that there was nothing left of value.

Nhat was quiet for some time, and then she said, "I cannot believe it. You are not pale and weak like the other returning soldiers, despite the harsh war. You even look younger and … and very smart."

Ngoc Lan said nothing …

The next morning, Nhat spoke with her husband. "I am tired. This is the first time I have been able to allow myself to feel tired. In the years you were away, I worked night and day in the fields, knowing that this was the only way that I could help and support you; the only way in which I could be close to you. I used to secretly imagine this handful of rice would come to you and feed you. I never had the time to realise how tired I was until now."

They looked at each other and their eyes expressed their feelings far better than words ever could.

Ngoc Lan took his son to school for the first time and was saddened to learn that Khai did not have any warm clothes and the only shirt he owned already had holes in it. He also didn't have any shoes.

"Mummy said all the money we had, we needed to send to support you, Dad, and then you would come home," Little Khai said, as he explained why he didn't have shoes.

"Your Mummy is always right, son," Ngoc Lan answered.

"I don't need good clothes, Dad," Khai said, trying to be a good boy.

The old school had been destroyed by the bombing and the new school had no tiles on the roof. None of the windows had glass, so everything inside was covered in a thick layer of dust. There were not enough desks and benches, so many of the pupils had to sit on the floor to study. There weren't enough books, notepads, pens or teaching aids. There was no drinking water and all the children and teachers had to take water from the common well. In this unclean well, a frog opened its eyes wide, looking at the sky. After leaving his son at school, Ngoc Lan went to the market to buy him some clothes and a pair of shoes. Most of the people at the market were women, who wore old clothes, and most of them were without footwear as they sold their wares on the floor. All they had to sell were vegetables and fruit; no meat. Ngoc Lan felt uncomfortable, because his shoes were too shiny and his clothes were too good in comparison.

Ngoc Lan tried to help his wife by working on the farm, but he had never done farm work before. Immediately after leaving school, he had gone into the army, so he didn't have a clue about how to work the farm. So Nhat sent him to buy some meat, and when he had arrived at the council butcher shop, there had been such a long queue that he returned empty handed. The next day, he woke early and went back to the butchers at 5.00 a.m. to make sure he could buy some. In front of the closed shop, the children had laid a line of bricks and they sold them to people to represent their place in the queue. Ngoc Lan was angry, as he saw people arrive at 8 o'clock to pay the children and they had taken the places in front of him. When at last Ngoc Lan was inside the shop, there was no meat left.

"What did you do if you wanted to buy meat in Saigon?" Nhat asked, with a smiling face as she noticed that Ngoc Lan had arrived home again with empty hands and a long face.

"I just took the money and went into any butcher shop or market to buy it. It was simple."

"I'd like that," Nhat said.

They could never say more than that, because one was not allowed to criticise communism.

In the coming week, Ngoc Lan was kept occupied greeting many guests at their home. Ngoc Van came early one morning and stayed for the night. There was so much Ngoc Lan wanted to know about all that had happened while he had been away, but Ngoc Van answered all Ngoc Lan's questions with one answer, which was that Ngoc Lan would discover everything in his own way in his own time. However, what Ngoc Van did tell him was that after the war, many generals had become politicians. For Ngoc Van, the generals were only good when they were fighting; they didn't have the skill to organise the country in a way that would improve the lives of ordinary people. In Ngoc Van's opinion, some of the generals were not correctly posted according to their abilities. For example, General Giap was pushed into accepting the post of chairman in the head office of Women's Birth Control. However, in the Vietnamese people's hearts, General Giap would always remain a hero of the country.

On his return to Saigon after his two-month break, Ngoc Lan was shocked to find Rose Villa deserted. The gates were locked and it was the very first time that Ngoc Lan had seen his family's home empty. The drive leading to the entrance hall was neglected and covered with moss. The windows were caked with dust and bars had been fitted over them. The rusty gate showed that nobody had gone in, or out, of Rose Villa for quite some time. The note on the gate told Ngoc Lan that the house had been possessed by the council. He had always known that a house as big as Rose Villa could no longer belong to the Philippe family under the new law. Ngoc Lan blamed himself for not contacting Nicole for two months, because so many things had been going on in the North, but there were no telephones in his home village. Ngoc Lan had sent some letters, but he could not be sure if those had been received by Nicole.

Ngoc Lan went to the neighbours' houses to ask if they knew anything. He did not recognise anybody and as he asked about Nicole or any of his family, nobody knew, or was prepared to admit that they knew, anything. Ngoc Lan recalled how all his neighbours in Can Tho had been removed just before he had left on his mission and he started to worry. Where was his family? Where had they gone? Had they, like so many other people, been ordered to relocate to Lam Dong, because the new government officials wanted to turn the jungle there into agricultural land? If so, surely they would have left a note for him? Why would they not have been allowed to stay until he returned, so that they could all have gone together?

The City Military Administration Committee had also changed, and even the police department had been taken over by the regular police force. The Provisional Committee had been dissolved and all the officials had changed. Someone even advised Ngoc Lan that because he was a part of the Northern army, he should not have contact with rich people, because it would not be good for his career and he may never get a job if he was known to belong to a French family. In those years, all the jobs were given to ex-army soldiers first; then to the people who had been poor farm workers.

In the first week back in Saigon, Ngoc Lan went to the council offices every day to try and find out about the situation at Rose Villa. The lady behind the counter, an ex-farm worker, was unable to find any documents covering Mac Dinh Chi Street. The estimated waiting time was four hours, but most people had to wait until the following day or gave up. On Friday, the queue of people behind Ngoc Lan grew longer and longer and the lady became ever more flustered, and started to shout at the people in the queue. Eventually, Ngoc Lan and a few of the others became bored and disillusioned with the unhelpful council staff, so they left without anything actually having been resolved.

Ngoc Lan had so many questions about Ann, Nicole and the children that he did not know where to begin to look for them. Had Nicole become angry and left him when she found out that he had a wife in the North? He searched frantically for his family, but everywhere he went, he found the same answer; people were sorry, but they could not help him.

Even Mrs Tam had no idea. She had retired and no longer worked in the market. It was not the right way to do business now, because, under the new system, everyone worked together and got paid by the government. Only council-owned shops had the right to buy and sell goods to the people, so Mrs Tam had lost her livelihood. But she was getting older and for years now she had worked with one single purpose in mind: the reunification of the country. She had seen this achieved, and all the hard work and stress had finally caught up with her. Even she couldn't believe how her life had changed in such a way and so quickly. Mrs Tam even had to sell all her belongings to buy food; as did many others. So this created a situation where everything became available very cheaply; except for food, that is. It had been just months since the fall of South Vietnam, and everything had changed. The war was over, the Bietdong were no longer needed, and the new council was too busy to have time to look after all the people who had been in the Bietdong; or rather nobody actually cared about them.

Mrs Tam's children were not yet recognised as martyrs, because nobody had known about the actions of her family in the past. Moreover, the new government had no time to look after the elderly. Everyone was hungry and when people are hungry, they only think about their empty stomachs; even the council officers.

Mother Tam had spent all her money on the war cause. She had come from a middle-class background and she had now become a very poor person in a matter of weeks. Ngoc Lan could not help her, because he was even poorer than she was. That year, money no longer had the same meaning that it had in the past, as high inflation continued. Money that had previously paid for everything became worthless. Even the old currency was worthless, and all bank accounts had been frozen. Gold still retained its value, but the rich were now those who had access to food.

Mrs Tam told Ngoc Lan that her life was very different; former soldiers, the people who she had helped in the fight, had gone their separate ways. Those that had been in the Northern army had been sent to Cambodia to help in the overthrow of the Pol Pot regime and the Khmer Rouge. The boss of Ngoc Lan's team was still undercover to keep him safe, so he could not, or may not have wanted to, help him. The city was full of strangers. The life of the inhabitants of Saigon – now renamed Ho Chi Minh City – had become harder. Even though she was poorly, she was unable to go to hospital, despite having devoted her entire life to the cause. She was only able to obtain some Chinese herbal medicine. She had no idea why the Philippes had disappeared; the last time she had seen Nicole, she said she was looking forward to Tu's return. God bless her; she could never get used to calling Tu, "Ngoc Lan". Mrs Tam was as much in the dark as Ngoc Lan was. She also knew that whilst the army chiefs had been very successful fighting in the war, they had little idea on how to lead a ravaged country at peace.

Ngoc Lan left Ho Chi Minh City and travelled to Can Tho, but he no longer had any right to live at Tu's house. As he arrived in Can Tho, Ngoc Lan discovered that his villa had been taken over by the city council. There was still no sign of Ann, Nicole and the children, and the new residents of his villa were cold and unhelpful. They had moved into a large house for nothing, and did not want to do anything that could threaten their new livelihood. Looking for Nicole in Can Tho was like looking for a needle in a haystack. Everybody he asked denied knowing anything and made Ngoc Lan feel extremely unwelcome. Lacking money, food and shelter, Ngoc Lan finally admitted defeat. Full of despair, he returned to Ho Chi Minh City, only to hear further terrible news.

Mrs Tam had died peacefully in her sleep at the ripe old age of eighty. Having no children or relatives, the local council had organised a funeral for her. They had no idea where her family tomb was, so they put her grave in a different cemetery. Tu hoped that one day, if he had money again, he would move her closer to her children and Little Lien. With his heart broken, Ngoc Lan looked up his old friends in Saigon, hoping they could shed some light on the situation.

Ngoc Lan's friends were all busy, or at least they pretended to be busy. No one invited Ngoc Lan to stay with them even for just one night. Ngoc Lan started to think it might be because he was a former spy.

Just before the South fell, Ngoc Lan, had everything. Before 1975, he had been able to travel everywhere in Saigon with his car, and he had had a lovely life filled with happiness. Every house on both sides would open their doors to welcome him as a member of the Philippe family, but now everything had changed.

Having lost everything in Ho Chi Minh City, literally everything, being short of money and with nowhere to stay, Ngoc Lan had no choice but to travel back to the North again. He used the last of his money to buy a one-way ticket to the North. Ngoc Lan was heartbroken. During the three-day journey, he kept seeing Nicole's face etched in his mind. When Ngoc Lan had initially left Saigon, she had been happy and she had wanted him to return home soon. Did she blame him? Did she still love him? Would it have been better to tell her the true story? Now Ngoc Lan no longer had a good job with good pay and the smart uniform of South Vietnam, would she still love him? With this new way of life, he knew for sure that Nicole would think that the communist side must be terrible, and he was one of them. Unanswered questions went round and round in his mind, until he reached screaming point.

Over the past few months, there had been so many changes. Ngoc Lan was no longer in a position of importance; he was no longer rich with influence. He now had to forget the polite behaviour of the upper classes; he now had to beg for fresh water during the journey back to the North.

Some of his friends had survived the war, but they were not happy either. Ngoc Lan knew of people whose babies had been born disabled or deformed, due to exposure to Agent Orange. However, as soldiers, they were always unselfish and were always down to earth. Every family had lost somebody or something. Anyone, even soldiers and police officers, who dared to boast about their actions, would be viewed with suspicion or contempt. So Ngoc Lan decided to keep all his medals and commendations in his old backpack. He would not even show anyone his Certificate of Invalidity. He would follow the requirements of the new party and he understood all that his native province Ha Bac needed was to modernise.

Chapter Forty-Three

On July the twenty-first 1982, on Ngoc Lan's very last journey back to Saigon, the Hanoi to Ho Chi Minh City express train ran southwards in the murky light of dawn. Passengers sat with their heads nodding as they dozed. Some passengers who couldn't sleep went to the restaurant car to have a drink and a smoke. He had managed to get work in a brick factory for three months in order to raise enough money for a train ticket to Saigon. He had been contemplating not going to Saigon again. However, Nhat had told Ngoc Lan, after she knew the full story, that she wanted him to find Nicole and his two sons. Nhat hoped that she and Nicole could become sisters.

Ngoc Lan looked out of the window on to the quiet landscape. Outside the train window, under the moonlight, there were no fierce battlefields, no military bases with plywood houses, no combat trenches and no barbed-wire fences. He saw many tombs, both new and old. There were still many temporary graves marked only with a piece of wood. The old craters were now ponds full of lotus flowers during the summer; the changes happen so quickly, he thought. Many tears had fallen since that great day of liberation. During the past few years in his native village, Ngoc Lan had been overloaded with work in an attempt to the repair the war wounds. The North had taken its first steps in the cause of national reconstruction. After arranging his work, Ngoc Lan could finally afford the time to return to the place he had spent most of his time as Agent 022. Ngoc Lan remained quiet for most of the journey south. He thought about Nicole, Saigon and the past ten years ... Ngoc Lan could not believe what he had been through in all his time during the war as a spy. That life was associated with much sadness, happiness, and romance.

He recalled Little Trung's birthday, when Ann and Nicole had thrown a special party and they had invited everyone at Rose Villa and all of Ngoc Lan's colleagues, shipping company workers and friends from Little Trung's school. In the big room covered with lots of flowers was a big table full of parcels. Nicole and her mother were the centre of attention (as always) and Mr Lam was giving the guests the best of both Vietnamese and French foods. The servants never forgot to give Little Trung presents to show how much they cared for him and how much they loved him ... Those were lovely times, Ngoc Lan thought, but now they were only memories.

Ngoc Lan told his wife and his family about his second wife, leaving out some of the details. However, Nhat understood and she was the one who had now sent Ngoc Lan back to the South again to look for clues as to the Philippe family's whereabouts.

It took four days to travel the 1,000 miles and, one afternoon, Ngoc Lan felt tired and he nodded off to sleep, dreaming that he was outside Rose Villa. Through the window, he could see Ann and Nicole, his children and Mr Lam. He called out to them, but they couldn't hear him ... couldn't see him. He wondered if he was dreaming. The door was locked and Ngoc Lan tried to call for Mr Lam but he could not hear him. Ngoc Lan wanted to walk under the window so Nicole could see him but his feet were so heavy that he could not move. Instead, he stood and watched what was going on inside the house.

Ann was wearing grey clothes. For the first time, Ngoc Lan saw his mother-in-law in Western-style clothes, rather than the traditional Vietnamese *Ao Dai*s or a smart French outfit. Ngoc Lan saw his mother-in-law lose her self-control for the first time. Some big bags were ready and waiting in the sitting room. Mr Lam was still alive, but why had Nicole told him that he was dead Tu wondered, as he saw Mr Lam making a cup of tea for Ann.

"Nicole!" said Ann. "Listen to me. Be attached to nothing. It's time to leave."

"Mother, please let me wait for Tu," Nicole pleaded, as she stood leaning against the window. She wore a purple *Ao Dai*, a necklace of big pearls and high-heeled shoes. Her hair was done up high in a knot.

"How can we wait for him?" asked Ann. "In the near future, this house and our entire plantation, stock and everything we have left, will be confiscated. Where will we stay if we have to wait for him? We may even be sent to re-education camps, and who knows when we would be able to return home? I want you to follow me, tonight."

"Mother," Nicole prolonged the word "Mother" in a respectful and tender voice, "I am the wife of a communist man. We are the winners."

"Nicole, you can think that you are on the winning side if you want, but I cannot; I have lost everything. My friends were defeated, and your father has fled back to France and disappeared. I am dying to hear any news about him. The unrest still hasn't finished, and our relatives must present themselves to the new administration. How can I belong to the side of winners like my son-in-law? This is a tragedy of war; it is nobody's fault. I can't live here any more; I need to go, dear."

"Mother, please think of my love for Tu. He is the father of your grandchildren!"

Ann shook her head: "Nicole, I don't want to break your heart, but I must tell you the truth now. Tu had a wife in the North. To build up his cover, he had to marry you; he now has gone to the North and I don't think he will come back to you. In such a situation, how can I leave you here! I want to go to France immediately. I feel anxious about your father. In France, you will have a chance to travel to America; a country you love. The ship is waiting in the open sea. Tonight, we will go, my dear! Tu is staying with his wife and children in the North. Maybe he has forgotten about you and your children already."

Ngoc Lan could see that Nicole was badly shaken. The room was spinning around her and she had to hold on to the dining table to stop herself from falling. Her face and lips had turned pale. What a terrible shock!

Finally, she looked up at her mother. "Mother, is that true? Did he really have a wife in the North?"

"Not only did Mrs Tam tell me, but also Tu himself, just before returning to the North. He said whatever he did or said would never be enough to compensate for how truly sorry he was. He asked me never to tell you, because he did not want to hurt you."

"Then I have been cheated by all of you. Everyone has known the truth, except me," Nicole said bitterly. "Mother, I know that my husband loves me. For his duty, he had to sacrifice everything, even his integrity with me and our children. I admire him for that and I am proud of him. Deep in my heart, I know he loves me and always will. Now the reality is not as I want, I am heartbroken. But don't worry, Mother, I will get over it. In the American War, all Vietnamese women have lost so much. Each and every one of them has suffered so much misery. I was surprised that I was not one of them. But I don't feel sad, because I have contributed, however modestly, to the victory. My husband understands that I love him. He will understand that whatever I may do now, I will not wait for him any longer. I will leave; not because I am disloyal to him, but to make life easier for him. I now understand the real cost of the American war, Mother."

Nicole turned to Mr Lam: "Shall we go? Mr Lam, please could you carry my children?"

"Don't go!" Ngoc Lan shouted, trying to open the wooden entrance door, but he could not. He was heartbroken as he saw Nicole holding Ann and Mr Lam's hands. Mr Lam carried the children; all of them stepped into the sea. The black and wavy sea swallowed the entire small family, whole ... Only Ngoc Lan stood in the empty, large room, amongst the furniture covered with white sheeting and cobwebs.

"Don't go!" Ngoc Lan shouted again. But it was too late. They had all disappeared into the sea. "Don't go, I beg you, Nicole!" Ngoc Lan murmured.

He woke up in a cold sweat, with his heart pounding; he found himself back on the train. He breathed a huge sigh of relief to find that it had all been just a dream.

Ngoc Lan's sixth sense was used to working with high intensity and accuracy. Many of his dreams had come true. However, he hoped that this was not one of them. In a confused state, Ngoc Lan willed the train to go faster towards Saigon. He hoped Nicole had not taken their children on the route of the boat people. Surely not ... thought Ngoc Lan. He hoped Nicole was waiting for him at Rose Villa back in Saigon. This time, Ngoc Lan sincerely hoped that he would find information concerning his wife and the children. On the way to Saigon, Ngoc Lan could feel how much he loved Nicole! Finally, the train entered Saigon Station. Taking a motorcycle, Ngoc Lan hurried to Rose Villa.

He discovered that Rose Villa was still managed by the state. The heavy gate that was once covered with roses was still locked, and Mac Dinh Chi Street still remained a quiet area. Ngoc Lan stood outside his house and lost all hope. The strange neighbours looked at Ngoc Lan with suspicion.

Ngoc Lan went to Ann's native village; all of her relatives had gone, too. He did not know where they were; perhaps they had gone to Hong Kong, France or Thailand. Maybe they had gone to America; Ann and Nicole had a lot of friends and relatives in America. Nicole had told him many times that she would like to visit America.

Ngoc Lan could not believe that Saigon was so strange to him now. When he left the city, there had still been many of his Vietcong comrades living and working there. Now, they were dispersed and demobilised. He intended to ask the People's Committee permission to visit Rose Villa for the last time. Then he thought better of it, because he could not suffer the sorrow in his heart. Instead, he decided to go Mac Dinh Chi Street to look at his house for the last time.

Through the locked gate, Rose Villa's courtyard was empty and deathly, with the exception of the roses, which still looked alive. Behind the kitchen window, Ms Thi, Ms Lam and Mr Ba would no longer move back and forth. The library would never accommodate the big, black, charming man, Mr Mac , who used to sit in the small chair chatting with Ann, or with Mr Lam as he tried to smoke a cigar which he had stolen from his master. Ann would have to remind him that the library was not the smoking room. The closed dining room on the right side of the villa would never see Charles reading French newspapers or Little Hieu playing with his spoon, sulking, as he screamed, "I want my Mummy."

"I want your Mummy, too, son," Ngoc Lan thought, aloud.

Above the library was his bedroom on the first floor. Behind the closed window was no longer his cosy room, where Nicole used to embrace him in the morning. Now, nobody lay there. He would never go in, never. Even if someone was kind enough to understand and give him the chance to see his own house just one last time, he would never be able to enter such an empty and desolate Rose Villa. Standing at the cold gate, his blood seemed to freeze because of his sorrow.

One of his old friends working at the city police department told him that Nicole once worked as a shop assistant at the department's canteen, then suddenly left her job without telling anyone. Nobody knew why or where she had gone. There was no information about her. Someone said that she remained somewhere in Saigon. His oldest son, Little Trung, would now be at the height of an adult's shoulder. Ngoc Lan was a policeman, so he did not believe everything he was told, but he knew someone must know something. However, Ngoc Lan never met anybody who had actually seen any of his family first hand. He hoped that Nicole had taken their children to France. He hoped that she did not leave on any of the dilapidated ships. Thus, with a broken heart, Ngoc Lan left Rose Villa's gate.

During his visit, Ngoc Lan was invited to a special meeting with the other secret agents. Here, he discovered that his boss, General Co, had been fighting for the North. He did not know whether he should laugh or cry, because his boss had turned out to be the manager of the Bietdong team.

At that meeting, Ngoc Lan discovered why Rang had died. Everyone knew that his boss, General Co, was different. This general was cold and hard. He congratulated everybody except Ngoc Lan. However, before he left, General Co asked if Ngoc Lan wanted to continue with his mission. However, Ngoc Lan did not trust his boss any more and decided to opt out. How could General Co do that to him and Mrs Tam? He must only have cared for himself. The war was over, and General Co continued in his position as general of the new country. Living the life of a general, he would never understand Ngoc Lan's life. This man must have been the one who had questioned Ngoc Lan's CV; if not, why else did Ngoc Lan not have that job? General Co still lived in the big house and the Americans thought he was working for them, so his children were allowed to live and work in America. Everything was just perfect for General Co.

Ngoc Lan thought back and remembered many occasions that Mrs Tam had almost said too much. Ten years on, he now understood that Mrs Tam had been protecting General Co's identity. He was hurting. If he had known that General Co had been a spy on his team, Ngoc Lan's life as Agent 022 would have been a lot easier. It was no use complaining; no one wanted to listen to someone complaining.

Ngoc Lan could not leave Saigon without visiting Han, the wife of his colleague, Vinh. Unlike Mother Tam, Han's house was more luxurious and richer than under the old regime. Dressed smartly, Han smoked a cigarette while preparing Ngoc Lan a cup of coffee. She still called him by his false name when she spoke. "I thought you had forgotten us, Tu," Han said accusingly.

Chapter Forty-Three

"How could I forget you? Tell me, how is Vinh?"

"He was sent to a prison for re-education in the North for an unspecified period," Han said, sighing, "so I don't know where he is or when he is coming home. I am so terrified."

"What are you doing now?" Ngoc Lan asked, changing the subject.

"As you know, I was not re-educated, because I was an unimportant secretary and guaranteed by you. What else could I do other than work on the black market? How could the wife of a renegade lieutenant colonel on the side that had lost be recruited into a state-run office? Vinh's family has lost everything now, too. Vinh blighted the whole family, because he was a big police officer from the losing side. None of his relatives could find decent work; even his brothers who were doctors. All of them are now working on the black market, including me. Many people feel ashamed of the word 'trader'. How strange that I am now a trader and earn good money. Brother Tu, tell me, how is Nicole?"

"My whole family has disappeared," murmured Ngoc Lan. Then he changed tack, because did not want to make Han sad. "Maybe she took my children and mother to France. If possible, I will reunite with them one day!"

"You should do that, Brother Tu. This system has no place for the upper class. The rich and the foreign people such as the Chinese are leaving Vietnam for good. I wish, one day, that I will have the chance to go to America to find my own son. Many half-blooded children who went to America are with the wrong families. Their families were treated badly and continually faced hunger. So the upper classes used some of their money to adopt the mixed race children, so that the rich families would automatically have rights to emigrate to America. The real parents and families of the mixed-race children remained in Vietnam, while their beloved children flew to America with their adoptive family. I have heard that a lot of the children were dumped once they arrived in America. Why is America always so blind to the truth? Anyway, where are you staying at the moment?"

"Rose Villa is managed by the State and I am not permitted to own such a big house. I am staying temporarily at the former police headquarters," Ngoc Lan replied.

"How does it look now?" Han asked curiously.

"Much simpler; the former police tried to burn as many documents as possible to destroy evidence, so most of furniture was also burnt."

"After returning to the North, promise me you will find and visit my husband at the prison. He must be longing for news from me and the children."

"I cannot promise," said Ngoc Lan, "but I will try. He was a good friend to me."

Han burst out crying "Brother Tu, try to do something for him, I beg you. I know my husband very well, and you also know him. He only carried out his duties as a police officer. He saw you 'favouring' the communists on many occasions and he turned a blind eye; as did I. I thought, rather than being a spy, you were being charitable; that you wanted to save as many lives as possible, because all of us were Vietnamese. Why do you, the communists, not think so? Your words are good, but your attitude makes us feel like we are dirt and worthless! My husband was trying to save all the documents at police headquarters for the new government, rather than just burning them all. We all knew we could fight, but we decided to do nothing and save the people's blood that fateful day on the April the thirtieth, 1975. And after everything, your winning side just locked my husband in prison! It has been two years now and I have heard nothing from Vinh. How dare you!"

"Han!" Ngoc Lan turned serious. "What is the matter with you? Surely you of all people would understand that the new, young Vietnam has many problems to deal with? You should not speak in such a hostile manner."

"I don't need great things!" Han sobbed. "All I want to know is when my husband will return to me. You could tell me, couldn't you? You're on their side!"

Ngoc Lan felt wretched. Did Nhat, his first wife, wait for him in sorrow like this? Suddenly, he wanted to go home to his family in the North. "Family". How sacred that word was. God, please forgive me, I've only just realised how important that word is, he thought to himself.

"Han!" Ngoc Lan consoled her. He softly tapped her on the shoulder and as he did so, his memory flooded back of that occasion, several years ago, when Han had first arrived at police headquarters. She had worn a short skirt and was walking amidst police officers in the office. Dozens of men's eyes had admiringly followed her charming body! Now, in front of him, was a pitiful woman ... Nobody was to blame. Why must there be two sides; winner and loser. He wondered which side he belonged to. Oh God, he belonged to both sides and yet, at that moment, he felt that he did not belong to any side. Why didn't the people understand how he felt? Maybe they will one day, given time. The problem is time, not now but maybe later, perhaps later ... he thought.

When they parted, Han gave Ngoc Lan a large sum of money.

"Please take it. If possible, please visit Vinh and buy some provisions for him! I really want to visit him, but my children are so young that they can't travel to the North. Brother Tu, to travel to the prison in the North is not easy for me. I can only arrange a trip once a year, and they kept changing the prison. I am concerned that the wining side didn't like the wife of Vinh, so it not easy for a woman like me."

Han carefully wrapped the money she had risked her life to earn. She had accumulated it to support Vinh, and as she wrapped the money, she wrapped her love to be sent to her husband with it. She hoped Tu could find and visit him. Maybe Tu could even help Vinh return home earlier. Ngoc Lan decided not to take the money, because he was a North Vietnamese soldier; it would be difficult for him to explain why he was friends with a dangerous South Vietnamese prisoner. He felt ever so guilty and asked the Gods why life should be so difficult. He could feel Han's blazing fury behind him and he wanted to apologise to her, but he could not; he was on the winning side, and he couldn't apologise to the losing side. Sometimes, life can be odd – very odd– and Ngoc Lan knew he was a bad person. Who could want to have a friend like him? Ngoc Lan felt like he wanted to die; he would love to die. God, please take me, he thought. Vinh never did return home.

Suddenly, Ngoc Lan thought about all the prisons, where the new government kept all the prisoners of war. Those prisons were in the jungle, with no roads nearby, and far away from human habitation. Everybody was so hungry that he wondered how all the Southern prisoners could survive the cold weather of the North. Ngoc Lan just wanted to do something ... anything that he thought might help. That night, after he had left Han's house, Ngoc Lan went to church. He had not been to church for such a long time. After the war, Catholics were not made welcome in Vietnam, because of what President Diem had had done to the Buddhist people; he had painted a black picture of the Catholics.

From 1960 to 1963, under the government of Diem, he and his brother Vicar Ngo Dinh Can killed 25,000 Buddhist people. The church at Tan Yen was closed, but not that in Saigon. Ngoc Lan prayed for the people who had died at the hands of the war. He prayed for everyone who had touched his life and the last person he thought about was Vinh. "Dear God, please save Vinh."

He crossed himself and wanted to cry before he left the church, because he had no idea where to go next. In the past, he had had accommodation at the police headquarters, Rose Villa and the farmhouse at the rubber plantation with many cottages and houses, within which hundreds of workers lived. They had always welcomed him with open arms. Sometimes, if Nicole and Ngoc Lan had had time to stop at any door of their farm workers, the people had always been pleased to offer them a cup of tea … Mrs Tam's house was always open for him, even though she knew that he could never return … Ngoc Lan even had Rang's apartment key … But that was all in the past now, and for the time being, he had nowhere to go.

Before returning the North, Ngoc Lan visited Little Lien's tomb.

"Only you and me left," murmured Ngoc Lan. "All of our comrades have dispersed in their separate directions. Saigon is so different now, Little Lien. Nobody is familiar; all of my relatives have gone. Only you remain in Saigon for me. The places where I used to live are strange now. I am alone in this city; the city we and our comrades fought to protect and liberate … Something unusual is going on, sister. I must do something, but what can I do? I don't mean this city must express its gratitude towards our comrades and us, but the people are so cold to me it's all so unfair … Why don't you answer me?

I still love Saigon. The city where I lived, fought and loved for many years. In the past, I was protected, so I still love Saigon for that. Saigon has now been renamed after Uncle Ho. Did you know that, my little sister? In the past few years of my life, I have been through too much. I am sure you could imagine this, because you knew; but I still believe that we have had more happiness than sadness. I will go back to the North tomorrow, where

I will enter a new fight. America's embargo cannot wear down the Vietnamese nation's strong will. I promised to devote myself to the party's ideals. I know that the future fighting will also be very fierce. The fight to modernise our economy, the fight to rebuild our country, and we will succeed, as we did when we won the war, won't we, Little Lien? Well, my little sister, you do know, don't you, that I love Nicole with all my heart. How strange that it was only after losing her that I realised how much I loved her ... I want something simple. I want to love and be loved. Nicole and my sons have left, taking with them half of my heart. I am so sad. I feel such great sorrow ... but I will not cry, because I am a soldier. I am no longer Agent 022, nor a member of the Philippe family, nor a special police captain. Today, I wear the military uniform of Uncle Ho's army. Can you see that, Little Lien? Do you see the peaceful sky above? It has been blue over the past few days. The grass that is growing beneath me is growing fast, covering all the scars of war. The children are even swimming in the bomb craters. Did you know that, my dear, sweet little sister?"

Chapter Forty-Four

It was two years since the war had ended and millions of soldiers had returned to their homes. Whilst adjusting to domestic life, the soldiers found it impossible to find work and with the help of General Giap, who was the head of birth control, the population of Vietnam had grown from 32 million to 54 million in a short space of time.

Ngoc Lan took over from Nhat and became a farmer. Nhat, in turn, reverted to her role as housewife and mother, and looked after their three children; Khai, Cun Con and Cun Lon. Every year, Ngoc Lan needed to give to the council 400 kilos of rice and 100 kilos of meat in taxes, but because of the heavy storms, he struggled with the quota and earned very little. As a result, the only food on the table was a small bowl of vegetables. Nhat never complained, but the children cried at night, because they were so hungry.

Life was hard, but Ngoc Lan never complained; he even helped the people to understand why they were hungry. For him, the problems were caused by the destruction of the war, and the embargo imposed by the Americans after the war. It just made an already difficult job almost impossible. Many Vietnamese starved and thousands died as a result. The Vietnamese just wanted to forget the war and build a stronger country, so everyone could look to a brighter future.

Ngoc Lan had a good life before, and he saw no reason to accept poverty now. He wanted to make a fresh start for Nhat and his children, and the only way for Vietnam to heal its wounds was to bring the population of Vietnam together. Eventually, he wanted a job so he could earn money, and so he could enjoy a cup of tea and think about Nicole and their sons, Little Trung and Little Hieu, but that day never came.

When Cun Con and Cun Lon were born, they were both very ill. They had both contracted leukaemia. Their doctor told Ngoc Lan that it was because he had been travelling down the Ho Chi Minh Trail, and every time he took a drink from the river and every time he took a mouthful of food, he had been poisoned by Agent Orange. It had seeped into his body, changing his DNA, and now he had passed it on to his sons. Ngoc Lan tried to do everything he could to help his children. He sold everything he had and borrowed money from everyone he knew; he wanted nothing more than for his children to die a peaceful death. Cun Lon died when he was just three years old, but Cun Con was the stronger of the two, and his body fought every step of the way to stay alive, which prolonged his life and made his death the most painful. When the doctor visited him, he was astounded by how ill it could make someone. He spent weeks lying in his bed and developed bedsores, which turned gangrenous, which was both painful and made the room smell of death.

Two weeks before his death, Cun Con whispered to his father:"Daddy, I'm going to die."

"You will not, son," Ngoc Lan answered.

"Daddy, I will go to heaven and there, I will look after my brother. In the evening, I will bring my brother home to see you and Mummy. But you must open the window, so that I can find you and Mummy."

"The window will always be open, son."

"If you are home from the field, could you please light the lamp, and then I will know you and Mummy are at home."

"I will, son. But you will be ok."

"Daddy, when the doctor told you to bring me home, he told you to let me eat all my favourite foods – I knew then. Then Grandma came every night to tell me stories about Jesus and everyone who came to visit me left with tears in their eyes."

Ngoc Lan waited for his son finish and then he ran to the field to weep. Everyone in the village heard him cry; because he howled and the wind carried his cries to the village. Some people that heard him went to the field to comfort him, but decided to leave him alone; everyone knew that no word could reduce the pain in Ngoc Lan's heart that day. They just wanted to let him know they were there for him.

During the week leading up to Cun Con's death he could not eat, he could not speak, and he could not breathe. Nhat knew that he was dying, and when he did eventually pass away, she hysterically tried to resuscitate Cun Con, simply believing that if she did so, she could keep her son alive and with her for a little longer. Both Ngoc Lan and Nhat were consumed with grief.

After weeks of living in his own world of misery, Ngoc Lan realised that he needed to pull himself together. His eldest son and Nhat still needed him. Ngoc Lan tried to look for a new job as a policeman, as he hoped for a better salary. But every police office he approached gave him the same answer: "no". At the time, Vietnam didn't have enough police officers, so Ngoc Lan couldn't understand why he couldn't get a job. Struggling with no job, and no money, Ngoc Lan's life became worse. His younger brother, Mai, who had a good job, helped him a little. However, Mai's wife did not like her husband helping him and one day, she spoke with Ngoc Lan.

"You were living in Saigon for ten years as a double agent. God knows if you were good or bad, but if you were so good, why does no one want you to work for them? We can't help you forever. Every single person in this province is starving."

She was right, Ngoc Lan thought, and he never asked his younger brother for help again. At the end that year, Ngoc Lan's luck changed. His friend Nguyen Van Dien became Communist Party Secretary in Ngoc Lan's hometown and Dien tried to help Ngoc Lan as much as he could and gave him a position as the co-operative's deputy chairman. Based on his experience of the production contracts with labourers in the rubber plantation, he and Dien bravely experimented with the soya bean and groundnut crop production. The yield was raised from 200 kilos per acre to 1 ton per acre. Looking out on the green fields, Ngoc Lan knew that his troubles were coming to an end, and a beautiful life was on the horizon. However, it wasn't to be. The council was not happy. Dien and Ngoc Lan had done something new and without prior permission from the council. Because of this, Dien was expelled from the party and removed from his post as the cooperative chairman, along with Ngoc Lan. Ngoc Lan was distraught and wanted to commit suicide, but when he thought about all the people who had died for peace, he knew his actions would paint a black picture of Ho Chi Minh's army.

Time passed terribly slowly and eventually, spring arrived. It was still cold and orange trees were budding and blossoming in the garden. Ngoc Lan had a high fever, and all he could think of was how much he wanted a bowl of hot chicken soup. He lay on the bed in the front room and pitifully looked outside, where his wife was putting rice seedlings into baskets for transplantation. Her ragged conical hat was covered with a layer of old nylon.

Seeing her husband watching her, she turned, sobbing, "We are so poor!"

Ngoc Lan was very moved. "Your poverty is the country's glory. You should be proud, darling."

"I don't need glory, Ngoc Lan. I only wish I could do more for you. I am sorry, because I don't even have enough money to buy you some medicine."

Later that morning, Dien passed by and paid a visit to his friend. Leaning his old bike against the jackfruit tree at the gate, he hurried into the house, smiling at Ngoc Lan.

"I have just come from a meeting with the council and they have decided to withdraw their judgment. Your experiment is to be officially applied throughout the whole of the country. I was restored to my post and the party suggested that I stand for election as the communal chairman. They have also voted you in as the deputy chairman for the next term."

Ngoc Lan jumped up despite his fever, "I was feeling very unwell, but now I suddenly feel better. When the new system is in use, we will become well off, Dien!"

Dien embraced his close friend and their eyes were wet with glistening tears.

One month later, Ngoc Lan and Dien retired, because the council said they were too old and it was time for young people to run the farm production. It didn't matter, because Ngoc Lan was due to receive compensation for being a victim of Agent Orange. A year later, the officer in charge of his compensation decided to withdraw his claim, because he thought Ngoc Lan looked fit and well. On his forty-six birthday his wife made him a birthday cake, the French cake that she knew he always loved.

Having lots of spare time on his hands, now that he had retired, Ngoc Lan visited his cousin Ngoc Van. He welcomed him outside his house. Inside were many police officers getting on with the job at hand; they were taking a tally of all of Ngoc Van's possessions in order to decide what should be taken for distribution amongst the poor.

"It is not right that I am rich and that I need to share things with those less fortunate than me," Ngoc Van told his cousin. "They have even taken away my wallet and look, this gate doesn't belong to my family any more because the land it enclosed has been taken away so the council can give it to the poor people. Without our own gate, we'll need wings to fly if we need to go out of our own house for anything."

The idea of having the poor people and farmers employed within the council was turning sour already. The cow herder became chairman of the province, the farm worker became an officer or a policeman, and thus the policemen like Ngoc Lan were made unemployed. Ngoc Van was no longer a city engineer, because the ex-army troops had taken all the building jobs. The preference for the old-style of French villa was discarded, and army houses became the new fashion. They were like a tunnel rather than a house, with narrow sides, no windows, no kitchen, and no toilet.

"It's all wrong!" Ngoc Lan sighed.

"Everything is wrong, but I hope things will change soon, when the country recovers. Anyway, life could be worse."

"How?" Ngoc Lan asked, with a note of tiredness in his voice.

If Ngoc Van thought that being poor was better and right, he must be mad. Maybe he was hiding his real thoughts. Ngoc Lan just wanted to be rich again, so that he could travel to Saigon and Paris to resume his search for Nicole and the children and for Ngoc Lan this couldn't come soon enough.

"I don't know, and I am too tired to wait for that," Ngoc Van answered. "I don't want the burden of rebuilding our country any more."

"Don't give up, brother," Ngoc Lan told him. "Nobody can accept the situation as it is, but it will change. Our government is still too young at the moment and we have to help it. Then everything will be ok again."

Ngoc Van looked at his cousin: "I have always supported the communist party; I even taught my children the communist way. We must have something to believe in, to hope for. Did you know your wife knew you were safe and well? While you were away, she told me that she had a dream that you had a South Vietnamese wife ..."

"She was right."

"I beg your pardon?" Ngoc Van could not believe his ears.

"I will tell you one day; it was not as bad as you might think."

"When we have time, a happy time, then perhaps we could talk about the past," Ngoc Van said with happiness in his eyes.

However, Ngoc Van never did get time; he died in a work-related accident that winter. It always went back to the past; everything nice had been in the past, Ngoc Lan thought, as he attended the funeral of Ngoc Van, his favourite cousin, his best friend and his loyal supporter. However, by the same token, Ngoc Lan began to support Ngoc Van's wife and her children. He travelled between the two villages in the years to come to help Ngoc Van's family. He couldn't do much, but the fact he was there meant a lot to Ngoc Van's children; they felt as if they had another father.

He used to tell bedtime stories at night when he stayed, when the children couldn't sleep because they missed their father. Books were quite expensive, so Ngoc Lan used to tell stories of his times in Saigon and he would weave exciting, thrilling adventures. He told them he was scared, scared and scared again, but he did it! He never let it get the better of him. He also told the children that they should become good people. Bad people would be sent to prison and the prisoners lived behind iron windows – they missed their family, they missed the blue sky and they missed daily life. He told his cousins that if he had known his boss, General Co, was also a spy, and if he had known that man was his secret boss, he could have done even more for the cause, in which case he would not have been scared at all.

"One day, I will write your story, Uncle," Huong his second cousin, told him.

"It was an impossible job, but I did it," Ngoc Lan said. "When I was young, I was very handsome. I was charming ... always smartly dressed and there was a beautiful French lady in love with me, but please don't tell Aunt Nhat what I tell you now."

The children looked up at the poor man in tattered clothes and wondered whether Ngoc Lan could ever have been smartly dressed.

Ngoc Lan tried to hide the hole in his shirt and said, "Now we dress much more simply, just like the Chinese; but we used to dress stylishly, like the French and Americans ..."

Ngoc Lan.

General Duong Van Minh.

Presidents Thieu & Nixon.

General Cao Van Vien.

Party of Ngoc Lan's group after the war.